CHAOS

LUCY ROY

Chaos

Tessa Avery Book One

ISBN (hardcover): 978-1-7353385-2-1

ISBN (paperback): 978-1-7353385-6-9

ISBN (ebook): 978-1955556088

Cover art: Denise Worisch

Edited by: Jenifer Knox

Formatting: The Swamp Goddess, Book Formatting and Design

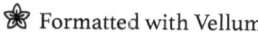 Formatted with Vellum

To my daughters.
Your sparkly mermaids will be turned into real characters one of these days.

ALSO BY LUCY ROY

Major Greek Gods

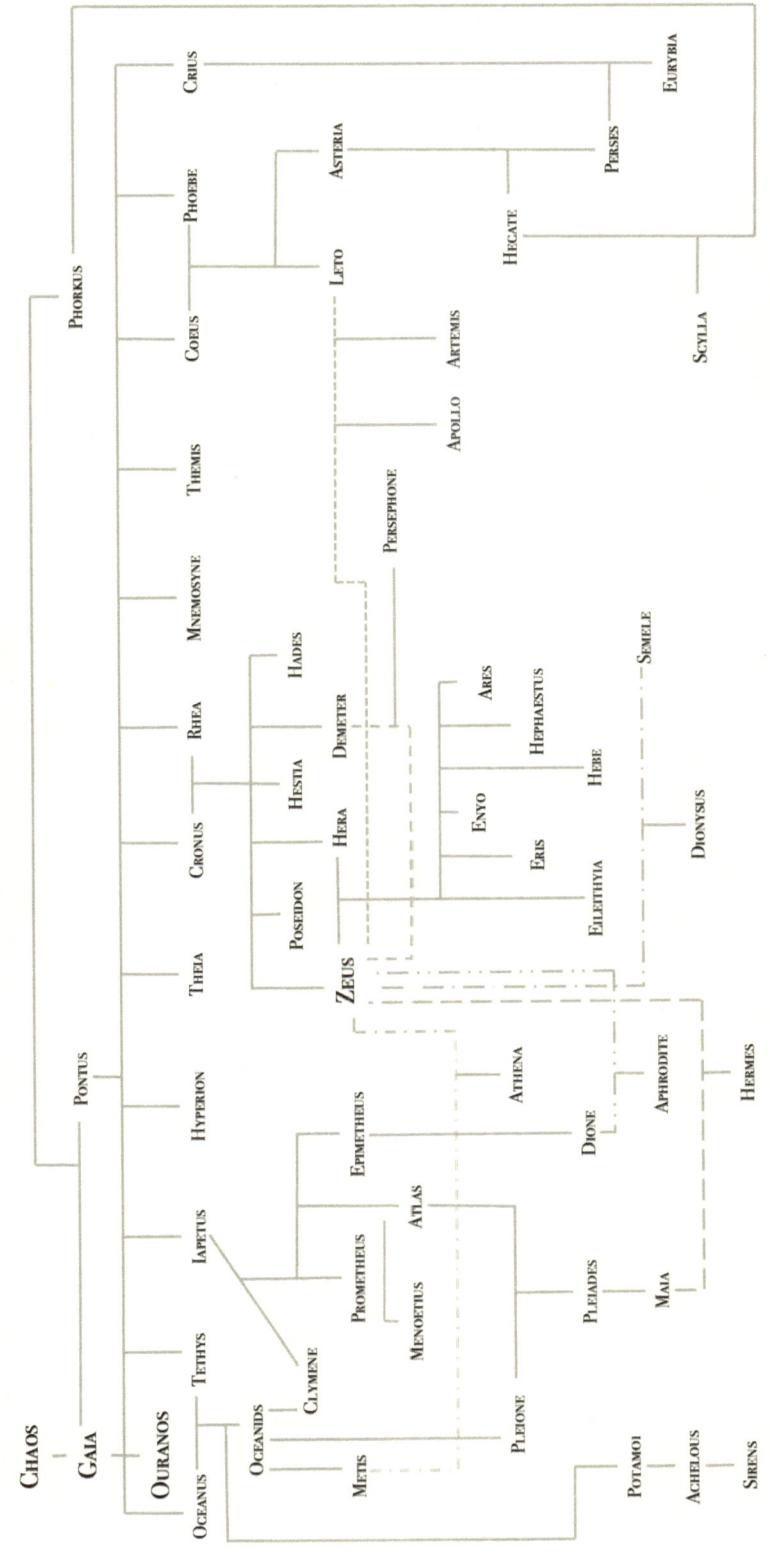

1

TESSA

My opponent hurled his staff toward my jaw, giving me barely a breath to throw my own weapon up, stopping his staff's momentum with a satisfying *crack* when it was mere centimeters from shattering my cheekbone.

Too close. I pushed back, swinging my smooth, wooden staff upward to crash against his once again.

As we moved, the rhythmic sound of our weapons colliding rang through the basement. It was oddly pleasant, despite the early hour, and usually worked to set my mind at ease.

Not this morning, though.

"You're letting your anger guide your movement, Tessa."

I clenched my teeth and increased the speed of my attack. "It isn't anger," I huffed, not breaking pace as I attempted to maneuver around his blocks. "It's irritation. Big difference."

He lunged for me again, so I pushed forward with my right arm, cursing when I felt the pressure of his staff under my chin.

"Damn it." My eyes fell shut in defeat. No, not defeat. Disappointment.

John stepped off the mat, signaling the end of our sparring session, and pulled his own staff out of range. The small furrow between my guardian's brows told me he was equal parts annoyed and concerned, which was never a good combination. "Okay, that's enough for today."

"Fine." I let my sparring weapon clatter to the concrete floor, the sound echoing off the cinderblock walls. John had already laid me out three times; I wasn't itching for a fourth. Trying to mask the stress that had been building the last few days, I picked up my water bottle from the bench against the wall and raised it to my lips.

John waited for me to lower it before speaking. "Tessa—"

I held up a hand to stop the oncoming lecture. "I know. 'Things that are out of my control cannot take control.'" The mantra was one of many John had drilled into my head over the last eighteen years.

"Yes. Yet here you are, letting a few bad dreams dictate how you train." He crossed his arms. "Why?"

"What do you suggest? I can't help that I wake up in a crappy mood."

I refrained from saying what was really bothering me; that the effects of the nightly barrages of agony and fear that came to me in my sleep were making me question my mental strength. Poor mental strength was unacceptable in my future line of work, which ultimately led to my morning brattiness.

"And that's fine. However, you need to funnel that 'crappy mood' into something positive." He pointed at my staff, which had rolled to a stop next to the treadmill. "I knew exactly where you were going to aim. Do you know how?"

"Because I always drop my shoulder?"

"Exactly. You may have the strength of an immortal, but fighting like that makes you predictable. Do you want to be predictable, Tessa? If you come across an empousa in battle, do you want her to *predict* when to sink her fangs into you?"

I let my head fall back and let out a groan. "No." It was no use mentioning that, once I transitioned, it would be nearly impossible to kill me, because I knew what his response would be.

Anyone can be killed. You just need the right weapon.

"Good." With a grin, he put an arm around my shoulder. "Now,

buck up, and let's go get some breakfast. I think Analise said something about blueberry pancakes."

I softened a bit at that. "See, all you had to do was lead with
pancakes. That would've killed my bad mood on the spot."

He smirked. "Somehow I doubt that."

TWENTY MINUTES LATER, showered and dressed, I found myself
staring absently into my messy makeup drawer. It seemed the
thought of Analise's blueberry pancakes wasn't enough to dissipate
the funk I'd fallen into.

As I absentmindedly dug through the various cosmetics, I
contemplated the nightmares I'd been having recently–if I could even
call them that. I was certain they had something to do with my
upcoming transformation, but I hadn't figured out how or why yet.

In just a few days, I would complete the transition from an eigh-
teen-year-old high school student to a full-blown Ischyra, one of the
many immortal forces that protected the realms of Earth and Olympus. Soon, I would join the soldiers who kept the various demons,
witches, and other evil beings from threatening the human world.

But no pressure.

I pulled out my concealer and began dabbing it under my eyes,
letting my thoughts drift to what everyday life after my transformation might be like. As had been the case recently, questions about the
mundane aspects of immortal life began to form in my mind.

Will I still need to trim my fingernails? Shave my legs? Wear
deodorant?

What will happen to my scars? Will the one I got on my chin from
riding a bike with no hands finally heal? Will the filling that resulted
from too many Jolly Ranchers in middle school fall out, the cavity it
filled suddenly repaired?

Will I just be a lower-maintenance version of myself with the
added benefit of superpowers?

They were simple questions with undoubtedly simple answers,

yet I'd never bothered to ask them. Of course, I knew the big things, like that I would continue to age for a few more years after my transformation, that any injuries would heal almost immediately, and that I could only have children with other Ischyra. I was also fairly well-versed in the history of our world, but that was because John and Analise had been giving me regular lessons since I was five, when they'd first told me the Fates had chosen me to become a soldier for the gods. I'd never really taken it upon myself to find out more than what my guardians required of me, mainly because I was far more interested in learning how to fight.

As I looked in the mirror above my dresser, I pulled at the dark circles under my eyes and speculated whether eternal life would relieve me of my frequent and desperate need for concealer. I considered those pesky shadows telltale characteristics of my humanness. Somehow, I doubted immortal beings suffered the same problems when they had a rough night's sleep.

"Tessa! Breakfast!"

"Just a minute!"

Forcing my face into a neutral expression, I finished layering on the concealer. Once the stubborn circles were covered, I brushed on a sparkly pink shadow that highlighted my green eyes. A few coats of mascara later, I looked much more awake. I threw on a pair of denim shorts and a turquoise tank that showed off my late-spring tan, then wound my long blonde hair into a bun.

As I leaned down to grab my phone, I caught sight of the three wavy, white lines on the inside of my wrist that marked me as an Ischyra, and a jolt of nerves shot through me.

In just a few days, I'd become immortal, and my mark would take on the vibrant purple of Olympus. I'd be ready to defend humans against the creatures the gods had released on Earth thousands of years ago. Or at least, that was the plan. After this morning's training session, I was beginning to question just how ready I was.

I ran my thumb contemplatively across the mark. Hopefully, I'd be able to manage the responsibility the gods were about to put on my shoulders without screwing it up.

∾

WHEN I REACHED the kitchen in our old farmhouse, I grabbed a mug from the drying rack on the counter and poured myself a cup of coffee, letting music from the "Relax" playlist on my phone pump into my ear. Despite my exhaustion, I was on edge, so the soothing music helped ease me out of the panic I'd felt when I woke up in a cold sweat just two hours earlier.

In an attempt to avoid conversation, I sat down at the table and opened the local paper, *The Renville Gazette*. As I chewed on a blueberry pancake in silence, I mentally crossed my fingers that no one would bring up my nightmares or training. It wasn't that I didn't want to talk to my guardians–I loved them wholeheartedly. I was more hoping I could suck it all up for the next few days and hope things changed after my transition.

"Tessa!" Analise's voice snapped me out of my ruminations.

"Huh?" I broke away from the paper and met her icy gray eyes, which were narrowed in frustration.

"I said, is there anything you want to talk about? John said he beat you three times this morning." She tucked a lock of short platinum hair behind her ear, concern etching her features. "That's unlike you."

I gave her a tight smile and looked back down at the paper. "Nope. Just tired, that's all."

"Tessa." John's voice was a bit more commanding than Analise's, but when I glanced up, the firm set of his jaw was offset by the warmth in his brown eyes. "Take out the earbuds."

With an eye roll, I obliged, although I wanted to point out I technically only had one earbud in. When I looked at my guardians—my parents, for all intents and purposes—I saw Analise's concern mirrored on John's face.

"You had trouble sleeping again last night." Analise shared a worried look with John. Something passed between them as he slipped his hand over hers and squeezed. Fear for my sanity, most likely.

"No, I had nightmares that *kept* me from sleeping. There's a difference." Absently, I fiddled with the edge of the classified section, setting creases through an advertisement for a local cleaning service.

"Do you want to talk about it?" John asked, running a hand over his stubbly chin, a common sign he was stressed.

"You know you can," Analise added. It was clear my problems were wearing on them just as much as they were on me.

"What's there to say? I'm bugged because these stupid nightmares about absolutely nothing are keeping me up all night. That's basically it."

"You're sure they're about 'nothing'?"

"I don't know. It's hard to tell."

John's answering frown told me he knew I wasn't being entirely forthcoming.

Wanting to avoid any further discussion, I folded the newspaper and set it back on the table, then busied myself by wrapping two more pancakes in a napkin and pouring my coffee into a travel mug.

"Tessa—"

Before Analise could push any further, I held up my hand to cut her off. "Listen, I appreciate the concern, but like I said, they're just nightmares. Not the end of the world. I have to go. My bus is almost here." I grabbed my backpack off the back of my chair, then made for the door.

"Just let us know if you want to talk," John called after me.

"Will do," I mumbled around a mouthful of pancakes as I slid my feet into a pair of flip-flops before slipping outside. The sound of the old screen door slamming followed me as I headed down the driveway to catch my bus to Renville High, the only high school in our small town on the southern edge of Lake Erie.

As I walked, I thought wistfully about how the number of family breakfasts with my guardians was now in the single digits, and I was surprised to feel a lump forming in my throat.

Like the other Ischyra, my birth parents were not a part of my life. By one twist of fate or another, we'd all been orphaned or abandoned as children. My birth mother had dropped me off at a police station in New Orleans when I was an infant, wearing nothing but a dirty diaper. As soon as the officer who found me saw my Ischyra mark, he'd contacted the local liaisons' office, which facilitated contact between Earth and the Elders' Council on Olympus. After that, two human guardians had been assigned to raise me.

Although being abandoned had led me to John and Analise, two of the most wonderful people I knew, I still felt a bit resentful when I thought about how I'd been dropped off like an unwanted pet. Apparently, the Fates and the Elders had other things in store for me, though, so I tried to keep that in mind.

My guardians were only twenty-two when I came to them, just a few years older than I was now. Tomorrow I would graduate high school and move on to Olympus, and after that, their duty to me would be done. They were still relatively young, and once I was gone, they'd be free to live out the rest of their human lives however they wanted.

There was no question they cared about me and my well-being, but pretty soon they wouldn't be there for me every morning when I woke up from a bad dream. I wasn't quite sure how I felt about that.

Who knows? Maybe immortals don't have dreams.

Glancing down the street, I saw my bus turn the corner. A moment later, it came to a stop in front of me in a puff of black smoke. Stuffing the last bite of breakfast in my mouth, I climbed aboard.

2

TESSA

Mary Miller, my lifelong best friend, was waiting for me when I stepped onto the sidewalk outside the large, two-story brick school. She took one look at my face and immediately pounced.

"What's wrong?"

I smiled wryly. "Is it that obvious?"

"Yes. You look terrible."

"Thanks." I rolled my eyes then downed the rest of my coffee. I slid my travel mug into my backpack and hoisted it onto my shoulders. "I had another dream last night."

"Same one?"

"Same one."

"Have you been able to make anything out?"

"Nope," I said, shaking my head slowly. "Just lots of noise, some red flashes."

"Okay, let's go over this again." She flipped her wavy chestnut hair over her shoulder and began pulling it up into a messy bun. "Tell me what you saw."

"That's the thing. All I remember is that it's loud and hot, and sometimes I see these bright flashes of red and white, like fire or lightning or something, and I wake up feeling like I'm having a panic attack. I wake up every morning exhausted from tossing and turning all night, with this weird sense of déjà vu. It just seems so familiar, but it's like it's... right on the edge of my memory."

"Hmm." Mary pulled out her magenta lip gloss and started to slick it on. "The déjà vu makes sense since you've been having them so much. Oh! Maybe they're prophetic! Maybe you're dreaming about some kind of fight or something."

"Eh, maybe. It doesn't feel that way, though."

She sighed, looking deflated. "Okay, so that's one mystery we have no answer for."

Mary reached down to pick up her bag, and as she stood, I took in her full outfit. She wore ripped acid-wash jeans and black, knee-high leather boots topped with a black off-the-shoulder t-shirt. Despite our school's dress code, the shirt left about three inches of her midriff visible.

Her style always oozed confidence, but I wondered how she was going to feel once we were required to wear the traditional black Ischyra training uniforms every day.

I'd just started walking toward the building when Mary cocked her head to the side. A look of interest came into her eyes.

"Who's that?"

I followed her gaze to a guy who looked to be a few years older than us, leaning against the wall next to the building's entrance. He was tall with light brown hair trimmed short on the sides and longer on top. One foot was propped against the wall behind him, and his eyes seemed to be scanning the crowd of students funneling into the building.

"Hmm." I tilted my head to the side and eyed him speculatively. "I'll bet he's from Olympus. I wonder which one of us he's here for."

"Well I'm pretty sure Eric's already here, so it's got to be one of us," Mary said, referring to our friend Eric Anderson, the third in our group of three Ischyra who would be traveling to Olympus in two days to make our transitions.

Just then, our two closest human friends, Leila Malone and her boyfriend Josh Harper, stepped off their bus and walked over to join us.

"What'cha doin'?" Leila asked, twining her fingers through Josh's as she looked toward the building. "Ooo, who's that?"

"A hot guy from Olympus," Mary replied.

"How do you know he's from Olympus?" Josh asked, brushing his dark blond hair out of his eyes as he looked in the new guy's direction.

"Because he's completely out of place," Mary replied. "Look at him. He looks about as comfortable here as I would at an Elders Council meeting."

Leila grinned and tucked her dark, curly hair behind her ears as she checked him out. "So does that mean he's here for one of you guys?"

Mary shrugged. "Probably. Come on, let's get inside."

Leila linked her arm through mine, keeping her other hand in Josh's as we started slowly making our way toward the entrance.

"So speaking of hot guys," she said, sliding me a look, "are you two even going to have time for boys once you're out protecting us from the evils of the world?"

"Mary always has time for boys, Lei, you know that," I said, laughing as I ducked to avoid Mary's smack to the back of my head.

Josh snorted.

"Okay, ladies, as fascinating as this conversation is, I'm going to head inside," he said dryly, dropping Leila's hand.

Mary waved absently. "Yeah, yeah. Just because we found someone hotter than you to ogle."

"Ha!" He reached over and ruffled her hair, causing her bun to fall to the side. "Totally not possible."

"Jerk!" She swatted his hand away as Leila ducked to avoid the crossfire. "Now my hair's a mess!"

Josh's brown eyes crinkled in a grin. "It was already a mess, loser."

"That wasn't nice," Leila said, nudging his muscular chest. "Mary's going to be gone in a couple of days. You should be nicer to her."

Mary sent him a scathing glare and stuck her tongue out at him as she adjusted her bun.

"Uh huh. On that note..." Josh leaned down and pressed a kiss to Leila's temple. "...I'll see you at lunch."

"Love you!" Leila called as he jogged toward the building, leaving us to slowly follow.

Suddenly, her eyes widened. "Oh, here he comes!"

As I watched the tall mystery guy approach, I tried to get a feel for him. Considering our transformation was just a few days off, it was kind of unnerving to know he was here to talk to one of us.

As he came closer, I took in more of his appearance. His skin was tan, his lips full, and he had a strong, sculpted jaw that gave him a bit of a don't-mess-with-me vibe. His eyes were dark, but it was hard to tell what color. Fitted dark jeans and a blue t-shirt hugged a frame that was both slim and muscular, and on his feet were a pair of beat up gray Vans.

"Ladies," he said with a nod as he approached, then turned his gaze on me. "Ms. Avery?"

I heard Leila suck in a breath.

I tried to hide my surprise at the mention of my name, and instead, met his gaze as steadily as I could.

"That's me," I replied, squaring my shoulders as I sized him up.

He flashed me a quick smile, then gave me the same once-over I'd given him. "My name is Nathaniel. I'm a liaison from Olympus. Do you have a moment?"

His voice was refined; a little formal, even, which completely contradicted his appearance. With his looks, I would've expected to see him on a poster promoting a college, not on an errand from Olympus.

"Sure. What do you need?"

I cast a quick glance at my friends and forced back a sigh when I saw their expressions. Mary was trying not to laugh, and Leila was gawping like a fish.

He looked at them warily, then cleared his throat. "Could we speak privately, please?"

"Sure, of course," I said, tucking a stray lock of hair behind my ear. "Let's walk."

I started walking toward the main entrance. With a farewell nod in the girls' direction, Nathaniel fell into step beside me.

3

NATHANIEL

No matter how many centuries went by, it never ceased to amaze me just how odd human girls could be.

And while I knew the incoming Ischyra weren't technically human, they maintained friendships with many of their mortal classmates, so they still had a peculiar, human way about them. When congregated in groups, it seemed like all they did was laugh and whisper to each other.

Shaking my head, I turned to the pretty young woman walking beside me. I was surprised that, after years of training to become an immortal soldier, she maintained a softness to her looks, not the harsh, angular lines one would expect from the strength she obviously possessed.

"Thank you for speaking with me. I know this is probably a bit odd," I admitted.

Tessa smiled, revealing a small dimple in her left cheek. "Yeah, maybe a little. So why are you here?" Despite her confident outward appearance, I heard trepidation in her voice.

"Nothing to worry about," I said, trying to make my tone reassuring. "Every so often, the Elders, usually Zeus or Hestia, get curious about the emerging Ischyra. They pick one from an incoming generation and send a liaison down to get a feel for what the newest group might be like."

Her eyes widened. "Oh. Wow. Okay... Not that I'm not flattered or whatever, but aren't there like, fifty other incoming recruits this year? Why me?'

I did a brief perusal of her thoughts and found her mind teeming with curiosity.

I shrugged. "Why not?"

She narrowed her eyes. "And if I said I didn't want to talk with you?"

"That would...not be a good thing?" This was not starting out well. Before I could attempt to read her mind again, she laughed.

"I didn't say I wasn't going to! I'm just curious to know what would happen if I just decided I didn't want to have a chat with some random stranger first thing in the morning. I mean, if they just pulled my name from a hat or something, can't they just pick someone else? And how do I know you are who you say you are, anyway?"

She was three steps ahead of me before I picked up my feet from the pavement and caught up to her.

"I know that they wouldn't take kindly to being refused. And why would I lie?"

"Who knows?" She shrugged. "You are a random stranger, after all." She flashed me a bright smile. "And don't worry, I'm not going to kick off my immortality by pissing off the Elders, trust me. Ask away. And please, call me Tessa."

"Okay, Tessa," I said, sliding my hands in my pockets. "What's been your favorite aspect of growing up as an Ischyra?"

She was quiet for a moment before responding.

"Well, I like how strong I am, and I love working with weapons."

I heard pride in her voice as images of her practicing with a staff flashed though her mind.

"And I'm really excited to find out what my powers will be," she continued. "Oh, and John and Analise—those are my guardians—they're really great."

"Do you have any thoughts on what your affinity might be?"

"Not a clue, but I think I'd prefer something Elemental than Mentalist."

"Oh? Why is that?"

She shrugged. "I just like having a physical weapon to fight with, that's all."

I pressed my lips together to keep from smiling as visions of Tessa wielding fire appeared in her thoughts. New recruits always thought fire was the most interesting of all the elemental affinities.

"What about your purpose?" I asked. "You'll be training to protect Earth from being corrupted by malevolent creatures. How do you feel about that?"

She fiddled with the strap on her backpack for a moment before responding. "I mean, I'm definitely proud of the fact that I'll be helping protect humanity. I didn't choose to become an Ischyra, though, so sometimes I feel a little annoyed that my entire future has already been chosen for me."

I considered her response as I reached out and opened the door to let her pass into the building. "Do you think that annoyance will prevent you from successfully performing whatever duties the Elders assign you?"

She stopped and gaped at me. "Absolutely not! I'm totally on board, but that doesn't mean I can't be annoyed about *why* I'm on board."

"What do you mean?"

"Well... it's not exactly the Ischyra's fault that there are all these freaks roaming the planet. The only reason we exist is to fight the evil creatures the gods let escape into the world when Pandora died."

I frowned. "I don't think that's entirely fair. Pandora was—"

"Created by the Elders and given to the Titan Epimetheus to punish the humans."

"Well yes, but Epimetheus was warned not to marry her. He chose not to listen to Prometheus when he told him she was a trick."

"It doesn't change the facts, though, does it?" She smiled. "You don't need to argue their side, Nathaniel. I've heard it all my life. I'm just saying, I'm more than happy to do my part, but I can't help but be a little irritated about the circumstances that got me here, you know? Zeus and the other Olympians tricked Epimetheus, and Epimetheus was stupid enough to trust them. It's a bit irksome that my future has been decided because one god was pissed off and another had terrible decision-making skills."

"That's an interesting take," I said after a moment. "Wouldn't you agree, though, that the release of those creatures in such a way may have been a bit beneficial?"

She arched a brow. "Seriously?"

"The gods used their powers to create the original Ischyra because they acknowledged their fault in Earth becoming overrun with monsters." I shrugged. "If Epimetheus hadn't accepted Pandora as his wife, the Elders would have had no reason to take responsibility for what her death released. She would've lived out her life unnoticed, the malevolent creatures on Earth would have multiplied on their own over time instead of all at once, and Earth would be left with less protection. Her death on her wedding night merely accelerated the process."

She cast a sideways glance at me. "I suppose that's a somewhat valid point," she conceded.

I bit back a smile, and we continued to walk in silence for another moment. The halls were congested with students, so I was forced to fall behind her while she navigated the crowds.

"So, do you have any questions for me?" I asked once we'd made it through a particularly large group of students and were able to walk side by side again.

"Actually, I do." She pressed her lips together, as though working out how to best phrase her question. "Before your transition, did you have...dreams? Or nightmares? Or just trouble sleeping in general?"

"What kind of dreams?" I asked, dodging a large student in a letterman jacket. The press of students around us made it hard for me to get a handle on her thoughts, but I was able to make out a few bright flashes.

"Bad dreams. Nightmares."

"About?"

She began to look a bit uncomfortable. "I don't really remember seeing much, but it's kind of loud, and there's this weird burning feeling. I feel like I should know what I'm seeing, but it's just out of reach, you know?"

Puzzled, I gently pressed into her mind to see if I could see any of her memories, but there were only brief flashes of light and a roaring sound.

I leaned against the wall next to her locker while she spun the lock.

"No, that doesn't sound typical. Do you think this has to do with your transition?"

She shrugged and pulled up on the latch before yanking the door open.

"I've had this same nightmare almost nightly for the last two months." She began pulling textbooks from her locker and stuffing them in her backpack. "I've never in my life had recurring dreams until now. I'm graduating tomorrow, and I'll be in Olympia training by next week; it would only make sense that they're related."

She huffed out a breath and slammed the door shut, then started walking down the hall.

I hurried to catch up with her.

"Well I suppose that makes sense, but I don't know what the purpose would be. The Elders typically aren't the type to send nightmares to transitioning Ischyra for kicks. It would be, well, *beneath them* would be the best way of phrasing it."

"Obviously." Her tone implied she thought I might be dim. "I didn't say I thought it was because of the Elders." She wrinkled her nose and tucked her hair behind her ear. "Are you sure you never had any?"

"I've never heard of pre-transition dreams. Jitters and nerves, certainly, but not dreams." We came to a stop in front of a classroom a few doors down from her locker. "Are you sure it's not—"

"It's not jitters," she snapped. "*Or* nerves."

I didn't need to read her thoughts to know the irritated look on her face meant she'd heard this before.

"I'm sorry," I offered. "I'm not sure what else to tell you. I'd say talk with your mentors after your transition ceremony, but at that point, I guess it might not make much of a difference."

She smiled wryly. "They teach you those words of wisdom in training?"

"If only they did." I sighed and stuffed my hands in my pockets. The bell overhead blared shrilly, followed by a beat of silence.

"So, did you get what you needed out of this three-minute conversation?" She hovered in the doorway, eyebrows raised in question.

I shrugged and smiled down at her. "I guess we'll see."

"Okay." She turned to walk inside, then paused. "Hey, Nathaniel?"

"Yes?"

"What's your affinity, anyway?"

I hesitated before responding.

"I'm a Coercer."

Her eyes widened, and a small smirk formed on her lips. "A mindreading thought manipulator? I guess they keep you pretty close to Olympus, huh?"

"That they do," I responded, relieved by her response. The typical reaction when my power was revealed was apprehension, but I didn't get that from her.

"So if you can read minds, wouldn't you have heard my thoughts before you'd walked up to us? Why bother even stopping for a chat?"

I laughed. "The options would've been to approach you for a discussion or hover around until you gave me some thoughts that were worth noting. I don't like to leave my mind open in a place with so many voices, so I went with the former and only focused on you."

She nodded, brow furrowed. "You can close off your mind? How?"

A second bell rang.

"We can discuss that another day. You should get to class." I smiled. "We'll talk soon."

"Ugh, fine," she said with a grin. Then she turned and disappeared into the classroom.

4

TESSA

By the time lunch rolled around, Nathaniel was all the girls wanted to talk about. I'd met up with Leila in second period and had given her a quick play by play; by fourth, she'd notified Mary and Josh.

"So let me get this straight," Mary said as she plopped into a seat at our normal corner table. "The Elders—Zeus, Athena, Apollo, the whole lot—actually send liaisons to meet with Ischyra beforehand? Why?"

"Yep," I said, unwrapping my PB&J. "To see what the newest generation will be like. Whatever that means."

"So, Tessa," Leila said, her eyes wide with excitement. She rested her elbow on the table, propping her chin in her hand. Josh sat next to her, absently tracing circles on her back. "I meant to ask you. What color were his eyes? Were they even more dreamy up close?"

I rolled my eyes. "Dark blue, and no one says dreamy, Lei."

She arched a brow. "And if they did?"

I felt my face flush a little. "His eyes were... very nice."

"Who's got nice eyes?"

I glanced up when I heard Eric's voice.

"The Ischyra that met with Tessa this morning. The Elder council sent a liaison from Olympus and *I* think he likes her," Mary said with a laugh as she dug into a massive bowl of salad, the green leaves crunching as she stabbed them with her fork.

"She's not the only one," Leila teased as Eric took a seat next to me. "You should've seen the way he eyed her up."

"Wait, what?" Eric faced me, brushing his light blond hair out of his eyes, and scooted closer.

Eric was the stereotypical high school hottie. Tan skin, bright blue eyes, tall, athletic build. A smattering of freckles across his nose were accented by high cheekbones and a killer smile. He never let his looks go to his head, though, despite the attention he got from girls.

He'd also had a less-than-subtle crush on me for the last two years, which I tried very hard not to acknowledge.

I sent Mary a withering look and tossed my napkin at her.

She stuck her tongue out at me before shoving a piece of cucumber in her mouth.

"So, hold on. Some dude from Olympus came down to talk to you?" Eric asked as he unwrapped his own sandwich. "About what?"

"The Elders are checking up on you guys," Josh said with a smirk.

Eric paled. "Are you serious? Why?"

I rolled my eyes at Josh. "They're not 'checking up on us.' He said sometimes the Elders like to get a feel for the new generation. I guess I drew the short straw. It's really no big deal."

Liar, I thought.

"Oh." He frowned, then looked at Mary. "Then why do you think he's got a crush?"

"Eric, did you really just miss the part where she said he was here to meet her so he could report back to the Elders?" Mary snapped her fingers. "Focus!"

"He's like a spy or something," Leila said, wiggling her eyebrows.

"I don't think a spy would actually say he was spying, babe," Josh said with a sigh. He frowned at me. "Honestly, though, do you really think what he says will affect anything? I mean, right now you're still just a human girl."

"Yeah," Leila said. "Once you get some training under your belt, you'll probably be a completely different person."

Slowly, I started peeling the crust off my sandwich. "I don't know. A lot of factors go into where the Elders place us after our training year. I guess at the very least, it could affect where I end up."

Josh nodded, a contemplative frown remaining on his face as he took a sip of soda.

"Relax, Tess," Mary said after swallowing a massive bite of salad. "He was probably just showing off. 'Ooo, I know the Elders, woo.'" She rolled her eyes and popped an olive in her mouth.

"Mary!" Leila laughed.

Mary gave her a wide-eyed shrug in response.

I smiled in spite of myself at Mary's attempt at nonchalance. I knew that visit weirded her out just as much as it did me.

"Okay, so wait," Eric began, running a hand through his hair. "Are you saying that the Elders are now, at least in part, basing their first impression of us on you?"

"Gods, don't sound so worried, Eric." I frowned at him. "It was a pretty mundane conversation."

"No, sorry, I'm just saying—"

"Yes, yes, it's serious," Mary grumbled with a wave of her fork. "No one's saying otherwise. As long as Tessa didn't come off as a murderous rebel, I'm sure we're fine."

I UPDATED John and Analise on my meeting with Nathaniel later that night.

"So you guys have never heard of liaisons meeting with newbies?"

John pushed away the remains of his chicken parm and spaghetti, then leaned back and rested a hand on his stomach. "I haven't, but I suppose I can see the logic."

"Yeah, I guess." I twirled a bite of my spaghetti around my fork. "It's just kind of nerve wracking, you know? To know that some guy is talking to the Elders about me?"

Analise leaned forward and placed a hand over mine. "Tessa, your whole life—no, your whole existence, from here on out, will be nerve wracking. I don't think you need us to tell you that."

I laughed. "Is that supposed to be comforting?"

"No, honey, just realistic."

"What about you guys?" I finished the last of my pasta and pushed my plate away. "What was it like for you when you knew you were getting assigned to me?"

Their selection as guardians and assignment to me was something we hadn't really discussed much over the years. I think they'd both been focused on being a family and wanted to avoid "shop talk" outside of my lessons. Now that we were down to the wire, there wasn't much else to talk about.

Analise chuckled as she shot John an amused smile. "It wasn't easy, that's for sure. I was...resistant at first. Of course, our parents saw it as a good thing."

I smiled. "Why did the Elders Council choose you?"

She waved a hand dismissively. "Oh, they said I had 'great potential' as a parent for future Ischyra. I won't lie, I was upset. I wasn't terribly crazy about the idea of my future as a parent having been decided for me."

"Why? I thought being chosen as a guardian is a huge honor."

"Oh, it is!" She smiled and curled her fingers around mine. "But I was young. My parents told me what was in store for me, but I think... well, I guess I was in a bit of denial. I wanted to go to college and be a vet, but instead, I had to begin training for my guardianship right after graduation."

She looked at John before continuing, her eyes not leaving his. He had a small smile on his face, as though remembering a fond memory.

"When your Gramma and Grandpa told me I would be partnered with John, I knew things would be okay."

"You were still in high school when they told you about John, right?" I'd always been hesitant to ask for details on how their relationship began, only because I knew it hadn't been of their own making.

John nodded. "According to the Elders, Analise and I are kindred spirits," he explained. "They paired us because, at our core, we were in sync.

"We'd known each other for a while, and knowing I wouldn't be paired with a stranger to raise a child, eased my nerves quite a bit," Analise said.

"I won her over our freshman year of high school," John interjected with a grin. "So when my parents told me sophomore year that the most beautiful girl in school would be my partner, I was thrilled."

Analise rolled her eyes. "I don't know that I'd go that far," she said with a smile, her cheeks flushing at the compliment. "I knew he was a good person. I knew he would be good to me and to whatever child was assigned to us. We'd already developed a... friendship, so it made things easier." She started to get a bit misty-eyed, and I was surprised to see that John's looked a bit red, as well. "And then, when we got the call that our charge—you—had arrived..."

She sniffed and wiped her eyes with the heel of her hand. "Well, I was scared at first. Your arrival meant my life as a guardian was officially beginning. When I saw you, though...Tessa, when I looked into those big green eyes, I knew immediately that you were *ours*."

Now it was my turn to tear up. "How?"

John rested his arm on the back of Analise's chair and gave me a soft smile. "I would imagine in much the same way any parent does when they look at their child for the first time."

Tears were flowing quietly down Analise's face, but the smile that reached her eyes told me they were tears of happiness. "The point to this story, honey, is that, what's fated for us is not always a bad thing. It's frustrating to know that, if Epimetheus had just made a better decision, listened to Prometheus' warnings about Pandora, we might not be having this conversation." She smiled. "But it's because of his actions that the Elder council formed the Ischyra, so by extension, he's the reason we have you. Maybe that's selfish, I don't know. I do know there is no doubt in my mind that you'll be able to embrace your own future just as we did ours."

I smiled at how similar her sentiment was to Nathaniel's. Both were able to see the silver lining to Zeus' cunning, which made accepting their fates a bit simpler.

"Try not to worry," John said as he began clearing the table. "You'll be faced with things that seem impossible, things that you think are too big for you, but I'm confident there's nothing you can't do."

Once he set the dishes on the counter, John came back and crouched down so he was at eye level. "I won't sugar coat things for you, sweetheart. I never have. This is not going to be easy, not by a long shot. You will face terrible things. Just remember where you came from, remember your training, and remember that we love you."

We were all quiet as I considered their words, the only sound in the kitchen coming from the ticking cuckoo clock above the back door.

After a moment, I gave Analise's hand one more squeeze. "Thank you, guys. Knowing you both had these feelings really helps."

"Any person in your situation would have these feelings, sweetheart. It's perfectly normal."

I sighed, then gave her a smile. "I think I'm gonna go up and pack, maybe watch TV for a while," I said as I got to my feet. "I haven't packed anything yet, and this day kind of wore me out."

"Do you want a hand?" John asked.

"No, I think I'm good to do it alone. What should I do with the stuff I'm not bringing?"

"I suppose we'll donate what you don't need, right?" He looked to Analise for confirmation.

"Yes, I think that makes the most sense," she said quietly.

"Okay." I gave them each a hug. "Thanks for the talk. I feel a lot better now, really."

John cupped my cheek and smiled down at me. "Anytime, sweetie."

When I got to my smallish bedroom, I stopped and looked around. The hardwood floors, smooth with age, and lavender walls had been home to me for as long as I could remember. Pretty soon I'd be sharing a dorm room with another recruit, which was something I wasn't really looking forward to.

I brought up Netflix on my computer and put the newest season of *Supernatural* on as background noise, then started picking through the last eighteen and a half years' worth of possessions to figure out what I'd be taking with me when I left for Olympia.

As Sam and Dean fought demons onscreen, I began to sort through my belongings. I started with scaling my clothing collection down to a manageable amount. I packed a toiletry bag filled with my favorite makeup, brushes, and mini straightening iron. Unsure how soon I'd be able to take advantage of the shops in Olympia, I threw in travel bottles of shampoo, conditioner, lotion, and body wash. After a moment's consideration, I threw in my razor and a few extra blades, too.

I didn't realize until I'd started packing just how nervous I was. As I went through my things, I was hit with the uneasy realization that the changes I was facing went much further than my musings this morning. I'd always known my future, of course, but now that my transition was just around the corner, its life-altering nature was becoming much more real for me. There was no question that I was excited to see what the future held, but as I watched my "donate" pile increase in size, I saw it as a physical reminder that I could only bring so much of "me" into my next life.

When I turned to face my bookshelves full of books and framed photos, a lump formed in my throat.

The photos represented the good memories of the last eighteen years. My sweet sixteen party down at the lake two summers ago when my friends and I had spent the entire day kayaking and swinging into the water from a rope swing. My first day of kinder-garten, clutching my backpack tightly in small hands as I stood next to Mary, whose hazel eyes were wide with first-day terror. My second birthday, where I stared in amazement at the flickering candles on the cake in front of me.

My three favorites sat on the top shelf.

The first was of me, John, and Analise in a subdued driftwood frame. In the photo, I was an infant, and John and Analise were only twenty-two. A liaison from Olympus had just brought me to them, and they stood in front of our house, grinning brightly as Analise clutched me in her arms, her eyes shiny with tears. John's face wore a mixture of pride and terror that I still liked to tease him for.

The second was a picture from eighth grade graduation in a blue and green mosaic frame. Mary, Eric, and I all stood in front of the stage in our navy-blue caps and gowns, arms around each other, grinning. Eric had just gone through a growth spurt, so he towered almost a foot over Mary and me. I shot up to five foot eight by the end of freshman year, but Mary never made it past five three.

The one next to it was in a shiny silver frame and had been taken just a few weeks earlier at our senior prom. Eric and I, along with Mary, our friend Kellan, and Leila and Josh had all gone in on the cost of a limo. Just before we climbed in, Alan, Mary's guardian, had insisted on a photo of us "all glammed up." Instead of smiling, I pulled Eric into a headlock, Kellan scooped Mary up in his arms, and Leila pretended to push Josh's face away as he leaned in for a kiss. Alan had been annoyed and forced us to stand for a normal photo next, but this one was the one I'd deemed top shelf-worthy.

Smiling, I took the pictures, wrapped them in t-shirts, and added them to the "keep" pile.

An hour later, I'd officially whittled my life on Earth down to the size of a rolling carry-on suitcase. I zipped up the bag and set it near the door, then turned to face the piles of rejected items on the floor.

I picked up the box of black trash bags John had left on my dresser and slowly began filling them with the things I wouldn't be taking with me. Once I was done, ten trash bags sat next to the door, ready for donation.

I sighed and put my hands on my hips as I stared at them.

"That's not depressing at all," I muttered. Turning away, I grabbed my pajamas off my bed and put them on, then climbed in, rolling to face my computer. I was able to distract myself with Sam and Dean's antics for barely half an episode before sleep finally took me.

~

"Tessa, honey, I need you to wake up."

That's not Analise.

My eyes snapped open and confusion washed over me.

"What the-- Where'd my room go?"

I wasn't sure who I expected to answer, but I assumed someone had brought me to the vibrant garden I was presently standing in. A low stone wall surrounded a space that was about half the size of a football field, and flowers of every shape and color bloomed around me, their scents wafting through the air. There were vibrant red poppies, violets, lilies, roses, hyacinths, narcissus, and fragrant herbs. A bright magenta flower I didn't recognize grew in beds all around the perimeter, and bushes of pink, white, and yellow honeysuckle lined a narrow stone path that led away from where I was standing.

I frowned as I stared at the small blossoms. I used to love picking the small flowers when I was a little girl so I could suck the nectar, but the scents here were overpowering. It smelled off somehow, almost cloying.

My perusal came to a halt when my eyes landed on the woman standing in front of me. She appeared youthful, no more than twenty-five, but her eyes held the wisdom of someone who'd been around much longer. Her hair was a flowing mass of red that shimmered against skin that was pale, almost translucent. She wore a long sundress that was a thin layer of sheer white over blue that mimicked the cornflower color of her eyes. Delicate straps crisscrossed over her chest and wrapped around her slender neck.

The silver clasp in the shape of a flame that rested at her throat where the straps intersected identified her as Hestia, goddess of the hearth. Flipping through my mental flashcards, I remembered that she was the one who helped keep the rest of the Elders' council functioning as a family and not a bunch of rogue politicians.

She took a step closer and her piercing blue eyes searched my face.

"Tessa, are you listening to me?" Her voice was lovely and melodic.

"Um, yes," I said, trying to get my bearings. I was beginning to feel a bit lightheaded as I frantically tried to guess why an Elder was standing in front of me.

"I'm Hestia," she said with a smile.

"Yes, I know, I recognize the flame," I said, gesturing toward her throat.

She gave me a warm smile and touched the shining flame.

"You remember the symbols of the Elders. I'm pleased to hear that. I wanted to introduce myself before your upcoming transition."

I felt my eyes go wide.

"Oh." I massaged my temples to try and ease the wooziness. "I mean no disrespect, but why?"

She gave me a reassuring smile, then linked her arm through mine and started to lead me down the stone path.

"Nothing to worry about, I promise. Tessa, the other Elders don't know I'm speaking to you, but I thought it best we meet." She turned her head to face me, her porcelain brow furrowed with concern. "You seem troubled. Why is that?"

"I...um..." How was I supposed to answer that?

I decided changing the subject was the best tactic at this point.

"Where are we?" It was a beautiful place; something meant only for the gods to enjoy, certainly. Humans likely wouldn't know what to do with such beauty.

"We're somewhere between my mind and yours. It's what we call a dream walk. I've opened a portal connecting your mind with my own." She gave me a conspiratorial wink.

"Oh. Yeah, I've heard of those. That's...interesting. But *where* are we? This place is beautiful."

"Ah. This is one of my ambrosia gardens on Olympus. It's one of my favorite places to visit when I need some peace." She gestured behind her. "My home is just up there."

I turned in the direction she was pointing and saw a sprawling, tan stucco mansion a few hundred yards away just up the mountain. I frowned as I turned back to her.

"Wait. Ambrosia?" I suddenly realized what the unidentifiable magenta flowers were. The scent wafting through the air wasn't honeysuckle; it was the nectar of the gods. Anyone who consumed it that wasn't an immortal would just get sick, which explained my lightheadedness.

"Yes, I do apologize, I know it's probably making you feel a bit off-kilter. I'll be quick, I promise."

"Okay, but can we sit down, please?" We were still walking but putting one foot in front of the other was becoming difficult. "I'm kind of getting a contact high from this stuff."

Rubbing my forehead and not waiting for a response, I plopped down in the middle of the path.

After a moment, I felt Hestia's skirt brush against my leg as she sat down next to me.

"Now, tell me what's bothering you."

"Right." I rested my forehead on my knees and focused on my breathing. The mountain air that flowed into my lungs felt cool, but the sticky sweetness of the garden polluted every breath.

"Um...that guy—Nate—no, Nathaniel—he just randomly showed up at my school asking questions. And I keep having these weird dreams, but they're not really dreams because I don't really see anything, I kind of just wake up terrified. And I'm scared because, in two days, I'm not going to be human anymore and you guys are going to send me off to fight monsters."

I snapped my jaw shut, cutting off my ambrosia-induced babbling.

"I see."

I snorted, my slight delirium making me forget who I was speaking to. Realizing I'd just sassed a goddess, I quickly added, "Sorry."

She gave me a gentle pat on the back. "Not to worry, dear. I do think it's a bit more than that, though."

I thought hard. I couldn't think of anything else that had been really bothering me, aside from the thoughts that I'd been turning over in my mind for days now, and those were hardly pressing.

Without realizing what was happening, I opened my mouth and let the first words that came to mind fall out.

"Will I still be me once I have my power? After I'm not human anymore?"

"Of course!" She wrapped an arm around my shoulder. "You will be the same Tessa you are now, just complete. Your whole human life has been building to this; all you're doing is gaining a piece of yourself that's been dormant for some time now."

"I guess that makes sense." I opened one eye and gazed at her suspiciously. "Hey, how did you get me to say that?"

She winked. "Not me, honey; it's the ambrosia."

I rested my head back on my knees. I was just about to ask if I could go home when a different question shot out.

"Hey, will I be able to do what you're doing?" I lifted my head to face her. "This dream walk thing?"

She gave me a quick smile.

"Only gods and goddesses are able to do dream walks, dear."

"Oh. Bummer."

Hestia went silent, and when I opened my eyes, I saw that she was fidgeting with the fabric of her skirt, folding it and unfolding it repeatedly.

Gods fidget?

I sat up and leaned back on my hands.

"You know, it's been my experience that when someone is fidgeting, it's usually because they're avoiding saying something." *Or flat out lying, but what do I know?*

"You are incredibly perceptive, aren't you?

"I try." I gave her a weak smile. "So? Are my perceptions accurate?"

"I wanted to speak with you because I wanted to ease your

concerns after today. I can see you have some uncertainty regarding Nathaniel's visit, but I assure you, that meeting was perfectly normal." She dropped the pretty blue fabric she'd been playing with and mimicked my position, extending her legs out in front of her and crossing them at the ankles. "Since the creation of the Ischyra, the council of Elders has sent liaisons to meet with new recruits. Zeus has no hidden agenda; he wouldn't send a liaison to meet a new recruit for nefarious purposes, I promise. He may have earned himself a formidable reputation, but his ways have calmed since the end of the war with the Titans."

The thought that the ruler of Olympus had sent Nathaniel to speak to me left me speechless. I would've thought he'd be too busy for something like that.

"Not too busy at all," Hestia said.

Had I said that out loud? "Huh?"

She smiled.

"Ohh. That's right. You guys can read minds, right?"

"Yes, we can, although most of us don't make a habit of it unless we're given cause. It gets quite noisy up here, otherwise," she said, tapping a long, thin finger to her temple.

Remembering that I'd basically called her a liar in my head a few moments ago, I cringed.

"Not to worry, Tessa. I've been called worse things than a liar in my time."

"Geez, I'm sorry, that was—"

"It's already forgotten." Her smile made me think she actually meant what she said.

"How come you're reading my mind, then, if you don't normally keep yours open?"

A frown flickered across her face, so fast I barely saw it. "Sometimes it can be difficult to convert our thoughts to words, that's all. I thought it might be helpful to see your thoughts in this instance."

I stared at the light reflecting off the pathway stones. I wanted to ask more questions, but my dizziness was quickly turning to nausea.

"Please let me wake up," I said, rubbing my temples. "My stomach hurts."

"Of course. I am sorry about the ambrosia."

She reached out to touch my face, then paused. just before making contact

"And Tessa?"

"Hmm?"

"It was very nice to meet you." Her smile was warm as she reached a hand toward me.

"Hey, wait!" I jerked backed quickly. "What about my dreams? What are they all about?"

She opened her mouth as if to speak, then immediately closed it. After a moment, she smiled at me. "Unfortunately, I can't help you with those, although I wish I could. Dreams are outside my area of expertise."

Of course. The one thing I needed her to answer, and she can't.

Her expression softened a bit. "I'll see you soon." With a small smile, she touched my cheek. "Sweet dreams, Tessa."

When I jerked awake, I was back in my room. Disoriented and still dizzy, I closed my eyes and counted to ten before sitting up. Slowly, the ambrosia haze began to fade.

Something about my conversation with Hestia niggled at my mind, but I couldn't place my finger on it.

The clock on my phone showed it was three in the morning.

"So much for a power nap," I grumbled.

How in all the realms was I supposed to sleep now?

5

NATHANIEL

Wanting to get a report on my visit with Tessa, Hestia had summoned me just before dawn, which was unlike her. As I sat before Hestia in her private quarters, I noted her troubled expression.

"Is everything alright?" I asked.

"I've just come from a meeting with Tessa, and I would like to know your thoughts on her."

I raised my eyebrows.

"No need to look so surprised, Nathaniel." She smiled softly, resting a pale hand on the mantle. The fire she'd set in the hearth flickered across her soft furnishings, giving the cream-colored walls an orange glow.

I cleared my throat. "Alright. She was quite outspoken, and based on what I overheard, those who were with her struck me as similar. She seemed to have no qualms with voicing her opinions on certain aspects of our world, and it appeared that at least two of her close acquaintances were human."

"Hmm." She drummed her fingers on the mantle. "This generation seems interesting, don't they?"

"They do."

"I suspect this round will surprise us. Was there anything else of note?"

"Just one thing. Tessa mentioned some dreams that have been causing her trouble."

Hestia faced me, a stormy look in her eyes. "Yes, she mentioned those. Did she tell you what was in these dreams?"

"No, and her memory of them was quite muddled."

"Did you see any latent memories when you examined her mind?"

"No, there was nothing more than a few flashes of light."

She nodded slowly, then turned to stare out a large, gold curtained window that overlooked her courtyard garden. "If you don't mind, I'd like you to meet with her tomorrow and report back with anything you feel worth discussing. I have a feeling she may have some questions."

"Consider it done."

As per Hestia's request, I was waiting when Tessa stepped off the school bus the next morning. She was immediately greeted by the friends I'd seen her with the day before. When she saw me, her human friend—Leila, I recalled—nudged her, and all four stopped walking. The hulking male hovering behind Leila eyed me curiously.

Tessa turned and muttered something to them that sounded like "It's cool, I need to talk with him" before walking over to me.

The others stared after her for a few seconds, then began walking toward the building's entrance, quickly lost in the crowd of students.

"Morning," she said, sounding apprehensive.

I smiled. "Good morning. Come on, let's walk."

I began heading away from the students crowding the sidewalk. We made our way down the block and stopped in front of a house that bore a short concrete wall in front.

"So, I hear Hestia came to you," I said, taking a seat on the wall and motioning for her to sit beside me.

"Right to it, then." She let out a breath and nodded. "Yes, she paid a visit. In my dreams, which was super weird," she added with a frown as she sat down.

"Dream walks are often easier than using the portal systems or teleporting, especially if you're looking for privacy," I explained. "What did you think of her?"

She cocked her head and smiled. "You're a Coercer. Can't you just read my mind and find out?" Her tone rested somewhere between resentful and amused.

"I can, but I try to avoid doing so. Truth be told, I find it fairly rude."

"Well, yes, I would agree. And somewhat intrusive."

"So?"

She sighed, then stretched her legs out in front of her. Her denim shorts showed off the tan that seemed requisite for those living near the water.

"So... Hestia. She seemed pretty nice, I guess. But she's the first goddess I've met, so I don't really know. She could be totally faking it, right?"

"She could be, certainly, but she's not. Hestia is one of the most benevolent of the goddesses on Olympus. It would be nearly impossible to speak poorly of her."

Tessa let out a derisive snort that belied the prettiness of her face. "Okay, I have to know. How old are you? Sometimes the way you speak... it sounds so formal, but other times it seems totally normal."

I sighed. I'd been wondering when she'd get around to asking. "Old enough. I apologize if my twenty-first century vocabulary isn't quite up to par."

Her eyebrows shot up and she gave me an amused smile. "Sarcasm, huh? I think you've been spending too much time around us humans. How long have you been working in the US, anyway?"

"I was assigned to North America not long after settlers arrived in the sixteenth century. This has been my 'territory,' so to speak, since 1595."

She smirked. "So you're pretty old, huh?"

"We're immortal, Tessa. Four hundred and fifty years isn't a terribly long stretch of time."

"I suppose. Why do you need a territory, anyway?"

"All liaisons are assigned one." I shook my head. "Weren't civics part of your lessons?"

"I've got a decent knowledge of our history, but the civic aspect didn't stick terribly well. I know the basics, like Ischyra get assigned to certain areas or for certain tasks, but I didn't know liaisons got specific territories. No offense, but I kind of thought you all were basically errand boys."

"I see." I rubbed my brow, a bit frustrated at her lack of understanding. "You know that liaisons are the go-between for Olympus and humans, correct? The main conduit for all inter-realm interactions with the Elders?" The relations with humans were one of the main reasons all Ischyra had a normal human upbringing prior to their transformations.

"Yep."

"Well, when the gods sent a group of Ischyra over to the New World to help manage the immortal creatures involved in the early conflicts, I was assigned as their liaison to ensure the Elders were kept up to speed on all that was happening. More conflicts on this continent were influenced by the surplus of immortal beings created by Pandora's magic than humans in the centuries prior to the arrival of Europeans. That meant more Ischyra were assigned, which in turn meant additional liaisons. I was the first."

She smiled wryly. "You guys didn't do a very good job keeping things under control over here, did you?"

I bristled at her insinuation. "Actually, we did. Most of what played out here was the work of humans. It would have been far worse had Ischyra not been involved in keeping the malevolent beings at bay."

"Huh. Interesting."

I didn't know why she was so surprised. In all my years, I found humans to be nearly as horrible as the creatures the Ischyra helped protect them from.

"It's unfortunate you didn't take more of an interest in your history lessons. A lot of it is quite fascinating."

She slid a sideward glance at me. "Uh huh. So anyway. Back to Hestia. Are any of the other gods and goddesses as nice as her?"

I paused before answering, considering the most diplomatic way to phrase my response.

"Since the war with the Titans ended, most of the older gods and goddesses have mellowed out a bit, for lack of a better phrase. Even still, all gods and goddesses have their own way about them. In that sense, they're quite like humans."

"In other words, not so much?"

The corner of my mouth twitched involuntarily. "Not so much."

"So why are you here, anyway? I'm assuming it's not for a history lesson."

I laughed. "No, that's not the reason. I'm just checking in. Hestia thought you might need to talk."

She began tapping her fingers on the concrete wall. "I see."

"Are you alright? I know dream walks can be a bit unnerving."

She kicked a small stone toward the curb and sighed. "Yeah, I guess. It's just weird. I mean, how would you feel if three days before your transition, a liaison showed up to chat and a goddess—an Elder, no less—decided to dream walk into your head?"

"I suppose I would feel a bit uneasy, as well."

"But your transition was about a million years ago, so you don't really know if you'd be 'a bit uneasy' or weirded the fuck out, right?"

I turned to face her directly and placed a hand on her arm, turning her toward me. "Just because I'm older doesn't mean I don't understand—" My words halted as my eyes met hers. An image flashed in my head, too quickly to make out. I frowned, then closed my eyes as I tried to recall it. When I opened them, Tessa's eyebrows were raised expectantly. Another image flashed, this time clearer, along with a feeling of sheer panic.

Then I felt a slight tug from her mind.

"You don't understand what?" she asked.

"Tessa—" I frowned, staring into her eyes.

"What?" She reached up and touched her nose, then her chin. "Is there something on my face? *What*?"

"Tessa, what exactly did you and Hestia discuss?" I tried to control the hardness in my voice.

"Are you reading my mind right now? I thought you said you didn't do that unless—"

"Unless circumstances necessitate me doing so, I know. And I'm not reading it, you're projecting. Forcefully."

Without hesitating or breaking eye contact, I pushed myself into her mind, responding to the sudden sense of urgency that was rippling off her.

"What the—I'm not 'projecting' anything!"

Reflexively, she tried to pull away. As she did, I felt another mental tug, more insistent. This time it didn't let go.

"Just wait," I snapped, gripping her arm to keep her in place. No longer waiting for permission, I quickly flipped through the memories of her conversation with Hestia. When nothing immediately came forth, I pulled back, considering my next option.

She glared at me, rubbing her arm as though I'd burned her.

"I need to look into your mind," I finally said.

"Didn't you just do that? *Without* my permission?"

"Yes, but—" I struggled with my words. "There's something... else. I need to look deeper. Please."

I cringed at the thought of digging into her subconscious, knowing how uncomfortable it could be. Getting a feel for someone's thoughts was one thing—digging into the recesses of their mind, even when I had permission, was something I despised doing.

It was the most hated of my abilities.

"Yeah, I don't think so." She stood as if to leave, and the pull from her mind grew even stronger, almost desperate.

Before I could think twice, I grabbed her arm and pulled her back down. The fury coming off of her was palpable, like nothing I'd ever felt before.

"Hey!"

"Just wait." Trying to ignore the fear and anger in her eyes, I gripped her arms tightly, using my coercive powers to hold her in place. Then, crossing my own boundaries, I dove into her mind.

6

TESSA

Feeling someone else in my head was one of the most disorienting and infuriating things I'd ever experienced. Nathaniel had told me he'd read my thoughts before, but I hadn't actually felt anything then.

But this?

This was downright intrusive. A violation.

I tried to pull away, but it appeared Nathaniel had me in some kind of mental straight jacket.

'What the—Nathaniel, let me go! Is this really necessary?'

I assumed he could hear the words I directed at him. I tried again to push back against his presence but there was no budging him.

'Yes, this is necessary, I'm sorry. Something isn't right. Now please, be quiet. And stop trying to kick me out, it isn't going to happen.'

Well there was something to add to my to-do list.

Then a third voice, quiet and female, entered my mind.

'Watch.'

My entire body stiffened, and Nathaniel's hands tightened on my shoulders.

He was watching my conversation with Hestia. Just as he reached the part where Hestia touched me, sending me back to sleep, it all changed.

The dream I'd had so many times was back, but this time I was finally given permission to see what was behind the darkness and the heat I'd been experiencing.

There was fire everywhere. Lightning surrounded me, close enough to touch. Amidst the sounds of destruction, I heard shouting, but I couldn't see where it was coming from. A woman screamed, then blinding white light flashed in front of my eyes and suddenly, I felt weightless.

There was a movement in my periphery. Turning my head, I screamed. A massive shape, blurry but human in form, was running toward me. I tried to move, but my body was frozen.

"*Take her,*" a cold voice said from behind me.

I tried drawing on whatever power was hidden inside me to force my body to move, but it felt as though the entire void of Chaos itself had infiltrated my being. There was nothing there but emptiness.

'Nathaniel, get me out of here!'

But I no longer felt his presence in my mind.

There was no help for me here.

Just as I was about to be overtaken, there was a burst of light. I heard one last scream and felt a hard pull, like I was being stretched in all directions. The pain was absolute, burning me from the inside out. My entire body was at its breaking point, my bones reduced to nothing but splinters.

Then, when I felt as though I couldn't take anymore, it went quiet.

The sights and sounds of apocalyptic destruction had vanished; the silence that remained, deafening. There was nothing. And in the dark, terrifying void of nothingness I was suspended in, a voice spoke very quietly.

"*This is not the end.*"

The female voice was as soft as a warm breeze, but all I heard in those five words was fear. All I *felt* was fear. I reached out with my mind, searching in vain for Nathaniel's presence. Now that I wanted him there, he was nowhere to be found.

Then I was falling.

Falling, falling, deeper into the gray-black nothingness. The further I fell, the more hopeless I felt.

Alone. All alone.

Desolation and panic washed over me in waves as pain began to rip through me once again. The sensation of it all shattered my previous notion of what pain was.

The voice spoke again, smaller, quiet, but just as fearful.

"This is not the end."

I started to fall faster. My panic finally overtook me, and just as I opened my mouth to scream, everything went black.

I WAS PULLED from the memory gasping, terror coursing through me as I clutched at the soft material of Nathaniel's shirt. As I crumpled to my knees, pulling him down with me, I felt his strong arms wrap around me.

"Tessa? Tessa!"

His voice forced its way into my thoughts. I pushed him away, then braced both hands on the ground as I attempted to keep my breakfast down. My nails scraped against the pavement as my fingers curled into fists. Leaning forward, I let my forehead rest on the rough cement and took several deep breaths.

I'd had intense dreams before; some more vivid than others, but this had been visceral. I felt it to my core. Those feelings, the fear and panic and desperation, were mine.

I couldn't stop shaking.

"Tessa!"

Slowly, I pulled myself into a kneeling position, then lifted my face to meet Nathaniel's. He was sitting on the ground in front of me with his arms resting on his knees, his blue eyes wide. The tears in my eyes caused his image to wobble, but I could see that his mask of professionalism had vanished, and in its place was a fear that mirrored my own.

"What was that?" He leaned forward as if to brush my hair from my eyes.

Before he could touch me, I slapped his hand away and scrambled to sit on the retaining wall, then rubbed my hands over my face. My cheeks were wet, fully coated with tears, and I saw streaks of black on the backs of my hands, telling me my mascara was running. I took a few more steadying breaths, then let my hands drop to my lap.

I glared at him, anger and fear causing my voice to tremble.

I wanted—so badly—to hit him.

"Why don't you tell me? You're the Coercer. Wouldn't *you* know why a random vision just showed up in my brain?"

It probably wasn't fair to put this on him, but I was a few counties beyond logical at the moment. I looked down and saw that his hands were shaking.

"I don't know, I swear! I just saw a flash of something..." He ran a hand roughly through his brown hair, causing it to stand almost completely upright. It might've looked kind of hot, under ordinary circumstances.

"No clue at all? Because I only saw that when *you*—" I sniffed and jabbed a finger in his direction "—poked around in my head."

He stared up at me, confused. "Tessa, I have no idea what that was, believe me. Hestia just told me she talked to you and that it was time to meet with you again."

"Yeah. Her." I snorted. "I thought she was supposed to be the nice one? Or are you going to try to tell me she had nothing to do with whatever the heck that was, either? It had to have been one of you."

I'd finally stopped shaking, but a migraine was beginning to drill its way through my forehead, so I reached into my backpack and retrieved my water bottle, then chugged half of it in one gulp.

When he spoke, his voice was quieter, confusion replacing the panic in his voice.

"I promise, I don't know what that was."

I frowned. He seemed pretty sincere. But then again, so did Hestia.

"Are you sure?"

"I truly don't." He frowned. "Obviously this was Hestia's doing—"

"No shit, Sherlock," I muttered.

"—but I just can't fathom why." His midnight blue eyes bore into me. "Was that your dream?"

"I don't know. I think so."

Half a block away, the bell rang, dragging me back to reality.

I slipped my water bottle back into the side pocket of my bag. "I've gotta go." I attempted to get up, but my legs wobbled, and I stumbled back onto the wall. He jumped to help me, but I held up a hand to stop him. Gritting my teeth, I waited a few seconds, then forced my body into a standing position.

"Tessa, wait—"

"No. It's my last day, and we have one more round of practice before graduation tonight. I'll just talk to you later or... whatever."

It was a horrifically lame excuse, considering the circumstances, but I needed to be done with this conversation and far, far away from him.

Nathaniel moved as if to walk me to class again, but I took a few steps away from him and shook my head.

"I'm good. Really. And there's nothing to talk about. You don't know anything, remember?"

Maybe being snarky wasn't the most polite response, but the violent images replaying in my mind were making it hard to focus on etiquette.

"Right, of course," he said quietly, hurt flashing through his eyes. His concern for me was evident, but I couldn't worry about that right now. I just needed to get into the building without falling over.

I turned back toward school and walked away as quickly as my legs would allow.

Once I was inside, I stopped and pressed my back against a row of lockers. I needed to spend more time going over this on my own before I shared it with any of my friends, and there was no way I could see Mary without her knowing at once that something was up.

Thankfully it was a half-day, so I wouldn't see her until graduation practice that afternoon.

I was already late for homeroom, so I decided to just spend the next ten minutes in the girls' bathroom instead of calling attention to my disheveled appearance by walking in after the bell.

I'd only taken a few steps down the hall when the image of darkened woods flashed through my mind, followed by the sound of distant screaming.

"What the—" I pressed a hand to my forehead in an attempt to soothe away the drilling pain. Squeezing my eyes shut, I braced my hand against the wall to keep from stumbling.

Calm yourself, Tessa.

The words swirled in my mind, soft, yet commanding, so I took a few deep breaths, attempting to do just that. Once I felt slightly more steady, I continued making my way to the bathroom.

When I stepped into the dimly lit, pink-tiled room, I checked all the stalls before dragging the large metal trashcan over to block the door. Dropping my bag on the floor next to me, I rested my head against the cool tile. As I replayed the vision I'd just seen, I struggled to find some bit of recognition, but nothing came to me. Considering Nathaniel had seen most of it with me, I assumed it hadn't *all* been some bizarre out-of-body experience.

Nathaniel.

I let anger beat back the reasonable part of my brain that knew full well Nathaniel hadn't done anything wrong. He'd seemed so sincere in his shock. I didn't think he'd have the ability to put those images in my head, but he was a Coercer, so what did I know?

The fear of my current predicament gave way to aggravation and anger, and I walked over to the sink and looked in the mirror. When I saw my reflection, I scowled.

I looked terrible. Tendrils of blond hair had fallen from my ponytail and stuck to my cheeks, the tears that had fallen acting like glue. Black streaks trailed from my lower lashes and smeared from the outer corners of my eyes where my mascara had run. The light brown freckles scattered across my nose were completely obscured by the blotchy flush brought on by my hysterics, and the whites of my eyes were so red that the green of my irises looked fluorescent.

"Why can't you be that green on a normal day?" I muttered to my reflection, turning on the cold water.

The moment I closed my eyes to wash my face, the distant screaming I'd just heard moments before echoed through my mind once again.

Gritting my teeth, I splashed cold water on my face, neck, and arms in the hope that it would bring down the swelling and redness, rubbing a bit to get the ruined eye makeup off. When I moved to dry my hands off on a paper towel, I realized they were shaking.

I squeezed them into tight fists, willing the trembling to stop. Once it had, I yanked my hair out of its ponytail, then dug through my backpack until I found a small hairbrush, spilling the contents of the bag in the process. The water had loosened up the hair that had been stuck to my face, so I brushed it all out until it was smooth, then wrapped it up in a high bun.

As I slowly began picking up the items that had scattered all over the floor, I replayed my conversations with Hestia and Nathaniel again, searching for any clues to what was going on with me.

Then a memory pricked at my mind; something Hestia said.

'Zeus has no hidden agenda. He wouldn't send a liaison to meet a new Ischyra for nefarious purposes, I promise.'

Zeus, from what I knew of him, was an honorable leader. His past was certainly checkered, but nothing in recent history indicated he would've sent Nathaniel for anything other than legitimate Ischyra purposes.

But there were twelve other Elders on the council.

What if it hadn't been Zeus who'd sent him?

7

NATHANIEL

What I'd seen in Tessa's mind wasn't sitting well with me. I could still feel her fear, her panic, and my own helplessness when I couldn't remove myself from her mind to stop the onslaught of visions.

Seeing that tortured look on her face again was simply not an option for me.

It was clear that Hestia had planted that vision in Tessa's mind, but I didn't think she'd be too forthcoming with information if I went directly to her. She would've mentioned it the night before if she'd wanted me to know.

I needed time to think, so I made my way back to my home just outside Olympia, the small village on the lower portion of Mount Olympus.

On the surface, Olympia resembled Earth in many ways. A tree-lined thoroughfare housed a number of small shops and restaurants, and houses and apartments were built along the smaller side-roads for those who lived here permanently. The streets were arranged like spokes on a wheel, each leading back to the central square where the doors of Olympia's portal field, the main point of access for all

Ischyra and inter-realm travelers, were arranged around a statue of Zeus.

A large stone arena, the main training facility for the Ischyra, sat just on the outskirts of the village. In the background, soaring thousands of feet in the air, stood Mount Olympus, the top of which was almost always encased in clouds. Scattered up the mountain were the homes of demigods, lower gods, and far beyond the cloud cover, the palaces of the Elders.

My home, a sprawling cabin in the forest that separated Olympia from the uppermost parts of the mountain, was peaceful, and most importantly, private.

I climbed the short set of stairs to the front door, lost in thought. As I stepped over the threshold into the large great room, I was so focused on what had happened with Tessa that I almost didn't notice my visitors.

My back immediately went up when I saw that Apollo and Hestia were waiting for me.

Hestia sat on the leather sectional in front of the fire place where she'd set several logs ablaze. She appeared tense, her back rigid and her mouth set in a firm line as she watched Apollo wander my living room, looking perfectly at ease. His pale, high cheek-boned face and casual expression betrayed no true emotion.

To humans, he might be considered striking or statuesque. In moments like this, when he appeared in my home unannounced, I saw him as nothing but intrusive.

I took a seat at the other end of the sofa and arched a brow expectantly.

"Nathaniel," Apollo said with a nod, not meeting my eyes. "I'll cut right to the chase. Hestia tells me that you met with Tessa Avery."

Hestia's eyes met mine and she gave me a barely discernable nod. *'He already knows what I've asked of you.'*

I shifted my gaze back to Apollo, who had moved to sit next to Hestia.

"Yes, I just left her a short while ago."

Apollo pursed his lips and absentmindedly tapped his finger on the arm of the sofa for a moment before giving me an expectant look. He raised his eyebrows when I didn't immediately respond. "And how did that go?"

"It went...as well as to be expected. When I left, she was quite upset."

"About?"

I tapped my thumb on my knee as I considered what to tell him. "She said that Hestia visited her in a dream walk last night. As we discussed what they spoke about, I saw flashes of what looked to be latent memories. When I pushed into her mind, something—a vision, maybe—took over." I paused, still ashamed that I'd forced my mind on hers, despite the apparent necessity of the action.

I cast a quick glance at Hestia before continuing. "I'd seen no evidence of it when I met with Tessa yesterday."

Apollo gave Hestia a look of annoyance before continuing his questioning. "What exactly did this vision show you?"

I leaned back, propping my foot on my knee. "It's difficult to say. There were some flashes of lightning, a lot of screaming. Someone ran toward her, then she was sucked into someplace... dark. I felt her emotional response, but by her reaction, it seemed as though it was physically painful for her as well."

The look of agony on her face when I was finally able to release myself from her was seared into my mind.

Apollo's composed expression faltered, and his gaze flicked to Hestia again. Something passed between them that caused Hestia's tense expression to turn irritated.

Apollo cleared his throat and turned his attention back to me. "Nathaniel, I think you would do well to not pursue this."

"I—what?" I frowned in confusion. "You don't think—"

"I said—"

"He heard what you said, Apollo," Hestia said, breaking her silence. "Now let it be." She stood and straightened her pale blue dress. "He was only doing what I asked. You and I can discuss the memory I passed to Tessa later."

The air in the room suddenly felt very heavy. Apollo was second in command after Zeus, and while he was quite skilled at concealing his emotions, the hard set of his jaw made it clear he didn't take well to being chastised.

Apollo stared at me as if he wanted to push further, but Hestia placed a hand on his arm before rising to her feet. "Come," she said sweetly. "You've gotten your information, now it's time to leave."

He stood and straightened his white suit coat. "Nathaniel, I trust we won't be speaking of this again." The subtle threat in his tone was impossible to miss.

"If that's what you want," I replied, staring into the fire and refusing to meet his gaze.

Without another glance in my direction, he teleported away.

Hestia gave me a small smile, then she, too, was gone.

I rested my head on the back of the sofa as I thought over Hestia's words. It didn't appear that Apollo had caught the hint she'd so carefully dropped.

She'd given Tessa a memory.

Not a vision of what's to come, but a memory of past events.

How in all the realms could that be possible? The girl was only eighteen.

And Apollo expected me to simply leave it be?

I felt certain that was damn near impossible.

8

TESSA

A few hours later, I stood on Mary's front stoop, biting my lip as I waited for her to answer the door.

When she opened it, she rolled her eyes, then pulled me inside.

"Ugh, there you are! Where've you—" When she saw the look on my face, her expression stilled.

"What happened? You skipped our last practice! You'll be lucky if Principal Sharp lets you walk tonight!"

I craned my neck to look into the living room. "Chris and Alan aren't home, right?" I wasn't ready to go to my own guardians with this yet, much less Mary's.

Her brow furrowed as she took in the look on my face. "Nope, they're at school helping set up for graduation. What's up?"

"Can we go to your room?" I dropped my bag on the bench by the door and rubbed my hands up and down my arms. "I need to...I don't know. Talk, I guess"

"Sure, come on up."

The second the door closed behind her, Mary marched me over to her unmade bed and sat me down with a bit more force than necessary, then took a seat next to me.

"Now, tell me what's wrong."

Forcing the shakiness from my voice, I detailed the disturbing vision I'd seen when Nathaniel had entered my mind.

When I was finished, she sat in stunned silence. After a few seconds, her expression turned incredulous.

"So, hold up. A Coercer pushed himself into your mind without your permission?" She shook her head. "This isn't even remotely okay, right?"

For whatever reason, I felt as though I needed to come to Nathaniel's defense.

"No, it wasn't like that. Well, I guess it was, I don't know. He said he only did that in situations where it was 'absolutely necessary.'"

"So he says," she scoffed. "How do you know he was telling the truth?"

I shrugged. "I don't, I guess. But if you could've seen his face, Mare."

"I'm sure," Mary responded, her voice dripping with sarcasm.

I sighed in exasperation. This was the last thing I needed right now.

"So, you're positive this was your nightmare? Or the parts of it that you haven't been seeing?"

"Yeah, all the stuff that I'd seen already was there – the flashes of fire, the heat, the sounds, that awful falling sensation." I shivered as I recalled how it had felt to plummet toward nothing. I began slowly tracing the pattern in Mary's blue paisley comforter with my finger.

"The first part was pretty clear; it looked and sounded, or at least I think it sounded, like a battle or something. It could've easily been a normal old nightmare."

I took a deep breath before continuing.

"The second part, though, the falling..." I raised my eyes to her. "Mare, it was the most terrifying thing I've ever experienced."

"So how do we find out what this was? How do we track down Nathaniel? He has to know something."

"I don't know. I was furious afterward; I wanted to kill him, and I mean that literally. I've never been so angry at someone in my life. I just don't know, though. If I could've seen my own face, I think it probably would've looked a lot like his right then, if that makes sense."

Mary frowned. "He didn't give any inkling that he might know what this might mean?"

"No, none at all." I shrugged. "Maybe he really doesn't know anything. I mean, I get that he's a Coercer and *might* have been able to fiddle around in my brain, but something that visceral seems far outside what his skillset would be."

"Or he's just a really good actor who gets his kicks scaring the newbies," Mary said dryly. "I mean, what do you even know about him? For all we know, he could be one of the original Ischyra. A freaking demigod."

"Eh, doubtful. A first gen wouldn't be Zeus' errand boy. No way."

"Well, he could be! What do you even know about this guy? Are we even sure the Elders sent him? How do we know he isn't working for one of the Sirens or something?"

I groaned. "Mary..."

The Sirens' only business was at sea, not on land and certainly not involved with new recruits. It was incredibly rare to even see them anymore. They dealt solely with the gods. Mary knew that as well as the rest of us.

"What, Tess? I don't understand why you're so quick to assume all's totally kosher here—"

"I didn't *say* that—"

"—when it's completely freaking obvious, to me at least, that this guy—a fucking Coercer—popped up out of nowhere, claimed to be on business for the Elders, screwed around in your brain, and sent you into a panic attack." She threw her hands up. "How can you possibly defend him?"

"I'm not defending him! But I certainly don't think the freaking Sirens suddenly decided it would be fun to mess around with some unsuspecting teenager!"

"Okay, fine. Then what do you think it was?"

I dropped my hands in my lap. "I don't know, but I really don't think Nathaniel put it there. Just because he's a Coercer doesn't mean he can plant visions in my head."

"No, but he can sure as shit make you think you saw something that didn't exist."

"No, I don't think he could."

I pulled a piece of folded up notebook paper from my back pocket.

"Look, Mare, these are the notes I took when John and Analise were teaching me about the different Mentalist abilities. I went home and dug them up before coming over. They told me that Coercers can manipulate people into doing or saying something outside their control and they can communicate telepathically, but they didn't say anything about creating visions like that. He used Coercion to keep me from running off; I felt that very clearly. I didn't feel anything like that when that vision started."

I flipped the paper over and pointed at a different set of notes. "It seemed more like the kind of thing an Illusionist would do. They'd absolutely be able to make me see something that wasn't there."

"Okay, fine, then how do we know he's not an Illusionist?"

I shrugged. "We don't. But like I said, his reaction seemed genuine when we were finally pulled from my head. I really don't think it was him."

Before Mary could interject with her opinion, I rushed ahead. "And listen, there's something else. Last night, I had a visitor. In my dreams."

"Like a dream walk?" Mary asked.

"Yep."

She looked confused. "But the only ones powerful enough to do a dream walk are the original Ischyra or—" She gasped. "The gods. Shit, Tess. Who was it?"

"Hestia."

There was a beat of silence before either of us spoke.

"Holy shit," she said, letting out a shocked laugh. "I cannot believe we're having this conversation. Elders don't do dream walks with new recruits. This just—it doesn't happen. Okay. Start at the beginning."

I detailed my entire encounter with Hestia, from waking up in the ambrosia garden at Olympus to Hestia's hand on my face as she sent me back to my own mind.

"She had to have been in on it," Mary said flatly. "If it wasn't Nathaniel, it had to have been her."

"Yeah, that's what he said, and it seems like it would make more sense. I don't know what to do here, Mare. We're graduating in—" I glanced down at my phone "—three and a half hours, and tomorrow we're supposed to show up at the portal field ready to travel to Olympia. Suddenly I'm feeling *not* so ready for this."

"It'll be fine. We'll figure this out. Maybe once we're in Olympia and training, we'll find some answers. We can hit up the other newbies and see if anyone else has had encounters like this."

"Do you really think that's safe? We don't know any of them yet."

Mary frowned as she considered my point. "Fair enough. Okay. New plan. Corner that dung-eater Nathaniel and demand answers."

I choked back a laugh.

"Are you insane? He answers directly to the Elders! Hestia sent him specifically to talk to me. If he had anything to do with that vision, who do you think sent him to do it?"

"Well, we can't do nothing!"

I stood and stuffed my phone in my back pocket. "I know. We'll figure this out, but I need to go. I promised John and Analise we'd do dinner before graduation. I'll see you in a couple of hours."

She squeezed my hand. "Okay."

"Thanks." I smiled but could tell it didn't reach my eyes.

I'd come here hoping my friend could help me rationalize all this insanity, but I felt worse leaving than when I'd arrived.

I just couldn't win today.

TWO HOURS LATER, I stood in line with Mary and my ninety-two fellow graduates, all wearing identical navy caps and gowns, waiting for our ceremony to start. Students and families were still flooding through the wide double doors that opened into the corridor, packing the beige carpeted hall to the brim.

I leaned against the wall and listened as Mary made plans with Leila and the others to go to Josh's after-party, still unsure of whether or not I wanted to make an appearance. After this morning's events, I really just wanted to burrow in my bed and do one last mindless *Supernatural* binge.

"So are you gonna go to Josh's?" Eric asked as he leaned against the wall next to me.

Trying to force away memories of the visions I'd seen, I smiled up at him. "I don't think so. Tomorrow's going to be so hectic, I don't want to deal with it when I'm exhausted from being out all night, ya know?"

"Yeah. Rudolfo came by earlier for dinner," he said, referring to an Ischyra who was a good family friend of his guardians. "He told me to take it easy tonight, get a good night's sleep so I'm 'well-rested' when I get to Olympia."

"And you're going to listen to him, right?" I arched a brow. "Seeing as he's ancient and might know a thing or two?"

Eric laughed. "I don't know. It's our last night. You don't want to hang out with everyone one more time?"

"No, I do. I'd just rather go to Olympus at full capacity, that's all. Which you should, too," I added, poking his side.

Eric clucked his tongue in disappointment. He draped an arm over my shoulder and laid a loud kiss to the side of my head. "You're gonna be missing out, Tess."

While he and the others continued to make plans for the night, the hall slowly began to empty as families and friends took their seats. A few bars of music wafted through the open double doors at the back of the auditorium, giving us our cue to line up. Principal Sharp came out to make sure we were all in order, then motioned for us to begin walking. Slowly, we marched to the stage, our final journey as students at Renville High.

"So," Mary whispered once we were situated on the risers. "What did John and Analise think about your encounter with Nathaniel?"

"I didn't tell them anything," I whispered back, avoiding her gaze.

"You really think that's the best idea?"

I gave her a wide-eyed look of surprise. If there was anyone who would encourage keeping guardians in the dark about my vision, it would be Mary.

"It's our last day together and I didn't want to worry them with something they can't control, you know?"

"Yeah, but even if they don't have actual answers, they might have some advice." Mary shrugged. "They may be human, but they're still part of our world."

I chewed my lip as I considered this, then shook my head. "No, it's not worth it at this point. We'll figure it out on our own."

A moment later, Mrs. Sharp took the stage to begin the ceremony. She spoke for a few minutes about how our class did a wonderful job keeping up the traditions of the school and a whole bunch of other things she undoubtedly said at each year's graduation. She spent a few moments thanking those of us who would be moving on to transition as Ischyra, something she only had to do once every four years. I couldn't help a pang of jealousy as I thought about how excited my human classmates were as they prepared to go off to college next year. Maybe it was silly, considering I was going off to live on Mount Olympus, surrounded by gods and demigods, but sometimes I wished I'd had a little more time to be a human.

As Jessica Landis, our valedictorian, gave her speech, I ruminated on whether I was right to leave John and Analise out of this. I thought it would have caused unnecessary worry. After all, as of tomorrow, it would be rare that I would see them, if at all.

Yet another relationship casualty of our world.

"Motherfucker," Mary whispered through clenched teeth, jolting me out of my bout of self-pity.

"Mary!" I hissed.

"Look!" She jerked her chin in the direction of the audience.

I quickly scanned the crowd, and when I saw what had drawn her attention, I sucked in a breath.

Nathaniel was standing at the back of the room, arms folded across his chest, leaning against the wall by the doors.

"For gods' sake, what is he *doing* here?" Mary looked as though she was about to storm off the stage and confront him, so I put a hand on her arm to keep her in place.

"Relax," I said, frowning at her as she glared at him. "Maybe he just feels bad about earlier or something."

"Doubtful," she scoffed.

Mrs. Sharp called for our row to stand. One by one, she called us forward to shake her hand and receive our diplomas. She cast Mary the stink eye as she handed her diploma over, clearly annoyed that she had ruined the alphabetical order of the ceremony by sitting next to me. Mary grinned sweetly, then headed back to her seat.

I kept my eye on Nathaniel as I walked, but I couldn't tell where his eyes were focused.

"Mare?" I said when I returned to my seat. Her focus was back on Nathaniel. "What are you doing?"

"Giving that little shit a piece of my mind," she whispered, her voice barely audible over the applause.

"Seriously?!" I jerked her arm, forcing her to focus on me. "Are you insane? He could report you!"

I hesitantly cast a look in his direction and saw he'd stepped a bit further into the light, resting his hands on the half-wall that ran along the back of the auditorium. Surprisingly, the side of his mouth was quirked in a slight smile.

"He's not going to report me. See?" She pointed at him. "He's smiling. He thinks this is a big joke."

"Or he thinks it's funny that you aren't even going to *get* to Olympus before they kick you out!"

I was struggling to keep my voice low, so I took a few calming breaths before continuing.

"Mary, you need to stop."

She shrugged. "Too late now, he's gone."

My gaze snapped toward the back of the room and, sure enough, Nathaniel had disappeared.

Well, that was weird.

'Not really. I just wanted to make sure you were alright.'

I jumped as a voice spoke in my head.

"What the—" I said aloud. *'Nathaniel?'*

"Tess?" Mary touched my arm.

'Your friend is giving me an earful, you should probably tell her to relax.'

"I...um..."

This was not normal.

'I'm a Coercer and you're about to gain super powers. This is perfectly normal.' Amusement rang clear in his tone.

"Tessa, what is it?" Mary was staring at me, brow furrowed.

I cleared my throat. "Nathaniel is talking to me...in my head."

"What?" She whisper-shrieked, getting a few curious looks from those around us. "He's talking to you? Wait, what's he saying?"

"He thinks you should relax," I whispered.

She snorted. "Okay, tell him to stop screwing around in your brain and maybe I will."

'She wants you to stop screwing around in my brain.'

So weird. So, so weird.

'It's not that weird. And I'm not 'screwing around' in your brain. I'm just talking to you.'

'It's totally weird. And you should really warn people before poking into their minds, you know.'

'I'm not reading your mind, I'm only hearing what you direct at me, and you tend to yell.' He paused. *'Are you alright?'*

'I think so.' I glanced over and saw that the last row was getting called down to get their diplomas. *'I don't suppose you happened to figure out what the heck that vision was?'*

'No, I'm sorry. Tessa, I promise, I had nothing to do with—

'I know. Or at least, I think I know. I paused, debating whether or

not to tell him about the additional flashes I'd seen after I'd gotten inside school.

'There were more?' His thoughts took on a more serious, no nonsense tone.

'Shit. You weren't supposed to—ugh!' I started reciting the alphabet, hoping it would keep him from seeing what I'd seen.

'Nice try. I'm going to come by later so we can talk.'

'No, you really don't—"

'Goodbye, Tessa.'

I felt a soft push in my mind, then nothing but silence.

"Shit."

"What is it?" Mary asked. "Is he still talking to you?"

"No, he's gone," I muttered. "Talking to him like that just gave me a headache, is all."

She frowned at me. "Uh huh," she said dubiously.

A few minutes later, Principal Sharp called for our class to stand. The music began to play, and she gave us the signal to toss up our hats for one final class picture.

Thoroughly weirded out by my first-ever mental conversation with someone, I was relieved when we finally descended the stage.

HOURS LATER, after John and Analise had given me one last kiss goodnight and gone to bed, I made myself a cup of tea and went to sit out on the front porch. Our house sat just on the edge of the woods, so the only source of light was the half-moon that hung over the trees. Cicadas and crickets warred with each other for vocal dominance, a sound that, while annoying to some, was one I'd miss once I was living on Olympus.

I sat down on the porch swing and propped my feet up on the railing, then rested my head against the back and gazed up at the stars as the swing slowly rocked back and forth. Directly in front of our house, stretching from the tree line, was my favorite constellation; Taurus, the bull. Squinting, I could just make out the Pleiades on its outer edge—seven stars that were easy to find but nearly impossible to truly see.

"Stargazing?"

I jumped when a voice spoke beside me, causing me to splash tea onto my hands. I looked over and saw Nathaniel walking up the porch steps.

"Geez, you scared the shit out of me," I complained, wiping my hands off on my t-shirt.

He smiled, then sat down on the swing next to me, propping his feet up on the railing, mirroring my pose. A gentle woodsy scent floated toward me as he adjusted his position.

"Sorry, I didn't mean to startle you. I was worried earlier when you told me you'd seen more after you left this morning." He shrugged and met my eyes. "Considering your initial reaction, I wanted to check in."

"Oh." I took a sip of my tea. "Well thank you. How did you know where I lived, anyway?"

He raised his eyebrows. "You think we don't know where our recruits live before coming to Olympus?"

"Ah. For a minute there I thought you were turning stalker on me." I smiled to let him know I was joking.

He laughed. "It's nice to know you have a sense of humor after this morning."

I took another slow sip of tea. "Honestly, I'm trying not to think about it." I wrinkled my nose. "That's the smart thing to do, right?"

"We can go with that if you'd like." He eyed me speculatively for a moment. "Do you want to talk about it?"

I turned so I was facing him more directly, pulling one leg up on the swing and leaving the other to dangle over the edge. "I'm not really sure what to say. Aside from what you saw, the others were just flashes; hardly more than my dreams."

He frowned. "Different than your dreams, though, right?"

I raised an eyebrow. "Don't pretend like you haven't already poked around my mind and seen them."

He opened his mouth, then closed it and pursed his lips. "Okay, I won't. You never saw or heard any of that in your previous dreams?"

"Nope, and I'd remember if I had. There were different emotions attached to them, if that makes sense. Just as strong, but different."

"What do you mean?"

"It's hard to describe. Obviously you know how panicked I was when I saw that vision with you. The others... I felt just this pure terror. It was almost painful."

"I'm sorry," he murmured after a few moments as he stared off into the trees.

"For what?"

His deep blue eyes searched mine for a moment before he responded.

"I'm as confident as you that Hestia planted that vision in your mind for me to bring forward. I don't know what her purpose was, but regardless, I was the one who threw it in your face."

"You didn't throw it in my face, Nathaniel. If everything you say is true, this is on Hestia, not you."

"If?" The corners of his mouth turned up in a smile. "I thought we established my trustworthiness already."

I narrowed my eyes, then nudged his leg with my toe. "It's still up for debate, so don't push it."

"I suppose that's something," he said with a laugh, swatting my foot away.

We sat for a few moments in companionable silence listening to the night singing insects attempt to drown each other out.

"How do you sleep with that racket?" he asked.

"I grew up with it. It's nothing but background noise for me."

"I suppose that makes sense."

"What's it like on Olympus?"

"Quiet," he said with a smile. "Very quiet. It'll probably take some getting used to if this is your nightly serenade."

I set my empty mug down and pulled my legs to my chest, then wrapped my arms around my knees.

"No, I mean what's it really like? Do you get to see the gods often?"

"Sometimes," he said. "Not as often as I used to."

I smiled. "Do the Elders just stay in their castles high in the sky?"

He laughed. "Zeus and Hera do, but the rest all have their own jobs or interests elsewhere. You'll meet Athena, Ares, and Hermes tomorrow."

My eyes widened. "All three? Why so many?"

"Athena and Ares because they're in charge of all Ischyra dealings, Hermes because he facilitates all inter-realm travel. He'll be there to make sure your first trip through the portal goes smoothly."

Right. Because tomorrow I would be traveling through a portal to a different realm.

I let out a shaky breath and tried to figure out how to keep my nervous thoughts to myself.

His expression turned concerned. "It's nothing to worry about," he said, his voice reassuring. "Really."

"I know. It's fine,' I said, not meeting his gaze. The last thing I needed was to look weak in front of him.

"It's not weak to be fearful of what's to come," he said.

"Can you stop reading my mind, please? Or teach me how to stop doing that projecting thing?"

"Sorry," he said with a smile. "You'll have to work on building up your mental walls once you transition."

I huffed. "Do people normally shout at you with their thoughts?"

"Not as much as you."

"I'm not sure if I should be flattered or concerned that I'm some sort of freak," I said, forcing a grin onto my face. "What do you think it means?"

He shrugged. "If I had to hazard a guess, I'd say that you'll probably end up with Mentalist abilities."

"Oh," I said, feeling a little deflated.

"Hey!" He poked my leg. "Mentalist abilities can be pretty amazing."

"Says the Coercer," I muttered. "What are there, five of you? Of course you'd think it was awesome."

"I've known and helped train Ischyra with plenty of other mental powers. Trust me, it wouldn't be the worst thing."

I sighed and looked up at the moon. "I don't suppose you could coerce me into a coma for a few hours, could you? I don't know how I'm going to sleep tonight."

"You mean the forest symphony isn't enough to lull you to sleep?"

I raised my eyebrows. "I guess that's a no?"

"That's a no."

I groaned. "What use is having a Coercer friend if I can't even benefit from his powers?"

"Ah." He nodded and smiled at me. "So I've gone from debatably trustworthy to a friend, all in the span of a conversation. I'd say my day is complete."

I had no response to that, so I just stuck my tongue out at him.

He chuckled. "Alright, I'll let you get to bed. And try not to worry about tomorrow. Nothing much happens on the first day. It's the second day you have to worry about."

"Jerk," I said, picking up a pillow from the swing and tossing it at him. "That's not helpful!"

He laughed as he caught the pillow and set it back down on the swing. "I'm kidding. Really, go try to get some sleep. You've got nothing to worry about."

"Fine, but if I don't get any sleep tonight, I'm blaming you." A thought occurred to me just then. "Hey, wait a sec."

He raised his eyebrows. "Hmm?"

"What would you have done if I hadn't been sitting on the porch? Rang the doorbell?"

He laughed, then pointed to my bedroom window above the porch. "What they do in movies. I'd have thrown a pebble at your window. Or just yelled in your head for you to wake up."

I arched a brow. "And how do you know you wouldn't have been hitting my guardians' window?"

"Are you telling me yours isn't the room with the pink and purple striped curtains?"

"Oh." I frowned. "Fair enough."

He chuckled and walked down the steps. "Goodnight, Tessa. I'll see you tomorrow."

"Goodnight, Nathaniel," I said, unable to help the smile that formed on my lips as I watched him walk down the driveway. Once he was out of sight, I picked up my mug and went inside, positive I wasn't going to get a single wink of sleep.

9

TESSA

Surprisingly, I fell asleep relatively quickly after Nathaniel left, and for the first time in more than two months, my sleep was dreamless.

Despite my best efforts, I hadn't been able to convince Mary or Eric to stay home after graduation. When we got to the portal field at seven the next morning, Mary climbed out of Chris and Alan's blue Honda in black leggings, a fitted gray *Charmed* t-shirt, and flip flops. Her wavy brown hair was wound into a top knot, Ray-Bans firmly in place, and her skin had the tell-tale pallor of someone who'd over-done it the night before.

I couldn't help facepalming when I saw her walking toward me on the sidewalk. My best friend was about to become an immortal soldier, and she showed up in an outfit that practically screamed "hangover."

With a shake of my head, I turned my attention to the portal field that sat about one hundred yards away. A dozen white doors stood in the middle of a small grassy clearing in the woods, each bearing a golden number and leading to a different location in the realms of Earth and Olympus. The area immediately around it had been spelled by one of Olympus' witches to repel anyone who wasn't an immortal.

I hoped whenever our escorts arrived, they wouldn't take Mary's outfit as a sign of indifference to her position.

"Mary's certainly going for an interesting first impression," Analise whispered.

John laughed beside her. "She's always been her own girl. They'll probably like that about her."

Analise and I shot John identical dubious looks. I looked down at my own black capris and sleeveless white button down. I'd blown my hair out that morning, so it hung perfectly smooth to my lower back.

"Well, I'm glad some of us remembered to dress for the occasion," I teased as Mary and her guardians approached.

Mary scratched the top of her head and wrinkled her nose. "Whatever. Aren't we supposed to be getting uniforms there or something?"

"Not until the transition ceremony, dummy."

"You guys!"

I looked over and saw Leila running toward us, still in her plaid pajama pants and a pink tank top, her long curly hair flowing behind her. Josh trailed behind her, looking a bit worse for wear. His blond hair was messy, and his eyes were a bit glassy, as though he'd just rolled out of bed.

"Wow, they actually made it," I said, laughing. Leila had sworn they'd be here to see us off, but I figured they'd be sleeping off Josh's party most of the day.

She crashed into us, wrapping us in a huge hug.

"I'm going to miss you two so much," she sniffed as she pulled back and brushed her hair out of her eyes. "I'm so happy we got to be friends."

I gave her a tight hug as tears pricked my eyes. "Me too, girlie."

I opened my arms to Josh, and he wrapped me in a tight hug, lifting me a good six inches off the ground.

"I'll miss you, Tessie Bear," he said, using Leila's stupid nickname for me.

I patted his back and gave him a loud kiss on the cheek. "I'll miss you, too."

He set me back down and draped an arm around Leila's shoulders.

She gave a watery laugh and leaned into him. "What am I going to do without you? Who—Mary, what the fuck are you wearing?"

Her face was incredulous as she turned toward me.

"You're letting her meet the *gods* looking like that?"

"Letting her!" I scoffed. "She's the one that decided to go out drinking last night."

"I don't know how this surprises any of you," Josh grumbled, stifling a yawn.

"Oh, you guys suck," Mary grumbled. "Hmm. Let me see..." She started digging through her suitcase. After a moment, she pulled out a thin-strapped blue and yellow flowered dress. "What about this?"

Josh snorted.

"For one, it's wrinkled." Leila sighed. "And two, it barely covers your ass. So no, not that. You've had ages to pack. Why'd you even bring that?"

I bit my lip to keep from smiling. I was really going to miss spending every morning with those three.

"Just forget it, Mare," I said. "You don't have time to mess around with getting changed."

Leila's eyes grew wide. "Crap, we should go. They probably won't want me here." She looked at the doors with narrow eyes.

"Who's coming for you guys, anyway?" Josh asked, sending a furtive glance over my shoulder.

"I think Ares and Athena," I responded, not divulging how I knew that. I really didn't care to get into a discussion about Nathaniel showing up at my house, considering Mary's actions toward him at graduation. "They're the ones in charge of the Ischyra."

Leila gave us a tightlipped smile before diving in for another hug. "You two are going to be the best immortal soldiers this world has ever seen."

"Damn right." Mary grinned cockily. Her face softened as she pulled back and looked at Leila. "I'm going to miss you so goddamn much," she whispered.

"Will you ever be able to visit?" Leila asked, her voice quiet.

Mary and I exchanged a look.

"I don't know," I replied. "I guess it all depends on where we get assigned."

"But we'll try," Mary promised. She looked up at Josh and grinned. "Do I get a hug, big guy?"

"I probably have one to spare," he said, laughing. He pulled her into a one-armed hug and ruffled her hair, then blew a raspberry on her cheek, knocking her sunglasses askew.

She let out a yelp and pushed him back, wiping her cheek with the back of her hand. "Dammit, Josh, you got morning breath on me! You know what? I lied. I'm not going to miss you one bit." She pulled the tie out of her hair, then flipped her head upside down to gather it back up.

"Your love for me will never die, Mare," he joked, grinning as he glanced toward the doors again. "We should probably go, Lei. I doubt they're gonna want us civilians here."

Leila let out a deep breath and nodded.

"Yeah, you're right." She grinned as she looked between us. "Good luck. I love you guys!"

We gave her one last farewell hug before they turned and jogged back to her car. When she climbed into the passenger seat, I saw her wipe tears from her eyes, and Josh reached out a hand and rubbed her back reassuringly.

"Gods, I'm gonna miss her," Mary said wistfully. "Her and her stupid boyfriend."

"Oh, Josh isn't so bad."

"He's always messing up my hair," she grumbled as she secured her hair on top of her head. "It takes a lot of effort to get a messy bun this cute."

"Very true," I agreed. "Here comes Eric."

Eric grinned as he walked up to us, his guardians trailing behind him.

"Hey, guys. You ready for this?"

"As ready as we'll ever be," Mary said, stifling a yawn.

"When do you think they'll be here?" he asked us.

Mary shrugged. "Who knows? They said we needed to be here by eight, so hopefully soon. I'm antsy to get moving."

"Gee, I wonder why?" I muttered.

"You're really not nervous at all?" Eric asked.

"Kind of. I don't know. I mean, I feel a little pukey, I guess." Mary said as she put her hand to her stomach.

"I have a feeling that's tequila, not nerves," Eric said, laughing.

Before she could respond, I sucked in a sharp breath. "They're here!"

Four figures had appeared in the middle of the portal field. All conversation died out as our entire group faced them as one.

"Holy shit, is that—" Before Eric could finish his question, Mary cut him off.

"Hermes! Oh, my fucking *gods*, that's Hermes. I always knew he'd be hot," she whispered.

Mary stood gawking at the roguish looking Elder who'd just arrived with three companions. His deep tan and butterscotch hair gave him a golden glow, accentuated by his loose, white, button-down shirt and pale khaki pants. Strapped to his feet were tan leather sandals, nearly the same shade as his skin. He looked more like a frat boy on spring break than a god.

Beside him stood a tall, slender man with white blond hair and cheekbones to die for, wearing a blindingly white suit. On his right, arms folded across her chest, was a small, fierce looking woman.

A tall, muscular man stood beside her, his hands on his hips as he took us all in. His eyes were sky blue, visible from my spot ten feet away. His cropped hair was the color of dark coffee, and he had a chiseled jaw most male models would probably kill for.

"Welcome, recruits. Guardians as well," the woman, who I assumed to be Athena, said, her clear voice loud and almost musical.

She looked to be a few inches shorter than me and moved with the grace and strength of a dancer. Her light brown hair was pulled back from her delicate face in a simple bun, and she was dressed in a sturdy-looking, navy blue tunic and white leggings. A silver bow and a quiver of arrows rested against her back. Without having to look, I knew her eyes would be the color of steel. A silver clasp in the shape of a shield was pinned to her dress

"I am Athena, overseer of all Ischyra dealings and coordinator of military tactics. This is my brother Ares, who oversees all aspects of physical and weaponry training," she said, indicating the man on her left. She gestured toward the blond man on her right. "This is Apollo, Olympus' second in command."

The stern looking god inclined his head in our direction, betraying no emotion at all.

"Welcoming" was not the word I'd use for him. Intimidating, maybe. Or terrifying.

"Hermes here handles all inter-realm travel," Athena continued. "He will help ensure your first time using the portal system goes smoothly."

Hermes grinned and held up a hand in greeting.

Athena clasped her hands behind her back and looked at the ground for a moment before facing us again. 'Although you may have awaited this day all your lives, we know it may be a bit difficult for you. It is important to remember that you are embarking on a journey that is far greater than what you have experienced the last eighteen years. Tomorrow you will become soldiers, defenders of the human realm. Your mortal lives and all that they contained will be left behind."

No need to sugarcoat it, I thought.

"In just a few minutes, we will be sending you through to your new home. Once through, you will meet your trainers who will give you your dormitory assignments and all further instruction."

She smiled warmly and held out her hands. "Now, are there any questions?"

We shook our heads. For once, Mary didn't have anything to say.

"Wonderful. We will give you a few moments to say your farewells. Please take your time."

I turned to face John and Analise, who had come to stand behind me, and felt my lower lip begin to tremble. John opened his arms and pulled me into a tight hug, and I felt Analise place a hand on my back, her forehead resting on my shoulder.

"I'm going to miss you guys so much," I said, trying to force back sobs that were forcing their way up my throat.

"Us, too, sweetheart. Us, too." John's attempt to control his tears was failing as miserably as mine.

John set me down so that Analise could draw me into a hug. I buried my face in her shoulder and inhaled the familiar, comforting smell of her mint shampoo. Tears silently dripped down my cheeks onto her shoulder.

"You're going to do wonderfully," she whispered. "I need you to know how much we truly believe that."

Her words were meant to calm me, but all of my insecurities reared up, pushing her soothing words aside.

Will I be strong enough?

Will I be able to control my powers?

Will my nightmares continue their nightly torment?

Will the vision of fire and destruction come true?

"You are going to be amazing," Analise whispered fiercely. "There isn't anything you won't be able to achieve."

"Remember—" John began.

"'Things that are out of my control cannot take control.'" I gave him a watery smile and took a deep breath. "I know. I won't forget. Thank you."

He grinned. "Just remember, anytime you're feeling homesick, look to Taurus. That will be our common point, alright?"

"Sounds like a plan," I agreed, quickly wiping the tears from my cheeks. The massive K-shaped constellation had long been one of my favorites.

"Alright, then. It's time to put your game face on," he said.

I took a deep breath and nodded, forcing all evidence of nerves off my face.

I closed my eyes and counted to ten as I tried to steady the heavy beating of my heart. After a few more deep breaths, I felt my body settle down.

John and Analise each gave me one final hug, then resolutely, I squared my shoulders and turned to face the gods before me. The four Elders waited a few more moments before calling us forward.

I walked toward the four beautiful gods waiting next to the door that had a shining golden 6 in the center. On Athena's right, Apollo stood stock-still in his white suit, staring at the three of us curiously. When he caught my eye, he looked away, leaning to whisper in Athena's ear before stepping through a door with the number four inscribed on it, allowing Hermes to take his place.

Well, that was odd.

Before I could think on it further, Ares spoke.

"Hermes will explain the process of crossing between realms." His voice was deep and imposing—the complete opposite of Athena's.

I joined the rest of the group and waited as Hermes gave us a blow-by-blow on inter-realm travel. I was surprised to hear how much he sounded just like any other twenty-first century guy.

"Alright everyone, listen up. This shouldn't be too complicated, but I'll walk you through it so there's no confusion. This door—" he gestured over his shoulder with his thumb "—will take you directly to Olympia, where your trainers will be waiting just on the other side. The other doors will take you to other areas throughout the realms, but you'll learn about those in time. I know it looks a bit intimidating, but there's no need to be afraid."

He grabbed the brass knob and pushed, opening the door onto what looked like a swirling mass of white, then turned back to us and grinned mischievously.

"Who wants to step into the swirling vortex first?"

I looked around at my friends and saw that neither immediately jumped to action. Rolling my eyes, and trying to remember Analise's words, I tightened my hand on the strap of my black suit case.

"I will."

"Damn, Tessa, you go, girl," Mary whispered behind me.

Eric gave my shoulder a quick squeeze. "I'll be right behind you, Tess," he whispered.

"Tessa, right?" Hermes gave me a sparkling grin as I stepped forward.

"That's me," I said as I eyed the swirling whiteness inside the door.

"Alright, then. In you go!" He held out a hand and I grasped it, its warmth oddly comforting. For some reason, I'd expected the gods to be cold.

Slowly, I stepped up to the door. I hesitated for a moment, then a small voice, far in the back of my mind, urged me on.

'Never doubt yourself, Tessa. You will move mountains.'

I faltered, unsure if I'd actually heard those words or imagined them.

Shaking my head to clear my cluttered mind, I stepped forward to meet my fate.

10

NATHANIEL

I was oddly proud to see Tessa come through the portal from Earth first, stepping easily onto the reddish brick of the small village square. I couldn't help but smile at her wide eyes as she took in her first view of Olympus.

Her friend Eric came next, stumbling a bit as he stepped through, followed by Mary. Hermes stepped through last, pulling the door shut behind him, then came to stand beside me.

"Athena and Ares headed home. Apollo went wherever it is Apollo goes," he said with an eye roll. He jerked his chin toward Tessa. "Is that the one you met with?"

"Yes."

He gave her an appraising glance, and I elbowed him.

"What? I'm allowed to appreciate a beautiful woman."

"Fine, but do you have to ogle her?"

"Quiet, both of you," Chiron said from my other side. The centaur was the lead trainer for the Ischyra, and as I had already encountered two of the Renville recruits, he had requested I be present at their arrival.

I stole a glance at his feet and was a bit disheartened to see that he'd come in his human form; no hooves in sight.

Over the years, the newer generations of Ischyra had needed more of an adjustment period when it came to seeing a half-man, half-horse upon arrival, despite previous knowledge of his kind. I often blamed it on the stigma entertainment had placed on shapeshifters of all types, classifying them as creatures to be feared. Sooner or later, they would be exposed to his true form, but at the beginning, he contented himself with runs through the forest when he wasn't focused on training the recruits.

For now, his broad, seven-foot frame, bare torso, and mass of wild black-brown hair were the only indication that he wasn't quite as tame as the rest of us.

As Chiron stepped forward, I hung back. As entertaining as it had been, I had no desire to relive the reaming I'd received on Tessa's behalf the previous evening. By the looks of it, Mary wasn't leaving her side.

When Tessa's eyes met mine, she smiled, but the look of resolve on her face appeared forced. She wasn't aiming her thoughts at me, though, so I didn't try to read them.

The tired looking brunette at Tessa's side followed her gaze, and when she saw me, her lips set in a thin line.

'Try anything funny, and the second I get strong enough, I'll rip you limb from limb and choke you with your own arm.'

I bit back a smile. The mentors were going to have fun with this one, that was certain.

"She's feisty, isn't she?" Hermes whispered, clearly having caught Mary's message.

I slid him a sideways glance. "It's rude to listen in on people's thoughts, you know."

"New recruits are far too entertaining to ignore," he replied, laughing. "And don't act as though you don't want to hear what that pretty blonde's thoughts are of you."

I didn't respond.

He was right. He knew it as well as I did.

When Tessa saw Mary's expression, she elbowed her in the ribs and gestured toward Chiron, who had begun his welcome speech.

"Welcome to Olympus, everyone!" He rubbed his hands together. He always enjoyed the arrival of the new recruits.

"I'll get right to it. As it stands, there will be fifty new Ischyra coming in. Over the course of the last twelve hours, recruits have been arriving from other areas around the world. Your new living quarters are just up there. The three of us will be escorting you there shortly."

He gestured toward a U-shaped building just down the tree-lined street that stretched to our left.

"At seven o'clock this evening—about four hours from now, considering your time change, so keep that in mind—you will attend the arrival feast for new recruits, during which time you will be able to get better acquainted with your fellow recruits. You'll also meet Ischyra from previous generations who will be assisting with your training, which will begin the day after tomorrow at the training arena just outside the village."

Their heads all turned in unison up the mountain, where the stone walls of the arena were just visible behind the village's outer-most buildings.

"Now, if you'll follow me, we'll be heading just up the hill here."

Chiron began leading the way up the hill, and Hermes nudged me.

"I have to go check in with Chiron about the next round of recruits. I'll be back."

He jogged to catch up with Chiron, the rest of us trailing behind. A moment later, I was surprised to see Tessa fall into step beside me.

"Hey," she said quietly. Her small black rolling suitcase clattered on the cobblestone as we walked.

Mary was on her other side and looked to be focusing intently on putting one foot in front of the other. Eric walked behind us, taking in the sights.

"Hi." I gave her a smile. "How are you?"

"Eh, you know, living the dream. You?"

"Can't complain," I said.

"I don't suppose you happened to look into...things, did you?"

I opened my mouth, wanting to tell her what I'd learned during my meeting with Apollo and Hestia, but snapped it shut before any words came out.

It just wasn't worth the aggravation of a fight with him. Not yet, anyway.

"I haven't found anything out, but I'll do what I can," I said, smothering my irritation.

"Thanks."

I slid my hands in my pockets. "Were you able to get some sleep last night?"

"Yes, surprisingly." *'No thanks to you,'* she mentally added with a smirk.

'I told you that you'd be fine,' I replied. *'Any dreams?'*

'Nope, none.'

'That's good to hear.' Speaking aloud, I asked, "So how was your departure?"

"It was rough, emotionally, but now that I'm here, I'm dealing."

"And coming through the portal?"

"Easier than I thought it'd be." She gave Mary an elbow to the ribs. "How about you, Mare?"

When I looked at Mary more closely, I noticed she looked pale.

I opened my mind to hers and smiled when I saw what was bothering her. "Are you feeling alright, Mary?"

Sliding her sunglasses up onto her head, Mary gave me a scrutinizing look. I was on the verge of annoyance when she finally shrugged. She wasn't forcing thoughts on me like she had been earlier, so I didn't attempt to read whatever was going through her head now.

"I'm fine and it was okay."

"Well, I'm glad to hear all went well."

She gave me a brief smile, then gave Tessa a pointed look as she fell back to walk with Eric. He put an arm around her, and she closed her eyes and rested her head on his shoulder as they walked.

I barely had time to wonder how she was going to manage walking with her eyes closed when Hermes joined us then, forcing himself between me and Tessa, throwing a casual arm over her shoulder as he grinned down at her.

She looked up at him wide-eyed, then turned to look at me.

I rolled my eyes and shook my head. *'Ignore him.'*

'Not fucking likely!'

"So you're Tessa." Hermes' grin turned wicked. "Nathaniel told me about you."

A look of confusion crossed her face. "He did?"

Hermes leaned down and pressed his lips to her ear.

"He thinks you're pretty," he whispered.

Her eyes darted to me, and a flush spread across her cheeks. *'This is mortifying.'*

'I'm sorry. He's incorrigible, but you get used to it.'

"Don't you have recruits to meet?" I asked him pointedly. *'This isn't helpful. Go away,'* I sent to him.

Hermes smirked before responding. *'It's been ages since you've liked a girl. Let me have my fun.'*

He grinned down at Tessa. "He's deflecting. That definitely means he has a crush."

Mary muttered something unintelligible, pressing a hand to her mouth as a sour look crossed her face.

Hermes looked back at her warily. "Is your friend going to vomit?"

"It's—Mary isn't feeling well this morning," Tessa explained.

"Mary's fucking hungover," Mary muttered, shooting me a glare. Her eyes widened when she realized who'd actually spoken. "Oh shit."

Hermes dropped his arm from Tessa's shoulder, then turned to walk backward. He folded his arms across his chest and arched a brow.

"You're braver than many gods I know, girl. Coming to your first day so hungover you don't realize an Elder is in front of you? That's just asking for trouble."

Tessa pressed a hand to her face and shook her head.

"Right. Um, well, I think the portal might've made it worse," Mary said, her words rushing out.

Hermes started laughing. "You're talking to the god in charge of inter-realm travel. Portals don't make people sick." He narrowed his eyes at her, then grinned. "Cheap beer does, though. Especially mixed with tequila."

Mary's eyes widened as she realized Hermes was reading her mind.

Just then, Chiron called my name.

I grabbed Hermes' arm and pulled him forward.

"Come on, let's leave the recruits alone," I said.

"Always ruining my fun," he muttered. He flashed Tessa one last grin, then turned back around.

Chiron was waiting for us just outside the gate to the smallest of the five apartment complexes dedicated strictly to Ischyra recruits.

"Let's get them settled in," he said as he opened the gate, leading the recruits into the open stone courtyard of the dormitory. "We've got to go get ready for the next round to come through. Argentina, I believe. Are you alright to take these three on a quick tour?"

I nodded. "Of course. Are their dormitory assignments already on their doors?"

"Yes, they were put up earlier. The others are already in there getting settled."

"Not a problem."

"No funny business while we're gone," Hermes warned, jabbing a finger at me.

"Wouldn't dream of it."

With one last wink in Tessa's direction, he vanished.

"That was awesome!" Eric said, staring at the spot where Hermes had just stood. "Can you all teleport like that?"

"Just the gods," I replied. "Everyone else has to use the portal fields. Come on, I'll show you to your rooms."

Tessa reached down and pulled her friend to her feet. Mary had been lounging on one of the stone benches that surrounded the central fountain, somehow managing to look perfectly at ease, yet completely out of place.

Rubbing the bridge of my nose, I wondered how she would fair over the next twelve months of training.

I took them through a stone archway to the covered hall that wrapped around the courtyard. As we walked, I showed them the way to two large common rooms, two small workout facilities, and a laundry area, before finally coming to a stop at the entrance to the women's residence halls.

"Nearly all of the other recruits have arrived, so it's more than likely your roommate will already be present. Your room assignments will be inscribed on your door, so once you find your name, go on and get settled."

I paused before opening the door.

"Now remember," I said, turning to the girls. "Olympus expects the Ischyra to be a team. This won't be a competition, so you should not look at each other as opponents. Rooming with someone new, someone you don't know, is a way to foster that sense of comradery."

"Can we—" Mary started to speak, but I cut her off with a wave of my hand.

"And no, you may not coordinate with other recruits to switch." I smiled wryly. "Your assignments are made by the gods, and they don't like their decisions being questioned."

Her mouth snapped shut.

I pushed open the door. "Your rooms are just through here."

11

TESSA

When we entered the hallway for the women's dormitories, I was surprised to see how much it looked like a regular human university. Seven heavy wooden doors ran down either side of the gray carpeted hallway, and colorful paintings of various Olympic beings were hung on the white walls. I ran my fingers along their rough texture as I scanned the gilded nameplates until I found my name on the last door on the left.

I hesitated before entering, wondering if I should knock. Technically it was my room, but what if my roommate – Ms. Mariana Comsa, according to the fancily scripted nameplate – was getting changed or something?

After a moment, I rolled my shoulders back, then knocked lightly before slowly opening the door.

When I entered the room, I saw that it, too, seemed modeled after a normal college dorm room. A large, blue, curtained window on the wall opposite the door looked out onto a wide, grassy lawn that acted as a buffer between our building and the one behind it. Matching beds and nightstands sat on either side of the window. Each nightstand held small alarm clocks and lamps, and spanning the space between the two, was a squat bookcase that already held several books and a few framed photos. On either side of the room was a door that matched the one I'd just walked through. The one on the right was open slightly, revealing a pale blue tiled floor. The one across from it was shut tight.

A black-haired girl was lying on her bed with one arm draped over her eyes and her legs crossed at the ankles. Quietly, I tiptoed over to the other bed and set my suitcase down on the floor, then sat down, still reeling a bit from my encounter with Hermes. Before I could think much on it, a heavily accented voice came from the girl, causing me to jump to my feet.

"You can speak. I am not asleep."

Dragging her arm away from her face, my roommate sat up and faced me, and for the briefest of moments, we assessed each other. She looked to be about my height with enough definition in her arms to tell me she spent a lot of time working out. There was a very severe look about her – sleek black hair cut in jagged edges at her shoulders, pale skin, with a perfectly bow-shaped mouth and angular jaw. One black eyebrow arched delicately as her bright blue eyes scanned me from head to toe. Finally, she stood and extended her hand.

"I am Mariana, but you can call me Yana. I am from Bălanu, Romania. You are from the United States, yes?"

Standing up, I gave her hand a quick shake. "Yep. Pennsylvania. I came through the portal field in Renville. I'm Tessa."

She flashed me a quick smile and put her hands on her hips. "It is very nice to meet you, Tessa. I hope you do not mind I chose the bed on the right."

I gave her a quick smile. "Of course, no problem at all."

I sat back on the edge of the bed and kicked off my black flats. I was anxious to get out of the stiff capris I'd worn for my trip through the portal. Glancing at Mariana, I noticed she was in black leggings and a thigh-length sleeveless white tunic, making me wonder if I'd underestimated Mary's casual comfort look.

"So how was your trip through?" I asked her. "Do you have a portal field in your town, or did you have to travel?"

"No, I had to travel about two hours to get to the field in Craiova. Andrei, the boy who traveled with me, lived much closer."

"Oh, bummer."

I dug through my suitcase until I found my own black leggings and a purple, loose-fitting tank top that was just long enough to cover my butt. I stepped into the bathroom, leaving the door partially open as I changed.

"You guys didn't know each other, then?"

"No, we had never met before this morning," she replied. "You knew the other Americans?"

I quickly pulled my long hair into a ponytail and stepped back into the room. "Yeah, we've all known each other pretty much forever."

"That must have been nice, growing up with friends who shared a similar future."

She looked a bit wistful, and I wondered if that meant she'd only ever been able to talk to her guardians about what lay in store for her.

"Did you have many human friends at your school?" she asked.

"Yeah, some." I sat down on my bed and crossed my legs. "What about you?"

She smiled ruefully. "A few, but my guardians did not really care for it. I think they were concerned bad human habits might rub off on me."

"Really? Like what?"

Before she could answer, there was a loud knocking at the door.

"Tessa, let me in!"

Speaking of bad human habits...

I rolled my eyes in Yana's direction. "Sorry about this."

I'd barely opened the door before Mary barged in and flopped onto my bed, pulling my pillow over her eyes. Yana looked at me in understandable confusion.

"Something wrong, Mare?"

She yanked the pillow away from her face and glared at me.

"Yes. Ms. Anette Johansen. She's the freaking problem. I hope you got a cool roommate because mine sucks." She lifted her head slightly and noticed Yana staring at her. "Oh. Hey. I'm Mary."

Yana gave a small smile. "Yana."

"Cool." Mary sat up. "So anyway, this chick, she must've brought her entire freaking bedroom from home, because half of my room is covered with boy band posters and knick knacks. How she even fit all that crap in that dinky little suitcase she brought is beyond me. Tess, there are New Kids on the Block bobbleheads on her nightstand. Do they even exist anymore? I'm pretty sure my guardians listened to them back in the 80s."

I couldn't help grinning. "Okay, but what is *she* like? Is she nice?"

She shrugged. "Maybe. I don't know."

"Mary..."

"What? I'll chat her up at dinner. Or better yet, you chat her up and tell me how it goes." She gave me a thumbs up and flopped back down on the bed. Almost immediately, she sat back up.

"Hang on. Can we please talk about that thing with Hermes earlier? Why did he have his arm around you?"

"Hermes had...what?" Yana glanced between us, confused.

I rolled my eyes. "I have no clue. Clearly, he and Nathaniel are friends, but I didn't expect him to be so..."

"Handsy?" Mary offered.

I snorted. "Casual."

"Who is Nathaniel?" Yana asked.

"A liaison who came to talk to Tessa the other day. He's got a thing for her now."

"It's a little more complicated than that," I said, shooting Mary a glare.

Quickly, I gave Yana a blow-by-blow of my first meeting with Nathaniel, leaving out the part about the vision.

"And now he likes you?"

"He totally likes her," Mary said, grinning.

"I don't know about that," I said, the blush I'd felt earlier returning. "He doesn't know me."

"An Elder said he likes you. An Elder agreed with *me*, Tess, so I'm totally right." She shifted her gaze to Yana. "Just wait. When he sees her tonight in her little dress and those sexy heels, you watch how he reacts."

"It's knee-length," I said. "Not little."

"Yeah, yeah. What time do we have to be at this thing tonight?"

"I think seven? I'm pretty sure that's what Chiron said. We've got a few hours still."

"Awesome. I'm taking a nap." Mary closed her eyes and pulled a pillow over her face.

"Uh uh, no." I gave her ankle a hard yank. "Get up, we're gonna go meet some of the others."

"What? Why? That's what this dinner is for, right?"

"Come on, grumpy. Let's at least get out of these stuffy rooms. There's lots to explore around here." I gave her foot another tug. Then, knowing her fondness for canned soda, I added, "They might even have a soda machine in the common room."

It had the desired effect. She pulled her foot from my grasp and swung her feet around to the floor.

"Fine. Let's go." She glanced over at Yana. "You coming?"

Yana's eyebrows rose. "Oh, yes, of course I'll join you."

"Don't worry," I whispered as we were leaving. "Mary's not usually such a brat. She just decided to go out and get drunk last night and hasn't quite recovered."

Mary stuck her tongue out in response. "Whatever. At least I had fun."

"You are braver than me." Yana placed a hand on her stomach. "My stomach has been in knots all day, and I did nothing last night."

Mary shrugged and stood up. "It'll pass, don't worry. Let's go, I want sugar."

WE WERE PLEASANTLY surprised to find that the common room did, in fact, sport a few vending machines that held a variety of drinks and snacks. I didn't recognize any of the labels, so I assumed they were specific to the Olympic realm. Fortunately, they didn't require actual money—one of the perks of living in Olympia.

To Mary's disappointment, the closest thing to canned soda was bottled carbonated fig juice. Yana and I went for plain honeysuckle water.

After we'd each picked out our snacks, we sat down on two of the four couches set up around the room.

"So, Yana," Mary began, crunching away on her freeze-dried pears. "What's Romania like?"

Yana took a sip of her sweetened water. "It is a beautiful country. My home was near the Danube River in the south, just on the border of Bulgaria. The commune I grew up in is very small, and we did not travel so much. I'm hoping after our training year I am assigned someplace exciting." Her eyes seemed to brighten at that thought.

The three of us snacked our way through another ten minutes of conversation before some of the others started filtering into the common room, including Eric and a dark-haired recruit who looked to have a permanent scowl on his face. They made their way over to join us, then were quickly followed by a third guy who hopped over the back of the couch to sit next to Yana.

Introductions went around. The dark-haired guy turned out to be Eric's roommate, Andrei Capreanu, the one who'd traveled from Romania with Yana.

The recruit who'd landed next to Yana introduced himself as Igor Federov from Tura, a small town in Russia. Despite the naturally downturned look to his face, the smile he gave me when he shook my hand made him seem a lot friendlier than I'd initially thought.

"Igor, where's your roommate?" Mary crumpled up her empty bag and glanced around for a trash can.

"It's just here, look." Andrei took the bag and walked quickly toward a metal circle, about twelve inches in diameter, built into the wall next to the vending machine. "It's an incinerator, see? We've got one in our hallway. You have probably got one in yours, as well."

He pressed a small button on the side of the circle and a hole opened, allowing him to toss the bag inside. It snapped shut, and I could just make out a muffled *whoosh* that I assumed was the bag being burned to ash.

"Huh. Cool, thanks." Mary gave him a quick smile, then sat back down and looked at him expectantly as he reclaimed his seat next to Yana. "So. Who's your roomie?"

"Demir is around here somewhere, although he's been very quiet," Igor said, exchanging a look with Andrei.

Andrei scanned the room, then lowered his voice to just above a whisper. "We get the feeling he does not care to be here."

Yana smacked his chest. "*Taci*, Andrei! That is not your business."

He waved her off. "What? You tell me to be quiet, but I worry that there is a recruit here who does not wish to be." He looked to the guys for backup. "I am correct, no?"

Eric shifted uncomfortably, but I was pretty sure he agreed with Andrei.

"Maybe give it a bit more time before passing judgement," Mary said, arching a brow. "We just got here."

Andrei shrugged. "I suppose."

The six of us hung out and talked for another half-hour before dispersing to get ready for dinner. We'd just split off from the guys with the intention of taking a nap, when a tall, peppy blonde came bouncing down the hall, her sleek ponytail swaying behind her.

"Mary! I was just coming to look for you." She grinned, flashing a set of dazzling white teeth.

"Hey, Anette." Mary gave the girl a tight smile, then gestured at Yana and me. "This is Yana and Tessa. What's up?"

"I was beginning to think you'd forgotten what time dinner would be! When would you like to start getting ready?"

Mary forced a smile. "Oh, that's so sweet...thanks. We still have a few hours, right? Like, three?"

Anette pushed open the door to the hall and held it as we walked through. I heard music wafting through an open door that sounded vaguely like 1990s pop. I gave Mary a questioning look and she arched a brow as if to say, "What did I tell you?"

"Oh, yes, we do, but I thought maybe we could hang out a bit before, you know? We are going to be living together for the next year, after all!"

"Uh huh. Well, I'm totally cool with that...after I take a nap." Mary looked at me, then back toward her open door. "Which I think I'll do in Tessa's room. Softer sheets and all."

Anette frowned. "Well, okay, but would you like me to come get you? It would be a shame to not have enough time to get properly ready to meet the Elders."

"I'll make sure she makes it back with enough time," I said, cutting Mary off before she could come up with anymore lame excuses. "She's just a little homesick."

I ignored the glare I could feel coming from Mary.

"Oh..." Anette nodded knowingly. "Yes, that will happen at times, I am certain." She gave Mary a look that showed a bit more sympathy. "We will talk after you've napped."

I nudged Mary with my elbow, and she sighed.

"Look, if you want, you can come to Tessa's room later, we'll get ready together."

"Oh, that sounds wonderful!" Anette smiled at both of us. "I will see you in a bit, then."

I couldn't even be annoyed that my best friend was offering up my room as pre-party central. Getting ready to go to dinner with a bunch of girls actually sounded like a lot of fun.

AN HOUR LATER, I opened my door to find a bouncing Anette on the other side. "Ladies, it is time to wake up! The feast begins in just two hours!"

Glancing at the clock on my nightstand, I saw that she was right. Rubbing my eyes, I looked over at Mary, still asleep against the wall in my bed, and Yana, who was sprawled out across her own.

I gave her an appreciative smile. "I'll get them up. Thanks for letting us know."

"Oh, it's no problem. I'll be back soon to get ready with you all."

I gave the leg of my bed a swift kick to wake up my best friend. She grumbled in response and threw a pillow at me, but she was awake, so my duty was done. Leaning over Yana's bed, I hesitantly shook her shoulder.

"Yana, we need to start getting ready."

"*Da*. Okay," she mumbled sleepily, her eyes drifting shut again.

"Do you need to shower first?"

I'd never had to share a bathroom with anyone before, so I wasn't sure of proper etiquette. I was still surprised at how human my experience at Olympia had been so far. I felt as though I'd just been dropped off at college, not a village at the foot of Olympus in an entirely different realm.

Yana sat up and shook her head. "No, it is all yours. I showered when I arrived."

When I opened the closet to look for towels, I heard the water turn on in the bathroom. Looking back to my bed, I saw that Mary had snuck into the bathroom before I could.

Brat.

~

ONCE WE WERE ALL SHOWERED, Anette joined us, and odd bits of makeup and clothing began getting passed back and forth as everyone worked out what to wear.

I was loving the quintessential girly-ness of the entire process. I'd expected training uniforms and practical clothing to be the norm, yet here we were sharing Anette's stash of MAC eyeshadow and taking turns with Mary's curling iron.

"Is this even a fancy thing?" Yana asked as she sprayed flowery hair spray in my hair to set the gentle waves she'd just put in. She picked up a gold clip she'd borrowed from Anette and slid it along my temple, pulling the hair on one side back from my face.

"I guess? I mean it's a dinner with the gods, so I don't see how it wouldn't be." I grinned. "Even if it isn't, when's the next time you think we'll get to get all pretty like this?"

"This is very true," she said with a smile. "I like your dress."

I looked down at the purple pencil dress I'd bought a few weeks earlier. When John and Analise told me I would need to bring one formal outfit, I jumped at the chance to go shopping. It was the last shopping trip I'd done with Analise, and we'd had a blast going from store to store in the nearby mall on the hunt for the perfect dress. I'd even managed to snag some gold bangle bracelets and super cute strappy gold heels while we were there, which set off the pink quick-dry polish I'd borrowed from Anette perfectly.

I smiled fondly at the memory.

"Thanks," I said to Yana. "It's a little outside my normal fashion comfort zone, but I love it. I like yours, too."

The dark gray smoky eye she'd donned to accent her short, flowy charcoal dress made her blue eyes stand out like beacons.

"Thank you." She smiled as she set down the can of hairspray. "There, I think you are all set."

I looked at my reflection in the mirror and bit my lip. "Yana, this looks amazing. You might need to do my hair every day," I said, running my hand over the long blonde waves. "I can never get my hair to do this. Or anything, really."

"Okay ladies, let's go," Mary said loudly, clapping her hands. She'd borrowed a knee-length, off-the-shoulder dress in a deep navy from Anette who'd somehow managed to bring an obscene amount of clothing from her home in Norway. Her brown hair was straightened for once, and she'd put on my pink sparkly eye shadow, bringing out the green in her hazel eyes.

"Hey, Anette?" I asked, moving to walk beside her. "How'd you manage to pack so much stuff? I mean, my suitcase is a decent size, but you seem to have brought everything."

She grinned and tucked her bright blond hair behind her ears. "Ziploc bags. I folded all my clothes flat and rolled them up. I was able to fit a lot more than if I'd packed them normally."

I frowned. "Wasn't everything all wrinkled?"

She laughed. "I brought a fabric steamer."

I raised my eyebrows and smiled appreciatively. "That's pretty awesome."

When we entered the courtyard, I saw that the rest of the girls, as well as the boys, had beaten us there and were waiting expectantly with Nathaniel.

Mary let out a low whistle when she saw him. "Well damn, doesn't he clean up nice?"

"You can say that again," I murmured as I took in how he looked in his slim fitting gray pants and pale blue dress shirt with the top button undone. Before I could appreciate the perfect fit of his outfit, Eric jogged over and came to stop in front of me, followed by Igor.

"Hey, guys!" He grinned down at me. "You look great."

"Thanks, you guys do, too."

Similar to Nathaniel, the guys were all wearing dress pants and button downs. A few were sporting ties or blazers, too.

"Sit with me at dinner?" Eric asked.

"Um, su—"

Mary grabbed my elbow. "Sorry, Eric. Yana and I already called dibs on this one. You guys can have Andrei and whoever that guy is he's talking to," she said, gesturing toward where Andrei was laughing with a lanky blond guy.

Eric rolled his eyes. "Come on! I'm not sitting and playing wingman all night."

Mary laughed. "Then go hang out with the other recruits. Make new friends. It'll be good for you."

Before he could voice any more disappointment, Nathaniel addressed us.

"Alright, everyone, let's get going. We'll be heading back to the portal field to take the door to the Agora. It's about halfway between here and the deity residences and will be where all formal gatherings and meetings will be held. Tonight, you'll meet the Elders for the first time, and you'll have the opportunity to talk with some Ischyra from past generations. Most of those who will be present at dinner will become your mentors for the next year."

Elders. Right.

Suddenly my purple dress and gold heels seemed massively inadequate for a dinner with the gods.

Silently, we followed him through the outer gate and down the hill to the portal field, forcing me to navigate the cobblestone like a minefield in my stilettos.

Stupid shoes, I thought. What had I been thinking wearing four-inch heels?

'You look fine. Stop worrying.'

I bit back a smile when I heard Nathaniel's voice in my head. I looked up to where he was walking, but he looked wrapped up in conversation with one of the male recruits.

'This is kind of intrusive.'

'It's not my fault you project your thoughts when you're worried.'

'I'm not sure if I buy that, but I will say your ability to carry on two conversations at once is pretty impressive.'

'What can I say? I'm good at multitasking.'

"What's got you so smiley?"

I looked down at Mary and saw that she wore a suspicious expression. Her eyes flicked toward the front of our group then back at me.

"You're talking to him, aren't you!"

"Talking to who?" Yana asked.

"No one," I muttered, giving Mary the stink eye.

Just then, we arrived at the portal field and I was saved from further questioning.

Instead of going to the plain white door from which we'd entered Olympia, Nathaniel led us to a shimmery golden one.

"Who's first?" He caught my eye, and I saw one eyebrow raise slightly. Almost immediately, I felt a hard shove to my back.

"Tessa is!"

I glared at Mary. "I'm wearing heels, you jerk!" I hissed.

"Like your balance has ever failed you," she said, making a shooing motion with her hands.

I shook my head, then went to stand beside Nathaniel in front of the door.

He smiled down at me. "First again?"

"I guess so," I said with a sigh. I eyed the open doorway warily. "Same deal as when we arrived?"

"Yes. Just step through to the other side. Once I get the rest in, I'll be right behind you."

"Sounds good."

Focusing my eyes forward, I put one foot through the door, bracing myself for the same coldness I'd experienced on my first trip through a portal.

When I stepped out onto the rocky mountainside, I stood in front of an opulent building built on an outcropping that overlooked the Valley of Olympus far below. It was about four stories tall with a colonnade of gleaming white columns around the perimeter, interspersed with statues of the gods. A dense forest rose up behind it, ending far off in the distance just below the wispy ring of clouds that circled the summit. Rose and honeysuckle bushes were planted in beds along either side of the front, breaking up the monotonous white tone.

It was different than the typical Agoras of ancient Greece which were usually open-air meeting areas. This building reminded me more of the Parthenon in Athens, which I'd visited when I was twelve with John and Analise. I felt a quick pang of sadness as I was hit with the realization, once again, that I had no idea when I'd see my guardians again.

Shaking off the feeling, I stepped away from the door to wait for the others. I slowly turned, taking in the massive mountain range that surrounded me. Much like the night sky, its vastness reminded me how completely small I was in the grand scheme of things.

As I looked out over the expanse of Olympus, the voice I'd heard as I stepped through the portal when I arrived sounded in my head.

Never doubt yourself, Tessa.

I felt my brow furrow in confusion.

When I'd first heard those words as I'd left Renville, I'd thought it was just my own mind misremembering the words that Analise had whispered before I left. Now hearing it again, I noticed that the voice was distinctly male and sort of familiar, and the words were definitely not Analise's.

I jumped as I felt a hand on my arm. I turned my head and saw Mary frowning, looking concerned.

"Tess? What is it?"

I rubbed my forehead. "Nothing. My head kind of hurts, that's all."

"Oh, okay. Well, everyone's through. Your boy is taking us in."

I looked up at the building, and sure enough, the rest of the recruits were halfway up the steps. Mary moved to catch up, and I followed slowly behind. Two imposing blue and white mosaic doors swung open, and the quiet din of conversation filtered down the wide white steps.

I couldn't help but gape when I entered.

Opulent was too mundane a word to describe the inside of the Agora because it had clearly been built for the gods. All throughout the massive white marble room, mosaics depicting various deities glimmered, some so lifelike they appeared to be moving. The parquet floor was made of shining wood, inlayed with intricately carved flowers and vines.

Ischyra, distinguishable by their formal black uniforms, filled the straight-backed chairs at the elaborately carved tables that were arranged on either side of the room. Each seat was set with gleaming gold flatware, pearlescent plates, and crystal goblets. Scattered along the tables were tall pitchers of clear liquid with some type of white blossom floating inside.

The fifty Ischyra recruits took up five of the large round tables. Mary, Yana, and I snagged seats together, and we were quickly joined by Anette and two other girls I hadn't met yet. Eric drifted to the table next to us with Igor, Andrei, and the blond guy he'd been talking to, along with a few other male recruits.

"And here I thought you'd be the first one to find someone to hook up with," Mary whispered, giggling.

"I thought the same about you," I murmured as I looked around the room. "This place is insane."

At the end of the room opposite the doors, set in front of arched windows that rose from floor to ceiling, was a curved dais that featured fifteen thrones so beautiful they looked as though they'd been sculpted by Michelangelo himself. Running the length of the dais in front of them was a long table carved in the same style as the one we occupied. With a start, I realized those seats would soon be occupied by the Elders of Olympus.

A redhaired girl who sat on the other side of Mary leaned over. "Why are there fifteen thrones?" she whispered. Her accent reminded me a little of Anette's.

I shrugged. "No clue." I smiled at her and held out a hand. "I'm Tessa."

She grinned and shook my hand. "Sina."

For the next few minutes, none of us spoke, and I could tell by the way Yana was throwing furtive glances at the door and the way Mary was wringing her hands under the table, that I wasn't the only one with a bad case of nerves.

After a few minutes, one of the large tiled doors opened with a loud creak, and the room became quiet. A small man in a charcoal gray, double-breasted suit stood at the front of the room before the dais and cleared his throat.

"Hey, look, it's Rudolfo," Mary said. "I didn't expect to see him here. Think he's gonna play hypnotist again?"

I laughed as I remembered the previous year's after-prom party where he'd been hired to hypnotize students.

"You both know him?" Yana whispered.

"Yeah," I said. "He's friends with Eric's guardians. We've known him pretty much forever. Last year, our school hired him as a hypnotist for the party we had after our prom. You should've seen the things he got some of the kids to do."

"He is a Coercer, then?"

"Yep. He's a super cool guy."

I refocused my attention on Rudolfo as he began to speak again, his heavy Spanish accent ringing through the room.

"I would like to take this opportunity to welcome our new generation of Ischyra to our lovely mountain! For those of you who don't know me, I am Rudolfo, of the three hundredth generation of Ischyra! Each generation, we begin the Ischyra recruits' time here with a feast, a night to enjoy your first taste of Olympian food, mingle with the recent generations of Ischyra, and meet the Elders. This is a *most* special event, and I do hope you will enjoy yourselves as much as I will!" He cocked his head to the side, then smiled and clapped his hands together loudly. "Now, if you will please rise, the Elders have arrived!"

Everyone stood as the doors opened once more. It was a bit hard to see across the sea of bodies, but I didn't have to wait long to get my first glimpse.

Whatever I had expected when I pictured them was nothing to what was in front of me now. I'd been pretty star-struck when I'd seen Athena, Apollo, Ares, and Hermes at the portal field in Renville, but now, seeing all thirteen of them up close as they made their way up to the dais?

Nothing could've prepared me for the beings who passed in front of us.

Their youthful looks might make someone think they were no older than twenty-five, but their expressions, the way that they carried themselves, indicated that their experience was eons beyond that of any human.

Athena came through first, accompanied by Ares. As they came closer, I noticed a small silver shield clasped to the lapel of his navy blue suit jacket. Athena's matching shield glittered at her temple where it pinned her wavy brown locks away from her delicate face.

The two war gods were quickly followed by Hestia, wearing a flowing turquoise gown. As she passed by our table, I thought I saw a slight smile flit across her lips.

A tall, fierce looking man in a fitted gray suit with dark brown skin, almond shaped eyes, short black hair, and sharp chin came next. The small trident on his jacket indicated he was Poseidon, god of the sea.

I didn't know why, but he always seemed to be the most intimidating god in all the stories.

Hephaestus, the stooped, dark haired Olympian forger of weapons, limped slowly behind him, his black cane making a distinct tap on the marble floor with each step. His hair was nearly as black as his suit, yet when he passed beneath the gentle glow of the chandeliers, I saw that reddish streaks ran through the soft waves.

Aphrodite followed next, the train of her shimmery white gown trailing behind her, a sharp contrast to her russet skin. The straps of her dress were held together with matching silver doves. Her thick, black hair was piled high on her head with wavy tendrils that trailed down her back. There was a small upturn to the corners of her heart-shaped mouth, as though she were smiling at some private joke.

The next few Elders who walked past had the same ethereal presence. Demeter, the goddess in charge of the Olympic agricultural operation that supplied the mountain, was wearing a navy blue halter dress made of layers of sheer fabrics. She was tall and thin with full lips, light eyes, and perfectly arched brown eyebrows. Long, flowing blonde curls tumbled to her waist and were woven through with red poppies.

Hermes came next, and walking beside him was a confident looking male with light brown hair that fell across his forehead and deep, olive toned skin. He carried himself in a way that told me he knew he was good looking. Three silver leaves of ivy were pinned to the breast of his gray suit coat, identifying him as Dionysus, the youngest of the Olympians and brother of Hermes.

Nine Elders had come through and seated themselves at the curved dais. When I looked back to the door to see who would be next, I saw Apollo and a woman who I recognized as his twin, Artemis. They had the same pale features – white-blond hair, gray eyes, porcelain skin, and killer cheekbones. His double-breasted fitted white suit matched Artemis's shift dress perfectly. On his lapel was a shiny silver sun, while Artemis' clasp was in the shape of a small bow and arrow, indicating her place as goddess of the hunt. They didn't show the same friendliness as the other gods who'd accompanied one another. They walked about a foot apart from each other and both wore the same dour expression.

The last two to enter the hall were Zeus and his wife Hera, and Chaos be damned if I ever saw a more stunning pair.

Each wore a white toga fastened with a gleaming gold clasp in the shape of a lightning bolt, the fabric doing little to conceal Zeus's muscular physique. His sandy blond hair fell in waves to his chin, which bore a short, neatly trimmed beard. Even from a distance, I could see that his eyes were both warm and wise. His mouth rested in a small smile as he touched Hera's delicate hand, which laid lightly on his arm.

Dragging my eyes away from the ruler of the Olympic realm, I realized the fragile look of Hera's hand hardly matched the immortal strength that was clear on her face. Waist length brown hair a few shades darker than her olive-toned skin was pinned back, revealing a thin, regal nose, and dark, almond-shaped eyes. The calculating way she took in the room simply oozed power and left no doubt as to why she had such a formidable reputation.

Sina let out a shuddering breath once the Elders had taken their seats. "My goodness," she breathed.

I was just about to sit back down when two more men entered the room.

"Who is that?" Yana asked.

"Not a clue," I said, frowning.

I did a quick count of the gods and goddesses seated at the dais and saw that all thirteen were present, yet there were still two thrones that sat empty on the end. Zeus' mouth was pressed in a firm line, but he gave the men a welcoming nod. The two who were joining them looked to be brothers, possibly twins.

The first man who entered appeared confident, his square chin held high as he walked the length of the room, eyes focused on the dais. He wore a black suit over a white shirt, the top button left undone. His short blond hair and tall, muscular build made me think he was a soldier of some sort.

The other man was identical in build and coloring, but his hair was worn a bit longer, just brushing his shoulders and slightly unkempt. He wore khakis and a black, long-sleeved dress shirt with black shoes. Both men were handsome, but where the first exuded confidence, the second looked...uncertain—apprehensive, even—as he took in the crowd. His eyes jumped from face to face as though waiting for someone to approach or call out.

I heard Mary let out a muttered curse, and when I looked at her, I saw that she wore an expression of disbelief as she tracked the movements of the two men.

"What is it?" I hissed.

Mary tore her gaze from the two men and turned her wide eyes on me. "You don't recognize them?"

I shook my head. "No, who are they?"

"Tessa! Gods, didn't you pay attention to your lessons? That's Prometheus and Epimetheus." She stared at them as they walked past and made their way to the two remaining empty thrones on the dais. "What in all the realms are they *doing* here?"

My eyes went wide, and my jaw dropped. I probably looked ridiculous, but in that moment, I didn't care.

Prometheus and Epimetheus. Twin Titans, previously disgraced at the hands of the Olympians.

Epimetheus. The Titan whose foolish decision to take Pandora as his wife had led to the release of countless monstrous creatures onto Earth.

The same monsters that forced Zeus and the other Olympians to create a race of immortals designed for the sole purpose of fighting them.

"Holy shit."

12

NATHANIEL

Noticing the reaction of Tessa and her friends when the Titans entered, I quickly scanned the minds of the newcomers, curious if their reactions would be similar. For the most part, I found confusion mixed with some surprise.

Once the gods were settled, Zeus stood from his place at the center of the dais and motioned for the guests to take their seats, then began to speak with the thunderous voice of a seasoned orator.

"Welcome, all! I hope today finds you well and that all of your travels were smooth. Tomorrow morning, the transition ceremony for the new Ischyra recruits will take place, at which time the powers the gods have entrusted you with will be awakened." His eyes roamed over the crowd. "I acknowledge that this time in your lives may daunting, but know that older generations of Ischyra, as well as the gods and demigods of Olympus, are here to support you. We'd like you all to take this time to get to know one another before you meet your mentors in the morning."

He smiled and held out his hands. "Now, let's eat!"

I was surprised he hadn't mentioned the Titans' presence at all. I scanned the faces of the Elders and found Athena looking at me.

'Chiron will discuss the presence of the Titans at the first training *session. If anyone asks, you can tell them.'* Her eyes drifted toward the table of recruits next to me and landed on Tessa, who was talking animatedly with several of the female recruits. *'Hermes told me you met with that one. She's very pretty,'* she said with a smirk.

I sighed and rolled my eyes. *'You all gossip like old ladies.'*

She gave me a small shrug, then turned and began talking with Demeter.

Once Zeus was seated, servers dressed in white, high-necked shirts and black dress pants began distributing food to the guests.

"Music, Delia!" Dionysus called to a harpist in the corner. She began to play, the soft music just loud enough to be heard over conversation. He sat back down and immediately poured a goblet of ambrosia wine to the brim. Laughing, he turned to Hermes, who was seated next to him, and filled his glass as well.

I shook my head, knowing they would be inebriated and likely singing by the end of the evening.

A movement out of the corner of my eye drew my attention. I looked in the direction of the recruits' tables and saw that Tessa was snapping her fingers in my direction. Just beside her, Mary was deep in conversation with the black-haired girl Tessa roomed with.

I raised my eyebrows. These twenty-first century women were quite the demanding bunch. I motioned for her to come over. She excused herself from her friends and made her way toward me. When she saw that her friend Eric was in the seat just behind me at the next table, she jerked her thumb behind her.

"Eric, swap with me for a sec."

"What? Why?" His eyes darted toward me, then back at her.

I had a hard time not keeping a straight face when I heard his response. Fortunately, Tessa rolled her eyes hard enough for both of us.

"Because I said so. You'll get your seat back in a minute, relax."

He looked as though he wanted to argue further, but when Tessa put a hand on her hip and cocked an eyebrow in challenge, he just gave me a scathing look and stormed off to take the empty seat next to Mary.

Amused, I turned my attention to Tessa, trying not to openly admire how she looked in her dress.

Focusing my eyes on her face, I smiled. "How's your first day on Olympus going?"

"It's great." She adjusted her dress and sat down, then tilted her head in the direction of the dais. "What's up with that?"

"I'm assuming you're talking about the presence of the Titans?"

"You would assume correctly."

I took a sip of water, then set my glass down on the table. "They've been here for quite some time, so no need to worry."

She tapped her fingers lightly on her knees, frowning slightly. "Listen, I know I said that I'm fine with my future. I really am. I want to know what my powers are, and I want to do good for all the realms, not just on Earth." She turned her green eyes on me. "But Epimetheus is one of the reasons I have to be okay with all of this. So I guess my question is, them being here...does this mean we're going to have to work with them?"

"Most likely." I crossed my arms across my chest. "Tessa, if I remember correctly, when we spoke previously, you blamed the Olympians for Pandora's existence, not Epimetheus. Yet here you are, annoyed with a disgraced Titan. Why?"

"I don't know. I guess because Zeus and the rest of them were still fighting a war?"

"What do you mean?"

She shifted in her seat. "I mean, okay, on Earth, I never thought it was fair to fire rockets from the sky at people who are fighting with guns on the ground, but when you have the better weapons and better ideas, you come out the victor, right? That's the whole point of war—to win."

She sighed and shrugged.

"I just have a problem when some jackass's sex drive overpowers common sense and contributes to mankind's potential downfall. Zeus may have handed Epimetheus the bomb, but he didn't detonate it."

A smile twitched at the corner of my mouth. "That is...quite the oversimplification, but I do agree with you. And please, Tessa, keep your voice down. Calling a Titan a jackass isn't the type of first impression you want to make." I glanced at the dais, but it didn't appear anyone was paying us any attention.

She let out a small huff. "Sorry."

"You truly don't feel sympathy for Epimetheus at all?"

"Of course I do," she said. "Why are they here, anyway? Are you allowed to tell me?"

I hesitated for a moment, then tapped my finger on the table and nodded. "There have been rumblings lately of an uprising of sorts. The Titans—most of them, anyway—who are free and have been living peacefully for the last several thousand years want to avoid another war just as much as the Olympians, so a few have been reaching out, trying to rebuild alliances."

"Who's still around that can rise up against the Elders, though? And why didn't John and Analise tell me any of this?"

"All guardians were given explicit instructions to keep quiet about it. This isn't the kind of news that leaves the Mountain until necessary. As far as who can rise up against Olympus, well, there are still some Titans who haven't gotten over Zeus' rebellion, and a number of larger groups who'd be willing to offer their support."

"Okay...So which ones are still in a tizzy?"

"A few."

"Ah." She nodded. She looked around, seeming to feign interest in a nearby table of recruits. When her eyes darted back toward me in a movement that was so infuriatingly *female*, I couldn't help but smile.

"Alright. What do you know of the war with the Titans and the time surrounding it?"

She shrugged. "The basics, I guess. Cronus imprisoned his kids to keep them from killing him, Rhea hid Zeus so he could set them free, they rose up against Cronus and his allies, kicked their asses at Thessaly, booted most of them to Tartarus, and now the Elders rule Olympus instead. What else is there to know?"

"Well, to start, not many Titans who fought the Olympians are still locked away in Tartarus. As they were the figureheads for the Titans' side, Cronus and Iapetus—the twins' father—are the only ones who remain. Zeus released the others, including Menoetius, the twins' other brother, claiming the time they'd served was sufficient punishment but left Cronus and Iapetus to serve an eternal sentence." I took another sip of water. "It's why Prometheus is here and not suffering an eternity of torture chained to a rock."

"So wait, their father is locked down there with Cronus, and they're cool with being here to stand with Zeus?" She raised her eyebrows. "You guys seriously trust them?"

"They have other reasons, believe me, but all you need to know is that they recognize the crimes that their father committed and want to take their former places on Zeus' side. They were always his allies, despite what he may have believed toward the end. They all had the same ideas for what peace across the realms looked like." I cast a quick glance at the dais and saw Prometheus looking in our general direction. "And for the love of all that's holy, would you *please* keep your voice down? You're going to draw attention to yourself."

"Sorry," she muttered.

Tessa's eyes drifted briefly toward the dais. Following her gaze, I saw that Prometheus was looking directly at her, his brow furrowed.

Wonderful.

I was fairly certain that look had nothing to do with her attire, which meant he'd likely heard her not only question his allegiance but also refer to his brother as a jackass.

Shaking my head, I moved on. "Recently, Ares received word from one of the higher ranking Ischyra on Earth—a man named Cornelius, who's stationed in Athens—of rumors that some of the more malicious factions on Earth have been gathering. Demons, the Sirens, the empousa, and some others. We believe Menoetius has been attempting to round them up so he can form a coup."

"Menoetius as in the twins' brother?"

"Yes, and before you ask, he distanced himself from his siblings long before the war began. He and his brothers have been at odds for millennia."

Servers arrived just then, so she leaned aside to allow them to put plates of olives, goat cheese, and arugula in front of her. The pitchers on the tables were topped off, and carafes of wine were placed alongside them.

"So is that a legitimate concern?" she asked.

"Ares thought it important enough to bring to the Elders, and they felt it was credible enough to tell the rest of the Ischyra on Earth to keep their ears to the ground, so to speak."

She opened her mouth to respond but stopped when Eric appeared behind her and leaned down to speak into her ear.

"Can I get my seat back now?"

A look of annoyance crossed her face before she pasted on a smile. "Yup. All yours." She turned back to me. "Talk soon?"

I nodded, and after she moved back to her regular seat, Eric eyed me speculatively, then returned to the conversation at his own table and I turned back to mine.

Once the plates had been cleared away, I watched the Ischyra recruits as they began to mingle with the other guests, laughing and getting to know the mentors they'd be working with for the rest of their training year.

Tomorrow, they'd each find out what their powers were, and from there, they'd be sent off to their mentors to learn how to use them

They seemed solid enough. Each had their quirks, of course, but I could see that they were all loyal; they would do the job they'd been chosen to do.

Hopefully, once they realized what that job truly entailed, that wouldn't change.

13

TESSA

"Well that was interesting," Yana muttered as we walked from the portal field to our dorm. We all had been pretty quiet since we'd left the Agora.

"You mean the part where the twin Titans showed up?" Mary pulled open the door to the girls' hall and we all filed through behind her. "I'm not sure 'interesting' quite covers that."

Once we entered our hall, most of the girls went off to their own rooms, but Mary, Anette, Yana, and I were all way too amped up to go to bed. After saying goodnight to the others, we settled into the room Yana and I shared to recap the night.

"I don't know," Anette said, idly twirling a piece of her white blond hair. "I don't see why this is such a big deal. I think it is good to forgive crimes, yes?"

"Epimetheus didn't commit a crime, Anette," Mary snapped. "He made the most epic fucking blunder of all time when he accepted Pandora from Zeus."

"Yes, he may have made a mistake, but it's not as though he sought her out," Anette pointed out. "Zeus brought Pandora to him, offered her as a gift. It is not the Titan's fault that Zeus tricked him."

Yana spoke before Mary could respond. "Mary, do you not

consider Zeus' creation of Pandora an 'epic fucking blunder' as well? Why are you not more angry with him?"

With a sigh, I laid down on my bed and pulled a pillow over my face as I waited for the bickering to die down. This type of argument was longstanding; many of our kind felt Zeus was mostly at fault and Epimetheus was just a victim of his cunning. Others felt Epimetheus should have heeded the advice Prometheus had given him when he told him not to accept gifts from the Olympians. He didn't, so for some people, he carried the bulk of the blame for humans being plagued with evil.

Despite the amount of blame I placed on him for how things turned out, I often felt sympathy toward Epimetheus. He'd married the woman he loved, only to watch her die the moment they consummated their marriage. I couldn't imagine that kind of pain, especially considering the events her death set in motion. Malevolent creatures on Earth, previously limited in numbers, multiplied by the thousands, leaving nothing but chaos and destruction in their wake, all thanks to the magic released when she died.

"Of course I'm angry with Zeus!" Mary exclaimed. "What he did —tricking Epimetheus like that—well, it was awful. But he'd just come out of a really big freaking war. He thought he'd been betrayed by his allies, so he retaliated."

"But Epimetheus did not betray him!" Yana shot back.

"Zeus didn't know that."

"Mary, I think you are a smart girl," Yana said with a shake of her head. "You know as well as I do that the only reason Zeus was able to find forgiveness from humans is because he had more power and opportunity to make amends than any of the Titans."

"But did Epimetheus try? Tell me, Yana, what exactly did he do over the last three millennia to try and redeem himself? At least Zeus tried to make things right when he created the Ischyra."

"Ah, so that is where your problem lies!" My roommate threw her hands up. "He didn't try hard enough to redeem himself. What exactly would you have had him do? He was powerless! And we all know the only reason Zeus created the Ischyra in the first place was because the other Olympians forced him to!"

"Prometheus tried to help," Mary shot back. I could hear the tell-tale wobble in her voice that told me she was trying to force calmness into her tone. "He loved humans so much, he risked his life to help them when Zeus allowed all those monsters into our world. He was tortured for *years* for helping them. All Epimetheus did was run into hiding," she said bitterly.

Anette held up a hand to stay Yana's response, then faced Mary.

"So what do you suppose we are to do about it? Refuse to work with the Titans? That is hardly an option. We do not even know why they are here. For all we know, they will be gone tomorrow."

Mary rolled her eyes. "Oh, yeah, I'm so sure that's exactly what's going to happen."

I jerked the pillow off my face and sat up. "Fires of the fucking Underworld, Mary! Enough! It's late and I want to go to bed. Please save your sarcastic judgmental bullshit for tomorrow when we actually have some answers."

The other girls sat in stunned silence. Mary and I glared at each other for a moment before she huffed and turned away.

Yana cleared her throat. "There is no point to arguing whether we think they should be here." She held up her hands and shrugged. "The Elders would not bring them without cause, so don't you think we should just wait to see what their reasoning might be?" Mary shot a glare at her, but she ignored it. "Look, Zeus did pretty awful things to those two. I am betting something major has changed to bring them all back together like this."

Mary huffed. "Well, what do you think that is?"

I contemplated telling them everything Nathaniel had told me, but I was too tired to get into that hornet's nest. I hadn't even told Mary; I'd just given her a vague, 'He said we'll hear about it at training' answer after speaking with him.

"How should I know? I just got here," Yana shot back. "But we all know our own Elders are the ones who created Pandora in the hopes that she would royally screw up the human world."

"Yeah, well, I bet if Prometheus, the god of fucking *forethought,* had told them it was a bad idea, they might've listened," Mary grumbled.

"What is the point of being pissed about all of it now?" Yana asked. "It is done. They all did shitty things that led to us being here today. Period."

"Okay!" I raised my voice to cut the argument off where it was. "Again, I'm exhausted, and I think Yana is, too, so how about we all get some sleep?"

Mary looked like she wanted to argue, but she settled on shooting a death glare in my direction before following Anette out.

After we said our goodnights and got ready for bed, Yana and I sat in silence for a few moments.

"Did you have fun tonight?" I asked.

I couldn't come up with anything more creative, but I wanted to steer the conversation far away from Elders and Titans. Her pursed expression when the girls had left made it seem like she was still irritated.

She sighed and punched at her pillow to fluff it up. "I did. I met quite a few interesting people that I'm excited to work with. You?"

"Yeah, it was cool. I talked to this one guy—Christopher, I think his name was—who's an Elemental, a Tempest. I always thought I wanted to have an affinity for fire, but the stuff he was telling me he could do with wind—tornadoes to clear your enemies off a field, that kind of thing—sounded kind of awesome."

"Oh, that does sound interesting! I used to always think affinities involving wind were...weak or something, you know? This just reminds me how much I have to learn."

"Agreed. So do you have an idea of what kind of affinity you want? Is there something that's always fascinated you?"

She considered for a moment before answering. "Well, when I was younger, my guardians introduced me to a woman who was an Electrokinetic. I watched her shoot lightning from her fingers and hit a spot three meters away." She sounded a bit awestruck. "Could you imagine how useful that would be if you were in a battle?"

I laughed. "Could you imagine how useful that would be anywhere?"

She was silent for a moment, and when she spoke, her voice was quiet. "Are you nervous for tomorrow?"

"I am." I picked at a thread on the pale gray comforter that covered my legs. "I mean, it's amazing, right? We're about to become superheroes. It's kind of weird that I'm still so nervous."

She let out a small laugh. "Yes, I would say amazing is accurate. Did your guardians ever explain the ceremony to you?"

"Yeah, a few years back. You?"

"Only recently. They told me our powers will be...pulled from our minds? Is that correct?"

"More or less. They're already there, they just need to be awakened."

"By a Mentalist, correct?" she asked.

"A Coercer, from what I understand."

"Do you know if it will be the man who spoke tonight?"

I shrugged. "Rudolfo? Most likely. There aren't many and he has to be pushing fifteen hundred years."

I stood to pull some pjs out of my top drawer and thought back to my own experience with a Coercer. The vision I'd seen when Nathaniel had immersed himself into my mind had nearly shattered me. I shuddered to think what the reaction would be if that happened in front of a hundred other Ischyra and gods. The last thing I needed was for the Elders to see me buckle under that kind of mental pressure.

"Tessa?"

Yana's voice snapped me from my thoughts.

"Yeah? Sorry."

"Are you alright?"

"Yes, I promise, I'm just tired." I looked over at her and gave her a half smile. "I think I just need to go to bed."

My roommate looked dubious, but she didn't press further. "Of course. We should probably get some sleep. I hear having someone poke around in your mind can be quite an ordeal, so I'd like to be rested."

That's putting it mildly, I thought.

As we lay in silence, with only the light of the pale moon outside, I contemplated if or when I'd be able to share my nightmares with her. I knew there was almost no chance I'd be able to keep them from her if they started up again, but I also couldn't see myself feeling comfortable talking to someone I barely knew about the horrific things I'd seen with Nathaniel.

Taking a deep, steadying breath, I snuggled down in my bed and began replaying the events of the day in my head. So much had happened. I'd said goodbye to my guardians and old life and arrived at Olympus. I'd met other Ischyra and my fellow recruits. I caught my first glimpse of all the Elders in one place, traveled through not one but two portals, and discovered that our arrival was apparently timed perfectly with a brewing rebellion.

And tomorrow I'd travel to the Agora, where my powers would be awakened.

It was almost too much to wrap my mind around. I began to feel a trickle of panic stir within me, and I struggled to force it back down. After a few moments, I rolled over on my back and slowly fell into my old routine of counting backward from five hundred. It was a trick Analise had taught me and was always a surefire way to help clear my mind.

After a while, my brain finally slowed down enough for a deep sleep.

14

TESSA

I awoke the next day to the pale blue light of morning streaming through my window and birds chirping quietly in the trees out back. The clock on my nightstand told me it was half past seven; fifteen minutes before my alarm was set to go off. I groaned, hoping that I'd eventually be allowed to sleep in on a regular basis. At least until nine. Or ten.

I rolled onto my back and stared at the smooth white ceiling as I went over what the rest of the day might bring.

Today, I would find out what my affinity was. In just a couple of hours, I would be immortal. I would know what my powers were and who would teach me to use them.

"Are you awake?" Yana's sleepy voice sounded muffled under the comforter covering her face.

"Yep. Kind of. You?"

A grunt was her only response.

Neither of us made a move to get out of bed. As excited as I was, the knowledge that my human life was about to come to an official end was putting butterflies the size of dragons in my stomach. The doubts that had flashed through my mind as I departed Renville returned, causing me to question myself even more.

My conversation with John and Analise that day in the kitchen came back to me.

"What's fated for us is not always a bad thing."

Finding my resolve, I threw back the covers and stood up. I was acting like a wimp. John and Analise had given me love, prepared me as best they could for my life as an immortal, and I wouldn't let their efforts be for nothing.

No, I wasn't going to waste the final moments of my human life what-if-ing from my bed.

There was no place for human weakness in an immortal world.

I stalked over to Yana's bed and yanked the covers off her.

She let out something in Romanian that sounded like a curse and glared up at me.

"Come on, Yana. Get up. Let's do this. Let's go be immortal."

No hesitations.

"Ugh, you are as bad as my guardians. No such thing as a snooze button with them, either."

I smiled sweetly, then pulled the pillow out from under her head, a move I'd learned from Mary.

"Agh, I'm up! *Pula mea*, you are a pain in the ass!"

"I don't speak Romanian!" I laughed as she stormed into the bathroom and slammed the door.

I began getting dressed in the official training uniform for the Ischyra that had been waiting for us in our dresser drawers when we arrived. Slowly, I tugged on the black fitted pants before pulling on the matching, long-sleeved crew neck. The small purple symbol of the Ischyra was embroidered just above the hem, and a sense of pride washed through me as I stared at it. I glanced at the small white mark on my wrist and smiled, eager to see it change.

I eyed my ridiculous case of bedhead in the full-length mirror and struggled to figure out what in all the realms would be an appropriate hairdo for a day like this.

"Would you like a braid?"

I turned and saw that Yana had just emerged from the bathroom, looking fresh-faced and wide awake. Her black hair was done in a perfect French braid.

I gave her a relieved smile. "Yes, please. That would be fantastic."

"Of course. Here, sit on the floor. It will be easier."

I complied, and Yana quietly got to work brushing through my tangles.

"Your female guardian never taught you to braid?"

"No," I said, trying to keep my head still while I spoke. "Analise was the best mother figure I could've asked for, but things like hair and makeup weren't really her thing."

"I see. Well, I will show you so you can do this on your own. It is not so complicated once you've practiced some."

I grinned at her in the mirror. "That'd be awesome."

She returned my smile with one of her own. "You know, I wasn't sure I would enjoy sharing a room with a girl I did not know. You're far less annoying than I expected."

I arched a brow. "Ditto."

"There." She smoothed the hair on the sides of my head, then stepped back to admire her work. "Perfect. Now, go brush your teeth; your breath is atrocious."

I rolled my eyes. "Thanks." I put a hand on my stomach. "I'm starving. What's for breakfast?"

"I don't think they want us to eat prior to the ceremony," Yana said.

"Seriously? Why?" Being told I couldn't have food only made my stomach clench harder.

"I believe it is because they don't want us to vomit."

Lovely.

A short while later, all recruits were gathered in the courtyard, standing neatly in five rows, the air heavy with anticipation.

Mary stood beside me, bouncing on her toes. Eric was two rows in front of me cracking his knuckles, which had always been a nervous tic of his. Andrei was tapping his thumb against his leg, Anette was twirling the end of one of her braided pigtails, and Igor's jaw was so tight it looked like it was made of stone.

My bravado from just a short while ago was fading back into "holy shit" territory, and I was having trouble getting my emotions under control. I kept shifting nervously from one foot to the other before forcing myself to take a few small centering breaths.

Chiron, Ares, and Athena stood near the gate, quietly observing us. Ares and Athena wore subdued clothing that was a stark contrast to the formal attire they'd worn the previous night. Chiron looked just as wild as he had when we'd arrived. His coarse brown hair was drawn back into a thick ponytail, his torso was bare, and on his legs were dark brown pants that buttoned down the sides.

I was confused for a moment before I realized the pants were actually breakaway pants that wouldn't get ripped to shreds if he had to transform into his centaur form on the fly.

So cool. I wondered if we'd get to work with any of the other centaurs, although from what I knew of them, they didn't have the same level of humanity as Chiron did.

Athena stepped forward and clasped her hands behind her back, then smiled out at us. "Good morning, everyone." Her voice was clear and silken.

"I feel your apprehension, and I want you all to know that I—no, we—understand your trepidation. Being immortal will not take away those emotions, but do not despair. To be nervous or fearful is to be *wise*."

She began to pace back and forth as she spoke.

"When you were a child, your guardians taught you to put one foot in front of the other before you could take your first independent steps. Your affinities are much the same. You will need to learn to put one foot in front of the other before you are able to claim those gifts for your own. Do not go into this day with the belief you will have complete mastery over your powers or that you will become invincible, that no harm will ever befall you, or that the rest of your existence will be easy. They will make you stronger, faster, and more amazing than you could imagine, but they will not give you wisdom. They will not tell you right from wrong, and they will not be a crutch for you to rely on in battle. Immortality does not equate to invincibility."

She held out a small jar that contained a single purple flower, and several of the recruits let out a gasp.

"We all have our weaknesses, and this is your biggest one. Who can tell me what it is?"

I looked around at the other recruits, not wanting to be the one to answer. A lithesome brown-haired boy at the far end of my row slowly raised his hand.

"It's godsbane."

Athena gave a curt nod.

"Thank you, Jonathan. Godsbane. Your guardians likely taught you of its uses and the danger it poses to your kind. While painful to a god, it can and has been fatal to Ischyra. As part of your training, you will learn all there is to know about this lethal poison. You will learn how and where it is grown, how its poison is extracted, and how it can be weaponized against you and others. This may seem tedious, but like your powers, it is yet another tool for your survival. Learn to use the tools you are about to be given and never take them for granted."

Immortality does not equate to invincibility. We all have our weaknesses.

Her gray eyes searched our faces as her words sunk in. It was so quiet you could hear a pin fall. After a few moments, she stepped back and gave a nod to her brother.

Ares took a step forward and rested his hands on his hips.

"It is time to make our way to the Agora." His voice was forceful, exactly what you'd expect from a seasoned warrior. "When we arrive, you will be called forward one at a time and your affinity will be revealed. Some of you may be hopeful that you will have a certain affinity. But never put your trust in hope. Trust in the gods who have given you their power."

His eyes narrowed in warning.

"Do not be disappointed if you do not receive the power you want.

Focus instead on honing the powers you have been *given*." He looked around the entire group, ensuring that we'd all gotten the message.

The emphasis on that last word made his meaning clear—the gods gave us our powers; if we betrayed the trust they had in us, we'd be stripped of those powers quicker than you could say Elder.

Without another word, he turned and strode out of the front gate. Athena motioned for us to follow, and we silently made our way down the hill to the portal for the Agora, where, one by one, we filed through.

As I waited for the others, I took a few moments to look out across the mountain, just as I had the night before. I was surprised to see how different it looked under the morning sun. The forest that stretched upward from Olympia was almost entirely obscured by the thick morning fog that blanketed the distant valley. The sun cast an orange glow over the Agora as it made its way across the mountain to combat the mist below.

"Morning."

I jumped when a voice spoke next to me, and I turned to see Nathaniel standing just a few feet away. He wore jeans, but he'd ditched his normal t-shirt in favor of a pale blue button-down with the sleeves rolled to his elbows.

"Oh, hey." I smiled nervously. "Good morning."

Unsure of what else to say that wouldn't sound completely lame, I turned and faced the Agora, examining the beautiful structure as I tried to beat back my apprehension.

"You know, this is the only building left from before the war?"

I looked at Nathaniel in surprise. "I thought all the buildings from back then had been destroyed."

"Most were." He turned back toward the massive white structure. "Not this one, though. It's always been the main meeting place on Olympus."

"That's good, though. It would've been a shame to destroy something so beautiful."

"Yes, it would have." He smiled down at me. "Come on, they're going in."

I followed him up the smooth marble stairs toward the brightly tiled doors that were held open by two Ischyra. I recognized one was Chris, the guy I'd spoken to at dinner the previous night.

He raised his brow in greeting when he saw me. "Morning, Tessa. You ready for this?"

I took a deep breath. "As I'll ever be, I guess."

He grinned and gave me a pat on the shoulder before ushering me inside. By the time I got through the doors, Nathaniel seemed to have vanished into the crowd.

Chiron had taken over leading the recruits into the hall that had been cleared of all furniture but the Elders' thrones. Idly, I wondered why he always seemed to choose his human form over his centaur body. As the son of the Titan Cronus, he was the only centaur who could shift between forms, but considering he'd been born in equine form, I would've thought he'd prefer it to a human one.

He began directing us to form a circle around the inlaid wood floor, and I quickly moved to sandwich myself between Mary and Eric. My heart felt like it was about to beat through my chest, but having two lifelong friends on either side of me brought me a bit of calm.

I looked around the room and saw that there were far more attendees than I'd expected.

Ischyra crowded against the walls all the way around. Mixed among them were lower gods, many of whom I recognized by the descriptions I'd read.

Poseidon's son Triton, distinguishable by two small golden tridents holstered in the waistband of his gray pants and the conch around his neck, was speaking with his father at the foot of the dais.

A goddess I didn't recognize with tawny skin and wavy black hair that tumbled to her waist stood against the back wall, quietly watching the room. Three glittering silver moons pinned her hair back from her face.

One of the winged Harpies who'd been born to the Oceanid Electra was dressed all in blue, a silver comb in the shape of a winged woman clasped in her hair. Beside her stood a petite brunette. Both were speaking animatedly with Demeter, whose golden hair was braided into a crown on top of her head. By the way Demeter was smiling at her, I guessed her to be Demeter's daughter, Persephone, the wife of Hades and the main emissary from the Underworld.

There were so many of them it was dizzying. The powers some of them possessed made me terrified to share a room with them, especially when I was about to have my mind pried open.

Speaking of which...

"What's he doing?" Eric asked, his tone disbelieving.

I followed his gaze to the center of the circle we'd just formed around the room. Nathaniel stood there, whispering with Zeus, who was stunning in his knee-length white toga and crown of gold laurel leaves.

Of course.

"He's a Coercer," I whispered back. "Shit. I just assumed it would be Rudolfo..."

"Apparently, he's *The* Coercer," Mary muttered. "He's just full of secrets, isn't he?"

I nodded as a slight feeling of awe washed over me. I'd thought he was your run-of-the-mill Coercer. There weren't many, but he was by no means the only one.

He was quite possibly the most important Mentalist in all the realms, and he'd already seen the deepest parts of my mind.

How in Zeus' name had I not figured this out on my own?

I eyed Nathaniel shrewdly.

"I guess I'd rather it be him than someone I don't know, considering he's already poked around in my mind."

"He's been in your mind?" Eric hissed.

Shit.

"Oopsie," Mary whispered.

I'd forgotten that she was the only one who knew about his little trip through my brain.

"Yeah, um, long story. I'll tell you later, promise."

I felt his eyes burning holes through the side of my head, but I didn't turn to face him. It was *so* not the time to be recounting that experience.

Thankfully, I was given an easy out when Zeus clapped his hands thunderously.

"Welcome, recruits and distinguished guests."

His booming voice silenced the room in an instant.

"I know Ares and Athena have already given you the 'pep talk,' so to speak." He nodded toward the two Elders who sat serenely in their thrones. "So I will not bore you with further platitudes. I only want to add this: today is not just the day you discover your affinities or the last day you could die a natural death. From this point forward, *you* will be responsible for keeping Earth safe from all the creatures who would see it destroyed. *You* will work with the other forces across the realms to fend off the witches, demons, rebels, and the gods who threaten the integrity of the worlds in which we live."

He folded his arms over his chest, causing the muscles on his torso to flex, then looked out at all of us sternly, all the warmth that I'd seen the evening before gone.

"Do not let us regret entrusting you with the powers that are about to awaken in you. It is important that you remember the punishments you will receive should you commit crimes against the realms."

He held up two fingers.

"There are only two possible punishments when an Ischyra is convicted of a crime against the realms. The first is the revocation of all powers, which will return you to your mortal state and you will be banished from Olympus. The second is immediate death, either by beheading or poison. I can assure you, the effectiveness of both has been proven."

The way he spoke left no doubt in my mind that he had probably had to dole out a godsbane poisoning or beheading on more than one occasion.

I turned to Mary and saw that her wide-eyed look mirrored mine. I was stunned at the change in our leader today. The god standing before us had been so warm and welcoming the night before; today he was the formidable leader we read about in stories growing up, calmly discussing beheading and poisoning his soldiers.

Here was the god who struck down the Titans, who overthrew Olympus, who so carelessly allowed innumerable demonic creatures to roam free in the human realm.

"And now, let me bow out and allow Nathaniel to take over."

He gave Nathaniel a sharp nod and a pat on the back before stepping aside.

Nathaniel gave a nod in return, then turned to face the room. "Welcome, everyone. For those of you who do not know me, my name is Nathaniel and I'm the Coercer for Olympus." His voice rang with power.

"Damn, Tess," Mary breathed. "He just got way hotter."

"Definitely," I murmured. If there ever was a time for a facepalm, it would have been that very second.

"One by one, I will ask you to step forward in the order in which you are arranged. At that time, I will perform the ritual that will guide the gods' magic into your system, awakening the powers that have lain dormant in you for the last eighteen years. Please be forewarned, I will not just be accessing your mind. I will be opening the deepest parts of it in order to allow the magic to flow in. This part can be a bit uncomfortable, but I assure you, it's to be expected."

Uncomfortable, my ass. Try freaking terrifying.

I shivered at the thought that this could potentially be worse than the first time he'd cracked my brain open.

His lips quirked, giving me the vague impression that he'd heard me.

He gestured to the Asian boy who stood directly opposite me. "We will begin with Mr. Dishi Tsai. Please, come forward."

Dishi looked nervously to his twin, Hao, who stood beside him. Hao clapped him on the back and whispered something in his ear before giving Dishi a nudge toward the center of the room.

When the nervous recruit approached Nathaniel, he was greeted with a reassuring smile. I was still a bit shaken that I'd been so casu-

ally joking around with Nathaniel this entire time, completely igno-
rant of who he really was.

The most powerful Coercer on Olympus.

He'd been in my mind, and I'd been so sure that he was being
honest when he said he was clueless about that vision. His fear and
concern for me had seemed so real. I felt my breath hitch when I realized he'd likely had a good thousand years or more to perfect his
ability to lie.

Mary squeezed my hand.

"Shh. It's fine," she breathed. "Get through today, confront him
later."

I gripped her hand in return, thankful once again that my best
friend stood beside me.

I was so wrapped up in my internal freak out that I almost missed
what would likely be the most amazing sight of my entire existence.

Dishi was standing stock-still in front of Nathaniel, his eyes full of
fear.

Nathaniel gave him another reassuring smile, then placed one
hand on Dishi's cheek and let the magic begin to flow.

15

TESSA

At Nathaniel's touch, Dishi's body gave a jolt. His legs wobbled precariously, and his head fell back, face turned skyward. Shimmering light, the color of sunset, burst from the air around him. It washed over him like water, falling in cascading waves to the floor. It wrapped around him like a lover, embracing him with a smooth caress.

I'm not sure how much time passed; seconds, maybe minutes before the light began to fade. The magic danced across his body, conforming like a second skin before slowly absorbing into him.

When it was over, Dishi slumped to the floor. I saw Hao step forward as though to help him, but Zeus, seeming to expect that reaction, placed a gentle hand on his shoulder and shook his head. Hao gazed at him in awe for a few seconds before turning his attention back to his brother.

I turned my focus back to the newly born Ischyra in the center of the room and saw that Nathaniel was pulling him up by the hand. Dishi stood, and everything about him looked different somehow. He stood tall, his back straight, and a quiet confidence radiated through him.

Nathaniel looked him straight in the eye, and announced,

"Earth!" His voice rang through the hall with authority and confidence.

The room erupted into applause. I thought it was just the other Ischyra and my fellow recruits, but when I looked around the room, I saw that all the other gods in attendance, including the Elders, were clapping.

Slowly, all recruits were called forward, each more eager than the last. Elementals—Earth, Air, Fire, Light, and Water—and Mentalists, who came in a range of affinities, were all announced. The excitement in the room grew with each new awakening, with whistles and shouts erupting from some of the mentors when a recruit with their affinity was announced.

I was thrilled when I heard Nathaniel announce that Yana was an Electrokinetic—a fire user who could manipulate the natural electricity in the air. She looked my way as she walked back to her spot and grinned when I gave her a thumbs up.

"Mary Miller!"

My heart started pounding when Mary's name was called. I was next, and once again, the confidence I'd built back up started to waver.

Mary held her chin high and strode forward, as though she did this kind of thing every day. Nathaniel gave her a nod of acknowledgement, and based on his smile, she'd likely responded with something snarky.

When her light dissipated, she gripped Nathaniel's shoulder, refusing to fall to the floor like the others.

"Typical Mary," Eric muttered.

I nudged him. "I'd like to see you keep your cool afterward."

He snorted. "If she can do it, so can I."

"Water!" Nathaniel announced.

Mary grinned, then shook out her arms and rolled her head around before making her way back to my side. The afterglow of her body's acceptance of power still hovered around her, highlighting her natural prettiness.

She grinned a thousand-watt smile at Eric and me. "Holy shit, that was amazing."

"It totally was," I said, returning her grin with one of my own. My best friend, the water user. I couldn't wait to see what she'd do with it.

"Tessa Avery!"

My brain gave a jolt when I heard Nathaniel call my name.

Eric put a hand on my back and gave me a gentle nudge forward. Eyeing Nathaniel warily, I made my way toward the center of the circle.

I heard his voice in my head almost immediately.

'I'm sorry I didn't tell you who I was. I'll come find you later. We'll talk then.'

'And how am I supposed to trust you with my brain in the meantime?'

'There's not really much of a choice right now. Are you ready?'

I pressed my lips together, then threw his own words back at him.

'I don't have much of a choice, do I?'

He inhaled deeply and gave a nod. "Here we go."

He placed one warm hand on my cheek. When I looked into his eyes, I saw that the fear and concern that was there the last time he entered my mind was replaced with reassurance.

He closed his eyes and let his consciousness settle into my own. A bolt of electricity shot through my body, so powerful I thought I might collapse. When my head fell back, I saw pure white light flowing over me.

It was amazing.

With each wave of magic that came down, things awakened within me. Every cell in my body was being charged, given a long-awaited boost. I felt strength course through my muscles. It swirled around, zigzagging through, finding any empty space to occupy. I felt my body slowly change as my immortal strength awoke.

The magic began to move more quickly, and I felt it coalesce in my mind. My power, my affinity, slowly clawed its way out of the quicksand of my mind, desperate to be free. It felt like my brain was being prodded by a thousand pins. The mental pressure increased, as though something was trying to get in. My power wanted *out*, and something was blocking it from completing its mission.

I felt Nathaniel's hand start to shake.

'*Open your mind, Tessa. You need to let the magic in. I can only help you so much. Your fear is fighting against me.*'

With Nathaniel's encouragement, I focused on opening my mind fully. I had no idea how to do that, but when I tried, the magic that had taken root seemed to understand and came to my aid. The pressure released, and all the power that had been knocking at my mental doors settled into place, at ease in its proper home.

I let out a small sigh of contentment.

I was complete. It was as if everything inside me had shifted, making room for a whole new being. I was truly *me* now. Tessa Lynn Avery, an Ischyra of Olympus. Powerful, strong, and immortal. I was the person I'd been waiting to become for the last eighteen years. I wanted to use my powers now; I didn't want to wait until tomorrow. I wanted to run for miles and lift boulders and do absolutely everything my magic would allow me to do simply because I could.

I could do anything now, and I officially had forever to do it.

When I opened my eyes and stared into the midnight blue of Nathaniel's, he looked concerned.

'*Are you alright?*'

I took a deep breath, then looked down at my wrist and watched as those three white lines transformed into a shimmering purple.

I met his eyes and grinned.

"That was amazing!" I whispered.

He gave me a short, slow nod, then dropped his hand, still maintaining eye contact. The silence around us was deafening.

He cleared his throat before speaking. "Telekinesis!"

16

NATHANIEL

Three thousand, twenty-four years.

Seven hundred and fifty-six generations.

I had guided the gods' magic into the minds of thousands of new Ischyra, allowing it the freedom to awaken powers that had been dormant for the first eighteen years of their existence.

I've lived through some of the most wonderful and worst periods in the Earth's history. Wars, slavery, the rise and fall of nations, the annihilation of races and the emergence of new cultures. I thought I'd seen it all.

None of it prepared me for what I saw when I entered the deepest parts of Tessa's mind for the second time in less than one week.

As I opened her mind to let the magic flow in, images bombarded me, much like what I'd seen the last time I'd explored her psyche. They played like a movie in fast-forward. Emotions, vivid as the scenes that flashed through my mind, flowed from her mind into mine, nearly bringing me to my knees. Joy as she sparred with a blond man whose face I couldn't make out. Excitement as she hugged a faceless man and woman. Feelings of sadness, anger, determination, fear, happiness, pleasure, and horrific pain all tore through my mind as though they didn't know where to go or what to do. They bounced around, battering against my own mental walls as they sought a place to rest.

My hand shook as I struggled to maintain my hold on her. Somehow, the magic continued to flow. The images that had been running amok in my head finally found a path back home into Tessa's mind. I tried to pull away before they could come to rest, but my consciousness felt glued to her own. Her mind fought against them, blocking them with a mental barrier even I couldn't break down. The visions pushed against it, refusing to be hidden. Seeing no other option, I did my best to guide them to her deep consciousness, hoping they would be safe there.

Eventually, I felt the pressure of the magic slowly recede from my mind as it finally began to absorb into her body. Everything within her sang as the power of immortality changed her. Her mind had strengthened, making room for all the things she would learn. I felt her awareness when her senses suddenly sharpened, her shock when she realized who and what she was now becoming.

Then with a *snap*, the magic was no longer flowing through me, and my mind was quiet once again. All I could feel was the residual presence of her powers.

Before removing my hand to announce her affinity, I opened my eyes and looked into hers, the color as green as emeralds. I was shocked that she hadn't fallen to the floor in a heaving mess like the others.

I searched her mind, but nothing seemed amiss. She had the normal glow of someone who had just been bathed in magic, only hers went beyond joy. She seemed to radiate with pure magic and strength. Her expression was ecstatic, the small dimples in her cheeks accentuating the smile that lit up her face.

She wasn't terrified, as she had been that morning before school.

Did she not see what I saw?

The scuff of a shoe on marble shook me out of my reverie.

I cleared my throat and hoped my voice didn't sound as shaky as I felt.

"Telekinesis!"

Tessa grinned and squeezed my hand before quickly making her way back to her friends, excitement shining on all their faces.

The rest of the Elders looked impassive, patiently waiting for me to call the next recruit. Epimetheus' face was expressionless as his eyes flitted over the crowd, but Prometheus appeared to be looking in Tessa's direction, his brow slightly furrowed.

I shook my head to clear my thoughts, then called the next name.

BY THE TIME all recruits had been awakened, there were twenty Mentalists and thirty Elementals.

After the last recruit moved back to their space in the circle, Zeus gave a nod to Athena who rose to speak.

"Congratulations, Ischyra!"

The room erupted into applause. The older Ischyra who were in attendance stepped forward, forgoing formality to welcome the new recruits with handshakes and pats on the back. After a few moments, Zeus clapped his hands in the same deafening way he always did when he was trying to gain a crowd's attention.

Once everyone was facing the dais, Athena spoke again.

"It is time to assign the new Ischyra to their mentors." She waved a group of Ischyra forward. "Mentors, please come forward to accept your new charges."

I barely heard the mentors call out the names of their mentees. Now that my part was finished, my thoughts drifted back to all that I'd seen in Tessa's mind. The faceless people in those visions couldn't have been her birth parents; she'd only remained with them for a few days before being abandoned at a fire station in New Orleans.

I looked toward the dais, hoping to get Hestia's attention, but she was deep in conversation with Hecate, who'd ventured out of her home for the first time in years to attend the transition ceremony. I took a step toward where they were seated but was stopped when Apollo stepped into my path.

"Nathaniel."

My jaw clenched as I met his pale gray eyes and gave a short nod before looking toward Hestia again. Her gaze flicked up to mine, and she gave a small shake of her head before returning to her conversation.

Annoyed, I turned my attention back to the god before me.

"What can I do for you, Apollo? Are you unhappy with today's outcome?"

"Quite the contrary. It would seem we have a good deal of worthy recruits this generation." He clasped his hands behind his back and looked around the room. "Nathaniel, I don't say this often, but I want to thank you for what you do here. I know how difficult this job can be."

I arched a brow, unsure how to respond to his sudden niceties.

After a few seconds of silence, he cleared his throat. "Have you spoken to the Avery girl again?"

"Several times," I replied with a sigh. "Why do you ask?"

His jaw clenched. "Just curious, is all. Is she adjusting well?"

I shrugged and glanced over to where she was standing with her friends.

"I suppose we'll see soon enough."

"Yes, well, I expect we will be speaking again soon. Do well by the new recruits, this is likely to be a difficult transition for them."

"Agreed."

He opened his mouth as though he wanted to say more, but instead just gave me a tense smile before wandering back toward his throne.

I barely spared his retreating figure a glance as I looked back toward the dais. Despite what Apollo had said about letting the issue drop, if I was going to keep getting a mind-full every time I had to read into Tessa's thoughts, I wanted to know what was going on.

Seeing no use in approaching Hestia, and not caring about decorum, I took another quick look into Tessa's mind. She was occupied with her lead mentor, Charlise, so I wasn't terribly concerned that she'd notice. Even if she did, I couldn't stand the thought of her experiencing any more of these visions without knowing what they were.

Whether Hestia inserted that memory or not, I was the one who used my powers to dig into the deepest parts of her psyche to throw it in her face. Seeing her on the ground, hysterical and nearly sick with fear felt worse than any gut punch I'd received in my lifetime, and I'd received plenty.

Thoughts of what she could do with her abilities swam around Tessa's mind, one blending into the next, making it difficult to see exactly what she was thinking. I could still sense some annoyance at me, reminding me that I would have to find her at some point to try to explain my position. I was surprised to see her power was there, swirling in the foreground of her mind as though awaiting instruction.

I felt a slight nudge, as though it noticed the intrusion and was attempting to remove me. I felt my brow furrow in confusion. The only other time I'd felt that sensation was when I'd seen the memory Hestia had given her. This felt...protective. Her power was far more stable than I would have expected for a newly transformed recruit.

Suddenly, hidden just on the edge of her deep consciousness, was a spark. It was small and barely perceptible, as green as the color of her eyes, and no matter how close I tried to get, it seemed to slip further and further back. Just before it slipped out of sight, I heard a male's voice whisper to her.

'Never doubt yourself, Tessa. You will move mountains.'

Then it was gone, and all I was left with was her endless string of excited thoughts.

It was likely she was simply recalling words of wisdom one of her guardians had bestowed on her prior to her departure from Renville. I felt another nudge, slightly more insistent this time, so I severed the connection to her mind before she could notice I was there.

Frustrated, I wanted to go speak with her, but I had no explanation for what I'd seen. I saw no sense in worrying her until I knew what there was to worry about.

I stuffed my hands in the pockets of my jeans and turned to leave the Agora. Tessa was happy, all thoughts of her dreams hidden, and I wasn't going to disrupt that right now.

I hoped to all the gods of Olympus that whatever was lingering in the recesses of her mind didn't steal that happiness away.

17

TESSA

"Tessa!"

I looked behind me and saw Anette jogging across the Agora floor, her peppy blond pigtails bouncing behind her. The floor had quickly become crowded with recruits and Ischyra. She'd been announced as an Illusionist, which meant that we were both classified as Mentalists and would be assigned the same lead mentor.

"Hey!" I grinned when she reached me and gave me a hug. "How cool is this?"

She pulled back and I saw her smile was as wide as mine. "It is! I am so glad I know someone else in the group."

"Same."

"Mentalists! All Mentalists, over here!" a female voice coming from the entrance called.

"Come on!" I grabbed Anette's hand and led her through the crowd to where the rest of the Mentalists were gathering.

In the middle of the group stood a petite platinum blonde female with hair that fell in jagged edges to her chin. She had a stocky build, but her facial features were delicate—long, thin nose, pale skin, and wide brown eyes, with a warm, welcoming smile that immediately made me feel comfortable.

"Hi, everyone. I'm Charlise, and I'll be your mentor for the next year." Her voice was laced with a thick southern accent. She jerked her head in the direction of the door. "Let's head on out. It's quieter and we've got a lot to discuss."

Quickly, we all followed her out the front door and right toward the circular portal field. Without a word, she led us through the portal back to Olympia.

Once we were through, she turned to face us, her eyes appraising as she looked us over. "So. There are twenty of you, two with dual affinities. This generation we've got quite a diverse bunch. Two Telekinetics, two Illusionists, three Linkers, one Astral, one Remote, one Psychometric, two Trackers, one Teleporter, one Replicator, one Splitter, and three Telepaths."

Say what now?

I understood about ten percent of what she'd just rattled off. When John and Analise started teaching me about the various categories Ischyra could fall into, I'd always had trouble focusing. Once they reached titles like "Psychometric" and "Splitter," my brain would start to fuzz over.

Hopefully, the people who actually *were* those things had paid closer attention in their lessons than I had.

"I'll be your lead mentor, but two additional trainers will be joining us tomorrow. Tonight, we'll just do intros and get a feel for what the next year will bring. For now, let's head back to your dorms. We'll get some food and chat for a bit." She grinned. "Then we'll see what you can do."

We made our way up the hill to the dormitory, then Charlise led us directly to the largest common room. Glancing around, I noticed Sina, the statuesque redhead who'd sat with us at dinner, hovering near the door. Beside her was a tall, muscular guy with curly brown hair, dark eyes, and full lips. His eyes were scanning the room shrewdly.

"Come on, I see Sina," I said, grabbing Anette's hand.

"Oh, wonderful! She was so nice at dinner, don't you think?"

When Sina saw us heading over, she did a little hop and clapped her hands happily. "I'm so happy there are people I know in our group, aren't you?"

"Yep, totally." I looked up at the guy glowering beside Sina and reached out a hand.

"Hi, I'm Tessa."

He looked at my hand for a moment before taking it and giving it a firm shake. "Damien."

Ignoring his surly attitude, I grinned.

"So what affinities were called for you two?"

"I'm a Mindlinker," Sina said. "Which apparently means I can link my mind to someone else's and take over their body."

Before Damien could respond, Sina tilted her head to the side and her expression became perplexed. "Um, can someone please tell me what our Mentor is doing right now?"

I cast a glance over my shoulder, and sure enough, Charlise was standing in the middle of the room with her eyes closed. Silence fell over the room as everyone turned to watch her.

A minute or two later, her eyes popped open and she smiled.

"Pizza's on its way!"

Her smile faltered a bit as she took in our incredulous expressions, then she rolled her eyes and huffed out a sigh.

"Oh, come on! Three of you are Telepaths; did you really think you'd only use your powers to fight evil?"

Sina gave a quick shake of her head. "You just ordered pizza?"

Charlise gave her a patronizing smile.

"Yes, Sina, I just ordered pizza. The Ischyra who runs the pizza shop on Main Street and I are good friends, and he doesn't mind if I pop into his head to place an order. Besides, we need to get to work and don't have time to be making pizza runs."

There was another beat of silence, and I blinked a few times as I tried to actually absorb what had just happened.

"Wow." Sina laughed, looking impressed.

"Now." Charlise clapped her hands. "Enough talk of food. Let's get started."

With a quick flick of her wrist, she sent every piece of furniture back against the walls, leaving a wide-open space in the center of the room.

"Everyone form a circle and sit."

As everyone moved toward the center of the room, I wedged myself between Anette and a girl named Josephina. Charlise took a seat directly across from us between two of the girls I hadn't really gotten to know yet, Lara and Cho.

"I understand that you're excited to get going," Charlise began, "but you need to be patient. Your powers have just awoken. They need time to adjust to you, just as you need time to adjust to them, so it may take a few days to really get a feel for each other. I'm assuming you got the same talk from Athena that I did about learning to put one foot in front of the other?"

I heard a few answering grumbles, and when I looked around, I saw that I wasn't the only one whose shoulders were slumped in disappointment. Faces that had been alight with anticipation a few minutes ago were looking decidedly dejected.

"Well, she's right, especially when it comes to Mentalist abilities. For now, we're going to do introductions and some mental exercises." She held up a finger. "And do not even *think* about rolling your eyes at the term 'mental exercises.' You are Mentalists now. If you think for one second you'll get through the rest of eternity without exercising your mind to keep it sharp, you're sorely mistaken.

"So, introductions. I'm Charlise Abrams, originally from El Paso, Texas. I've been an Ischyra for twenty years. I've got affinities in four areas—telekinesis, telepathy, mind linking, and illusions." She looked around at us eyebrows raised. "Who can tell me what those mean?"

Hesitantly, a pretty brunette raised her hand. "Telekinetics can move things with their minds, Mindlinkers can inhabit the mind and take control of any living creature, Telepaths can converse with others mentally, and Illusionists can create illusions and manipulate those made by others."

"Good, Sylvi." Charlise stretched her legs out in front of her and leaned back on her hands. "We'll start intros with you."

Sylvi sat up a bit straighter as all attention turned toward her.

"I am Sylvia Arnesen, but everyone calls me Sylvi. I grew up in Rovaniemi, which is in the Northern part of Finland. I am a Psychometric."

"Wonderful!" Charlise clapped her hands. "Can you tell us what a psychometric does?"

Sylvi shook her head shyly. "No, I cannot remember. It was one of the few that did not stick," she said.

"No problem, Sylvi. We're here to learn. Can anyone here tell Sylvi a bit more about her affinity?" Charlise gestured toward Damien, who sat near the door. "Damien, what can you tell us about yourself and Psychometrics?"

Damien cleared his throat and gave us all a cocky smile. "I am Damien Maheras, and I am from Athens. I have dual affinities. Like Charlise, I am a Mindlinker." He gave her a simpering smile. "I am also an Astral, which means I can project my consciousness anywhere within the four realms."

He turned toward Sylvi and gave her a slightly patronizing look. "Ischyra with Psychometric ability are able to obtain memories or knowledge from persons or objects through touch. They can be quite valuable should information need to be extracted from an individual who can no longer communicate. Psychometrics are also very good at weapons training because they can pick up a weapon and tell how it is supposed to be used based only on touch."

He gave Charlise a conspiratorial smile before sitting back down.

I'd barely been around the guy five minutes and it was already painfully clear he was going to be *that* guy in our group.

"Exactly! Thank you." Charlise turned back to Sylvi. "Do you have any questions?"

Sylvi pressed her lips together and shook her head, her face flushing as though embarrassed she hadn't known the answer. I wasn't sure why, but based on the looks of confusion I'd seen when Charlise rattled off our affinities, it seemed like quite a few of our group hadn't taken that aspect of their lessons as seriously as others.

"No, not yet, thank you," she murmured.

"Okay, who's up next?" Charlise inclined her head to see around Sylvi. "Kieran! Tell us about yourself."

And so it went for the next hour. About halfway through introductions, five pizzas were delivered, and slices were passed around.

For the most part, the affinities were all pretty intuitive. Trackers could mentally track people. Remotes were Ischyra who were able to view anything from anywhere in all the realms. They were very similar to Astrals who could project their consciousness anywhere they wanted to go. The main difference between the two was that, in order to astral project, the person would have to enter a trance-like state, whereas Remotes just had to "look" at what they wanted to see.

The affinities I'd had the least amount of knowledge on—as in none, really—were Splitters and Replicators, which sounded more like electrical parts than supernatural affinities.

Both affinities were similar to Mindlinkers in that they could connect to another person's mind, but that was where the similarities ended. Replicators could transfer their own knowledge to others. Splitters could divide their consciousness between multiple people, causing a type of "hive mind" communication capability. I imagined it would be kind of like getting stuck in a massive group text, only a million times worse because it was happening in your brain.

Once everyone had eaten their fill and we'd gotten all the introductions out of the way, Charlise had us deposit our plates in the incinerator so she could show us how to do our mental exercises.

"Okay, so right now, here's what I want ya'll to do." She cracked her neck loudly, then sat down and placed her hands on her knees. "You start by doing a bit of deep breathing, like this."

She demonstrated taking deep runner's breaths: in through the nose, out through the mouth.

"Do that for sixty seconds, it'll help center your energy. Then we'll move on to some stretches."

This exercise was actually familiar to me, as John had forced me to do it any time my emotions got the better of me during training.

After we did our breathing, she had us do a bunch of sitting stretches—touch our toes, reach for the sky, knee to shoulder, and a whole bunch of others that I thought I'd left behind in my basement workout room.

We repeated the breathing exercise a few more times, each time extending it over longer intervals before she told us we were ready.

"Now that we're all relaxed and our minds are open—" Charlise looked around with a wicked grin "—let's see what you've got. Come on, get up."

Yes, I thought.

She jumped to her feet and pulled her short hair back with a clip. "So, the first thing you want to do is remember that your affinity is now just another one of your senses. When you access all of your other senses, there's an action-reaction that happens. For example, when you hear the sizzle of a frying pan, you sniff the air to see what's cooking. When you're reading small print on a page, you might squint your eyes to see better. You flex the body part that's attached to that sense and get a response. Your affinity is no different."

She pursed her lips and looked around the room.

"Okay, let's go with an easy one. Tessa!"

I jumped at the mention of my name.

"Yes?" I asked tentatively. *Please don't make me go first,* I begged silently.

"My fellow Telekinetic!" She put her hands on her hips and gave me a nod of encouragement. "Move something for us."

"Um—okay."

Everyone was looking at me expectantly, like I was supposed to know what I was doing or something.

I took a deep breath and looked around for something to focus on. My eyes landed on a small end table that Charlise had shoved against a wall next to the door that didn't look too heavy. Facing it, I narrowed my eyes and tried to "flex" my brain. I mentally poked at the power that I could feel swirling around at my head and tried to get it to react.

It's just another sense, Tessa, that's all. Just pretend your mind sees something on that table over there, so it's going to go take a closer—

WHAM!

The table flew across the room and slammed into the opposite wall, leaving a large dent in the plaster.

A stunned silence took over the room.

"Holy shit," I breathed.

"Seconded," Sina whispered.

"Awesome job, Tessa!" Charlise exclaimed, waving her hand to put the plaster back in place. "Only a few hours in and you're already putting holes in the wall!"

I laughed weakly. "You'd think the walls around here would be stronger than the ones on Earth."

"Oh, they are." Charlise gave me a wide grin. "You threw that bad boy *really* hard."

She threw her hands in the air. "Everyone, give Tessa a hand!"

The others gave me a round of applause, and as I looked around the circle, I saw that a lot of them wore eager expressions.

"Who's up next?"

Hands flew into the air.

"Sina! Come on, girl, link up!"

Hesitantly, Sina rose and wiped her hands on her pants. She cast questioning eyes at Charlise. "With who?"

Charlise tapped her finger on her chin as she looked around the room.

"Kieran. He looks like he wants to volunteer." She gave a wide smile to the red-haired Irish boy sitting directly across from her. "Don't ya?"

He smiled sheepishly. "Sure."

"That's the spirit!" Charlise clapped her hands. "Sina, I'd recommend holding hands for this first round. It's a bit easier with physical contact."

She waited until both were in place before continuing.

"Now, Kieran, I want you to open your mind to Sina, almost like you're imagining her psyche becoming one with yours."

"And what do I do?" Sina asked with a frown.

"Eh, it's tough to say." Charlise scrunched her face. "I think the best way to describe it would be taking him into a mental headlock. Once you get latched on, you can take over."

"A headlock. Got it." Sina gave a sharp nod, then narrowed her eyes in concentration as she tried to subdue Kieran's mind.

Half an hour later, Sina's flame red hair was plastered to her neck, and she seemed no closer to linking with Kieran's mind than she had when she started.

"Just give it a little nudge," Charlise encouraged. "You've almost got it."

"If you say so," Sina muttered. Her mouth was pressed into a thin line as she focused all her mental strength on Kieran. Finally, she succeeded in taking over long enough to scratch his nose.

"Great job, Sina!" Charlise said, patting her on the back. "Go take a seat."

With a breathless laugh, Sina gave Kieran a high five and sank to the floor in an exhausted heap. She looked up at Charlise. "When will it stop being so difficult?"

"It's different for everyone, really. Now that you've got the first one down, the second time should be easier," Charlise explained. "But don't worry, I'm not going to push you any further today."

"Oh, thank the gods." Sina exhaled loudly as she leaned back and rested her head against the wall. Her light, freckled skin was red and blotchy from exertion, so when Charlise handed her a bottle of cold honeysuckle water, she chugged it down like she hadn't had a drop in months.

"Okay, Kieran, take a break for a few, you'll have your turn in a bit." She scanned the circle, her eyes landing on Damien. "Damien, you're up!"

A self-assured smile spread across his face as he stood. "Thank you, Charlise. What would you like me to do?"

"This one'll be simple." She made a sliding motion with her hand

and the drink machine that had been pressed against the back wall slid forward a few feet, then gave him an easy smile. "I want you to project yourself behind that machine and read what's written on the back. Picture yourself where you want to go and will it to happen."

He clasped his hands behind his back and closed his eyes. "Uh huh," he murmured, not bothering to thank her for her attempt to guide him. Charlise pursed her lips but otherwise didn't react to the brush off.

After about thirty seconds, Damien's body crumpled to the floor, causing more than a few snickers.

"Oh, shoot." Charlise deadpanned. "I forgot to tell him to sit down first."

Walking over to him, she rolled him onto his back.

When Damien returned to his body, his eyes flew open and he was gasping for breath.

"Hey, there, buddy! How ya feeling?" Charlise's head was tilted in concern. "Sorry, I forgot to remind you to lie down before projecting. Once your consciousness leaves your body, there's nothing left in there to tell it to stand up, ya know?"

He struggled to sit up, but the quiver in his arms told me he'd probably been physically drained during his projection.

"Thanks," he whispered hoarsely, all the bravado he'd just boasted gone. "I will remember that for next time."

"So, what did it say?" Charlise asked after handing him a bottle of water.

He scowled. "Made you look."

Charlise beamed at him. "Darn right." She patted him on the back and helped him back to his spot in the circle. "You did great."

For the next several hours, we all took turns practicing our powers. Some got the hang of their affinities pretty quickly, while others struggled just like Sina. Finally, long after the sun had sunk below the horizon, Charlise called it a day.

"You all did great today. If you feel like you didn't get the hang of it, don't let it get to you. Your performance here doesn't necessarily indicate how you'll do tomorrow. Even if your success today felt minor, it was still a success. Hold on to that knowledge and carry it with you. Now off to bed, it's gonna be an early day. Chiron'll be out first thing."

She waved her hand and replaced all the furniture, then opened the door and let us out.

"Finally," Anette moaned. "I had no idea we would be there for so long!"

I bumped her with my shoulder. "Come on, let's go get some sleep. You'll feel better in the morning."

She tilted her head and rested it on my shoulder as we walked.

"I will pray to the gods that you are correct."

18

NATHANIEL

Sleep eluded me that night.

I felt as though I'd lost control when I'd awakened Tessa's powers, and that was not a feeling I was accustomed to. The visions that flowed from her mind into mine that I'd forced into the deepest parts of her were perplexing, to say the least, and I struggled with the decision to confront her with them.

She'd been terrified when she'd seen that dream; a memory, if Hestia was to be trusted, that had put her on the ground in a heap of pure terror. I didn't want to do that to her again without having more information first.

A memory.

It made no sense. My immediate thought had been that it was *her* memory, but I didn't see how that could be possible. It made more sense that it would be someone else's memory, planted in Tessa's mind for some unknown purpose. The more I considered that idea, the more logical it seemed. That memory, as well as those I'd seen during her transformation, had seemed to be from her perspective, but considering I hadn't actually seen her face, there was no way to be sure that it was actually her experience.

But whose was it? And why Tessa? Why *now*?

I needed answers and had no clue where to get them. Hestia no longer seemed forthcoming, and Apollo had been very clear in his desire to abandon the topic of Tessa and her dreams entirely.

I dragged my pillow over my face in an attempt to drown out the moonlight that washed across my bed through the picture windows in my bedroom. I needed to sleep, but my mind refused to quiet down.

Taking a deep breath, I closed my eyes and slowly began counting backward from one hundred, imagining each number being slowly drawn in the air in front of me. The exercise had the usual effect, and I barely remember reaching thirty before I started to drift off.

CHIRON DIDN'T BELIEVE in allowing the recruits a final day to sleep in before beginning their training, and I tended to agree with him. Best to just hit the ground running. They were no longer in the human world where snooze buttons and "just five more minutes" were acceptable.

What I categorically did *not* agree with was his use of a bugle to wake them on the first morning of training. For centuries, I'd tried to get him to abandon the obnoxious gold horn, but that seemed to make him want to use it even more.

Today, I was especially averse to the unimposing little instrument that hung at his waist. I was exhausted. Mentally, if not physically. Even though I'd eventually managed to drift off last night, my mind hadn't gotten the rest it needed. When I woke up this morning, I grew even more irritated when I realized I'd completely forgotten to go find Tessa last night.

The three blasts Chiron let out on that infernal horn the moment he opened the door to the girls' dorms pierced through my brain like an ice pick.

"Good morning, ladies! Up and at 'em!"

A loud crash sounded from one of the rooms, while vicious

cursing in Spanish came from another, causing Chiron to look at me in amusement.

"I swear, the expletives these recruits come up with just get better with each generation."

I laughed, trying to force back the groggy feeling that still hung over me. "Maybe they can teach a few to the older gods. I'm about sick of being told to feed myself to the crows each time Apollo or Athena gets angry."

Chiron snorted, then adjusted the buttons on his breakaway pants. "Because Athena gets angry with you so frequently."

"You'd be surprised," I muttered, then, lowering my voice, I asked, "How long will it be until you show them your centaur form this time?"

He shrugged but didn't look at me. "Soon enough."

He was quiet for a moment, then smiled and gazed fondly at the bugle in his hand.

"You know, Nathaniel, I don't know what you have against the bugle. I find it to be quite effective."

I chuckled. "That's all that matters, then."

Based on the rumblings coming from the rooms, I assumed all the females were, at the very least, out of bed.

"Come on, it sounds like they're all up," I told Chiron. "Let's go deal with the men."

He grunted, then sounded the bugle one more time, causing me to wince.

"Fifteen minutes, girls! Don't make us come back here and drag you out!"

Jerking his head in the direction of the door, we made our way over the male dorms to get the other half of the recruits up.

A SHORT WHILE LATER, the recruits had assembled in the courtyard, all clad in their black training uniforms, looking at us expectantly, albeit with more than a few groggy expressions. The Mentalist recruits especially looked exhausted, thanks to Charlise's insistence on working out their powers on day one.

"Now that we're all assembled," Chiron began, holding out his hands, "Welcome to your first day of training. In just a few moments, we'll make our way to the training arena, which, as I mentioned when you arrived, is just outside Olympia. Our transport awaits in front of the portal field, along with some of your mentors, the rest of whom will meet us there. We'll be going by carriage this time so you can get a tour of the village on your way."

He nodded toward me, giving me the go ahead to lead them down the hill toward five large, red carriages, each drawn by a massive white stallion.

Despite having seen them thousands of times before, I was always struck by the beauty of the Olympic stallions. They were stunning creatures, each a vivid white with bright blue eyes, standing ten feet tall with a wingspan of nearly twenty-five feet. They were highly intelligent and had always been friends to the Elders. Each generation, they were always at the ready to make the first journey to the arena with the new recruits.

Chiron clapped his hands from the front of the group to get everyone's attention. "Let's get moving, everyone! Twelve to a cart!"

As the recruits began boarding the carriages, I made my way to Chiron's side. He never felt comfortable riding the carriages driven by horses, so he always made the trip to the arena on foot.

Once the recruits were loaded up, Chiron murmured to the stallion on the first carriage, and they began moving slowly up Main Street, which stretched up the mountain directly away from the portal field.

The mentors began giving their charges a tour of the town, pointing out the various restaurants and shops that lined the cobblestone street.

The older buildings—mainly the library and a few businesses—dated back about eighteen hundred years to when some of the Ischyra decided Olympia should become a place for more than just housing. A few establishments—a tavern and a small restaurant—

were opened, and from there, Main Street slowly began to grow into its current form. The original stone buildings still stood tall, but they were now interspersed with the wood construction of newer structures, their thatched roofs replaced with more modern solar shingles that provided power to the village. I always appreciated seeing how the residents took pride in taking the village from its original stone-hut dwellings to a place that was enjoyable to live.

"So, have you worked out your plan with the Mentalist recruits?" Chiron asked from beside me.

"More or less. Charlise said they did well last night, although some will need quite a bit more work than others."

"I suppose that's to be expected. What are your thoughts on this generation overall?"

"It's difficult to say. They seem eager, that's for certain."

"I'll give you that. Eagerness doesn't beget talent, though. Plenty of our students have taught us that," he pointed out. "Remember a few centuries back, the boy who was so anxious to prove himself against the empousa?"

I thought for a moment before recalling the recruit he was talking about. "Yes. Jeremiah."

The sixteenth-century Ischyra had felt he could take on three of the vampiric females on his own. He'd come across their nest while on his first patrol in London. Rather than leave and seek assistance, he'd gone in on his own to face the creatures. There were no witnesses to his death, but based on the blackened flesh surrounding his wounds, it was deduced that one of the creatures coated her fangs with a serum made from the godsbane flower, a fairly common trick among their kind. His partner, who'd been patrolling just one lane over, had arrived only in time to see the predators flee.

"Eagerness combined with a hefty dose of arrogance," Chiron remarked, shaking his head. "I've seen quite a bit of it the last few days."

He cast a quick glance over his shoulder.

"The boy named Damien and that Mary girl, to start," he muttered.

I laughed. "You may be right about Damien. Charlise doesn't care for him, I know that much. I don't think you've got to worry about Mary, though. She's far more nervous than she'd like us to know, and she's much smarter than she lets on."

"You've seen their minds, then?"

"Yes, I've scanned them all, several times. We may need to keep an eye on some, but I'll withhold judgement for the time being."

"How do you think they'll fair once they know of the rebel threat?"

I grimaced. "I'm not so sure. A part of me worries that the idea of using their powers in the real world so soon will lead to sloppiness in their training, but we'll see."

"Then I will follow your lead," he clapped my shoulder, "...and hope that you're right."

"No pressure, though?" I smiled wryly.

He laughed. "None at all. Now, why don't you go over your training plan with Charlise one last time before we get there? She should be about done giving the tour by now. I'm going to go the rest of the way on my own."

"Will do. I'll see you at the arena."

I watched as the centaur made his way to the tree line so he could shift into his equine form for his morning run through the forest.

I always envied his ability to seek out solitude and let himself be free. No matter where I went, it felt as though that kind of peace would always elude me. Something would always be required of me because my gift was so very rare. My trips to Earth were the only reprieves I got from the hectic world of Olympus.

Sighing, I glanced back at the carriage Charlise was in charge of, which happened to be the one Tessa and her friends had boarded. I saw the recruits laughing with one another as Charlise passed around a box of granola bars—what she considered "brain food." Tessa's smile was wide as she bantered excitedly with the others, and I could only hope that meant she'd gotten a better night's sleep than I had.

19

TESSA

I couldn't help but grin as I took in the sight of my new home. Trees with fluffy pink and white flowers ran down either side of Main Street, casting shade across the stone and wood buildings that housed various businesses. A quick scan of the bright signage revealed a uniform shop, several clothing stores, a book store, a salon, a coffee shop, and a grocery store. Restaurants were scattered among them—Mexican, Indian, American, and of course, Greek, to name a few. I saw the pizza place Charlise had ordered from the night before —Nico's—and made a mental note to pay a visit. That pizza had been to die for.

The eating establishments were more for enjoyment than necessity. Immortals didn't necessarily need to eat for sustenance, but who didn't love a good cheeseburger or souvlaki now and then?

My mouth practically watered at the thought of the grilled meat on a stick that Analise loved to cook for us when I was growing up.

"As you can see, there are quite a few businesses along here. We've got restaurants, retail stores, and a uniform shop for when you finally don't have to wear those getups anymore," Charlise explained, indicating our fitted black pants and matching long-sleeved shirt. They were made of this weird, soft, stretchy fabric that reminded me a little of spandex but sturdier. Our shoes were black slip-on sneakers with a grippy rubber sole.

"Where does everything come from?" I asked.

"Everything is made from produce, grain, and livestock from the farming valleys that surround the mountain. That's also where the stables are located, and there are a few weavers who make fabrics for all of our textiles."

"Well, that's convenient." Mary turned toward me. "Where're we going for dinner? We don't need money, right?"

Charlise smiled. "Nope. One of the perks of a self-sufficient society."

"I want a cheeseburger," Eric deadpanned. "No arguments."

I snorted. "Of course you do." It was a known fact that Eric would eat cheeseburgers on a daily basis if given the opportunity.

I felt a quick poke on the back of my head.

"So what *is* for dinner?"

I turned in my seat and saw Yana sitting right behind me.

"Yes! Great minds think alike!" Mary exclaimed, turning and giving Yana a high five. I was glad to see that their argument from the night before seemed to have been squashed. "Eric wants cheeseburgers. You in?"

Yana clapped her hands and rubbed them together. "I hope they have bacon. Bacon on a cheeseburger is delicious."

"Couldn't agree more," Eric responded.

"Hey, so who runs the businesses?" I asked.

"Ischyra who petition to take charge of Olympia's upkeep," she responded. "We need people to keep the village running, otherwise it would be overgrown and crumbling by now. After two centuries of service, an Ischyra can request to be put on village duty—open a business, maintain gardens, work at the farms in the lower valley, that kind of thing. The older ones are allowed to request permanent Olympic duty as guards or servants for the gods."

"Really?" Eric sounded incredulous. "Why would anyone ask to do those things? I mean, working for the gods sounds awesome, but the rest?"

Mary threw an elbow into his side and shushed him. "What our incredibly rude friend is trying to say is, it's surprising that they would ask to do something so mundane when they've been gifted such amazing powers," she said.

Charlise shook her head. "You say that now, but after a few hundred years, you may feel differently. And besides, they're allowed to trade off if they decide they want to go back into the field. It usually isn't too difficult to find someone who wants to take over a business for a century or two." She smiled at us. "Here, have some breakfast."

She handed a box to Igor who'd claimed a seat in the front row. "You may not need food to keep you in good physical health, but it helps keep you sharp mentally."

When the box made its way to my seat in the third row, I saw that she'd brought us breakfast in the form of granola bars and fig juice. I took one of each and passed the box on to Mary before pulling off the thin parchment paper the bar was wrapped in.

"So wait," Eric spoke around a mouthful of granola. "What if no one wants to volunteer to work in the village?"

"There's a lottery system, just in case. It helps to balance things out a bit, so that those of us who benefit from the labor of others eventually give back. It's pretty rare that we actually need to use it."

Eric nodded, his mouth too full to respond.

"Okay, so most of these side streets contain homes and apartments for permanent residents, but just down this street—" Charlise pointed toward one of the many side streets that stretched off of Main "—is where you'll find the library. It was the first building built in Olympia after the earlier generations started expanding, about eighteen hundred years ago. It has a decent collection of human and Olympic works."

I craned my neck to see down the street and was able to make out a large, gray square building with a domed roof sticking out among a stretch of row houses.

She turned and pointed down the street directly opposite.

"And down there is a larger gymnasium than what you all have in your dorms. It's typically used by Ischyra who aren't in daily training anymore, but there are instructors there who offer classes in other forms of combat fighting. Professor Luiz teaches a great *Jiu jitsu* course, if you're ever interested." She gave us a wide grin and held up her hands. "So that's the town. Any questions?"

As a few recruits raised their hands, I turned to Mary. "So what's your group like, anyway?"

"They're kind of great, actually. There are only six water users. You?"

I shrugged. "There are so many of us right now. Twenty all together I think, so it was kind of hard to get a feel for everyone. Did you guys get to try out your powers yesterday?"

"No. Jacob—our Mentor—said it can take a while to work out water affinities, so we're going to be working on that today." She rolled her eyes. "I really hope this doesn't turn out to be a boring affinity. I tried to draw water from the air this morning and got nothing."

"Oh, stop. I'm sure you'll do amazing things. I always thought wind was a weak affinity until I met Chris the other night. Dude creates tornadoes. *Tornadoes*, Mary. So you never know. You could be making monsoons by the end of your training year."

She looked slightly mollified at this. "I guess that would be pretty kickass, huh?"

"Totally kickass." I gave her hand a quick squeeze. "Seriously, don't stress. You never know what you'll be able to do until you do it, right?"

She gave me a wry smile. "You sound like John, you realize that, right?"

I laughed. My guardian had definitely been known for his inspirational one-liners.

"Yeah, I guess he taught me well."

We rode the rest of the way in silence, watching as Main Street gave way to the dense forest that stood between Olympia and the upper mountain, turning from cobblestone to hardpacked dirt. Our carriages wound through the forest for another mile or so before we came into the massive clearing that housed the arena.

It was one of the biggest structures I'd ever seen. Like the Agora, it was rectangular and made of gleaming white stone, but its size rivaled that of the Colosseum in Rome. Even that historic structure paled in comparison to the beautiful white monstrosity that stood before us.

As we walked through the massive archway that acted as an entrance, I was able to take in its true enormity. There were four levels of covered walkways that encircled the arena, the lowest of which opened onto a few dozen rows of seating descending down to an arena floor that stretched the length of two football fields. The main area was made of sand, with squat wooden benches running along the left and right sides.

I stepped away from the crowd and looked in awe around the arena, feeling a broad smile spread across my face.

When I first woke up that morning, I felt my power stir. It was odd, feeling its existence, almost companionable. As I gazed down the length of the sandy field, I gave my power a tentative mental poke and felt it swirl slightly in response, as though telling me it was ready to go.

That made two of us.

20

TESSA

"Okay, recruits!" Chiron bellowed once we were all inside. "I want you all lined up with your specialties so we can get started."

Yana gave my shoulder a quick squeeze. "Good luck!"

Her eyes sparkled, and I could tell she was excited to start working with her Electrokinesis. She looked to Eric, who'd been announced as a Pyrokinetic, another fire user. "Come on, let's go see what we will be doing."

Eric beamed in excitement. "Heck yeah," he said, and the two of them marched off to find their group.

"Crap, do you see the water people?" Mary was jumping up and down, trying to find where her group was located. It seemed like almost everyone towered over her small frame.

I placed my hand on her shoulder and pointed toward a group that was standing about twenty feet away. "Relax, jumping bean, they're over there."

"Awesome, thanks. Catch you later!"

I stood on my toes to find which direction Charlise had gone, but she'd already been lost in the crowd. I spotted Sina's bright-red hair on the other side of the arena, so I headed in her direction. Anette had already found her and was hovering by her side.

Sina waved when she saw me getting closer. "Tessa, hi! Over here!"

"Hey, guys." I glanced around. "Where's everyone else?"

Sina gestured behind me with her chin. "They are coming now. Come on, let's line up."

Once we were all facing him in orderly rows of ten, Chiron addressed us. "This is how things are going to go. Each morning, you will arrive here and line up just as you are now. The first part of your training will consist of a warm up, of sorts." He looked around at us, hands on his hips. "Can anyone tell me the purpose of an immortal doing calisthenics?"

A petite Asian girl named Cho quickly raised her hand.

"Cho?" Chiron gestured for her to answer.

"Because we need to hone our physical skills as well as our affinities. Speed and strength can only be beneficial if they are controlled."

"Very good. Contrary to what some of you might think, the ability to use those aspects of your power efficiently is not innate. Immortal strength and speed have been given to you, but much like your affinities, they are not truly yours until you can control them."

He paused, allowing that to sink in.

"So," he continued after a few seconds, "the first thing we're going to do today is work on your speed. Come, let's head out back."

"What's out back?" Sina whispered.

"Not a clue." I watched as Chiron moved toward a pair of large double doors that opened at the opposite end of the arena.

Chiron had made "out back" sound like a small thing, maybe a training area without walls where we would have a bit more freedom.

When we exited the arena, I saw that technically he wasn't wrong.

"Holy shit," Sina whispered.

"Yeah," I breathed. "Definitely."

Extending from the back of the arena and up the rocky mountainside was a running track clearly designed with immortal speed in mind. Carved to follow the gentle incline of the mountain, it was about four times the length of a normal track and twice as wide, with a flat, stone field spanning the interior.

There was no padded running area in sight, so I could only imagine how badly it must hurt to take a tumble during a run.

"Well, this is gonna suck," Mary said, coming to stand beside Sina and me.

"I'll say," I murmured, still gazing at the massive field in front of us.

"So do you think we're gonna find out why the Titans are in town?" Mary whispered, leaning closer. "That's what your boy said, right? Did he ever come find you last night?"

"He's not my boy, and yes, he said that they'd fill us in at some point. And no, he did not." I was still trying not to be annoyed at the last part.

"Come on, everyone, over here!" Chiron motioned for us to join him near the edge of the track. "We don't have all day, and I want to see what you can do!"

Quickly, we all took a seat on the low stone wall that surrounded the track, the mentors forming a line behind us.

I heard a muffled snicker from behind me, so I stole a look over my shoulder at the mentors who formed a row behind us. I saw that several of them, including Charlise and Nathaniel, seemed on the verge of laughter.

"Well, that can't be good," Mary muttered, following my gaze. "Since when does he laugh?"

"Since always, I'm guessing. Now be quiet."

She grinned mischievously. "Why? Do you think he can hear us?"

'I can definitely hear you.'

I rolled my eyes and smiled. "He can definitely hear us."

"Focus, people!" Chiron bellowed, snapping us back to attention. "You're going to be divided into five groups, then you'll be running a few laps."

Based on his tone, I had a feeling "running a few laps" as an immortal had different connotations than doing the same as a human.

He moved to the end of the bench and started counting us off like he was picking us for squads in gym class.

Thankfully, I ended up in group number five, so I'd be able to watch quite a few runs before I had my turn on the field.

Yana had been assigned to the same group so she came over and sat down next to me. "So who do you think will be the first to fall?"

I bit my lip and tried not to smile as I scanned the crowd. "Honestly? I don't know, but I'm kind of hoping it's Damien."

She snorted. "*Da.* What's that saying you Americans have? He seems like he needs to be 'taken down a peg'?"

I snickered. "Or two. You should've seen him last night when Charlise had him try to astral project. He was so cocky. Then once he actually did it, he dropped like a lead balloon because Charlise 'forgot' to tell him to sit down first."

"Ah, I would have loved to have seen that," Yana said wistfully. "Oh, they are starting."

I turned my attention back to the running field, hopeful I could learn something by watching the groups that ran before us.

Chiron directed the first group to the starting line and spaced them about ten feet apart.

"How would you recommend we begin?" Valentina, an Earth user, asked from her spot on the end.

Chiron grinned appreciatively. "Well, since you asked, I would recommend starting slowly, then gradually increasing. I want you to get comfortable with this drill because it will go a long way in honing your reaction time and accuracy."

He stepped off to the side and put one hand on his hip and let the bugle dangle from the other hand. "The only other advice I will offer is this. When you fall, tuck in your arms."

With that, he let out a deafening blast from his bugle and they set off.

Their speed was incredible. Right off the mark, they were flying; their legs moving so fast they were nearly a blur.

It looked thrilling. I wanted to fly out of my seat and join them.

"Oh, one down!"

A male mentor behind us laughed as Igor went tumbling onto the track, having lost his footing when trying to take the first curve. Dishi, who'd been just behind him, stumbled as he tried to avoid tripping over him and was knocked into Anette. Within about thirty seconds, five other recruits had gone down.

Valentina and Damien both managed to make it about three quarters of the way through their laps without any problems. Unfortunately, just as she was making her final return to the start, Valentina lost her footing and fell, the momentum from her speed causing her to roll off the track and crash into the surrounding stone wall.

Damien turned his head back in her direction when he heard her cry and reduced his speed just enough for us to see the victorious smile on his face.

Which lasted all of one second before he crashed into the wall at the opposite end, toppling over headfirst.

Silence, save for a few scattered laughs from the mentors, hung over us.

"And that," Chiron called, "...is why you never take your eyes off the road, Damien!"

Damien rose from where he'd deposited himself on the ground, embarrassment coloring his face as he stalked back toward the starting line. Valentina lay on her side in the grass, groaning. Igor was slowly trying to pull himself up at the far end of the track but seemed to be having trouble with his arm. The others were trudging down the track toward the start, wincing with each step.

All of them looked banged up in some way or another, but the only one who looked seriously injured was Igor. As he got closer, I could see that he was cradling his right arm, which was rotated at an absurd angle, as though it had gotten bent beneath his body when he fell.

He walked up to Chiron, who was looking at him sternly.

"Igor?" he asked quietly.

Igor lifted his face to our trainer. "Yes, Chiron?"

"Did you not hear my advice when you began?"

"I did, but—"

"What was my advice, Igor?"

"To tuck my arms—"

"When you fell. Not if, *when*." Then he raised his voice, addressing all of us. "Because you *will* fall. Repeatedly. You will be absolutely miserable by the end of your many days here. But after this year is done, you will all be the better for it."

He turned his gaze back to Igor. "As for you, let's fix that arm."

He snapped his fingers in the air.

"Nathaniel! Get over here and show him how to deal with this."

Igor's eyes grew wide, but when he saw the Coercer striding toward him, he straightened his back and tried to look confident.

Nathaniel gave Igor a dubious look, then arched a brow at Chiron.

"Are you sure? He's only just started."

The centaur shrugged. "Better sooner than later, wouldn't you say?"

Nathaniel heaved a sigh. "Alright." He turned to face the rest of the recruits. "Pay attention, everyone. You'll have to do this sooner than you think."

He turned back to Igor and looked him square in the eye. "Igor, this will hurt, but I'm going to walk you through how to fix this."

Igor swallowed, then nodded quickly. "I...appreciate that."

"Yes, well, you may not in just a moment." He crooked a finger, indicating for Igor to hold out his arm. "First, wrap your hand around your arm with your fingers going in the direction of the twist, like this."

"Oh, gods, I might be sick," Mary whispered, slapping a hand over her mouth.

Sina pressed her forehead into my shoulder. "Tell me when it is over, please?"

"Uh huh," I muttered, unable to look away.

"Now, I want you to very quickly twist in the opposite direction. The bone isn't broken, just out of place, so this will reset it."

Igor blanched. "Do I—Can't I—" He hesitated, staring down at his arm, then looked back at Nathaniel, his brown eyes wide with fright.

"It's like ripping off a bandage," Nathaniel explained. "It would heal on its own in a few hours, but it'll be more painful, and you need to be able to train today. So, you're going to fix it now so you can get back to work."

Taking a deep breath, Igor tightened his grip on his arm. He squeezed his eyes shut and gave a vicious twist.

I tried to cover my ears to close out the sound, but the loud crunch was impossible to miss.

Igor's chest was heaving, but he had a relieved smile on his face.

"Better now?" Nathaniel asked.

"Much. Very much." Igor shook out his arm, which had been pulled perfectly back into shape. "Thank you."

Nathaniel gave him a quick smile before stuffing his hands in his pockets and strolling back to stand with the mentors.

I was still having trouble reconciling the guy that had come to meet me that day before school with this confident and assertive immortal standing in front of me now. Maybe it was unfair, but the impression I got of Nathaniel when we first met was that of a worker bee—he did what he was told, when he was told, and didn't ask questions.

Now, having seen him rubbing elbows with Zeus and watching as he helped teach recruits how to heal themselves, I began to wonder what else I'd yet to learn about him.

21

TESSA

"Having fun yet?"

I groaned and looked up from where I'd just fallen for the fifth time, closing one eye against the blazing sun. I scowled when I saw Nathaniel grinning down at me.

He reached out a hand and pulled me up to my feet.

I dusted off my black pants, which had become coated with powdery gray dust from the stone track. I was surprised that they weren't shredded to bits at this point.

"Yep. Best day ever." I smoothed back my hair and checked that my braid was still in place.

He smiled, amused. "Well, at least you remembered to tuck your arms. Any injuries yet?"

I shook out my arms and made my way back to the start line. "Some scraped knuckles, but they healed right away."

"Good to hear." He gestured with his head toward the arena. "Come on, we're heading back inside."

I frowned. "But we didn't all finish."

I looked out over the practice area at my group mates, many of whom seemed to be dragging themselves up from their own falls. I was curious what their missteps had been. I'd done exactly what

Chiron had said—I'd started off slow, at a human pace, but my body seemed unaccepting of that, so I regularly found myself accelerating too quickly. I'd tripped over grooves in the rock three times and stumbled over my own feet twice. The four groups that ran before mine hadn't fared much better.

"Yes, well, we've decided that's enough for today. It's already been three hours."

My eyes widened. "Seriously? We just got here!"

He laughed, then pointed up at the sky. "Not exactly."

Sure enough, the sun was more than halfway to its apex.

"Oh." I put my hands on my hips and started heading inside with the other recruits. "I guess time flies when you're having fun, huh?"

"You'll get the hang of it, just give it a few days."

"Days?" I gave him an incredulous look. "*Days?*"

"It's all muscle memory, Tessa. Your body will adjust much quicker than when you were human." He paused for a moment, looking around awkwardly. "Listen, I know I said I would come talk to you—"

I held up a hand to stop him. "It's fine. Really."

He shook his head. "No, I misled you and that's unfair. Can I come find you later? I'll try to answer any questions you have."

I narrowed my eyes. "Why would you do that?"

He sighed and ran a hand through his light brown hair. "Like I said. I misled you. It wasn't my intention, but it happened, regardless."

A smile pulled up the corner of his mouth. "Besides, you're kind of stuck with me for a while, so I'd like to clear the air, if possible."

"Stuck with you?" I arched a brow and grinned at him. "So does that mean you're one of the other Mentalists who'll be helping Charlise out?"

He cocked his head to the side. "You say that as if you expected it."

"The way you keep popping up, it certainly doesn't surprise me." I slid him a sideways look. "But why, though? Isn't mentoring stuff for the younger Ischyra?"

"Eh, yes and no. The Mentalist abilities are much more complex than the Elemental ones, so sometimes we bring in more experienced mentors to help with that training."

"I guess that makes sense." I blew out a breath. "I think I'm having dinner with some friends later, but I'll be around after. I'm not really sure what time that'll be, though."

"That's alright, I'll find you."

"Cool. So how'd you get out of wearing the uniform?" I gestured toward his faded jeans and white T shirt. All of the other mentors were wearing dark gray track suits. "Isn't that a requirement or something?"

"Only for the regular mentors," he replied. "I've got to go check in with the others. We'll talk soon." With a small wave farewell, he jogged over to where the rest of the mentors had assembled behind Chiron, in the center of the arena floor.

The hard, sandy practice area had changed since we'd gone out back. Ten square tables ran along one side, each holding a large wooden box. A square enclosure that looked like an adult-sized sandbox filled with cushions sat near the middle of the arena, and closest to the entrance was a long, shallow pool filled with shimmering water. Twenty glass boxes, slightly larger than phone booths, sat off to the side opposite the row of tables.

"Hey, what was that?" Mary had just come up behind me. She grinned and nudged my side with her elbow. "What were you guys talking about?"

I smiled, noting her wide-eyed, curious expression. "Nothing important. How was your run?"

She rolled her neck, letting loose several loud cracks, then reached up and adjusted her ponytail. "Painful."

I laughed. Mary had fallen at least ten times during her group's turn.

"You're too anxious to prove yourself, Mare. Take a step back."

"Easy for you to say. You got to practice with your powers already," she huffed. "And John always ran you ragged during your training."

"Yeah, yeah," I murmured. My training sessions with John had always been intense. Whether we were focused on weapons or calisthenics, he always insisted on putting out a one hundred and ten percent effort. It had been grueling, but I certainly appreciated it now.

"You'll get your chance today, don't worry."

"I know!" She squealed, clapping her hands together. "I'm so freaking excited I could puke."

"Um, okay?" I shook my head. "That's not weird."

She stuck her tongue out at me. "Whatever. You'll see."

While we waited for Chiron to address us, I looked around, taking in my fellow recruits. We looked nothing like the teenagers who'd crossed to Olympia just a few days ago. Here, lined up in our matching black training gear, we really looked like Ischyra. It was a heady experience knowing that we'd officially met our fate.

"Alright everyone, that was a great first attempt," Chiron said once we were all settled. "This will be our typical warm-up each morning, although after a few days we'll be adding in a strength component."

A few muffled groans rose up from the recruits.

"No, I don't want to hear any of that. I promise each day will get just a little bit easier. The rest of today will be spent with your mentors. On Monday, one week from today, our schedule will begin to rotate to include hand-to-hand combat and weapons training as well. For the first few days, though, we'll be focused solely on getting comfortable with your new powers."

"Gods, have we really only been here for three days?" Sina whispered, leaning in close. "It feels like it has been weeks!"

"Right? I completely lost track of time," I whispered.

Chiron cleared his throat.

"Now, before I send you off to your mentors for further instruction, let's take a seat. I wanted to give you an idea of what you'll be dealing with, once your training year is complete."

Within seconds, the arena was silent, and we were all seated, backs straight, waiting like obedient school children.

"As I'm sure you all noticed," he began, clasping his hands behind his back, "Prometheus and Epimetheus have joined us. I acknowledge that some of you may have...thoughts about the presence of the latter of these two, so I will be very clear."

He let his eyes traverse the crowd.

"Your thoughts on their presence are of no matter to them, to me, and especially not the Elders. They are here because they will be joining us in facing a common threat. Your guardians, if they performed their duties adequately, would have educated you on the decade-long war with the Titans. When the war ended, Cronus and many of his supporters were locked in Tartarus. Eventually, Zeus opted to release those who he believed had paid their penance. As of today, the only two left in Tartarus are Cronus and Iapetus, the twins' father."

He sighed and shook his head.

"The war with the Titans was about rebelling against an oppressor. Ousting a Titan who had no place ruling the Olympic realm. Cronus was a despicable creature, and Zeus was able to remove him from power not only with the help of his siblings but with many of Cronus' brethren as well."

"Prometheus and Epimetheus were two of our Titan allies, and despite certain events that took place after the war, they have come to an agreement with Zeus and the other Elders. They have rejoined the ranks of Olympus, not as guests, not as disgraced gods, but as allies."

"Certain events?" Mary muttered, crossing her arms. "That's one way to phrase it."

"Shh!" I whispered.

"Recently, it has come to our attention that someone is attempting to organize a coup, another rebellion, not unlike the one Zeus led against Cronus and his allies. While most of the Titans who are free wish to live their lives peacefully, there are some who would see Zeus usurped and his father brought back to power."

"Who?"

I craned my neck to see who had spoken and saw Damien sitting near the front.

There was a pause as Chiron assessed the recruit who'd interrupted him.

I watched the two with interest, wondering how Chiron would handle Damien's rudeness. As the seconds ticked by, I began to feel uncomfortable, as though waiting for a bomb to go off.

Finally, Chiron smiled.

"Well, Damien, it appears there are a number of factions who have merged. Not everyone is as amenable to peace as Prometheus and Epimetheus." He narrowed his eyes at the recruit. "Now, go run one lap for interrupting me. One of your fellow recruits can brief you on what we're discussing."

Damien gaped at him and tried to sputter a response, but Chiron dismissed him with a wave of his hand.

Red faced, Damien stormed off toward the running field.

Chiron waited until he was out of sight, then began pacing back and forth as he spoke. "Menoetius, the twins' brother and one of the Titans Zeus released from Tartarus, appears to be the one leading this rebellion. He has managed to garner the support of a number of the more malevolent beings across the realms who wish to free his father and Cronus from Tartarus.

"Let me assure you—" he spoke firmly "—Menoetius seeks nothing but power and has no thoughts or cares for anything but his own goals. If he succeeds in freeing the Titans from the Underworld, Cronus will seize the opportunity to take back his 'throne' from Zeus. We cannot let that happen. What this means for you is that you will be facing a brewing war, if not an active one, once your training is complete."

He folded his arms and glared out at us. "Understood?"

A heavy silence hung in the air.

A brown-haired guy who I recognized as Andrei's roommate Demir cleared his throat. "Why should we trust them to fight their father and brother on our behalf?"

"Excellent question," a new voice remarked.

The other recruits and I turned to see who the newcomer was, and more than a few gasps went up when we saw the tall, hulking forms of Prometheus and Epimetheus walking toward us.

The twins were a study in contrasts. Prometheus wore dark khaki pants and a long-sleeved blue shirt that stretched across his muscular frame, his close-cropped blond hair styled neatly. He smiled easily as he approached, somehow managing to look professional, formidable, and approachable all at once. Epimetheus wore jeans and a black t shirt, and his own dirty blond hair was pulled back in a short ponytail at the base of his neck. Nothing about him seemed remarkable. He looked just as stoic as he had the first two times I'd seen him, so I assumed his brother had been the one to speak.

"Prometheus, Epimetheus. Good of you to join us!" Chiron grinned as the twins came to a stop beside him.

Prometheus nodded. "Yes, well, we thought we'd get the awkward introductions out of the way sooner rather than later." He flashed a grin at the group of recruits.

I couldn't help but smile as he acknowledged the mixed feelings of the new recruits toward him and his twin.

"As to your question, Demir," Prometheus continued, his voice a gentle baritone, "I don't expect you to trust us. You're only just meeting us, that would be foolish. I only ask that you let us earn your trust. We still believe in Zeus' original purpose. Cronus is an unfit ruler for Olympus. Allowing him to reclaim his seat would be detrimental to us all." He glanced at Epimetheus, who stood beside him, arms folded across his chest, eying the recruits.

"As for our relationship with our brother and father... well, that's a bit of a complicated mess. Suffice to say, we do not wish to see those three reunited, so it would behoove us if we could ensure that does not happen."

He smiled at Demir. "Does that answer your question?"

Demir nodded, wide eyed. "Y-yes s-s-sir."

I recalled what Andrei had said about Demir seeming too apprehensive for life as an Ischyra. Based on his reaction to the Titans, I could sort of see what he was talking about.

"Where are the rest of them?" Kieran spoke up from the back row. "The rest of the Titans who survived the war?"

"Some still live in the Olympic realm," Chiron responded. "Hyperion and Theia actually assist Demeter in running Olympus' agricultural operations. Many of the others chose to take up residence on Earth. You'll likely meet them in time."

"What about your other brother? Atlas?" Sina addressed the twins directly.

A small frown flickered across Epimetheus' forehead, and for a moment I thought he might actually speak. Instead, Prometheus responded.

"Atlas is currently unavailable," Prometheus responded, his expression hard. "That's all the information we can provide on him at the current moment."

"Alright, everyone," Chiron held up his hands to indicate the time for questions was done. "I know that you probably have many more questions, but just trust that they will all be answered in time. We simply do not have the time to take them all today."

He waved the mentors over to stand beside him.

"Now, let's move on. For the rest of the day, you're going to split off with your mentors for further instruction." He stepped back and began speaking quietly with the Titans, while the mentors stepped forward and began directing us to different areas of the arena.

Whispers broke out among the recruits as we stood.

"Is this what you talked to Nate about the other night?" Mary whispered.

I arched a brow. "Nate?"

She waved her hand dismissively. "Nathaniel is too much of a mouthful. He's Nate now."

I snorted. "I'm sure he'll love that."

"So? Was that what you guys talked about?"

"Yeah."

"Why didn't you tell me?" She sounded hurt.

"I'm sorry. Things just got so heated that night when we got back. I didn't really want to get into it."

She gave me a dubious look. "Okay..."

"Mentalists, over here!"

I squeezed her hand and smiled. "We'll talk later, K?"

She gave me a reluctant smile. "Fine."

I grabbed Anette's hand and followed the sound of Charlise's southern drawl to where she, Nate—the nickname was totally sticking from here on out—and another male Ischyra were hovering by the tables.

"Let's move it!" she bellowed.

"This feels like boot camp," Sina muttered, coming to my side.

"This *is* boot camp. This is literally basic training." I sighed as I looked at our mentors. "They're going to run us ragged every damn day."

"Morning, everyone," Charlise greeted us. "I mentioned last night that two other mentors would be joining us. You've all met Nathaniel, of course, and this is Fletcher."

"Hello, everyone."

Fletcher had a heavy British accent, and with his lanky frame, dark skin, and friendly smile, he kind of reminded me of Will Smith from his Fresh Prince days.

"I'm Fletcher Hughes, but you can all call me Fletch. I went through my transformation five generations back with Charlise," he said, giving her a cheeky grin. "I've got affinities for psychometry and astral projection."

"Alright, let's get going," Charlise barked, getting right down to business. "Everyone join up, two to a table. We're going to expand on the exercises we did last night."

We scurried to grab tables, and I ended up with Damien, who'd just returned red-faced from his lap. We were at a table on the end, not too far from where the water users were set up.

"Right, then. Fletch, Nathaniel, start going down the line to get them started. I'll take these two," Charlise said, gesturing with her chin at me and Damien.

Fletch and Nate each started moving to the other groups to dish out instructions, and Charlise came over to stand with us.

"Tessa, Damien." She gave us a friendly smile. "How are you guys doing so far? You enjoy that run?"

Damien's sharp-featured face was pinched in annoyance at Charlise's obvious dig, and I bit back a smile.

"It was...great?" I hedged.

Charlise gave a hearty laugh. "Oh, it sucked horribly, and you know it! Don't worry, though. Chiron was right, it'll only get easier from here. Tessa, I think we'll start with you since you did so well last night."

She waved a hand toward the mystery box that sat between us.

"Open the box."

I blinked. First again. Of course.

I tried to remember how I'd gone about throwing the table the night before.

It's just another sense. Go to the box and open up the damn thing.

I took a deep breath and focused all my energy on the smooth brown lid.

"You're pushing too hard. You did great last night. See if you can find that same headspace."

I nodded and closed my eyes. I inhaled deeply through my nose and exhaled through my mouth.

I pictured the box in my head, sitting innocuously on the square table. It was stained a dark brown and in the shape of a perfect cube. The lid appeared to be a slider, so I wouldn't have to lift it to open it; I would have to slide it toward me.

Steeling myself, I opened my eyes. Staring intently at the lid, I pictured a handle in the center and made that my focal point.

Pull!

The lid flew off, sliding out so quickly that I had to jump out of the way to avoid getting hit.

I looked at Charlise and beamed.

"That was so freaking cool," I squeaked.

She beamed at me. "You're a rock star, Tessa," she said proudly. "You really are."

"Can I do something else?"

She laughed. "Let's give your partner a shot. Damien?"

"Yes?"

"I'm going to ask you to try to mind-link with Tessa so *you* can pick up the object in the box using her hands."

He nodded sharply. "Of course." Jaw clenched, he looked me up and down, his pale blue eyes appraising.

"Now, Tessa... remember, your first instinct will be to shut him out. It will be very hard to go against that instinct, but you need to let him in. Remind yourself that this isn't malicious, it's an exercise. Put your mind at ease and you shouldn't have a problem."

She turned her eyes to Damien. "As for you, take your time with this. There's no rush. I'm going to move on to the next group, but one of the others will be over to check on ya'll in a few."

Giving us a thumbs up, she moved on to Anette and Sina who'd taken the table next to us.

"I'll apologize now if this is uncomfortable," Damien said, not sounding at all apologetic. "I have heard it can be."

I sighed. "It's all for the sake of learning, right? Just do your thing."

He gave a curt nod, then folded his arms across his chest and closed his eyes. For a few seconds I felt nothing, then finally, I felt a slight nudge in my mind.

It was nothing like when Nate entered my mind. That had been forceful, like a physical push. When Damien tried to link with me, it was weaker, more annoying. I felt like my brain was getting hit repeatedly with a fly swatter. Each time his power smacked at my mind, my own affinity would rear up, pushing back like some kind of guard dog.

After what felt like an eternity of an internal battle of wills, Damien let out a frustrated groan.

"Tessa, you are blocking me!" he accused. "Stop!"

"I am not!"

"You are, I can feel it! Every time I get close, you push me out." He made a sound of disgust and threw up his hands. "I do not think I can work like this."

"It's not like I'm doing it on purpose!" I crossed my arms over my chest. "And who says I'm the problem? You're the one trying to enter my mind." I arched a brow, daring him to challenge my logic.

He squeezed his eyes shut and ran his hands through his thick brown hair. After letting out a few deep breaths, he dropped his arms and met my eyes.

"Fine, we will try again, but *please* try to keep your brain under control."

"*My* brain isn't the—"

"Having trouble?"

I rolled my eyes as Nate came to a stop next to our table, cutting off my retort.

Damien huffed, then jerked his chin toward me. "She keeps blocking me out of her mind."

"Oh, real nice, Damien. You're acting like I'm doing it on purpose!"

"Perhaps if you tried harder—"

"I am trying!"

"Okay, enough!" Nate barked, causing us both to jump. "What is the problem?"

"Damien can't link to my mind and he's blaming me for it." I gave my partner a scathing look.

"I cannot link to her mind because she keeps pushing me out!"

"I am not!"

I felt another hard push on my brain and glared at Damien, kicking him back with all my mental might. "Gods, Damien! Can you at least wait until he gives us a little guidance? Forcing it clearly isn't working."

He frowned, then opened and closed his mouth a few times. No sound came out.

"Are you done?" Nate asked, his tone measured. He pierced us both with a glare.

Looking back at Damien, who still wasn't speaking, I realized Nate must be using his Coercion to keep him from talking.

"If he is," I snapped.

Nate pinched the bridge of his nose, then pointed toward the back of the arena.

"Damien, take a walk."

Damien heaved out a frustrated breath, then stormed off without a word.

Sighing, I faced Nate. "I'm sorry, I just—"

He held up a hand to stop me.

"It's fine. It's not abnormal for recruits to argue like this, especially when it comes to mental abilities." He gripped the back of his neck with one hand and pursed his lips. "Tessa, you were blocking me, too. What's going on?"

"What are you talking about?"

"I was using Coercion on both of you, and you blocked me."

"Oh. Hey! You're not supposed to do that!"

"You two were at each other's throats and words weren't doing the trick. You need to train, not bicker. So, yes, I used Coercion to shut you both up so I could help."

So apparently, he was assertive and a hard ass.

I huffed. "Well, I thought it was Damien. Sorry."

Although, I really wasn't.

Screw him and his stupid Coercer powers, I thought.

"You're shouting," he said, a small smirk playing on his lips.

"Well stop listening," I muttered, bracing my hands on the table and kicking the sand with my toe.

"I'm not listening, you're projecting. Again."

"So what, now I'm not even in control of my own thoughts? I thought I was a Telekinetic. Shouldn't I just be moving things around?"

"Technically. I'll talk to Charlise, but I think it's something we should explore a bit further." He flicked a glance over my shoulder so quickly I almost missed it. Frowning, I turned to see what had caught his eye, then immediately turned back.

Shit.

Apollo, looking stern and godlike, was standing in the second story walkway, looking right at us.

"What is he doing here?" I hissed, panic welling up inside of me as I turned back to face Nate.

"Ignore him," he said gently. "He's just here to see how things are going."

"Easy for you to say," I grumbled as I watched Prometheus and Epimetheus observing the recruits beside him. I felt my face flush as panic gave way to mortification. "You didn't just get into a shouting match with one of the recruits."

"Don't let his presence shake your resolve, Tessa. This isn't the last time Elders will be here to see how their recruits are doing. Let's just get back to the task at hand."

I took a deep breath and nodded, not missing his clear attempt to change the subject. "Fine. Where's Damien?"

He jerked his chin toward the other end of the row of tables. "Speaking with Charlise. I asked her to give him some guidance."

I looked down the row of tables and saw Charlise whispering animatedly to Damien who had an annoyed scowl on his face. They were about ten feet from where the water users were practicing with the pool. I caught a glimpse of Mary holding a basketball-sized ball of water between her hands, a look of deep concentration on her face.

"Oh, hey, look at Mare. She figured out her powers." I grinned. "She was really nervous this morning when I told her I got to practice mine last night."

"The Mentalists are the only group that really got to work on their powers last night. Charlise tends to dive right in," Nate explained, following my gaze.

"Huh. Interesting."

Just then, Mary glanced up and saw me looking at her, so I gave her a thumbs up. She grinned, a look of excitement on her face, but almost immediately, the ball of water fell back into the metal bucket at her feet. She shot me a look of annoyance, then closed her eyes and began reforming the ball in her hands.

I sighed and pushed a stray lock of hair behind my ear.

"Great, she's totally going to blame that on me distracting her. Can this day be over yet?"

Nate laughed. "You've still got a few more hours to go. Let's get

Damien back and see what you two can do now that you've had a chance to cool off."

As he called Damien back over, I felt a drop of water on my face.

"Is it raining?" I asked, wiping the water from my cheek. I looked at Damien, who'd just walked up, and saw he was staring at me wide-eyed.

"What is it?" I asked him.

He smirked, and his eyes drifted above my head. "Tessa, you should probably move," he said, looking like he was holding back a laugh.

I looked up, and directly above my head was a ball of water, undulating precariously. I flicked a glance at Mary who had a smug grin on her face.

Going on instinct, I used my mind to bat the ball of water back in her direction, just like I'd done with the box lid. I'd intended for it to go back into the pool, but my brain got the better of me. Before I could stop it, the entire thing fell apart right over her head. A few water users who were standing nearby jumped out of the way, narrowly avoiding getting splashed.

I clapped my hand to my mouth, stunned. Then I laughed as I watched her sputter, water pooling at her feet.

"Real nice, Tess!" Mary called. "I'll remember that one."

I grinned, slightly pleased with myself. I'd just used my powers without having to do any intense focusing. At least that was one thing I could call an accomplishment for today.

Alex, one of the mentors for the water users, turned at the commotion and glared in Mary's direction, not having seen that I was the one who threw the water.

"The water is supposed to stay over the buckets or in the pool, Mary," the auburn-haired mentor said. "Dry off and get back to work."

Suddenly slammed with the realization that Apollo had most definitely seen what had just happened, I clapped a hand over my mouth and faced Nate.

"Oh gods, am I going to get punished for that?"

"No, you won't be." He tilted his head to the side, a curious expression on his face. "How did you do that?"

"Do what?"

"Push the water like that?"

"I don't know? I focused and gave it a push, like Charlise taught me. Why?"

"Just curious." He frowned, then waved at us to continue before folding his arms across his chest. "Go on, try again."

I stared at him for a second longer, and just as I was about to return my focus to Damien, I saw Nate's midnight blue gaze drift behind me. I glanced over my shoulder and saw that Apollo was staring stonily at Nate.

Damien turned to see where we were looking and groaned. "I hope he didn't just see you yelling at me. I do *not* want to look bad so early in our training."

"I'm sure you're fine," I muttered. "Let's just try again."

I looked to Nate, hoping he could offer some guidance. "Any suggestions?"

His gaze snapped back to me, and when I looked behind me, I saw that Apollo was gone.

He cleared his throat. "I'm sorry, what?"

I gave him a questioning look. "You okay?"

He smiled and waved a hand carelessly. "Yes, sorry. Apollo can be quite demanding at times. Tessa, you had similar problems with your transformation, so think back to how you opened your mind to me then."

"Got it. Open minds." I looked across the table and met Damien's eyes. "Whenever you're ready."

As soon as Damien's eyes were focused intently on my own, I worked to open my mind like I'd done during my transformation. It had been easier then because my mind was still mostly human; my affinity hadn't fully awoken yet. Now I felt it fighting not only Damien's persistent knocking on my brain, but also my own attempts to push it back and let him in.

"Dammit, I cannot work like this!" Damien yelled after another half hour. We were both dripping with sweat, and my head felt like it had been squeezed in a vice grip.

"It's not me! It's my stupid power," I complained. "It doesn't want to let you in."

"It is not sentient, Tessa, and the whole point of this is to get *control* of our powers." He put his hands on his hips and faced Nate. "Right?"

Nate was quiet for a moment, his fingers pressed into his eyes. He took a deep breath then looked up.

"Yes, that is the point of this exercise, in addition to cooperation with one another." His voice dripped with irritation. He rubbed one hand across his forehead and put the other on his hip. "Tessa, what exactly are you feeling when you try to open your mind to Damien?"

I opened my mouth, then frowned, unsure how to explain it. "It's like—I don't know, it's like my power is fighting against me. It responds to me, but it also feels like it has a mind of its own." I scrunched up my face. "Does that make sense?"

Nate let out a frustrated sigh. "Not particularly. Okay, let's try to change this up." He crooked his fingers at my partner. "Damien, switch with me."

"Seriously?" I asked as Damien moved off to the side, a slightly relieved look on his face.

"Seriously. My powers are stronger than both of yours. I should be able to help."

"Didn't I just block you out?" I asked.

"Yes, but I didn't push. I was only trying to get you two to stop arguing." He took a deep breath and gave me a pointed look. "This will feel more intense than the last time."

A chill ran through me as I thought back to when he'd use his Coercion on me before, when I was still human. It felt so long ago, even though it hadn't even been a week. The memory of the fear and panic I'd felt caused my breath to hitch.

I saw Damien give me a curious look.

"Give me your hand," Nate spoke softly, holding out one of his own. I reached across the table and clasped it. "Take a deep breath."

I did as he said, then gave him what I hoped was a confident smile.

"I'm good. Go for it."

I felt the forceful push as Nate's power slammed into my own. Instinctually, I pushed back before remembering I was supposed to be letting him in.

'Try to stop fighting.'

'I'm trying!'

I could feel beads of sweat dripping down the back of my neck as I worked to tamp down my power and open my mind. I tried to flood my thoughts with trust and confidence in him. Nate wasn't a threat and he wasn't trying to harm me. He was trying to help, make me stronger.

I felt his fingers lace between my own, and he gave a comforting squeeze.

Slowly, I began to get control, just enough to let him in. I felt the same strange rifling sensation as he explored my mind.

'You're doing great, just a few more seconds.'

I wanted to respond to his reassurances, but it was taking every ounce of my willpower to keep my mind open even just a sliver. Conversation wasn't an option.

As I felt his power moving out like feelers through my mind, I realized Nate was far more powerful than I'd initially thought. That morning before school, he'd pushed me aside and gone through my memories and shown me a vision. Looking back, it seemed so simple in comparison, even if it had been wildly intrusive.

Now I felt like my brain was under attack. Understanding dawned as I saw the true power of a Coercer.

I wanted to crawl out of my skull.

I only lasted a few more seconds before the spidery feeling of his power got to be too much to bear and my powers rebelled against us both.

"Enough!" I let out a massive huff and forced my eyes open. "This isn't working," I gasped, wiping sweat from my brow and bracing my hands on the table. I squeezed my eyes shut, trying to forget the feeling of him crawling through my brain.

"It just isn't working," I said through gritted teeth.

I felt his presence exit my mind, leaving me with a horrible migraine. I raised my eyes to him, meeting his gaze.

His mouth was set in a firm line, and I saw beads of sweat glistening on his forehead.

"Agreed." He looked at Damien, who was standing next to me looking perplexed. "Go find Charlise; tell her I said to put you in the sandbox with one of the telepaths."

"The sandbox?"

"Yes." Nate's voice was full of frustration. "The box over there with sand and cushions. It's soft and comfortable and a good place to practice your astral projection without hurting yourself."

I let my body sink to the ground, then propped my arms on my knees so I could put my head down. There was a slight breeze coming through the arena, setting goosebumps across my skin where the sweat hadn't dried. The cool air felt glorious.

Once Damien walked off to find Charlise, I looked up at Nate, squinting against the sun. "So am I totally failing?"

He sighed and looked around the arena, then sat down next to me, his arm just brushing mine. "Not at all. Your power is incredibly strong, but it's going to take time to train it to respond *to* you instead of for you. Try not to worry."

"Easy for you to say. You probably figured your powers out right away, Mr. Coercer of Olympus."

The corner of his mouth turned up in a half smile. "And here I thought I was going by Nate now."

I rolled my eyes and laughed. "Well... Mary's right, Nathaniel is kind of a mouthful. We're lazy on Earth. Any name with more than two syllables has to be shortened."

"I don't suppose I have any say in this?"

"Nope. Now tell me, what do I need to do to fix myself?"

"Take a break. Go run some laps. You're pent up and need to let off some energy. I have to go check in with Charlise."

He stood, then reached down and pulled me to my feet. When I was up, he put both hands on my shoulders and crouched a bit so he could look me in the eye. "Look at me, Tessa."

I raised my eyes to meet his.

"I know this is frustrating for you, but we will figure this out, alright?"

I nodded, feeling tears prick the corners of my eyes. It was so much easier when he was frustrated. Now I just saw pity, which felt about ten times worse.

"Stop that. You're stronger than this."

"Thanks," I mumbled, stepping back. "I'll talk to you later." Before any tears could actually escape, I stormed off toward the track.

22

NATHANIEL

Teeth gritted, I made my way quickly down the main hall of Apollo's home. Despite the mix of irritation and confusion swirling through me, I couldn't help the feeling of gratification as my sneakers squeaked on the smooth marble floor, undoubtedly leaving small scuff marks on the perfect white surface.

Despite being twice the size of a typical mansion, the two-story gray concrete home was quite possibly the most boring of all of the Elders' dwellings. Its only charm came from the occasional view of the farming valleys below, visible through the rear window-wall that looked out over the eastern side of the mountain range on days where cloud cover was scarce. On the inside, everything was white; white walls, white floors, white furniture.

There was truly nothing remarkable about his space at all.

I didn't bother knocking when I reached the doors that opened into the main living area. I found Apollo staring silently out of the window, watching as the vivid colors of the outside world assaulted the starkness inside. Light from one of the many skylights shone down on him, bathing him in sunlight.

Prometheus sat in a high back upholstered chair near the fireplace where a fire quietly rumbled on the hearth. He, Epimetheus, and Apollo had left the recruits' training session nearly three hours ago, so I was surprised to see that he was still there.

"Prometheus." I gave him a brief nod of acknowledgment before taking a seat on the long white sofa facing the windows.

"Hello, Nathaniel," he responded with a smile. "Your recruits looked good today."

"Yes, well, they've still got a long way to go, but they seem promising."

I slid a glance at Apollo, still gazing out through the window and studiously ignoring me, before turning my eyes back to Prometheus.

"Will you be joining us again?"

Picking up the carafe of wine that sat on the small coffee table, I poured myself a glass. Today had been long and grueling, and having Apollo shout commands at me while trying to calm Tessa after my trip through her mind had left me with a sense of irritation.

'Let it go, Nathaniel,' he'd ordered as Tessa and Damien stood by, waiting for my instruction. *'Walk away now. You are nothing but a distraction to her.'*

Clenching my jaw, I took a sip of the sweet ruby colored liquid and tried to squash my frustration.

Prometheus nodded, slowly turning his own glass of wine back and forth on the arm of his chair. "Yes, I think I'd like that. As much as I've enjoyed living among humans, it's been so long since I've truly been involved in anything on Olympus, and I've missed it." He frowned, staring down at his glass. "I think the recruits handled news of the rebellion quite well."

I tapped the edge of my glass lightly with my finger. "Yes. I appreciate your candor with them. I think it's important they see that you're here to help."

He smiled sardonically. "I can't say that I blame them for feeling the way they do, can you?" He arched a brow in question. "Your leader did condemn me to an eternity of torture, after all."

"Of course. It will take time, I have no doubts about that."

"The girl you were speaking with at the Agora—the one who had difficulties today—she had some interesting thoughts, wouldn't you say?" He gave me a level gaze and took a sip of wine.

My body tensed. I had hoped that he hadn't overheard my conversation with Tessa at dinner, but I suppose it was unsurprising that he'd read her thoughts. I cast a glance at Apollo and saw that his jaw was clenched, his face fallen into a frown.

"She did," I allowed, turning my gaze back to Prometheus. "Tessa's mouth tends to run away from her at times, though. I hope you didn't feel disrespected."

Apollo snorted. "We don't need the respect of the recruits, Nathaniel, we just need their obedience."

Prometheus raised his eyebrows. "I have to disagree, Apollo." He turned his attention back to me. "And not to worry, Nathaniel, your friend has nothing to fear from me. She reminds me of my mother, in a way," he added, a faraway look clouding his face. "She always spoke what was on her mind."

"I never met Clymene," I said quietly. "I hear she was a true force to be reckoned with, though."

"That she was."

We sat in silence for a moment. Prometheus's expression turned troubled as he stared into the fire roaring in the hearth.

"I will do what I can to help gain the trust of your recruits, Nathaniel, I can promise you that. I know our presence complicates things quite a bit."

I waved a hand. "No need to worry. I was actually hoping you might be able to join us next week, once we move on to hand-to-hand and weapons training."

A grin spread across his face. "I would be happy to." He paused, looking uncertain, before continuing. "Epimetheus may also be of some use. Despite his shortcomings, he is a very skilled fighter. He's got a knack for weaponry."

I smiled, appreciating the gesture. "We'd be happy to have him, then."

I turned my eyes on Apollo. "Apollo, could we have a few minutes alone?"

"Yes." He kept his gaze fixed on the view outside. "Prometheus, will you excuse us please?" He turned and faced me, his jaw clenched. "I need to speak with Nathaniel privately."

Prometheus frowned as he looked back and forth between us, then stood. "Of course. I need to go find where my brother has run off to." He gave me a smile that didn't quite reach his green eyes. "Should I tell him to plan on attending training on Monday?"

"That would be great. I'll let Chiron know."

"Wonderful." He gave a quick nod to Apollo, then me. "Good day, gentlemen."

A tense silence hung in the air for a moment after he left. I could feel Apollo's eyes on me, but I stubbornly focused on the red liquid in my glass.

"You don't give up, do you, Nathaniel?"

"I'm not sure why you would expect otherwise."

"Maybe because I asked you to?"

I snorted and shook my head. "You ask me to go see this girl—"

"Hestia sent you, not me. I had nothing to do with that nonsense."

I gritted my teeth. "Fine. *Hestia* asked me to talk to this girl so I could try to get an inkling of what this generation of recruits would be like. That's it." I took a sip of wine. "And then suddenly, everything seems to be going to shit for her. And you're telling me to 'let it be'?"

"I'm not sure how many more times I need to tell you that, Nathaniel. It's really quite simple."

"You know as well as I do that there's something wrong with that girl."

He turned to face me but remained standing.

"No, *Nate*," he said, biting out Tessa's nickname for me. "We don't know that. She is a recruit, a soldier, and nothing more. She has had a few bad dreams, and if you continue to press this, it will only cause problems for her." He jabbed a long, pale finger at me. "You'd best get that through your head now before you cause yourself too much trouble."

I rested my elbow on the arm of the couch and pressed my fingers to my forehead, contemplating what his reaction would be if I spilled my glass of wine on his perfectly white carpet.

I sighed, frustrated that he was forcing me to spell this out.

"Aside from the memory she already saw..." I said slowly, "... which she still assumes was a vision or dream, as far as I'm aware, there are hundreds—if not more—that assaulted me during her transformation. She has also involuntarily blocked me from entering her mind *twice*."

His jaw twitched, but otherwise his face remained impassive.

"Is it possible your powers aren't as sharp as they once were?" he mused.

I gave him a withering look but refused to acknowledge his attempt to bait me. "She should not have been able to control water the way she did today."

"Why not?" He spread his hands in question. "She's a Telekinetic. Water is a physical thing."

"Stop taking me for a fool, Apollo," I snapped, setting my glass down on the coffee table with a thud. His eyes flicked down, then back up to me. "You know as well as I do that's not how telekinesis works. Unless that ball of water suddenly turned solid in midair, she should *not* have been able to move it like she did."

He folded his arms across his chest and glared at me, lips pressed together so tightly his mouth was only a thin line. "What would you like me to say, Nathaniel? That you're right? That there's something not right about her? Fine. However," he held up a hand, staying my response. "Contrary to what you may have been led to believe, I am not required to disclose anything to you about any of the recruits. That includes those who you may have developed a certain affection for. If you have a problem with that, then go take it up with your father," he snapped, leveling a glare at me. "Because I have no time for it."

I met his steely gaze with one of my own.

"And what will you do," I asked quietly, "when she starts asking more questions? When other strange things happen with her powers like they did today? Because I can assure you, that time will come."

"Are you a seer now, too, Nathaniel?" He smiled derisively. "Last I checked, you hadn't inherited *that* particular skill from your forbearers."

I rested my elbows on my knees and scrubbed my hands over my face, then sighed and stood to leave. "I can see this was a wasted trip."

"For once, we are in agreement."

Irritated at myself for thinking he might be at all helpful, I turned and stalked to the exit.

"And for future reference," he called when I was halfway through the door, "...I do not appreciate you coming into my home to verbally accost me, regardless of our relationship."

Without another word, I let the heavy white doors slam shut behind me.

23

TESSA

One would think, as an immortal, that eight hours of training would be a walk in the park.

As the hot water beat down on my face and sluiced over my sore body, I realized that person would be silly. My joints felt like they were on fire and my back muscles were full of knots.

In other words, I felt like utter shit.

I thought again how stupid I was for not asking questions prior to my transformation. Maybe then I would've known to pack some Tiger Balm and a heating pad when I came to Olympia.

"Tessa, hurry up!" Yana's voice came through the half-open bathroom door. "I smell like I have been burning shit all day!"

"That's because you have!"

"I am going to go lay on your bed until you get out," she warned. "The longer you take, the more your sheets will smell."

"You better not!" I yelled, just as the door clicked shut.

I brought my hand up to press the round silver button that controlled the water, but I paused, smirking. Running my fingers over the buttons that controlled the water temperature, I brought it down a few dozen degrees before turning off the spray.

When I stepped into our room in my maroon bathrobe, Yana was indeed sprawled on my bed, but she'd at least had the decency to take her shoes off.

I narrowed my eyes at her. "You're a horrible person, you know that?"

She laughed, her blue eyes twinkling. "Yes, this is true."

She hopped up and skipped into the bathroom.

"Don't worry, I left the water nice and hot for you!" I called as I began rummaging through my bottom drawer.

A moment later, I heard the shower turn on, and Yana let out a yelp as she was hit with the frigid water.

"Ack, Tessa!"

Snickering, I pulled on my favorite skinny jeans and a thin, pink sweater.

As I sat on my bed and started blow drying my hair, I tried to go over plans for working with Damien for the second day of our training. He'd been so irritated with me, and I think a little embarrassed when Nate had sent him away. We'd obviously had some major connection issues when he'd tried to link with me, but I had no clue what solution I could offer outside of "practice makes perfect" or "stop acting like a royal douche."

All I knew was that I didn't want to be wasting time fighting when we should be learning how to use our powers.

When I turned the hair dryer off, I found Yana scowling at me from beneath the pale blue towel wrapped around her head. "You call me horrible?"

I tossed her a hair brush and grinned. "Oh, stop. It's just a little cold water."

She pulled the towel off and started running the brush through her wet hair, then pointed a long finger at me.

"I will electrocute you in your sleep," she warned as she swept her hair up into a high, tight bun. "Do not doubt it."

I snorted. "I wouldn't for a second."

As Yana finished getting dressed, I put on some light makeup, then pulled on my black Chucks.

"You ready?" Yana asked, zipping up her bright blue hoodie.

"Yep, let's move. Mary told Eric that we'd meet them in the court-yard. Do you know if Andrei is coming?"

"I did mention it, but I am not so sure I am his type."

"Meaning..."

She pursed her lips. "I do not think he likes women."

"Ahh, that's right," I replied as I recalled Eric's "wingman" comment.

"I invited Igor, though."

My eyebrows raised in amusement. "Okay, then." I nodded slowly. "I can see it. He's got those big baby blues."

She laughed as she opened the door and stepped into the hall. "The rest of his face is very nice, too."

"Whose face?" Mary had just stepped out of her own room, show-ered and dressed in ripped jeans and a sheer white Henley with a green tank underneath. Anette stepped out beside her in gray leggings and a black hooded sweater.

"Yana has a crush." I grinned mischievously.

Yana's only response was to punch me on the shoulder.

"Ow, bitch," I winced. "That hurt."

Yana shrugged. "Serves you right."

I narrowed my eyes at Yana, then grinned at Mary. "She thinks Igor's a hottie." I laughed as I ducked out of the way of Yana's fist again.

"Ooo!" Anette squealed. "He *is* nice to look at, isn't he?"

I was shocked to see Yana actually blush fiercely.

"Ack, fine!" Yana threw up her hands in exasperation, then scowled at me. "You act like I am the only one with a crush," she muttered, looking at me pointedly as we exited our hall onto the covered walkway that surrounded the courtyard.

I stuck my tongue out at her and made my way over to the guys who were waiting for us in front of the large fountain.

"Finally!" Eric groaned. "What took you guys so long?"

"Stop your grumbling," Mary said. "Where are we going?"

"Someplace with cheeseburgers," he begged.

"Sounds good," Mary responded

"Okay, let's go," Eric said, waving his arms to herd us toward the door.

"Why are you so complainy?" I asked, moving to keep pace with him. "Food's only for fun anymore, remember?"

"Yeah, well, old habits die hard, I guess," he muttered, flicking his pale blond hair off his forehead in an annoyed gesture.

He glanced at me, and his expression softened. "You know how it was at home. After every training session with Evan and Joanne, the first thing we'd do was eat. It just became second nature, our normal routine, kind of like brushing your teeth when you wake up."

He shrugged, stuffing his hands in his jeans' pockets. "I guess it's like one of those—what is it? Pav-whatever responses to exercise."

I gave him an amused smile. "Pavlovian?"

"Yeah, that's it. The dogs, right?"

"Yep. So does that mean this is gonna be a daily thing, or do you think you'll get over it?"

"No clue. I guess I should try and get over it, but it's kind of a nice reminder of home, you know?"

"I definitely get that," I said wistfully.

I glanced up at the sky, but it hadn't yet darkened enough to see Taurus, my common point with John and Analise.

"This is our home now, though," Andrei said, falling into step beside us. "Our Earth lives are done."

Eric gave him a sideways glance. "Yeah, but it doesn't mean we don't miss the place we lived for eighteen years or the people who raised us."

"I suppose," Andrei said nonchalantly. "Our guardians were just doing their jobs, no? They helped to prepare us for our lives as immortals and now we are here. So why dwell on them?"

I cocked my head. "You don't miss them at all? I mean, mine were my parents, for all intents and purposes. The best mom and dad I could've asked for."

He gave me an incredulous look. "Truly?"

Eric cast a look at me as if to say, 'Is this guy *serious*?'

"I'm guessing your relationship with your guardians wasn't all that great?" he asked Andrei.

"No, it was quite fine. They did their jobs. They ensured I had a good education, trained me physically and mentally, taught me how to use a wide variety of weapons, and fed and clothed me. What more would they have done?"

"I could think of a few things," Eric mumbled as we reached the portal field and turned left toward Main Street.

We walked in silence for a few minutes before he pointed toward a building across the street.

"There, that's an American place. They probably have burgers."

Our group crossed the street toward the narrow cedar-shingled building. When we entered the small establishment, we were greeted by a curvy blond girl who bore the nametag 'Sissy.'

"Good evening, everyone!" She greeted us with a wide, toothy smile. "Welcome to Stefan's. How many will be dining this evening?"

Mary turned and gave a quick headcount. "Seven?"

"Perfect, right this way." Sissy grabbed a stack of thick maroon menus and led us through the semi-crowded restaurant.

It was so quintessentially American. Green vinyl-covered booths lined the walls, with about a dozen square tables organized in the center. Sports memorabilia in the form of autographed baseball and football jerseys covered nearly every inch of the walls. Interspersed between their glass frames were matted posters or photos of the players who wore them. There were glass cases set up throughout the restaurant that contained various awards, trophies, and championship rings.

The sounds of Bruce Springsteen surrounded us, blaring from speakers that were recessed into the white tiled ceiling, bringing back fond memories of some of the summer block parties we'd had on my street.

"Wow, this is crazy," Mary whispered from beside me. "I didn't expect it to look so much like home."

"Yeah, it's pretty cool," I agreed. "I wonder what the other restaurants will be like."

Sissy led us to two tables at the back of the restaurant, then smiled. "If you'll just give me a moment, I'll push them together for you."

She set the menus down and began shoving one table up against the other, then grabbed seven sets of rolled up silverware from a busser station that stood a few feet away. With a flick of her fingers, she lit the two candles that sat in the center of each table.

"So, you guys are the new recruits? How do you like it so far?"

"It's pretty awesome," Eric said, leaning against a nearby booth. I pursed my lips, trying not to laugh as I saw him very obviously check out our pretty hostess. "Have you been here long?"

I elbowed him, although I wasn't entirely sure whether it was still inappropriate to ask a woman her age or not.

"A while," she said, laughing. "I went through my transition in the early sixteen-hundreds."

She finished placing silverware down and motioned for us to sit.

"Someone will be right over to get you started. Welcome to Olympia! I think you'll really enjoy it here." With one last sunny smile, she walked back to the front hostess station.

"Well, she was nice," Eric said, opening his menu.

I cocked a brow at him and smirked before opening my menu. "Uh huh."

After spending a few minutes looking over the menu, we put our orders in with our waiter Sam—a shorter guy with a slight build and an easy smile. Much to Eric's delight, he left us with three heaping baskets of warm rolls and butter.

"So how was everyone's first day of training?" Anette looked around the table.

"Tessa's day was great," Mary snarked, although there was a teasing glint in her eyes when she glanced at me. "Apparently she's mastering her powers pretty quick."

I scowled at her and gave her ankle a swift kick. "Zip it, Mare, or I'll trip you next time we run laps."

"What happened?" Anette asked, looking between Mary and me in confusion.

"Mary is pissed because she thinks I distracted her while she was working with water," I explained.

"You did distract me! " She pointed a butter knife in my direction. "I had total control of it until you broke my concentration."

"It was just a thumb's up, for gods' sake!" I rolled my eyes. "And let's not forget your stupid ball of water. I'm still pissed at you about that."

"Oh, that stupid ball of water that *you* dropped on *my* head?"

"You dropped water on her head? I thought you were a Telekinetic?" Andrei asked, confused.

"I am. Water's a thing." I shrugged. "I move things."

He frowned, still not looking convinced.

"So, what does everyone do?" Igor asked after he picked up a roll and started buttering it. "I don't quite recall from the ceremony what everyone was specialized as."

I suppressed a grin when Yana cleared her throat.

"I am an Electrokinetic, a specialization of fire users." She jerked her thumb at Eric, the corner of her mouth pulled up in a wry smile. "This one is a Pyrokinetic, so he just plays with fire. You are a Tempest, correct?"

Igor nodded. "Yes, I am."

Anette's eyes widened. "Storm manipulation? That's awesome!"

He grinned. "It is. Today I was able to create a small tornado in a glass box. It only lasted a few moments, but it was thrilling."

As we waited for our food, we got the low-down on each other's powers. Of course, as time went on, we couldn't help showing off a bit.

"Tess, pass me the rolls?" Mary held out her hand for the basket that was in front of me.

Grinning, I focused on the basket, trying to lift a roll and send it toward Mary.

Just as it would've sailed past her, she reached out her hand and snagged it.

I winced. "Sorry. I'm still working out some kinks."

Her shoulders shook with laughter, and she set the roll down on the small plate in front of her. "You better start working harder."

"You guys want to see what I can do?" Eric sounded overly excited to show off his pyro powers.

"As long as it doesn't involve burning the building down," Yana muttered.

"Isn't that what I'm here for?" Mary wiggled her fingers. "Water user and all."

Eric pulled one of the small votive candles closer to him and focused on it. After a few seconds, the flame started growing taller.

And taller.

"Eric!" Mary snapped. "You can be done now."

He grinned. The flame was now about six inches high. "Anyone wanna toast their bread?"

The flame wavered a bit, and when Eric reached across to grab another roll, the sleeve of his red hoodie came perilously close to catching fire.

"Geez, Eric!" I focused my mind on the flame and batted it back down. "Just because we can't die doesn't mean I want to be cleaning soot from my clothes."

He looked at me wide eyed. "You ruined it!"

I rolled my eyes. "I did not, shut up."

"Tessa, how did you do that?" Anette was frowning.

"Do what? Put the flame down?" I asked.

"You're not a pyro. You shouldn't have been able to do that." She raised her eyes to mine. "So, Nathaniel—"

"We call him Nate now," Mary interrupted.

"Oh. Okay, so Nate announced you as a Telekinetic," she said skeptically, "but you were able to control water at your training? And now you are controlling fire, too? Are you sure he called you right?"

"I mean, yeah, I don't see how he would've screwed it up," I responded. "He's probably been doing this forever."

"That doesn't mean he didn't miss something," Eric muttered.

"I agree with Anette," Andrei piped up. "You might have multiple affinities."

"Isn't it super rare for a person to have Mentalist and Elemental abilities? I thought all the people with more than one affinity fell into the same group?"

"It is incredibly rare, but I believe it has happened once or twice," Andrei replied.

"Huh. But wouldn't Nate have seen that?"

"I would think so," Anette said. "What did he say about the water thing today?"

I shrugged, feeling a bit uncomfortable under their scrutiny. "He seemed a little weirded out, but he didn't really make a thing of it, so I figured it just meant I could push water with my mind, just like any other physical thing."

"That is not really how telekinesis works, though." She sat up a bit straighter in her chair, flushing slightly as all eyes turned toward her. "As a telekinetic, your mind... it's like another hand, okay? So anything you can manipulate or move with your hands, you can move with your mind."

She stared at me, waiting for me to respond, then winced when I didn't answer right away. "Does that not make sense?"

"Um...yes?" I frowned, not quite sure what she was getting at.

"What I mean is, you wouldn't be able to push a ball of water around with your mind any more than you would be able to push it around with your hands."

"Nate really didn't think it was weird?" Mary looked surprised. "He seems like such a stickler for things. You'd think he'd be right on top of something like this."

"No," I replied. "Well, I mean, he said some things were worth exploring, but then we just went back to our regular training."

"You should probably mention the fact that you just put out a candle with your mind when you go to training tomorrow," Yana said. "If you do have more than one affinity, you want to make sure you're training in the right areas."

"Yeah, I guess that makes sense." I took a sip of water. "I'll see what he has to say."

"Hey, you guys wanna see a cool trick?" Mary bounced in her seat.

"Probably not, if it's one of yours," Eric said, shaking his head.

An evil grin came over Mary's face, and then suddenly I was drenched. All the water that had just been in my glass was now all over my sweater.

"Shit!" I hissed, grabbing my napkin and attempting to dry myself off. "Mary!"

"Payback's a bitch." She blew me a noisy kiss from across the table.

I gave her a scathing look and went back to patting myself dry.

"Here, let me try," Andrei said. He walked over and stood beside me. "Stand up."

I narrowed my eyes and paused my blotting. "Why?"

"I can try to use my wind power to dry you off," he explained.

"Ah, okay. Worth a shot, I guess." I stood to face him, thankful I hadn't gone with a white shirt.

He took in my soaked sweater and bit his lip, as though trying not to smile, then threw a glance at Mary.

"Your aim is quite good, I must say."

She preened. "Why, thank you."

"Please don't encourage her," I groaned. I waved a hand at my soaked clothing. "Go for it, do your thing."

Andrei made a motion as though he was blowing out a birthday candle in the direction of my torso. I didn't feel anything at first, but after a few moments, I felt my clothing begin to dry as he slowly blew the water out of my shirt.

"Oh, hey! I think it's working!"

He paused, then smiled at me.

"That is good." After another moment, he stepped back and surveyed his work. "Better?"

"Much, thank you." I sneered at Mary.

I sat back down just as Sam delivered our food.

The cheeseburger he placed in front of me was massive. The patty was a good inch thick and loaded with bacon, lettuce, tomato, onion, pickles, and barbecue sauce. A heaping pile of curly fries, fried to perfection, shared the plate.

"Gods, this looks delicious." I looked up at Sam. "Is it as good as it looks?"

"It is," he said, grinning. "Our chef Stefan learned to cook from his guardian's father who was a master chef in France. His food is fantastic."

"France? Why didn't he open a French restaurant?"

He jerked his head toward the door. "Pierre up the street opened Fleur de Lis about three centuries ago. Stefan's second favorite cuisine is American, so he opted for that. We opened back in the nineteen-fifties." He looked up and down the table. "Does anyone need anything?"

We all shook our heads and dove into our food.

"So what do you guys think about the 'rebel threat'?" Eric spoke around a mouthful of his jalapeno bacon burger.

Mary shook her head. "It's crazy. Not gonna lie, I'm a little freaked out about it."

"Yeah," Eric agreed. He jerked his chin toward Andrei. "This jackass thinks it's great that we're going to get 'real world experience,' isn't that right?"

Several pairs of wide eyes turned on Andrei.

Igor snorted. "Is this true, Andrei? You wish to go into a battle so soon after our transformation?"

Andrei's cheeks flushed, but he tilted his chin up in a defiant gesture. "I do not think it is *great,* as Eric says. I just think that we will train more effectively if we know there is an imminent threat, that is all."

"Well, I suppose that makes some sense," Igor allowed after a moment of silence.

"Seriously?" Mary asked. "You think we'll be ready to fight witches, demons, goddamn *Titans,* after just one year?" She shook her head incredulously and stuffed a French fry in her mouth. "You're crazy."

"I don't think it's that crazy," Yana said, coming to Andrei's defense. "We are immortal now. It is not like we can be killed easily. And it is likely we will be training with two Titans."

"Exactly!" Andrei grinned at Yana, then put down his burger and rested his elbows on the table. "If you know that your training today could very well mean your life in one year's time, do you not think you might train harder if you knew a threat was immediate?"

Mary opened and closed her mouth a few times before finally responding.

"I—I don't know." She looked around at all of us and shrugged. "I guess I just don't want to think about it."

I contemplated Andrei's sentiment as the others went back and forth about his sanity.

"I don't know, I think it kind of makes sense," I said hesitantly. "I mean, I'm not really ready to picture all of us going into war, but since that's probably going to be the case, shouldn't we have every advantage possible?"

"Ugh, whatever," Mary said. "Like I said, I don't want to think about it right now. Let the gods deal with it for the time being."

"Agreed," Eric said as he stuffed the last bite of his burger in his mouth. He glanced around the restaurant. "Where's our waiter? I want dessert."

24

NATHANIEL

Several hours after I left Apollo's home, long after the sun had set, I found myself in front of Chiron's small stone cabin in the woods at the foot of the mountain.

When I was about twenty feet from his door, he appeared from the rear of the cabin in full centaur form. The equine half of his body was covered in dark brown fur with a long black-brown tail that hung to the ground. He stood nearly seven feet tall in human form, but that height, combined with the sheer mass of his centaur body, made him look larger than life.

"Nathaniel! What brings you over so late?"

"I needed to talk to you about one of the recruits, if you've got a few minutes."

"Of course, come in."

He moved toward the steps leading into his cabin, waving an arm for me to follow. His massive hooves clunked loudly on the wooden boards, echoing through the dark quiet of the forest.

Chiron's home was small, consisting of one sparsely furnished room. A bed of cushions in varying shades of brown took up about one third of the room, with a red and blue plaid couch resting against the opposite wall. Small, roughhewn end tables stood at either end of the sofa and next to his bed, and a table with two chairs was pushed under a window to the right of the entrance. Shelves lined the wall behind it, filled with jugs of wine, water, and a slew of dried meats and vegetables. As he had yet to adopt Olympia's solar technology, the only light came from a quiet fire in the hearth.

"I'm going to assume that this 'recruit' is Tessa?" He turned toward me and cocked one eyebrow in question. "I've seen you with her several times now."

"Yes, there was a bit of an issue today at training."

"Hmm."

He pulled a bottle of dandelion wine and two tumblers from a shelf and poured us each a generous portion. He set my glass down on one of the end tables, then curled up with his own on his bed of cushions, folding his four long legs beneath him.

"Sit," he commanded, then waited for me to comply before continuing. "Does this happen to have anything to do with that water incident with her friend?" He took a gulp of wine, downing half the glass in one shot.

I sat on the sofa and leaned forward, resting my arms on my knees.

"Yes. How did you know?"

"Although I worry about Mary's desire to prove herself, I also believe she exhibited enough control over her power today to avoid depositing a large amount of water on her own head."

"Then how did you know it was Tessa?" I picked up my glass and took a slow sip. The wine here was more earthy than Apollo's, who preferred his wine to be sweet on the verge of cloying.

"Just a hunch. I take it you were working with her at the time?"

"Yes, she and Damien were bickering. He was having trouble linking to her mind and it caused a fight. I sent him away to let off some steam, and when I went to call him back over, Tessa noticed Mary practicing. The next thing I knew, there was a ball of water hovering over her head."

I twirled my glass back and forth, watching as the pale liquid gently sloshed at the sides. "Tessa just...looked at it and used her mind to send it back."

He set his glass down and folded his arms across his chest.

"Do you think she's got dual affinities, then?"

"I don't know. It's possible, although I don't know why I wouldn't have seen that when I transitioned her."

I closed my eyes in an attempt to shut out Apollo's words, *'Is it possible your powers aren't as sharp as they once were?'*

"Nathaniel? Are you alright?"

When I opened my eyes, I saw my friend staring at me, his brow furrowed in concern.

"Yeah, sorry." I let out a heavy breath. "I went to see Apollo before coming here, and he was...less than helpful, to say the least."

Chiron barked out a laugh. "Why in all the realms would you do that to yourself?" He shook his head, clearly amused at my poor decision making.

I raised my eyes to the ceiling and looked through the large skylight that took up nearly half the roof. "Because I'm a glutton for punishment, clearly."

"Well, I won't bother asking what kind words of wisdom he offered you." He tossed back the rest of his wine and reached for the jug to refill his glass. "What I will remind you of, dear friend, is that you have not made a mistake or missed an affinity in all the years I've known you. Maybe there's something off about this girl, who's to say? Whatever it is, I don't think it has anything to do with your ability to guide the gods' magic. Zeus would not have entrusted you with that duty if he did not believe you were capable."

I tapped a finger on the side of my glass. "But how can I be sure?"

He shrugged. "Go see her. Look into her mind and see if there's anything lurking in the background."

I was shaking my head before he'd even finished his sentence. "No, me digging through her mind is the last thing she needs. I think I nearly pushed her over the edge today when I was trying to help her learn to let down her mental walls with Damien. Besides, if there was something there, I'm sure I would have seen it today."

"How did she react when you entered her mind today?"

"Not well. She couldn't open her mind. It was as though her power was protecting her from outside invasion, regardless of what my—or her—intentions were."

A frown flickered across Chiron's face as he took a contemplative sip of wine. "Her power seemed sentient?"

I thought back, remembering that Damien had used the same word when they were arguing.

"Yes, but not in the way it normally is for recruits. I've seen recruits whose powers were more alert, for lack of a better term. But hers seems like it's taken up residence in her mind, sharing the space with her like an additional consciousness."

"Does it seem hostile in any way?"

"Not at all. If anything, it seems protective of her, if that were possible."

Chiron leaned back against the window. "Why wouldn't it be? An Ischyra's affinity is a part of them, and some are more powerful than others. It would stand to reason that those with stronger powers might struggle to control them. It wouldn't be the first time we had a recruit who had to work harder to subdue their abilities."

I contemplated what he was saying. "That makes sense, I suppose, but it doesn't explain why she was exhibiting both Mentalist and Elemental abilities when the only power I'd seen in her mind was for telekinesis."

"That is a bit of a mystery, isn't it?" He gazed up through the skylight at the stars littering the darkness.

"It is."

"I wouldn't worry, Nathaniel." Chiron's eyes met mine. "If her powers are strong enough to fight both her *and* you, then they could be strong enough to subdue other aspects of her psyche, including other affinities. Once she gets ahold of her power, you'll be able to work out what else she has going on in that pretty head of hers."

"I suppose. I'll keep an eye on her."

"You do that."

I downed the rest of my wine and stood. "I'll let you get your rest."

"Yes, those recruits were a tough bunch today," he said, yawning.

I grinned. "I don't see that getting easier any time soon."

He huffed out a laugh. "Goodnight, Nathaniel. I'll see you in the morning."

I DEBATED whether or not to go see Tessa after I left Chiron's. I was exhausted and wanted nothing more than to go to sleep. I'd promised her, though, and I didn't want to go back on that.

When I reached the large wrought iron gate that led into the courtyard, I glanced down at my watch. It was nearly nine. Tessa had said she was going to dinner with her friends, so I took a gamble on her still being awake.

I'd just put my hand on the gate to push it open when I hesitated.

I really, truly, did not feel like dealing with Mary or the other girls asking questions, and I would have to pass the men's dormitories on my way. I was fairly certain I'd run into at least one person, and I was not in the mood for questions or speculation.

Grumbling to myself, I made my way around the building until I found Tessa's window. Keeping my eyes averted in case anyone was changing, I knocked quietly.

I saw movement in my periphery, and when I looked up, I saw Yana's face frowning at me. She opened the window, which was just the right height for me to rest my arms.

"Well, hello there," she said, giving me a lazy smile. "May I help you?"

"Hey, Yana. Is Tessa here?"

"Of course." Her smile turned mischievous as she turned and called to her roommate. "Tessa?" Her voice dripped with faux innocence. "What do you Americans call someone who shows up at your window at night unannounced? I forget the term."

"Uh, I don't know." Tessa's muffled response came from the bathroom. "Creeper? Stalker? Weirdo? Why?"

I covered my face with my hand and let out an annoyed breath.

"Ah, okay. Well, there is a creeper stalker weirdo at our window, and I believe he is looking for you?"

I arched a brow at Yana. "Really?"

She squeezed her eyes shut and fell back on her bed, her shoulders shaking with silent laughter.

"What are you—" Tessa walked out of the bathroom with a brush in her hand, wearing black pajama pants and a pink tank top, her long blond hair tumbling over her shoulder.

She gave me an incredulous look. "Dude. What are you doing?"

I rested my forehead on the sill, then brought my eyes up to meet hers. "Apparently being a 'creeper stalker weirdo.'" I shook my head. "I told you I'd come by. I didn't want to run into the others and have to deal with their nonsense."

"Ah. Yeah, probably a good call. I can hear Anette's music from here, so her and Mary's door is still open." She set her brush down and looked around awkwardly. "Uh, do you want to come in?"

She glanced at her roommate. "Am I allowed to invite him in?"

Yana's only response was to snort and bury her face in her pillow.

Tessa rolled her eyes. "What the—lemme get shoes. I'm coming out." She opened her closet and pulled out a pair of black Chucks, then threw on a white hooded sweatshirt, muttering to herself the entire time.

"...so freaking weird...climbing out a damn window."

"Agreed," I said wearily.

Once her sweatshirt was zipped up, she waved her hands, shooing me back from the window.

"Scoot back. I need to get out."

Yana pulled the pillow from her face and watched as Tessa hooked a leg over the sill.

"Should I leave the window unlocked or are you going to use the door like a civilized person when you return?"

Tessa gave her roommate a withering look. "Close the stupid window and leave the door unlocked." She quickly pulled the other leg through and hopped to the ground.

"You two have fun, now," Yana crooned before sliding the window closed.

I shook my head, then turned to Tessa, unsure of what to say now that she was standing before me in her pajamas.

"So, you wanna walk or something?" Tessa asked, her hands in the pocket of her sweatshirt.

"Yes, I suppose that would be the normal thing." I sighed.

She laughed. "I think we're a few steps past normal right now."

I smiled and started walking back toward the street. "I'm inclined to agree, Miss Avery."

25

TESSA

As Nate and I walked down the hill from my dorm toward Main Street, I realized I hadn't yet taken in the full night sky on Olympus. Most of the lights of Main Street had been turned off, bathing the small village in only moonlight.

I felt incredibly small and insignificant as I stared up at the sky, glittering with millions of stars.

"There are so many stars here," I murmured. "And it's so quiet."

"Told you," Nate said with a smile. "This is my favorite time to be out," he admitted.

"I definitely get it." I smiled as I stared across the expanse of darkened sky. "Growing up, we had this massive telescope. I loved begging John and Analise to take me to the lake at night to watch meteor showers or look for faraway galaxies. It was one of my favorite things to do with them."

A lump built in my throat as I thought back to the first time Analise had shown me how to use their huge telescope so I could see the rings of Saturn. I'd been six, but the memory was still as clear as day. Searching the sky, I located Taurus and smiled wistfully.

I pointed out the K-shaped constellation.

"Taurus is my favorite. My guardians and I made it our common point. Whenever I'm homesick, I look at Taurus and know that at some point, they'll look at it, too."

"What is it that appeals to you?"

"It's a bull, but it looks more like a person dancing." I shrugged. "And I've always thought the Pleiades were fun to look for."

He smiled. "The seven daughters of Atlas. They're difficult to see, aren't they?"

"Yeah, but I love how they're more defined when you look at them out of the corner of your eye. It's almost impossible to see them looking straight on." I sucked in a deep breath of the cool night air. "They're so big, but just out of sight, you know?"

He craned his neck up toward the sky.

"I've always found it to be quite humbling, myself."

I laughed. "John used to say the same thing. He'd say Earth was 'nothing but a speck in an ocean of other specks.'" I shrugged. "Not so eloquent, but it works."

"John sounds like an interesting man"

"Yeah." I sighed. "The greatest, really."

"So, how was dinner?" Nate turned left onto Main Street as we came up on the portal field.

"It was good. We went to Stefan's, that American place."

"Yes, I've gone a few times."

"Really?" That surprised me. "I mean, I know why we still eat— we're fresh from our human lives... food is just a normal thing, even if we don't actually need it. I'd have thought you'd gotten past that long ago."

He shrugged. "Food was never really my thing until recently because I couldn't find much I liked. Cuisines today are much more enjoyable than they used to be, so I like to try the new restaurants as they open."

"I see. So where are we going?"

"You'll see." The grin he gave me was almost playful, taking me completely off guard. "Come on."

He led me past the spot where the cobblestones met the dirt road and crossed into the forest where we were immediately enveloped in darkness. After a few seconds, my improved night vision kicked in and I was able to follow Nate without tripping over every root that crossed our path.

"There wasn't an easier way?" I asked as I pushed a thin leafy branch out of my face.

"No, but it's worth it."

He placed a warm hand in mine and led me further into the forest. Just when I was beginning to think we were never going to reach our destination, we stepped out into a large clearing, about the size of a football field, carpeted with soft grass. Tall wooden poles topped with wide platforms were scattered around the field, connected to one another with heavy ropes. When I squinted, I saw that more ropes continued off into the forest, quickly getting lost in the darkness. Ladders were propped against the poles, allowing access to the platforms at the top.

I gasped. "No way, is this a zipline course?"

Nate grinned. "It is."

I felt a dopey smile spread across my face, but I didn't care. "This is so freaking cool! I've always wanted to go ziplining. When do we get to go?" I bounced on my toes and grabbed his arm. "Can I try now?"

He patted my hand and smiled. "In a few months, most likely, and no, you cannot."

My shoulders slumped. "Then why are we here?"

Nate led me over to the center of the clearing and sat down on the soft grass. "Because it's one of the most peaceful spots around here, and after the day I've had, I need some quiet."

I sat down next to him and leaned back on my hands so I could look up at the sky.

"Bad day, then?"

He shrugged and mimicked my pose. "It could have been better. I've been meaning to ask you, have you had anymore dreams since you got to Olympia?"

"None. Like, literally no dreams at all since that vision." I bumped his arm with my shoulder. "You better not jinx me by asking." It had been so nice these last few days, waking up rested and refreshed.

"Doubtful." He sighed. "So, you've got questions for me?"

I took a deep breath.

Questions.

Right. Because he was the most powerful Coercer in all of Olympus, and he'd led me to believe he was just a regular old Ischyra, like some big jerk.

"You're shouting again," he said, laughter in his eyes. "You seem to have no problem letting your mental walls down when you want to yell at someone."

"Aren't you supposed to have yours *up* so you aren't bombarded with thoughts?"

He shook his head. "I only shore them up tightly when I'm someplace very crowded. Otherwise, I leave my mind open a bit so that others can contact me if necessary. I'll only hear you if you direct your thoughts at me, though, just like normal telepathy."

"Ah, I see." Interesting. "Anyway, about you." I kicked one of his sneakers gently. "Why didn't you tell me who you were? I mean, I know it's not my business, but...?"

He blew out a breath and laid back on the grass, interlacing his fingers behind his head.

"Honestly? I don't know."

I shifted my position so that I was facing him. "Okay... so then for my tougher question. How am I supposed to trust that you didn't put that vision in my head? Clearly, you're insanely powerful."

It felt weird to even voice my question. I didn't know him well, but looking at him now, relaxing in the moonlight, it was hard to imagine he could be that manipulative. Something deep inside told me I could trust him.

He sighed and closed his eyes. A few seconds passed before he spoke.

"Because I didn't do it." He sat up and faced me. "I'm not a bad person, Tessa. I think you know that."

I smiled wryly. "Because I've known you for such a long time now?"

He huffed out a laugh and ran a hand through his sandy-brown hair, causing it to fall into an adorable mess. "Fair enough."

"So?"

"I was just as caught off guard by that vision as you were."

"It did seem that way," I allowed. "But you've been around forever. That's definitely long enough to be able to perfect your 'holy shit' face."

He scratched his forehead and a look of consternation crossed his face. "Okay, that may be true, but—"

"Are you one of the original Ischyra?"

I clapped a hand to my mouth as the question I'd been asking myself since my transformation finally slipped out.

If possible, it seemed as though the field we were in had gotten quieter. Even the crickets who'd been serenading us seemed to whisper, as though they had suddenly decided to eavesdrop, instead.

Nate's jaw clenched, and I wanted to kick myself.

"I—I'm so sorry," I whispered. "That's...not my any of my business."

He closed his eyes and waved off my apology. "No, it's fine, I expected you'd ask sooner or later."

Holy shit.

I felt my mouth pop open.

There were only a few dozen Ischyra in the first generation. They were demigods, born with powers of their own from the union of gods and humans. And he was one of them.

"Holy *shit*," I murmured. I laid down on the cool grass and put a hand on my forehead. "I was only joking when I said you'd been around forever."

"Before you ask—" He held up a hand. "While, yes, I am powerful enough to plant visions in your mind, I promise I did not violate you in that way. Or any way. Whoever put that...vision there probably intended for me to pull it forward, but I was just the messenger."

"You mean Hestia?"

"Probably, although she's being quite close lipped on the topic now."

"Okay. I—believe you—I think?" I shook my head. "Gods, I'm sorry."

I wanted so badly to ask who his parents were, but at the same time, the thought of him being a demigod was almost too much to deal with. I didn't need to know which of the thirteen Elders had sired him.

Instead, I let the silence hang over us.

"Thank you," he said quietly after a minute. He laid down next to me and reached for my hand, giving it a light squeeze.

"For what?"

"Not asking questions." He gave me a flicker of a smile and kept his fingers laced in mine. "I know you want to, but I appreciate your restraint."

I swallowed hard and nodded. "Are you reading my mind again?"

He laughed. "No. I just know that, if I were in your shoes, I'd be overflowing with questions about me."

"Oh, trust me, they're there. I'm just not sure I want to know the answers." I pursed my lips. "Can I ask one question though?"

He looked at me speculatively. "One."

"Why does it bother you? Being gen one?"

He was quiet for a few seconds.

I held up my hands. "Never mind. I'm sorry I asked."

Stupid, stupid, stupid.

He smiled. "No, you're not."

"I'm not what? Sorry?"

"Stupid. You're not stupid for being curious." He ran his free hand over his face. "I'm sorry. It's just—the war with the Titans had just ended when the gods created the Ischyra, and there were many aspects that made it a...difficult time to be alive." He paused, considering me for a moment. "The gods didn't exactly view the Ischyra favorably."

"You really don't have to—" I started.

"No, it's fine. I told you I'd answer your questions, didn't I?"

"Okay. Why, though?"

"Zeus wanted an army. The others were happy to avoid getting their hands dirty, but once the Ischyra were created, they realized they didn't trust a bunch of demigods to effectively combat any potential rebel threats that might have arisen on Earth. In general, the gods felt demigods were inherently selfish. They didn't trust them to put their own desires aside.

"Most of the original Ischyra were very rebellious, so the Elders thought it would be easier to just allow them to leave, then start from scratch with something more pliable than demigods."

He smiled wryly.

"Most of the Elders don't like to admit it, but part of the problem was that some of their worst traits—self-centeredness and nasty tempers—were passed down to their offspring. On top of that, they tended to protect their own, so when fights broke out between Ischyra, their parents would ultimately get involved. It was stupid, and it's why they decided to turn things over to the Fates and create Ischyra 'artificially,' for lack of a better word, since they're the only other beings who can dole out godly power."

"Because we wouldn't directly inherit traits from them?"

"Exactly. You 'inherit' their powers but are spared the potential for inheriting their DNA or building a familial relationship." He let out a harsh laugh. "You couldn't imagine how much of an uproar there was when Zeus decided the traits passed down by his brethren were too much of a liability when it came to creating effective soldiers."

"So where are the rest? I mean, all we learn about the early years of the Ischyra is how they were created, but John and Analise never got into *who* the first generation were."

"After a few centuries, a lot of the first generation left Olympus, deciding to use their powers and immortality in ways that they saw fit. Many simply went to live among humans, leaving their lives as Ischyra behind them. They're a bit like the Titans; they keep to themselves and avoid getting entangled with matters of Olympus."

"Why didn't you leave?"

He gave me a small smile. "This is my home."

"I see." I sighed. "So, I'm going to go out on a limb and assume I'm to keep this to myself?"

He gave me a relieved smile. "Yes, that would be much appreciated."

A curious look came over his face.

"What is it?" I asked.

"You know, the first generation really aren't that special. More powerful, maybe, but other than that, no different than you."

"I disagree."

"How so?"

"Look at it this way." I adjusted my position so that I was laying on my side facing him, my head propped up on my hand. "I had this one teacher in high school, a history teacher, Mr. Forbes. He'd been working on his genealogy for years and was always talking about which ancestor did which cool thing."

I smiled, remembering the colorful family tree Mr. Forbes had spread across the back of his classroom that grew, year after year.

"Anyway, it was really cool to hear him talk about these people who lived hundreds of years ago, because it can be so hard to find information on them. It was a huge accomplishment for him. A lot of records didn't survive, and if they did, they're either not digital or are hard to locate. The first generation of Ischyra, well, it's kind of like Mr. Forbes great-great-whatever grandfather. The only difference is, you're still around to tell us about our past." I poked him in the side. "Which is really freaking cool, by the way."

"Hmm." A thoughtful look came over his face. "Oddly enough, I'd never considered it that way. I just assumed you all saw the first generation as superstars or something."

"You sure you didn't get any of those self-centered traits?" I teased. "Cause I'm starting to wonder..."

He laughed. "Fair point."

"Okay, so moving on..." I didn't want to pry too much into his past. "There was something Chiron said about Prometheus and Epimetheus having a messy relationship with their dad? And that's why they're willing to fight on our side? Are you allowed to tell me about that?"

"Yes, that's nothing but history." He rolled so he was facing me. "Back during the war, their mother, Iapetus' wife Clymene, spoke out against Cronus in support of Zeus' cause. Her own children were her life, and she saw Cronus' imprisonment of his own offspring as unforgiveable. She actually helped Zeus' mother Rhea hide Zeus when he was born to prevent Cronus from imprisoning him. Cronus was furious, obviously, and began to question Iapetus' loyalty. Iapetus distanced himself from his wife, but Cronus wanted her destroyed."

He rubbed a hand across his forehead and a pained look clouded his face.

"Do you know how hard it is to destroy a god, Tessa?"

"It's like a giant energy suck thing, right?" It had been something that was glossed over in my lessons.

"More or less. Gods are all, at their core, energy. Energy can't be destroyed, but when it comes to gods, it can...disassembled. Their life force gets sent back into Chaos while their soul is sent to the Underworld. It takes an incredibly powerful being to be able to pull off something like that."

"So Cronus destroyed her?" I felt my chest clench. "How heartbreaking."

"No. He demanded that Iapetus do it as a way to prove his loyalty."

I gasped and felt my eyes widen. "Oh, my gods, that's terrible! And he did it?"

Nate nodded somberly. "He did. Prometheus and Epimetheus loved Clymene dearly, so her death set them firmly against their father."

"But Menoetius didn't care?"

"He was on his father's side from the start. He craves power and still believes Cronus' side will win out."

"And what about Atlas? What's his deal?" I asked. His absence was niggling at my brain.

"It's expected that he will support the twins, despite opposing Zeus during the war."

"Interesting." I wondered if that meant he was avoiding detection intentionally.

Nate saw my hesitation and shook his head. "According to Prometheus and Epimetheus, Atlas and Clymene were very close. He was devastated at her death."

"Why didn't he change sides, then? Fight with Zeus instead of Cronus?"

"He did, toward the end, from what I'm told. As open as the twins are when it comes to discussing the Titan war, they tend to give us the bare minimum once the smaller details of family issues come up."

"Huh."

I rolled on my back and stared up at the starry sky as I thought about the twins' past. It brought me a strange sense of sadness. Their mother was dead, their father was locked away in the depths of the Underworld, one brother was missing, and the other was set to fight against them.

They were alone in the world.

Pushing the thoughts from my mind, I turned my head to face Nate and grinned.

"So, that was a nice depressing conversation. Sorry about that."

"It's not the worst conversation I've had today," he said, meeting my eyes. "Maybe next time you can tell me more about yourself?"

I arched a brow. "Next time, huh?" I couldn't help the small smile that formed on my lips. "I suppose that can be arranged."

He smiled, and I thought I saw his gaze drift to my lips, causing my heartbeat to speed up. I turned back to face the sky, unsure whether I was ready to be kissed by him. I hoped to death he wasn't reading my mind right now. Just in case, I started forcing random thoughts into my head.

Chairs. Baseball. Clowns. Jump rope.

He stood, and when I looked up at him, I saw he was trying not to smile. He extended a hand toward me. "Come on, I'll walk you back. We've got an early day tomorrow."

I reached up and grabbed his hand so he could pull me to my feet. Then I brushed off my pajama pants with my free hand, keeping the other locked in his.

"So, do you guys have coffee in this place? It's been a few days and I think I'm going through withdrawal."

He laughed. "Yes, there's a place on Main. Suzette's. I don't know how you stomach it, though." He made a sound of disgust. "Burnt bean water."

I wagged a finger at him. "*Delicious* burnt bean water. And give me time... I'll make a convert of you."

He reached forward to pull a branch out of my path, then placed a hand on my back as he guided me through the trees.

"Somehow, it wouldn't surprise me."

26

TESSA

I pulled myself up from the ground and glared in the direction of the male voice calling my name. His blond hair was back in a small ponytail, and his green eyes were bright in the sunlight.

"You are not fighting fair," I huffed, shoving my hair out of my face.

He sighed and leaned against his long staff.

"No one fights fair," he snapped. "You keep dropping your shoulder. It makes it too clear where you are going to hit."

"You just know me too well, is all," I protested.

"You are not trying hard enough," he shot back.

"I am!" I fumed. "I do not know what else to do!"

He sighed and turned his eyes toward the sunny sky.

"Stop focusing on your end game. Worry only about stopping my attack as it is happening. If your mind is focused on taking me down, you will not be able to focus on what's right in front of you."

I shoved the staff toward him. "Let's move to hand to hand. I feel the urge to punch you."

"Ha!" He took the staff and tossed it down along with his own. "I would like to see you try," he said, raising his fists. A smirk rested on his scarred face.

A grin spread across my face, and I launched myself at him, fist raised.

Suddenly, light flashed as fire erupted in the nearby trees, quickly encircling the clearing.

A large figure stalked out of the forest toward me, followed by a smaller, more slender one.

There was movement in the trees beside me, a flash of dark hair. I scrambled backward, tripping over something in my path. When I glanced down, I saw the man I'd just been sparring with lying on the ground, injured.

"No!" I cried. I slapped his face, hard. "Wake up!"

I glanced over my shoulder and saw that the figures had transformed into men. I couldn't make out the shorter one, but the other was tall, muscular, with short brown hair and evil eyes.

He was quickly closing in.

"It would be better for us all if you stopped trying to run from me." His voice was as smooth as silk as his dark eyes bore into mine. "If he—" he jabbed a finger toward the man on the ground "—had not turned traitor."

A bolt of lightning shot from my hand, striking him on his shoulder. He winced, then continued traversing the clearing.

Nothing can stop him, I realized as terror engulfed me. The fire around the perimeter continued to grow, boxing us all in.

I felt something brush my arm. I looked down and cried out in relief when I saw my companion staring back at me.

He grabbed my arm, digging his fingers in so sharply I winced in pain. "You need to run!"

"I am not leaving you here!" I sobbed.

"I will be alright," he assured me. He pulled himself into a sitting position and used his staff to stand. "It is not me he wants. Just go!"

A rough hand grabbed my shoulder and yanked me back, causing me to fall into the grass. Then a heavy arm wrapped around my chest and began dragging me backward.

"Leave her be!" A female voice cried from the opposite side of the clearing. She was standing at the edge of the forest, her long hair falling in a tangled blond mess around a sharp-featured face. Bloody gashes tore across her white dress as her chest heaved with exertion.

"*Take her,*" *the brown-haired man said coldly, jerking his chin toward her.*

The smaller man, thin, with light blond hair, stalked toward her, eyes narrowed in anger and determination. He held out one hand, palm up. White light began to pour from her chest as pure agony screamed from her throat.

"*No!*" *I pulled myself from the man's grasp and launched myself toward her.* "*No!*"

I stumbled, crashing into the smaller man.

Lightning sparked from my fingers as I wrapped my hands around his neck and jerked him backward, immobilizing him.

He fell to the ground just as the light finished leaving her body. She collapsed in a heap, unmoving.

A dark-haired woman appeared through the flames behind her. I saw her lips moving but couldn't make out the words.

A witch.

The light that had poured from the lifeless body was sucked from the blond man's hand. It began to swirl around me, forcing my hands away from his neck. I struggled uselessly as my body slowly lifted off the ground.

"*Chaos, take her!*" *the witch screamed.*

There was a furious roar from somewhere behind me.

"*No!*" *My companion was running toward me, but it was too late. No matter how hard I struggled, I couldn't move. The light around me grew brighter.*

Vicious pain ripped through me, then everything went dark.

MY ROOM WAS pitch black when I bolted upright in bed, chest heaving and tears streaking down my face.

I couldn't control the sobs that wracked my body. I tried to reach for the water on my nightstand, but fell to the floor with a hard thud, instead.

"What is—Tessa!" Yana cried, jumping from her bed. She fell to the floor next to me and gripped my shoulders. "What is it?"

"I... I...I" I latched onto the neck of her shirt and tried to steady myself. "Get—M-M-Mary."

Yana's eyes were wide with concern, but she nodded quickly, then flew from the room.

I closed my eyes and focused on my calming exercises.

A few seconds later, Mary barreled into my room. She crouched in front of me and put her hands on either side of my face.

"What happened?" Her hands moved to my shoulders and she gave me a shake. "Tessa! What happened?"

She looked up at Yana. "What fucking happened?!"

"I—I do not know. I just woke up and she was on the floor, like this."

"Did you have another nightmare?" Mary asked.

I took a deep breath and nodded. She reached over and grabbed my bottle of water and held it to my lips.

"Drink, then explain."

I did as she asked, sucking down the cool water. When I was done, I exhaled in relief.

"Thank you," I whispered.

"Is this how you woke up after every dream?" Mary asked.

I gulped and shook my head. My mouth felt dry again.

"Well that's not good," she said.

"Girls, what is going on?" Yana's voice was gentle but full of concern.

Mary raised her eyebrows in question, and I nodded.

"Tessa has been having nightmares for a while now," she explained. She frowned. "But she never actually saw anything until Nate pulled one from her mind."

"Nate—" Yana closed her eyes and shook her head. "I am confused."

I pulled myself up onto my bed and wrapped my comforter around my shoulders. Mary sat beside me, and Yana plopped down on the floor in front of me.

"Join the club," I muttered.

"Should I go get him?" Mary asked tentatively. "Do you think he might be able to help?"

I shook my head, not wanting him to see me like this. "It's done now."

"Have any more Elders paid you a visit?" Mary asked.

"No, not since Hestia."

"Wait, are you saying that Hestia visited you?" Yana looked incredulous. "When?"

"In a dream walk about a week ago. The next morning, Nate came to my school to talk to me and ended up showing me what I'd been dreaming about."

"And what was it?" she asked softly.

I explained what I'd seen with Nate as briefly as possible. Having just come out of a nightmare that felt a thousand times worse, I didn't want to dwell on what I'd already seen.

"What happened this time, hon?" Mary asked.

"It was like...what came before my other nightmare, I guess. What I saw with Nate was blurry... a guy running toward me, then just darkness. This time it was everything leading up to that, only none of it was blurry." I shuddered. "Everything, all of their faces were crystal clear."

"How many were there?" Yana asked.

I sniffed and wiped my nose. "Five, I think." I frowned. "I think there was someone else there in the woods, too, but I couldn't see who it was."

"What about the guy you were sparring with? Had you ever seen him before?"

"No, but he felt really familiar, if that makes sense."

"Like a lover?"

I shook my head. "No, I don't think so."

We sat in silence for a few more moments before Mary suggested I lay back down.

"Are you sure you don't want me to get Nate?"

"No, I think I'll be okay."

Her brow furrowed. "Are you sure? I can stay."

"It's okay." I wrapped my comforter tighter around me. "I'll be fine."

Yana cleared her throat. "Um, Tessa? You were out with Nate earlier. Do you think...?"

Mary's gaze snapped from Yana and back to me. "Wait, what? You were with him earlier?"

"Yes, I was, and no, before you say it, I don't think he did anything to me. It was really freaking obvious when he was going through my mind before, and that definitely wasn't happening tonight."

"Okay." Mary sounded unconvinced, but then she grinned. "If that's the case, you owe me details tomorrow, first thing."

I rolled my eyes. "Good night, Mary."

"HANG ON," I said to Yana as we entered the courtyard the following morning. "I told Mary and Anette we'd wait for them."

"Ah, okay." She looked around, then pointed toward the front of the courtyard. "I think I see them up there."

We made our way to the gate and found Mary and Anette waiting for us.

"Morning!" Anette beamed when she saw us, her pigtails bouncing as she waved.

"You guys ready?" Mary asked.

"Yup." I nodded. "Let's do this."

Mary eyed me speculatively. "You good?"

I took a deep breath and nodded. "All good, I promise."

She gave a sharp nod in return.

We were about halfway down the hill, heading toward the portal field, when I saw Nate walking toward us.

I heard Yana whisper loudly to Mary from behind me.

"So Tessa really did not tell you she had a date last night?"

Anette gasped. "Tessa! You had a date with him?"

Mary smacked my arm. "Yeah, what's that all about? Since when do we keep secrets?"

"It wasn't a date. Nate came by and we walked and talked." *And almost kissed.* "That's all. Now shut up, both of you. He's right there."

"Walked and talked?" Yana laughed. "Is that what you Americans call it?"

Pursing my lips, I stopped dead in my tracks, causing her to crash full force into me. The momentum had her stumbling sideways into Anette, who let out a surprised squeal.

"Bitch," Yana hissed.

I smirked. "You deserved it."

Just then, Nate fell into step beside us. "Morning, ladies."

"Good morning," my friends chorused in sing song voices.

I shook my head and raised my eyes skyward. They were going to be the death of me.

"Hey," I said, giving him a sunny smile.

"How'd you sleep?"

Yana elbowed me, and Mary cleared her throat loudly. I slid a glare at them.

"Not too great, actually. I think you jinxed me when you asked if I'd had any more nightmares."

Mary coughed, and I realized I hadn't told her that he and I had actually talked about my dreams.

"Really?" His voice was laced with concern. "What was it about? The same?"

"More or less."

"Tell him!" Yana hissed, poking my side. I swatted her hand away, but he'd already heard.

He raised his eyebrows. "Tell me what?"

"Later, okay? I don't feel like talking about it here."

"Of course." He paused. "You could've come to me."

"That's what I said..." Mary muttered.

"No need," I said. "It was the middle of the night and you wouldn't have been able to do anything, anyway."

"That's not the point," he murmured as he slid his hands into his pockets.

'If it happens again, you can call out for me. I'll hear you.'

'Really?' I was impressed. I thought he'd need to be nearby to hear me.

'Really. It's why I leave my walls down, remember?'

"Oh, Tessa! Did you tell him about your fire thing?"

I shot Anette a silencing glare, but it was too late.

Nate frowned. "What fire thing?"

I opened my mouth to explain, but Yana interrupted me.

"Eric almost started a fire at the restaurant, and she put it out."

"What?" He stopped in his tracks and turned to face us. "What happened?"

I grabbed the sleeve of his shirt and tugged him along.

"That's not what happened. He was playing with his candle, and the flame got kind of high. I got a little freaked out so I...might've pushed it back down with my mind," I said in a rush.

He ran a hand across his face. "Okay."

"That's it?" Mary asked. "Okay?"

He dropped his hand to his side and gave her a disparaging look. "'Okay' as in, we're going to go talk with Chiron when we get to the arena."

"Aw, come on!" I groaned. "It's only the second day!"

He shook his head. "Something isn't right, Tessa. We need to find out what's going on with you."

"I probably just have more than one affinity. That's totally normal," I protested.

"Not when we're talking about both Mentalist and Elemental affinities. That's not 'totally normal' and you know it." He blew out a frustrated breath. "I wish you'd told me about this last night."

"Sorry," I muttered, annoyed. "So what now?"

He scratched his ear. "As I said, I'll take you to speak with Chiron when we get to the arena." His expression softened a bit. "We'll figure it out, don't worry."

We reached the portal field, and he pushed open a stark white door with a glass handle. We came out at the rear of the arena, off to the side of the running field.

"You all go get settled inside with your mentors. They'll tell you what the game plan is for today." He raised his eyebrows at me. "Tessa, come with me, please."

Shoulders slumped, I followed him into the arena and toward our lead trainer who was standing near the main entrance.

"You know," I began. "Maybe there's just something wrong with me. Maybe I'm a dud."

He chuckled. "You're not a dud, I can assure you."

"Yeah, but how do you know? You also didn't see me using these other powers. Hey!" I brightened. "Maybe you're—"

"If you call me a dud, there's an excellent chance I'll get angry."

"You? Get angry? I don't believe it."

I saw the corners of his mouth twitch.

"Come on."

We were about ten feet from Chiron when I realized he was in centaur form, the sight causing me to stop dead in my tracks. Nate noticed and grabbed my arm to keep me moving.

'Don't make a thing of it, please.'

There was a half-man, half-horse standing in front of me, and I wasn't supposed to react?

Yep. Super easy.

Chiron turned as we approached and greeted us with a smile.

"Good morning! How did you fare after your first day of training, Tessa? I hope you got a good night's sleep; today will be a bit more intense."

I let out a weak laugh.

"Awesome."

He grinned. "I'm sure. So, what can I do for you two?"

His grin transformed into a smirk when he turned his gaze to Nate.

"Can we speak privately? We—I've got some concerns," Nate said.

"Of course, let's step outside."

Chiron made his way through the main archway, leaving large hoof prints in the sand behind him.

I gave my head a quick shake. Between Nate being an original

Ischyra, Eric's fire and my nightmare, and now seeing Chiron in his true form, I was starting to feel a little off kilter.

Once we were outside, Chiron turned to face us and folded his arms across his chest, his long black-brown tail swishing with the movement.

"So, I'm assuming this is about the water incident from yesterday?"

"I—" My gaze darted between him and Nate. "I didn't realize you'd noticed."

"Of course I did. It's my job to notice." He turned his deep brown eyes on Nate. "So what are you thinking?"

"She also manipulated fire last night," Nate explained.

Chiron faced me and blinked in shock. "Is this true?"

"Yes. But it was just a little." The words rushed out. "It's not like I was blowing dragon fire or anything. I just put a candle out."

He scratched his head and put his hand on his hip. Or, the part of him that would've been a hip if he'd been in human form. "Okay, then. We'll run some tests."

"Tests?" An edge of panic snuck into my voice. "What kind of tests?"

"Nothing invasive," Nate said, putting a hand on my back. "We just want to see what else you can do, that's all."

"What do you mean? Isn't this just a multiple-affinity situation? Rare but not abnormal?"

"Eh," Chiron hedged. "It's possible, but I'm hesitant to say so for certain." He turned to Nate. "Would you mind getting the recruits started? Once they begin running their laps, have Christopher take over and come join us."

"Wait, where are we going?" I had sudden visions of being dragged off to the Elders so they could poke and prod until they figured out what was wrong with me.

A wide smile appeared on Chiron's face. "To determine what your true affinity is, of course."

27

NATHANIEL

I was not pleased that Chiron sent me to start training in his place.

The look on Tessa's face was a mix of fear and confusion, her thoughts a jumbled mess. I hated to walk away from her before Chiron could find out what was going on.

I stormed over to the group of mentors that stood in front of the rear exit and turned to face the recruits who were milling around.

"What's up?" Fletch asked, coming to stand beside me.

"Chiron is occupied and asked that I get the recruits started for the day." I frowned and looked around. "Would you mind grabbing Chris for me, please?"

"Of course." He jogged off toward where the other wind mentors were congregated.

I let out a loud whistle. "Alright, everyone! Line it up!"

The fifty Ischyra before me hustled to line up with their affinity groups. The arena was silent within seconds.

"Chiron will be out shortly, so I'm going to give you a run through and then you'll get going on your laps." I looked around at the tired faces before me. "I hope you all got a good night's sleep, because today will be just as rough as yesterday."

I ignored the quiet groans that rippled through the crowd.

"I'm sure you're still exhausted. Learning to use your powers for the first time is a daunting task. Once you do your warm-up out back, you'll be joining your partners or groups to expand on what we did yesterday. Your mentors will give you specific details based on your first performance. If need be, groups or partners may be shuffled a bit."

I huffed out a breath and glanced toward the front of the arena to see if I could tell where Chiron and Tessa were, but there was no sign of them.

"To start, we'll be running five laps. You'll be with the same squad you were with yesterday." I clapped my hands twice. "Let's go!"

I turned and strode through the rear doors and waited at the stone wall that surrounded the running field. Christopher came to stand beside me.

"Fletch said you wanted to see me?"

I nodded. "Yes, I need you to take over for me here. I've got to go find Chiron."

His brow furrowed slightly. "Sure, no problem. Anything specific you'd like me to cover?"

"Just remind them to tuck their damn arms," I muttered, then jogged back to the main entrance.

When I stepped out onto the grassy lawn in front of the arena, I found Chiron and Tessa off to the side, deep in conversation. As soon as he noticed me, Chiron waved me over.

"Nathaniel, I was just telling Tessa that I would like to see if she's able to draw on or control any other powers,"

Tessa put her hands on her hips.

"I really don't think you'd say I controlled them, necessarily. I just kind of...I don't know, mentally swatted them?"

Chiron pressed his lips together and shook his head.

"No, you shouldn't have been able to manipulate them in any way. It's just not how telekinesis works."

"What are you proposing?" I asked.

He folded his arms across his chest and tapped a hoof absently in the grass. After a moment, he pointed toward the forest's edge about fifty feet away.

"Tessa, there's a stream just beyond those trees. Let's see if you can manage some more water manipulation."

"Okay..." She looked at him dubiously.

'*This is so not going to work, Nate.*'

"You don't know that," I whispered, putting a hand on her back and nudging her forward. "Come on, let's go give it a shot."

She heaved an exasperated sigh. "Fine. But am I still gonna have to run laps after this?"

Chiron chuckled. "It depends on the outcome."

When we reached the stream, only about ten feet wide and a foot deep at its center, Chiron stopped at the edge and held a hand toward the water.

"Try to draw it toward you," he directed.

Tessa's eyes grew wide. "And how exactly do you suggest I do that?"

He shrugged. "I don't know; I'm not a water user."

"Neither am I! I thought you were supposed to train me?"

A sly grin spread across his face, and before I could warn her, he gave Tessa a forceful push into the water.

She yelped as she slipped and fell onto the rocky bed.

"Shit that's cold!"

I pinched the bridge of my nose as Chiron started laughing beside me.

"Was that really necessary?" I asked, dropping my arm and trying not to smile.

"She talked back." He shrugged. "You know I don't handle talking back well."

"Well, now she's pissed off," I watched her warily as she stormed back to the bank.

Chiron held up a finger right before she got to shore. "Uh uh, you stay there."

"Seriously?" She dropped her hands to her side, water streaming from her fingers. "Why?"

"From what you've told me, you were irritated when Mary attempted to drench you and scared when Eric was toying with fire."

He gave her an easy smile. "Now you're angry. It's a nice, strong emotion."

She gritted her teeth, then took a deep breath and shook out her arms. "Okay, I'll try. Hang on."

She lifted one foot up and pulled off her sodden sneaker and tossed it onto the shore before repeating the process with the other one.

I exchanged a glance with Chiron. Immortal or not, that water would be freezing.

She stood perfectly still and closed her eyes, letting the steady stream of water flow over her feet, soaking her skin up to her calves.

After about a minute with no result, Chiron and I exchanged a glance.

"I don't think this is working," I whispered.

She held up a finger, but her eyes remained closed.

"Hang on," she whispered.

I felt my brow furrow as I watched her.

And then I saw it.

"She changed the current," I said, dumbstruck. "Chiron—"

"I see it."

The flow of the stream had reversed completely, flowing back uphill instead of following gravity toward the foot of the mountain.

Suddenly, Tessa let out a heaving breath and fell to her knees.

I splashed into the water and lifted her up before she became completely soaked. When I deposited her back on shore, I crouched down to her height so I could look into her eyes.

"Are you okay?" I asked.

She nodded quickly and raised her eyes to mine. "Yep." She let out a shaky breath. "Never better."

"Well that was certainly interesting," Chiron mused. "Okay. Let's see if you've got any ability with earth magic."

"Earth?" Her breathing had gone back to normal and she was facing him with a confused expression. "Why earth?"

A slow smile spread across my face as I began to see where he was heading.

"Just a thought. Maybe see if you can bring down one of those dead branches?" He pointed to the other side of the stream where a tree stood that had several dead branches toward the top.

"Okay, tree branch." She closed her eyes. "Got it."

"Chiron—"

"Hang on," he whispered. "Let's just see."

She focused her gaze on the pile of branches as though memorizing each one. After a few moments, she closed her eyes, resuming the pose she'd held in the water.

Another minute passed, then two, and still nothing happened.

"Alright, you can stop," Chiron said.

Tessa's eyes flew open.

"But I didn't do anything."

"Not to worry." He turned to me. "Nathaniel, can you please tell Genevieve to come out here."

A frown flickered across Tessa's forehead. "Who's that?"

Chiron patted her shoulder. "Just another one of the mentors, that's all."

"She'll be a big help, don't worry," I said. I reached out with my mind until I found Genevieve's presence.

'Genevieve, can you spare a few minutes, please? We're out front.'

After a moment, she responded.

'Absolutely. What's going on?'

'Chiron and I need your help with one of the recruits.'

'Ay, of course ye do.' Humor laced her Scottish brogue as she responded to my request. *'On my way.'*

Genevieve was one of our most gifted Elemental mentors from a few generations back. She had affinities for all five elemental power groupings. She'd been the first in ten generations to come through with more than four affinities.

As she made her way to us, I quickly briefed her on what was going on. By the time I'd finished explaining Tessa's situation, Genevieve was walking onto the front lawn.

"Gen!" Chiron exclaimed when she emerged. "Thank you for coming out, it's much appreciated."

"Bah," she said, waving him off, smoothing back the strands of her frizzy red hair. "It's not like I could say no, exactly, now is it?"

I laughed, then held out a hand toward Tessa.

"Gen, this is Tessa. We were hoping you could do a little demonstration for her, show her how your powers work."

She nodded, then smiled warmly at Tessa. "Certainly. How are ye, hon?"

Tessa's eyes darted nervously between us.

"I'm not really sure, exactly. Can any of you tell me what's going on?"

"Put simply, we want to see if your abilities change when you're in the presence of an individual who possesses that affinity," Chiron explained.

"Okay," she said, frowning as she reached back to tighten the messy bun that had come loose when I pulled her from the water. "Then I'll just trust that you all know what you're doing."

She turned back toward Genevieve. "Show me what you've got."

"Ay, with pleasure." Genevieve grinned mischievously. A moment later, she disappeared.

"Hey!" Tessa exclaimed. "Where'd she go?"

"I'm still here, hon, don't ye worry."

Genevieve's disembodied voice was about six inches from Tessa's face. She yelped and stumbled backward, nearly taking me down with her. I grabbed her arms and steadied her.

"Relax," I whispered. "It's just her light magic. She's made herself invisible."

Tessa's hands fell to her sides and her eyes widened in amazement.

"No shit?" She leaned forward and squinted, trying to see through the bends of light Genevieve used to make herself invisible.

"No shit," Gen said, popping back into view, laughing. "It's quite impressive, yeah?"

Tessa's eyes were as wide as saucers. "That's one word for it."

Chiron pursed his lips to keep from laughing. "Gen's a bit of a show off, aren't you?"

"As though ye don't enjoy showing those blowhards up who challenge ye to a race!" Genevieve laughed.

"They all deserve it," Chiron said. "They want to challenge a centaur, then they'll get centaur speed."

"Okay, so um, that was super cool, but what exactly was the point?" Tessa was back to looking confused.

I exchanged a quick glance with Chiron. "We'd like you to try to manipulate light."

"Manipulate—" She looked between the three of us as though we'd all lost our minds. "What are you talking about? Will one of you please tell me what's going on?"

I ran a hand through my hair, trying to work out the best way to explain. "Tessa, in your studies, did your guardians teach you about all of the different affinity groupings?"

She nodded. "Yes, of course. I wasn't exactly the best student, but they did their best. Why?"

I sighed, then glanced at Chiron, who nodded.

"Did they ever teach you about Mimics?"

Her nose scrunched up. "Mimics? Yeah, I think I remember Analise telling me a story once when I was really little. Aren't they made up? A superhero's superhero?"

"Ay, my guardian's mum used to tell me stories of the early days, and I recall the Mimickry affinity mentioned," Genevieve added. "But they were just stories. I never heard of anyone who actually claimed that one for their own."

"I've heard mention of this from reliable sources," Chiron responded. "Basically, they can mimic the power of someone else... borrow it, so to speak. An immortal who possesses the abilities of a Mimic would be nearly unstoppable."

"Right, I kind of remember." Tessa gestured toward Gen. "But like she said, they were stories."

"Not stories, Tessa." Chiron cast an uneasy look in my direction. "The affinity exists, and we think that might be yours."

28

TESSA

I couldn't help it. I laughed. "You two are crazy. Even if what you're saying is true and Mimics are a real thing, I couldn't do anything with earth magic, remember?"

"Consider it this way, Tessa," Chiron said. "In order to mimic a person's actions or voice, one would have to see those actions, hear their voice. Once they've heard that person's voice, they can still 'mimic' it, even when they're no longer in their presence."

"Hmm." I eyed Nate and Chiron speculatively. I was about one hundred percent certain they were wrong, but on the off chance that *wasn't* the case...

"Okay, then, let's give it a go." I threw my shoulders back. "Tell me what to do."

All three exchanged an uncomfortable look.

"Well, that's the thing, hon. I don't think any of us are able to tell ye what to do," Gen said gently.

"You figured out water. You'll figure out light, too." Chiron said.

"Hang on—" I held up a hand. "If all a Mimic needs to do is be in the presence of other power users to access their affinities, then why couldn't I use earth just now? Why can't I use all the affinities that were being used in the arena yesterday?"

Nate scratched his head. "Considering we're just going on conjecture here, I would say you were able to use Mary's water powers because she directed her powers at you. Eric was just across from you at dinner. Hang on." A smile crept across his face. "Tessa, who else used their powers at dinner last night?"

"What makes you think—"

He shook his head and waved off my interruption. "You're brand new. I know you were showing off for each other."

I rolled my eyes. "Fine. Mary drenched me with water, Andrei dried me off with wind—"

"Was there anyone with an Earth affinity?"

I thought back to the conversation where we'd all discussed our affinities.

"No, actually there wasn't."

"That's why she couldn't use any earth magic." Nate looked at Chiron, triumphant. "The Earth users were at the opposite end of the arena yesterday. She'd probably need to be focusing on them or vice versa in order to use their powers."

"Makes sense," Chiron agreed. "Let's see if that pans out. Tessa, you said Andrei used wind?"

"Yep."

"Alright, let's skip light for now and start there, then. How did you go about manipulating the water just now?"

"I just kind of thought back to yesterday, when I sent that water at Mary. I saw it and I wanted it to move, so it did. So, this time, I pictured the water moving in a different direction."

"Okay, then let's try to apply that same logic to wind and see if you can give us a nice breeze."

"I—ok."

How the heck was I supposed to do that?

I hadn't really thought about it when he asked me to use water; I just pictured the water moving, and it moved, which was exactly what I'd done the day before. I'd been angry when he asked me to do it, though, and Chiron seemed to think that emotional reaction would make it simple to access those powers.

This time, I had nothing. Aside from a little apprehension, no major emotion was flowing through me.

At a loss, I closed my eyes and reached back to the memory of Andrei using his breath to dry my shirt, hoping it would trigger something. My power stirred, and a feeling of curiosity washed through me. Small feelers, similar to what I'd felt when Nate had gone into my mind the previous day, began to examine the memory. As I watched Andrei slowly dry my soaked sweater, a pale magenta light seemed to follow the path his breath made. It traced itself down until it hit my shirt, enveloping it and sucking the moisture right out. Once the shirt was dry, the wind receded, and the light was sucked back in.

Only, it didn't all return. A small piece, barely more than a speck, remained. It hovered in front of my face, circling around, before drifting down to my chest. Then, without warning, I felt a small pinch as it was sucked right into my chest.

Holy crap.

"Tessa!"

Nate was calling me.

My eyes snapped open, and I saw that a strong wind was blowing across the lawn.

"Ha!" Chiron exclaimed, clapping. "I knew it!"

I squeezed my eyes shut, trying to figure out how to shut the wind down. The water had worn me out; I'd collapsed before I had a chance to turn it off. This time, I settled for just picturing the wind stopping, and when I opened my eyes again, I saw that it had worked.

When I looked at Nate, he was beaming. Seeing such happiness on his face was a bit disarming.

"Amazing." He shook his head and stared at me in wonder. "Absolutely amazing."

His smile is gorgeous.

The smile on his face grew wider, so before I could embarrass myself further, I turned to Chiron.

"So does this mean I can coerce him?" I jerked my chin toward Nate.

Nate's face turned serious, and he glanced quickly at Chiron.

"To be honest, I think you already have," Chiron said to me before turning to Nate. "You said she was forcefully blocking you yesterday? When you went into her mind?"

"Yes, I could feel her power beating back against my own. You think she was mimicking my power and using that to keep me out?"

I smirked. He did *not* sound pleased at that prospect.

Chiron nodded slowly. "I do. Considering we've just discovered she's able to manipulate other powers, it's the only thing that makes sense."

"True, but her powers have been erratic at best. How could she use something as powerful as Coercion so effectively?"

"I'm not sure." He looked at me speculatively before turning back to Nate. "You said her powers seemed sentient, correct?"

Nate gave a sharp nod. "Yes. As though there was an entirely separate consciousness at work in her mind."

"Tessa, is that how it feels for you?" Chiron asked.

"Very much so. I had to fight pretty hard when I was trying to let Nate into my mind yesterday. It's like my power is there with me and for me, but it hasn't really become a part of me, if that makes sense?"

"Hmm." He looked back and forth between Nate and me. "What did you see when you were drawing on the wind power?"

I explained what I'd seen when I recalled the memory of Andrei drying off my shirt.

"A small speck of power, you say?" Chiron's black brown eyes were sparkling, as though he was on the verge of a big idea.

I nodded quickly. "Yes, just a little bit, maybe the size of the tip of my pinkie." I held up my little finger.

"Interesting." He crossed his arms across his chest. "Nathaniel, didn't you say you used your powers on her when she was still human?"

Nate's cheeks flushed pink. "Yes, but—"

"No need to be ashamed," Chiron said, waving off his protest. "It's possible that this has something to do with the fact that you entered her mind while she was still human. You see—" he turned toward me, "—the human mind is very susceptible to manipulation, and if a power as strong as Nathaniel's is forced into the mind of one who is destined to become a Mimic, well, it's possible that power could leave a mark, much like Andrei's did. His power could've been the first you gained access to."

Nate snapped his fingers.

"*That's* why I saw Mentalist abilities at her transition." He shook his head and let out a laugh. "I seriously thought there was something wrong with my own powers."

I held up a hand and shook my head. "Hang on, that still doesn't make sense. I'm a Telekinetic. That's what Nate announced, and it was the first power I was able to use successfully."

Chiron tapped a finger on his chin and eyed me speculatively. "Did any Telekinetics use their power before you the other night?"

I frowned. "Yeah, actually. Charlise did."

He held up his hands and smiled. "There you have it. It's likely you wouldn't have been successful had Charlise not used her power in your presence first."

"Fine, but that still doesn't explain why Nate announced me as a Telekinetic and not a Coercer."

"Hmm." Genevieve put her hands on her hips. "Nathaniel, didn't ye tell me once that Telekinetics are the easiest Mentalists to both announce and train?"

Nate frowned, then nodded. "Yes, because their power doesn't rely on the presence of another living creature. It's the least complex of all the Mentalist powers. If she potentially has access to *all* Mentalist affinities, then it would make sense that the simplest of them would be the most evident at her transformation."

"That's certainly worth being explored," Chiron said. "If she is, in fact, a Mimic—"

"Right here, guys." I was starting to get irritated now. This was a big freaking deal and they were throwing around theories and talking as though I wasn't even there.

"I'm sorry," Nate replied, looking sheepish. He looked toward Chiron. "She's right. These are just theories, but—"

I narrowed my eyes at him. "I didn't say anything about theories."

His brow furrowed in confusion. "Yes, you did. Just a second ago."

"What are you talking about, Nathaniel?" Genevieve looked just as confused.

"Dammit." I put my hands on my hips and glared at Chiron. "Is there any way I can shut that off?"

"Shut what off?"

"The yelling thing. Nate said I'm always doing it."

"Not always," Nate said. "You just project. A lot."

"That's a different issue entirely," Chiron replied. "You'll need to practice building up your mental walls a bit more efficiently is all. It shouldn't be difficult, considering your power."

I sighed. "Considering we know next to nothing about my power, I don't find that likely."

"It'll just take some practice," Nate said gently. "I'll help you, don't worry."

I pressed my lips into a thin line and nodded, then looked up at him and tried to smile. "Thanks."

He gave my shoulder a squeeze, then frowned. "Are you alright?"

"Yeah, it's just a little weird, that's all. I was having a hard-enough time yesterday, and now you guys are saying I have to figure out this power that's about a million times bigger than I thought."

"We'll figure it out," Nate assured me, "...whatever it is. Did you want to try a few more things?"

I opened my mouth to respond, but Genevieve cut me off.

"Let's give the girl a break, shall we?" Genevieve suggested. "We can give light a try another time. I'm going to take her for a walk."

I gave her a relieved smile. "Yeah, I think that's a good idea," I said.

Nate's gaze drifted to Chiron, who nodded.

"Of course. Come back when you're ready."

I let Genevieve lead me toward the dirt road that would take us back to town. She waited until we were a few hundred yards away before speaking.

"Are you okay?"

"Not really," I murmured.

"This is an amazing thing, ye know? If it's true?"

I wrapped my arms around myself as I stared at the road ahead. Annoyance washed over me as I felt the sting of tears in my eyes. "I thought so, too, but the more I think about it, the more I'm starting to feel like a giant freak."

She smiled and slid her hands into the pockets of her fitted black uniform pants. "Oh, I understand that feeling, at least somewhat. When I was told I had five affinities, it was quite overwhelming."

"How did you handle it? With training and everything? Did people look at you weird?"

"Training was difficult," she conceded. "And there were others who felt I saw myself as above the rest." She pressed her lips together grimly. "They were wrong, of course, and they're all past it now, but I won't lie and say it was easy at first."

Her heavy Scottish accent had a soothing effect, and I found myself slowly relaxing.

"Well, maybe I'll get lucky and it'll turn out I've only got a bunch of affinities," I said hopefully. "And not some one-of-a-kind weirdo."

"Oh, honey, we're all a bunch of weirdos in this world. Don't let anyone tell ye different."

I couldn't help smiling. It was weird, hearing such heavy wisdom in her voice when she looked only a few years older than me.

"Hey, so can I ask a question? Not related to affinities?"

"Certainly."

"When did you stop aging?" I asked. "My guardians told me I'd keep aging for a few years until I reached 'full adulthood,' but how long does that take?"

Her brown eyes crinkled with laughter as she smiled over at me. "Your mind goes to funny places when it wants to be distracted, doesn't it?"

"I guess so," I said with a shrug.

"Well, to answer your question, I think it was about four or five years. Ye don't really notice that you've stopped aging at first, so it's tough to put an exact number on it."

"Huh. Interesting. So do I get to request to train with you, then?"

"If ye don't, I'd be quite insulted." She smiled and patted me on the back. "It will be quite fun to work with someone who can match me power for power."

I felt the corner of my mouth turn up in a small smile.

"That does sound pretty cool."

29

NATHANIEL

"Should we tell Zeus?"

The words felt odd coming out of my mouth. A week ago, I wouldn't have questioned whether to go to Zeus with news of a potential Mimic in our midst. We were on the brink of war, and someone with power like that could be invaluable.

Now, as Chiron and I stood watching as Tessa and Genevieve walked toward the dirt road that led back to Main Street, I struggled with it.

"No, Nathaniel, I think we should wait," he said quietly. "We don't know for certain what she is."

I let out a relieved sigh. "Agreed."

He nodded, looking pensive, then turned to stare at me with his formidable gaze. "If this turns out to be true, she's going to need support. I don't think I need to tell you how monumental this is."

"No, you certainly don't."

He put his hands on his hips and looked back toward the arena. From the rumblings within, it sounded as though the warm-up runs had just ended.

"For now, we need to keep this to ourselves."

"Her best friends live right here on Olympus, one just down the hall. If you think she'll keep this from them, you're crazy."

"That may not be such a bad thing, assuming they can keep it to themselves." He scratched behind his ear. "No offense to you, but I have a feeling support from someone like you may not rival that of the female she's known all her life."

"I suppose." Annoyed, I turned and started walking back toward the arena.

Chiron fell into step beside me. "This seems to be bothering you quite a bit. Why is that?"

"She's brand new, Chiron. She shouldn't have to deal with something like this."

He raised a brow and smirked. "It has nothing to do with the feelings you're developing for her?"

I stared at the ground for a moment, unsure how to respond. The feelings of caring for someone had become foreign to me, and it was something I was struggling to wrap my mind around.

"It might," I finally conceded.

"Ha!" He gave a little jump. "So you admit it!"

I gave him a wry smile. "Care to tell me what to do about it?"

Three thousand years old, and here I was asking for advice on women.

"It's not your first rodeo, Nathaniel." He grinned and clapped my back. "Isn't that what the humans say?"

I punched his shoulder, and he winced.

"Honestly, I don't know what you're so worried about. It's in our nature to love, to want to be with someone. You'd by no means be the first to start a romantic relationship on this blasted rock."

I laughed. "True."

Despite the rigorous training they went through, the Ischyra still had social lives, and their dating pool was quite large. Marriages were rare, children even more so, but romantic relationships were very common. Quite frequently, those relationships involved gods or even humans, in some cases.

"And I have no aversion. I just haven't had any interest until now, that's all."

"So what will you do?"

"First?" I held my palms up and shrugged. "First, I'm going to help you find out what she is. Then, we'll see."

"She cares for you," he said quietly. "You've seen that in her mind, I'm sure."

"I try not to invade her privacy like that. There are some things that come, through." I smiled as I recalled her thoughts on my smile earlier. "But ever since that day outside of her school...I just don't unless I need to."

"Understandable." He looked back toward the road and nodded in her direction. "It's time to bring her back. She needs to join training."

"I'll get Gen," I said, directing my thoughts toward her.

'It's time to head back in,' I told her.

'Ay, we'll be there shortly.'

"They're on their way," I told Chiron. Recalling my conversation with Prometheus the day before, I stopped him.

"I spoke with Prometheus yesterday when I was at Apollo's. He'd like to help with hand-to-hand and weapons training."

"I think that's a good idea. What about his brother?" he asked.

"He wants to see Epimetheus more involved with the recruits, if possible."

"I agree. He can't mope in his brother's shadow forever. The rest of us moved on from Pandora eons ago, it's time he did the same."

We stepped through the doors of the arena and were greeted by the site of Christopher attempting unsuccessfully to call order to the recruits.

"Unbelievable," Chiron muttered as he pulled out his bugle. "Thirty minutes. All I asked was thirty minutes." He raised the bugle to his lips and blew a single, long blast.

The crowd of recruits immediately grew silent, and Chiron and I made our way to the front.

"Now that we're all warmed up," Chiron shouted, "I'll give you a rundown of our upcoming schedule. For the rest of this week, we will be focused solely on getting comfortable with your affinities. Next week, we'll move on to a bit of hand-to-hand and weapons training, which you should have gotten a fair dose of with your guardians." He folded his arms across his chest. "Did anyone here not receive the requisite weapons training prior to their transformation?"

I followed his gaze as he looked out over the crowd. Aside from the academic and civic aspects, Ares and Athena also decreed that Ischyra were to receive training in all physical forms of fighting prior to their transformation.

When none responded, he gave a sharp nod.

"Wonderful. We'll be joined by Prometheus and Epimetheus for these lessons, as their skills in this area are quite extensive. Right now, let's split off into your groups from yesterday, and your mentors will tell you where to go from there."

'We're back.'

I turned toward the entrance and saw Genevieve and Tessa walking toward the crowd of recruits that was now splitting up into their affinity groups. Genevieve gave her a pat on the shoulder before heading off to join her group of mentees. Before I could take a step toward Tessa, Annette skipped over to join her, her blond pigtails swinging, and the two started talking.

"Where'd you all run off to?" Charlise spoke, having just appeared by my side with Fletcher.

"I had to help Chiron with something," I responded. "Let's get started."

Without another word, I strolled off toward the tables that had been set up for the Mentalist recruits. As I neared the tables, I glanced up and saw Apollo standing in the top level of the arena, gazing at the recruits below. A few seconds later, Prometheus and Epimetheus joined him.

'Anything you'd like to discuss?'

I gritted my teeth when I heard Apollo's voice in my head.

'No.'

Before he could respond, I closed off my mental walls entirely.

When I looked up at him, he was glaring down at me, his lips set in a hard line.

Just then, Fletch showed up beside me.

"Hey, Fletch."

"Morning, Nathaniel. Charlise and I thought it might be best to split them into three groups today instead of ten, see if we can give the Replicators and Splitters a bit more of a challenge. What are your thoughts?"

I glanced down at Charlise who'd fallen into step on my right.

"I think that makes sense. We'll begin with them, but I would like to see how the Illusionists manage when they're trying to hold up their illusion to multiple people."

"Alright," Fletch replied, nodding. "We'll set the Linkers up with the Telepaths and Telekinetics since they should be the simplest to infiltrate, and tomorrow I think we should give the Trackers, Astrals, and the Psychometric a solid focus."

"My only concern with combining the Linkers with the Telekinetics is that Tessa and Damien seemed to hit quite an impasse yesterday," Charlise said, looking up at me. "Do you think this is an issue of their ability to work together, or do you think one might have some kind of hindrance?"

I scratched my head. "I'm not entirely sure," I hedged. "I'll take them, see how they are today. If need be, I'll jump in and see what I can work out."

Charlise smiled cheerfully. "Sounds good, boss!"

She trotted off to sort the Mentalists into their groups, while Fletch and I waited near the sandbox, as it had come to be called over the years. It was a simple wooden structure with walls that were about two feet high. Instead of being filled with sand from the arena floor, soft cushions were spread around. We'd found that an enclosed space, even an open-air one such as the sandbox, helped certain Mentalist recruits focus. It also gave the Astrals a soft place to relax when they projected.

"Why don't you take the Illusionists," I suggested. "You can group them with the Astrals for today. I'll take the Linker group. Charlise can take the rest."

"Not a problem." He grinned, flashing a bright smile, then turned and raised his voice. "Illusionists and Astrals, come to me!"

I made my way over to the tables where Charlise had directed my group of seven.

I ran a hand over my chin and put the other on my hip as I looked at them speculatively. For the first time in a long while, I was at a loss as to where to begin. Most had done well with their partners, but Tessa and Damien's attempts to work together yesterday had been dreadful; I could only assume the same would happen today.

"Alright." I clapped my hands twice. "I think it might be a bit easier if we go someplace more quiet, so let's move this outside."

I turned to lead them toward the exit, and a small part of me hoped that Tessa would join me.

I felt a tentative poke in my mind. I let my walls down, hoping it was her and not Apollo.

'Thanks for letting me take a break.'

I smiled when I heard her voice in my head.

'So now this mindreading thing is alright?'

'Well, I can't exactly talk about this in front of the others.'

'Fair enough'.

The more the other recruits saw us talking, the more likely it was that some would begin to suspect favoritism. I'd seen it before. Genevieve had suffered through a good deal of negative attention during her training. Having five affinities, she required more rigorous training than the others, which meant she'd gotten to know more of the mentors than her fellow recruits. It was jealousy, pure and simple, and unfortunately, unavoidable.

'No need to apologize, it was a lot to take in. Are you planning on dinner with your friends again?'

'Not sure. Why?'

'We should probably talk a bit more about earlier, and I still want to hear about your nightmare.'

I could feel hesitation in her thoughts before she finally responded.

'That's fine, but do you think we could maybe just hang out? My mind is kind of full right now.'

'Of course, whatever you want.'

'Okay. Just give me time to shower after training.'

'Sure.'

'And Nate?'

'Yes?'

'Use the front gate this time, please? I'll meet you in the courtyard.'

I smiled.

'No problem.'

30

TESSA

Later that evening, as I stood in front of my mirror getting ready to meet up with Nate, I couldn't help the annoyance that flooded me.

Training had sucked royally. My telekinesis was on point, but every other thing about training was miserable.

First, I'd tried to work with Damien again; that was a miserable fail. My mind just wouldn't let him in. We'd switched partners, and I tried working with Sina, who was also a Linker, to no avail. Martin, our single Telepath, was able to make some headway, but Nate's theory was that it was because he was only trying to communicate, not take over.

After that, I'd been sent to the side to watch as the others worked with one another. Damien managed to infiltrate Sina's mind long enough to pluck five blades of grass from the ground, while Martin initiated a telepathic game of telephone with everyone else, sending a message telepathically to Josephina, who whispered it to Kieran, and so on, until it reached Anette, who proudly announced that "Sally sold seashells at an ice cream store."

I hadn't told anyone about Nate and Chiron's suspicions. I knew in my gut that they were probably right. They knew far more than I did about what affinities may or may not exist. I just didn't want to tell anyone, not even Mary, until I knew something for sure.

As I went to apply a sheer pink gloss to my lips, I paused. Squinting, I leaned in closer to examine my face.

I'd only done my makeup once since we'd arrived at Olympus, and at that point, I'd still been human. Now, as I examined my newly immortal face, I saw it.

My chin was smooth. The little scar I'd gotten in seventh grade had vanished, as though it had never been there.

Quickly, I opened my mouth and looked to my back molar. Sure enough, the small speck of silver that had resided there for the last five years had disappeared, the surface of the tooth unmarred by the tiny cavity that had once been there.

"Yana!"

My roommate stepped out of the bathroom, wrapped in a towel, her face coated with a mint-green facial mask.

"Yes?"

"Uh...Did you know our scars go away?"

She frowned at me. "Yes, of course. All injuries regenerate, even old ones."

"Huh. Neat. What's with the mask?"

She shrugged and stepped back into the bathroom, returning a moment later with her bathrobe on.

"The mask is for fun. It was something Jonna, my female guardian, and I used to do together each Sunday. It became our 'thing,' as you would say."

"That's cool." I smiled wistfully. "My guardians and I had a thing like that. Do you miss it? Those normal, human things you guys would do?"

She sat down on the edge of my bed and fiddled with one of my makeup brushes.

"At times. I am not as sentimental as you and Mary seem to be, but we were a family, just as you were. It is hard not to miss that." She smiled up at me. "Did your female guardian teach you how to do makeup? You are quite good at it."

I picked up my brown eyeliner and slowly began tracing a thin line along my top lashes.

"Not really. Analise was never one for makeup, really, but one Halloween, I dressed up as Cleopatra—"

"With blond hair?" She bit back a smile. "It must not have been a very good costume."

I shot her a glare in the mirror before moving on to the other eye.

"Ha ha. *Anyway*, she taught me how to do the most amazing cat eye with my liner. I don't really get a chance to do my eyes up anymore, though, so I never get to play with it. The rest I got from You Tube."

"I've always liked the way that looked," Yana said. "You will have to teach me. In exchange for braiding lessons, of course."

"Of course."

As I applied a coat of black mascara, I saw that Yana was watching me, smirking.

I screwed the wand back into the tube and turned to face her. "What?"

She shook her head, her smirk turning into a wide smile. "You are here one week and going on dates. I am jealous."

"They're not dates. We're just...talking or whatever," I grumbled, tossing the tube of mascara back in my makeup case and running my fingers through my hair. I'd taken the time to dry and straighten it, then I'd put on the same outfit I'd worn the night before since I'd only be in it a couple of hours.

"Whatever you say," Yana teased. "Hey, where did you go today? How did you avoid running laps with the rest of us?"

I froze.

"Uh...Chiron had some stuff he needed to talk to me about. Since I was having such a tough time linking with Damien this week, he wanted to help."

I knew the excuse sounded weak, and the arch of Yana's perfectly shaped brows told me she thought the same.

"Alright." She stood, then put one hand on her hip and rubbed the back of her neck with the other. "Tessa, if you need to talk—I know Mary is your best friend, but..."

I smiled and hoped my appreciation of her gesture was clear. "Thanks, Yana. I really appreciate that."

She waved a hand. "Do not mention it. Now go. If I cannot have boy stories of my own just yet, I will need to get by on yours."

I rolled my eyes. "I can't guarantee mine will be terribly interesting, but we'll see."

She wagged a red-tipped finger at me. "He will kiss you tonight, mark my words."

I raised my eyebrows and smiled. "You're crazy, you know that?"

She waved both hands in a "go away" gesture. "Shoo! Out the door!"

Laughing, I let the door click shut behind me, and I made my way out to the courtyard to meet Nate.

I found him sitting next to the fountain when I got there, staring up at the sky.

"Hey," I said quietly, sitting down next to him. "What'cha looking at?"

He turned his head toward me and smiled. "Nothing, really. Just thinking."

"I see. So...what do you want to do?"

He stood, then reached out a hand toward me. "Come on, I'll show you."

I narrowed my eyes at him and took his hand. "That sounds mysterious and creepy."

He laughed. "It's not, don't worry. You seemed to like the zipline field last night, and I thought of another place you might want to see. The view of the sky is even better."

I let him lead me down the street toward the portal field. He stopped in front of a very plain wooden door with a brass knob.

"That one doesn't look very interesting," I remarked.

He paused, his hand on the knob, and turned to me.

"Just wait. And close your eyes."

"Okay..." I did as requested, and when I felt him tug on my hand, I stepped over the threshold and felt something crunch beneath my feet. A cold wind swirled around me.

He put his hands on my hips and turned me to the right.

"Alright, open," he whispered.

I opened my eyes and sucked in a breath.

Sprawling before me was the entirety of the Olympic mountain range. Far beneath me, I could see the twinkling lights of the gods' homes, just above the wispy cloud-cover that separated them from the lower portion of the mountain. Rough, rocky peaks led off in the distance where I could see the thin crescent moon reflecting off the sea, miles away.

The only sound was the wind, blustering and cold.

"My gods," I breathed, slowly spinning so I could take it all in. There was almost no light up here, so all I could see when I looked up was the black sky, a blanket of millions of stars.

I let my gaze fall back to Nate who was standing with his hands in his pockets, smiling like the cat that ate the canary.

I couldn't help but grin. "This is amazing."

"I thought you'd like it. Come on, there's a shelter over here if you want to get out of the wind."

I looked around and saw a small, three-sided, wind-beaten structure with a thatched roof. The front was wide open, giving an unobstructed view across the mountains.

I followed him over to the shelter, our shoes crunching in the unmarred snow. Icy droplets slipped into my sneakers, sending a chill up my legs.

"You know, hanging out with you is starting to have some benefits," I joked. "You know all the best places to hide when you don't want to be bothered."

He slid a glance in my direction before pulling two blankets down from a shelf on the side wall.

"And here I thought you just enjoyed my company."

I wrapped myself in the thick wool blanket and sat down on the bench that ran along the back wall.

"I guess you're not so bad."

"Thanks."

I pointed a finger at him over the edge of my blanket. "Sarcasm will get you nowhere, buddy."

He swatted my finger away and sat down next to me, his long legs sprawled out in front of him. I kind of wished he'd hold my hand again, but the frigid air was keeping me from letting my hands out from under the blanket.

"So how are you? After today, I mean. You seem okay." He sounded apprehensive, as though he wasn't sure how I'd respond.

"Eh. I'm so-so. I don't want to trick myself into thinking I might be something that, up until now, I didn't think was real. It would be so amazing if that were true, you know?"

I took a deep breath, letting the crisp air flow through my nose and lungs.

"So I'm doing the mature thing and ignoring my problems until you and Chiron figure out an answer." I gave him a cheeky grin and pulled the blanket tighter around me.

"Ah, so you're leaving it up to us to figure out what you are?"

"Well, technically, you should've figured it out a week ago, but let's not split hairs."

He gave me a withering look but otherwise didn't respond.

"Listen," I said. "I'd really rather not talk about that right now. Let's just get with Chiron and you guys can have me do whatever tricks you think will prove I'm a Mimic. Until then, I just want to go about business as usual. I'll train with the others and work on my telekinesis, and we'll go from there." I nudged him with my elbow. "Okay?"

He sighed and rubbed a hand across his chin, then turned his head to face me. "Sure. But Tessa, this is something we need to figure out. If you've got more power inside you, it can't be pent up. It'll eventually force its way free, and you'll be in a whole mess of trouble."

I tried not to cringe at the "force its way free" part, but I couldn't help it. As if on cue, I felt my power stir, sending a feeling of restless-ness through me.

I sighed. He was right. The power that seemed to be a living force in my mind was far more than just telekinesis, of that I was certain.

"Let's just give it a few days, okay? Let me get through this week so I can at least try to work with my group at training. If nothing else, it'll give me exposure to other powers, which could come in handy when you guys perform your 'tests' or whatever."

"I can live with that," he conceded.

"Thanks."

"Now." He raised his eyebrows. "Tell me about this dream."

I pulled the blanket tighter around me as I thought back to the nightmare I'd had the night before.

"It was weird, almost like the precursor to what you saw that day before school." I contemplated telling him to just look into my mind so I wouldn't have to talk about it but figured that would mean I'd have to relive it, which was definitely not preferable.

He cocked his head to the side in question. "How so?"

I blew out a breath. "Okay, so do you remember how the last thing I saw before I fell into that...darkness or whatever...was someone running at me?"

He nodded and pulled one leg up on the bench so he could face me better.

"Well, this was everything up until that point." I stared at the collar on Nate's jacket, using it to keep myself focused as I detailed the dream and all of the people in it for him.

"It was so weird. The way we spoke, it was like we had been doing this every day. Then those men..." I shivered, then raised my eyes to look at him. "Crazy, right?"

Nate's brow was furrowed in confusion, and his mouth hung slightly open, as though he were trying to puzzle something out.

I snapped my fingers in front of his face. "Yoo hoo. What is it?"

"It's—it's just—I mean, I've only seen it happen once, but what you're describing...the way that woman was killed—it's like you're describing what happens when a god is destroyed."

I blinked, then laughed. "Gods, now *that* makes sense. We were just talking about that last night. I'm not surprised I dreamt about it. Hasn't that ever happened to you?"

He looked at me dubiously. "Hasn't what happened?"

"You talk about something or do something or watch something on TV, then you dream about it that night?"

"Yes, but I don't think that's what happened here. You're very clearly describing the destruction of a god."

"Oh, come on, there are only so many ways to imagine that happening! Don't you remember? I called it an 'energy suck,' and that's exactly what I saw. There is literally no other way to describe that."

"Alright, I might allow you that, but what about the part where you said it wrapped around you? Is that something you would imagine happening during an 'energy suck'?" He raised an eyebrow in challenge.

I pursed my lips. "I don't know, there's probably some weird psychological meaning to it that I haven't thought of yet."

"And the men and women who you've never seen before? What's your explanation there?"

"Who's to say I've never seen them?" I shrugged. "Maybe they were in the restaurant the other night and I just don't remember. Or maybe I just made them up."

Denial was seeming like an excellent vacation spot at the moment.

He scratched his forehead.

"Okay," he said after a few moments. "I'll shelve that for now because I don't really care to argue."

Before I could thank him, he held up a finger. "But if you have any more of these nightmares, Tessa, please let me try to help you."

"How? By digging into my brain again?"

He winced. "I don't know."

I was starting to get warm, so I let the blanket fall down around my waist so the cold air could wash over me. It was a revitalizing feeling.

I gave him my brightest smile. "So, tell me about yourself."

He blinked at the rapid change in topic. "Oh. Okay. What would you like to know?" He swung his other leg up onto the bench and leaned back against the wall. "I'm not terribly interesting."

I mirrored his pose against the opposite wall and laughed. "You're three thousand years old, I'm sure something interesting has happened along the way."

"Not much worth mentioning, really."

I rolled my eyes and lightly kicked his foot. "Fine. Tell me about your first girlfriend."

He raised his eyebrows and gave me a lopsided grin. "*That's* what you want to talk about?"

I shrugged. "Why not? And don't try to tell me you've never been in a relationship."

He rubbed the side of his nose. "Okay. The first girl I loved was an Ischyra named Karis. I was about five hundred at that point. She was one of the first generation who'd chosen to remain on Olympus, so we'd known each other some time."

"How long were you guys together?"

I don't know why I was so interested in his romantic past. Part of me didn't like to think of him being with another woman, but part of me also wanted to know that he was more than just a soldier.

"A few centuries. It was different back then, though."

A few centuries. Geez.

"How was it different?" I asked.

"Zeus felt I would make a good match for her, and surprisingly, I agreed."

"Wait... do you have *kids*?"

He barked out a laugh. "No! Like I said, it was different back then. Being together for a century or two, well, that would be the human equivalent of a decade. We were young, I was still very involved with the Ischyra, and she was often living on Earth, protecting the humans she'd been assigned to. We both agreed that choosing to combine our energy to create children wasn't something we wanted at that age."

I breathed an internal sigh of relief. A three-thousand-year-old potential boyfriend I could deal with. Kids were a whole other story.

Not that they'd still be kids, but that was beside the point.

"What happened to her?"

He tilted his head back against the wall and interlaced his fingers in his lap.

"She was killed." He tapped his chest. "Godsbane arrow, straight through her heart."

My own heart clenched at the look of sadness on his face. I reached forward and slid my hand over his.

"Gods, Nate. I'm so sorry."

He turned his hand so that his fingers curled through mine. "It was a long time ago." He gave my arm a tug. "Come here."

I let him pull me down so that I was laying with my head on his shoulder, then I wrapped my arm around his waist. He pulled the blanket tight around us, then rested his cheek on the top of my head.

"These things happen in our line of work. I'm sure you know that." He absently twirled a few strands of my hair around his fingers. "So what about you?"

"I had boyfriends all through high school for the most part, but only one was really serious. This guy Caleb and I dated a good chunk of junior year and most of last summer. We broke up right before he left for college."

His hand stilled for a moment before resuming its movement. "Why did you break up?"

I shifted uncomfortably.

"I don't know, it just wasn't...fun with him, if that makes sense? I knew he was leaving for school, and I never felt a need to push for the long-distance thing. I don't think he did, either. We just didn't work as a couple, I guess."

"Did he hurt you?"

I laughed. "Not at all. I'm the one that broke up with him. He's a good guy, just not for me."

"You don't strike me as the type to date men who aren't," he said quietly.

"Thanks." I smiled, inhaling his woodsy, comforting scent. "I like to think so."

WE LAID THERE for a while longer, talking about things that were much more benign than nightmares, training, and wars. I told him all about growing up in Renville, about John and Analise and how wonderful they were. He asked question after question about my likes, dislikes, and what I hoped my future as an Ischyra would bring.

By the time he walked me back to the dorms, it was almost midnight. The thin moon cast almost no light over the courtyard when we arrived.

When we reached the door that led into the girls' hall, I turned to face him.

"So maybe one of these days we can actually hang out during the day?"

He tucked a lock of hair behind my ear and gave me a slow smile. "I have some thoughts on that, actually. Did you happen to pack a bathing suit when you left Renville?"

"No, I didn't. Why?" I arched a brow in suspicion.

"Take your friends, go check out the shops in town, and get yourself one. There's a place I want to take you that I think you'll really like."

My lips curved in a smile as my fingers tightened around his.

"Hmm. So are we talking something practical or something fun?" Having grown up on the water, bathing suit shopping was one of my favorite things to do.

He gave me a slow smile, then rested one hand on my hip and ran the other through my hair. I stared up at him, eyes wide, suddenly very eager to feel his lips on mine.

He laughed quietly, then leaned down and gave me a light, slow kiss on the corner of my mouth. He moved his lips to my ear, and his warm breath sent tingles through my body as he whispered to me.

"Definitely fun."

When he pulled back, I bit my lip, heat rising to my face. He continued walking backward, giving me one last adorable smile before he walked off into the darkness.

Well, wasn't he just full of surprises?

I touched the spot on my cheek where he'd kissed me and did a little dance. Grinning like an idiot, I vowed to make sure that next time it was right on the lips.

31

TESSA

The next few days were brutal.

Every night brought a new nightmare. Some were similar to the one where I was sparring with the blond man, while others were reminiscent of the ones I'd had when I was human. Fortunately, after that first night, I'd managed to keep from waking Yana, and none of the nightmares had been so bad that I'd felt the need to call out to Nate.

On the plus side, by Friday—training day five—I'd finally managed to run a set of laps without falling, and I'd even let Damien into my mind, much to my relief. I was getting tired of his patronizing glares.

It was our last day of training for the week, which meant we actually got to sleep in the next day. The prospect of not waking up to an alarm was fantastic.

Saturday was also my bathing suit date with Nate, which I'd been slowly freaking out about all week.

So after training on Friday, Mary and Yana dragged me to one of the larger clothing stores on Main Street, *Goddesses*, which sold everything from cute winter pea coats to embarrassingly revealing lingerie.

"We'll skip that section for now," Mary said, smirking.

"Gods, Mare, he hasn't even kissed me yet!"

She waved a hand dismissively as she pawed through a rack of bikinis. "Oh stop, it's not like he'd be your first! You guys are consenting adults or whatever; you can do what you want." She bit her lip and arched a brow. "Besides, he looks like he'd be way more fun than Caleb."

I cringed, thinking back to the few awkward times my ex Caleb and I had actually slept together.

Yana gasped. "Tessa, I see that look on your face! Please, I need details!"

I rolled my eyes.

"Thanks, Mare," I muttered before facing Yana. "There's not much to tell. I dated this guy Caleb all last summer. He was a year older than me, and a few weeks before he left for college in Washington, we slept together. It was, I don't know. Awkward, I guess?"

"Awkward?" Yana repeated. "How?"

"I was his first, too. Neither of us knew what we were doing."

"Ahh. Well, hopefully, Nate will be different."

"I think I'll give it more than one date before sleeping with him," I said dryly.

"Maybe, but you should be prepared for all possibilities," Mary said, then paused in the middle of her search and leaned toward us, smiling mischievously.

"So I have it on good authority that my no-longer-annoying room-mate was able to acquire a few bottles of ambrosia wine. I told her to go grab pizza from Nico's and meet us back at your room at eight."

I looked up at the large, sunflower shaped clock hanging above a wall of shoes.

"That's in a half hour," I pointed out.

"Exactly, so let's get a move on."

We decided splitting up was the best course of action, and Mary and Yana each delivered two options to me in the dressing room. The ones I'd picked were a little more conservative—bandeau tops and cute boy shorts—but both girls vetoed those immediately.

"Those aren't even remotely sexy!" Mary exclaimed. "Gods, Tess, since when do you not want to look hot in a bathing suit?" She shoved her two options at me. "Try these."

I choked out a laugh. "These are more string than fabric. No way. Sexy I'm fine with, but pasties would cover more of my boobs than that top." I tossed them back at her, and she caught them, pouting.

"Here, this might work." Yana handed me a plum colored two piece made of an incredibly soft, stretchy material, similar to our training outfits. "It should cover a bit more than...that." She eyed the scraps of fabric still clutched in Mary's hands.

"Okay, fine." I pulled the curtain to the fitting room closed and maneuvered myself into the suit. When I finally got it on, I was surprised to see I actually liked it.

The top was a sweetheart-cut bandeau with thin purple straps and two long pieces of fabric that wrapped around my torso to tie in the back, keeping the girls locked down tight. The bottoms were a basic bikini style with slight ruching on the sides.

"Tessa?" Mary's voice sounded impatient. "We're running short on time, here."

"Coming!" I shoved back the curtain and stepped out. "Well?" I put my hands on my hips.

Yana looked me up and down speculatively. "I think it is perfect. They have other colors, so I may have to get one for myself."

I turned my attention to Mary. "Mare?"

She let her hands fall to her sides with a huff. "Fine, it looks great," she conceded. "You're lucky you got such a good tan when we were still in Renville. Where is he taking you, anyway?"

"No clue. Swimming?"

"It's freezing, though," Mary said.

"There are many hot springs further up the mountain," Yana said. "Igor told me about them on the way to training yesterday." Her cheeks tinged pink at the mention of Igor's name.

"Yeah?" Mary's face broke out into a wide smile. "He planning on taking you up there?"

Yana's mouth opened and closed a few times, and her face flushed even darker.

I smacked Yana's shoulder with the back of my hand. "Mariana Comsa! You did *not* tell us that!"

"Nothing has happened yet." She looked back and forth between Mary and me. "I will tell you when something does, I promise!"

I pointed a finger at her. "You better!"

On the way up to the register, a rack of dark-wash skinny jeans caught my eye. I began flipping through, searching for my size, but they all looked to be the same ridiculously small cut.

"Excuse me?" I called to the woman who was reading a book behind the counter. Her nametag read "Sofie."

"Yes?"

"Do you have these in a four?"

Sofie smiled and put her book down, then came out from behind the counter.

"These are actually one size." Her eyes sparkled with excitement. "Did you ever read that book *Sisterhood of the Traveling Pants*?"

I frowned. "Wasn't that a movie?"

"Yeah, the same pair of jeans fit all of them, right?" Mary asked.

The woman grinned. "Yes. Well, the idea for these came from that. The fabric has been spelled to fit whoever wears them."

"Shut. Up." Mary reached out and grabbed a pair. "How?"

"One of the witches who trained under Hecate has a thing for fashion." She held her arm out, gesturing around the rest of the store. "She's designed nearly everything here."

Mary draped one pair over her arm and thrust another pair at me. "Here. These will make your ass look fantastic."

Since there was no way I was turning down a pair of jeans that would fit me like a glove, I took them and followed the girl to the register.

"Hang on, I want to grab a shirt." Scanning the nearby racks, I found a cream colored off-the-shoulder top made of raw silk with lace trim along the bottom hem. I held it up to Mary and Yana for inspection.

"Perfect. Wonderful. Gorgeous," Mary said, her tone impatient. "Let's *go*."

"Did you girls find everything you were looking for?" Sofie began scanning the items so she could update the store's stock.

"Yep." I grinned at her. "Thank you!"

"Not a problem. Let me know how those jeans work out!"

ANETTE HAD, in fact, acquired several bottles of ambrosia wine from the local spirits store, and the four of us stayed up most of the night drinking and talking. We talked about boys mostly because we were suddenly surrounded by a whole new crop of them. The girls all pressed for details about the time I'd spent with Nate and were surprised when I told them we hadn't actually kissed yet.

And despite Mary's initial aversion to Anette, she'd slowly grown on her. It turned out she was actually a lot of fun to hang out with.

Especially when she got some alcohol into her system.

By the time Yana and I had dragged ourselves back to our room, it was three in the morning. Considering we'd been up since seven and had just completed eight hours of training, I was amazed we'd made it that long.

At least we got a good night's sleep out of it, and when I opened my eyes the next day, I was excited to see I'd slept until nearly noon.

I couldn't remember the last time I'd slept that late. Even better, I had somehow managed to avoid a massive hangover.

Thank the gods for small favors, right?

Suddenly, there was a pounding on my door. Yana let out a loud groan and pulled her pillow tightly over her head.

I jumped out of bed, and before I had my hand on the knob, Mary burst in, still in her pajamas, her wavy brown hair a mess. She stared at me, bug eyed.

"How are you not dressed yet?"

I rubbed a hand over my face and yawned.

"Because I just woke up. Why?"

"Ugh, Tessa!" She grabbed me by the arm and dragged me to the bathroom. "You need to get in the shower!"

"What? Why?"

She stopped in the middle of turning the water on and gaped at me.

"Bathing suit date, remember? Nate's going to be here in a half hour!"

I felt my eyes go as wide as saucers, and I suddenly became very aware of my morning breath, messy hair, and stubbly legs.

At warp speed, I whipped off my pajamas and hopped in the shower, washing and drying myself in record time.

When I left the bathroom, Mary was sitting on Yana's bed, poking her leg.

"You're going to get yourself electrocuted," I warned as I pulled my new clothes from their paper bag. "She's worse than you in the mornings."

"Well whatever, she needs to get up and help."

I unwrapped the towel from my hair and hung it over the bathroom doorknob.

"Why? I know how to get ready for a stupid date."

"Yeah, well—" Mary gave Yana's leg a shake "—this one needs to get up so she can do something super cute with—ow, bitch!" She stumbled back off the bed, landing hard on the wood floor.

"She told you that would happen, didn't she?" Yana grumbled, one hand sticking out over her blankets, still sparking with green electricity.

"Yeah, but I didn't think she was serious." Mary winced, rubbing the spot on her forearm where Yana had shocked her. "Whatever, now you're up. Can you make her hair look...not like that?" She wrinkled her nose as she examined my wet, tangled hair.

Yana rolled over onto her back and covered her eyes with her hands. "Ugh, fine. Why are you so damn chipper this morning?"

"My head is pounding, and I want to puke, but Tessa has a date in twenty minutes, so I'm powering through. Now get up."

Fifteen minutes later, Yana had twisted my long hair into a complex fishtail braid that fell over my shoulder and topped it with a cream-colored headband. The only makeup I'd applied was a few coats of black waterproof mascara to my upper and lower lashes.

"Am I good?" I held out my arms and let them inspect my outfit. I'd put on the new jeans—which were fantastic—and new top over my bathing suit, letting one purple strap peek out.

"Yes." Yana yawned. "Can I go back to bed now?"

I laughed and nudged her back toward her bed.

"Yes, I'll be back later."

"Wonderful," she grumbled, falling face-first onto the mattress. "I cannot wait."

I WAS ALMOST to the courtyard where I was supposed to meet Nate when I ran smack into Eric on his way back from the gym.

"Hey, Tess!" He smiled brightly. "Where ya headed? You wanna go grab lunch?"

"Oh, ah—" I put my hands on my hips. "No, I'm good. Just going for a walk."

He eyed me speculatively.

"You walk?"

"Yup!"

"In a—is that a bathing suit?" He frowned, then reached out and lightly snapped the purple strap that was in clear view thanks to my super cute top.

I took a small step back and cleared my throat. "Yeah, I was kind of—"

"Tessa?"

I cringed. Nate had just come up behind Eric, looking far too gorgeous in blue swim trunks and a white t shirt.

I stepped gingerly around Eric, and he turned and followed my movement, his eyes growing wide when he saw who'd addressed me.

"You're going out with *him*?"

"Yes, Eric, I am. Why?"

Nate folded his arms across his chest and leaned against a

column. There was an amused look on his face, but he otherwise stayed quiet.

'You're enjoying this far too much.'

'Just tell him you have to go. Or stay and continue to stutter out excuses, that's fine, too. I'm thoroughly enjoying his thought process right now, though. His imagination is quite vivid.'

Eric schooled his features and shrugged in an attempt at nonchalance.

"No reason. Have fun."

I pursed my lips as Eric turned and walked down the covered walkway, then slid a look at Nate.

"Well, that was weird."

"I found it entertaining," he said with a smirk.

"Do I even want to know what he was thinking?"

He smiled, then took my hand and led me through the empty courtyard. "Probably not."

"So where are we going, anyway?"

"The springs, just up the mountain. You'll like it."

"I see." I gave him a mischievous look. "Yana and Igor were talking about going there."

"Were they? I wasn't aware they were a couple."

"They're not, but she's totally got a thing for him."

We'd reached the portal field, and this time, we went through a door that was a pale lavender with a white glass doorknob and brass fixtures.

"This kind of looks like my bedroom door in Renville," I observed. "Purple's always been my favorite color."

"Each door reflects what's behind it, more or less," he explained as we stepped onto the flat granite surface on the other side. "This one is purple, well, because..." He held out his arm, and I gasped.

Aqua pools formed huge steps up and down the mountain, all surrounded by purple flowers in every shade and shape imaginable. Vines of wisteria grew up the rocky face of the mountain, sprouting directly out of cracks in the stone. The scent of lilac wafted over us from the bushes that clung to the outer edges of the pools, and bright purple Morning Glory vines crept along the ground beneath them. Steam rose from the water in lazy curves, giving the whole thing a misty appearance.

"This is one of Hestia's gardens, isn't it?"

Nate looked at me in surprise. "Yes, actually. How did you know that?"

I smiled, taking in the mountain view that acted as a backdrop for the garden before answering.

"When she came to me in that dream, we were in an ambrosia garden. She told me how much she loved them. This one has that same kind of beauty."

"Well, I'm glad you like it." He took my hand, and we climbed gingerly up the rough stone steps that led to the top.

As soon as we reached the highest pool, he kicked off his shoes and pulled his shirt over his head. Without any warning, he jumped into the pool, splashing hot water over my shoes and onto my legs.

When he resurfaced, the constant look of seriousness he always seemed to wear had washed away. Instead, he was grinning in a way that made him look like any other guy; happy, carefree, and able to have fun. His light brown hair was falling in his eyes, and I had the sudden urge to push it away.

As if reading my thoughts, he crooked a finger at me. "Come on."

I rubbed my hands up and down my arms, more in an attempt to calm myself down than warm up.

"Don't make me come up there," he warned. "You'll end up in here fully clothed."

"Okay, okay, I'm coming!" I held up my hands in a "please don't" gesture and started pulling off my black flats.

I wiggled out of my jeans but hesitated before taking off my shirt.

It was stupid. Growing up at the lake, I'd practically lived in bathing suits every summer, but right now, my shirt was long enough that it covered my whole torso and butt. Once I took it off, well, there'd be very little left to the imagination.

Screw it.

I pulled the shirt over my head and walked quickly to the edge of the pool. I sat down and let my legs dangle in the water, enjoying the feel of hot water as it clashed with the chilly air.

Nate was treading water in front of me, shaking his head.

"I know you're freezing up there."

I scowled at him and tried to ignore the goosebumps that had spread across my skin.

"Tessa..."

"Just give me a sec! It takes me a while to ease myself into hot tubs."

He swam closer and rested his hands on either side of my thighs.

"I don't need to read your mind to know you're full of it." He ran his hands slowly up my legs. "Now come on."

Before I could react to the feel of his hands on my legs, he'd grabbed me around the waist and pulled me in.

I went in so fast that my feet scraped against the bottom, nearly ten feet down. I broke through the surface sputtering.

"Asshole!" I splashed water in his face. "That was so not necessary!"

I brushed the hair that had escaped my braid behind my ears.

"You're in now, aren't you?" He drifted closer and rested his hands on my hips. "Isn't this better than sitting up there in the cold?"

"I suppose," I grumbled. We floated toward the edge, coming to rest on a natural underwater shelf formation that jutted out of the wall. I looked around, taking it all in.

"So, this is another of your favorite places? I can see why."

He gave me a soft smile as he floated in the warm water in front of me. "Did you have any place like this growing up?"

"Not really. There were some caves down on the beach that I liked to explore, and the lake at night was amazing. But no, nothing like this." I met his eyes. "Thank you for sharing it with me."

He pushed a piece of hair off my forehead. "You're welcome. It's been a long time since I've wanted to share anything with anyone."

"Why is that?"

He shrugged and looked out over the edge of the mountain. "I think I just needed to have something to myself. Plenty of others know about this place, but it's nice when I can come here alone."

I arched a brow. "And yet here I am."

"There you are." He gave me a wicked grin, then ducked under the rippling water.

I yelped as I felt a sharp pull on my legs as he pulled me under with him. He propelled us through the water until we were in a spot where the mountain curved in slightly, creating a shady space of water that was a bit less hot than the rest.

"You could've warned me, you know," I said, splashing water in his face.

The water was shallower here, so with his tall frame, he was able to stand without issue. He moved closer, then slid his hands down my sides and onto my hips, just brushing the waistband of my bikini bottoms.

"Sorry," he said. He gave me a wolfish grin as he gently pushed me back toward the rock wall.

I wrapped my arms around his neck and lightly ran my fingers through his hair.

"You know, I kind of like this other side of you."

He cocked his head in question. "What do you mean?"

"You're just always so serious. I like seeing you having fun. Seeing you smile."

"My *gorgeous* smile?" His tone was teasing, but I couldn't help but blush.

"You weren't supposed to hear that."

"All the more reason to figure out how to get your mind in check, right?"

I held up a finger. "Uh uh, no way. We are not talking about anything work related."

"No?" He raised his eyebrows and gave me a slow smile. "What should we talk about, then?"

"I don't know, you tell me." I bit my lower lip and arched a brow.

Bracing one hand against the stone, he ran his lips along my jaw, then down my shoulder and back up to my ear.

"Tessa?"

"Hmm?" My eyes were closed, and I was shamelessly loving the feel of him touching my body. My fingers dug into his strong shoulders, pulling him even closer.

"I'm going to kiss you now," he whispered, the rough tone of his voice turning my legs to jelly.

His lips traced a path down to my mouth, where he gently, almost hesitantly, touched his lips to mine. My arms tightened around his neck as his hand splayed against my back. Slowly, he pushed me back against the wall and deepened the kiss.

I sighed against his mouth, then brought my legs up to wrap around his waist, pulling him closer. His hand ran up the back of my thigh as he laid soft kisses down the sensitive skin of my throat. I ran my fingers through his hair and pulled his mouth back to mine, desperate for him to keep kissing me.

SPLASH! SPLASH!

"What the—" I jerked back, breathless, and craned my neck, trying to see who'd so rudely interrupted us.

"Oh, for fuck's sake," Nate groaned, his breathing heavy as he dropped his head to my shoulder.

I barely had time to be shocked at his use of profanity when someone spoke.

"You didn't think we'd let you come on a date and not harass you about it, did you?" The voice was male, almost musical, and very familiar.

"I'm so sorry about this," Nate whispered, his eyes full of regret. He took a few seconds to collect himself, then pulled me back out into the sun. The sudden brightness had me holding a hand over my eyes.

"Honestly, yes, I *was* hoping you'd refrain from that," Nate said, irritation lacing his tone.

"Why would you think—Oh, hey!"

As soon as I saw our guests, I realized where I'd heard the first voice before. It belonged to Hermes who was floating not ten feet away, with Dionysus at his side. Both wore mischievous grins.

Frowning, I drifted closer to Nate. He wrapped an arm around my waist and pulled me toward him.

'It's fine, they're friends,' he reassured me.

'They're Elders, and I'm in a bikini. I don't care if they're your friends.'

'It's a very nice bikini.'

'You're so very funny.'

Dionysus cast Hermes, whose brown eyes were laughing, a sideward glance. "Hermes, I think we're scaring her."

Hermes gave me a crooked grin. "Are we scaring you, doll?"

I forced a smile onto my face and tried to remember the ease with which I'd handled Hermes on my first day in Olympia. "Nope."

Dionysus sighed, his hazel eyes sparkling. "That's a yes. We're sorry." A disarming smile spread across his youthful face. "It's just been so long since Nathaniel's had a girlfriend—"

"So you felt the need to interrupt?" Nate laughed, and pulled me in front of him, wrapping his other arm around my waist.

Hermes grinned, his white teeth flashing against his golden skin as he eyed me curiously.

"We just wanted to get to know her, Nathaniel, that's all. You've been keeping her a secret," he chastised.

Nate's thumbs brushed lightly against my hip bones, sending tingles down my legs.

'You should probably stop doing that.'

His hands stilled as he saw what was going through my mind.

'Sorry.' He kissed my temple and I could feel his lips curving into a smile. *'Try to put your walls up, unless you want to get an earful from those two.'*

Frowning, I tried to do as he instructed, picturing a secure wall surrounding my mind. Hopefully, it worked.

"Yeah," Dionysus said indignantly. "Since when do we keep secrets from our best friends?"

I felt my eyes widen. I tilted my head back and glared at Nate.

'Best friends?'

He let out an exasperated sigh. "Fine. Tessa, obviously you know

Dionysus and Hermes. They're insufferable and intrusive and they're *leaving*."

Dionysus snickered. "No way. We want to get to know this girl you've been mooning over."

I couldn't help but smile.

'You've been mooning over me?'

He tightened his arms around my waist.

'Possibly.'

"Oh, look at that smile!" Hermes crowed. "Nathaniel, I think she's absolutely smitten!"

"So, Tessa." Dionysus swam forward and grabbed my hand. "Come talk to us."

He gave a gentle tug, and with a sigh, Nathaniel let me go.

Dionysus put his hands on my waist and guided me over to the shelf that jutted out from the wall and sat me down. He swam back a few feet and began to tread water in front of me. Hermes came to join him, and Nate sat beside me, tilting his head back to rest against the pool's edge and closing his eyes. His hand found mine underwater.

Dionysus looked at me expectantly. "Tell us about yourself."

A smile pulled up the corners of my mouth. "What would you like to know?"

A slow smile spread across Hermes' face.

Before he could voice his question, Nate cut him off. "Careful, Hermes," he warned, not opening his eyes.

Hermes laughed. "You spoil all my fun."

I blinked.

'What was he going to say?'

'Something far too inappropriate for someone who barely knows you.'

"Alright, I'll go," Dionysus said. He narrowed his eyes at me, and despite his boyish looks, he managed to achieve a somewhat threatening expression. "What are your intentions with our Nathaniel?"

I cocked my head to the side. "Intentions?"

"She has no intentions, you moron," Nate muttered.

"Is Nathaniel your first boyfriend?" Hermes asked.

"I don't think—" I cut myself off, not wanting to voice what I thought our relationship status was. "No."

Dionysus heaved an exaggerated sigh of relief.

"Well, that's good to hear. What did you like to do before you came to Olympia?"

I relaxed a bit, feeling a bit more at ease with the youngest of Zeus' sons. They didn't seem nearly as intimidating as the other Elders.

"Well, I grew up in a lake town, so I spent a lot of time at the beach in the summer. Most of my free time outside of school was focused on training, though."

"No hobbies?"

"Not really."

"That doesn't sound very fun," Dionysus commented. "Aren't humans supposed to be fun?"

I laughed. "I guess, but when your guardians drag you out of bed every day at five am for weapons training and push two more hours of training and lessons after school, it's easy to be too tired to want to do much else."

"Weapons training, huh?" Dionysus' mouth curved into a smile as he drifted a little closer. "What's your weapon of choice?"

"The staff," I responded without hesitation. "I started training with it when I was ten, and it's always been my favorite."

"Interesting." He nodded as he looked out over the valley. "That's an old weapon. What do you find so enjoyable about it? I would've expected some kind of projectile."

I considered his question for a moment. "I don't know. I mean, I've trained with projectiles, but—" I hesitated.

Dionysus cocked a brow. "But...?"

Nate and Hermes were watching me curiously.

"There's just...something satisfying about taking down an opponent up close and with such a rudimentary weapon. I mean, if you've got the weapons to take someone out from a distance, that's ideal, but I like the challenge of taking them on up close."

A grin broke across Dionysus' face. He wagged a finger toward me and looked at Nathaniel.

"I like her, Nathaniel. I like the way she thinks. I think we should keep her."

"I'm so glad you approve," Nate muttered dryly. He slid an arm around my waist and pulled me closer, and it was clear in that gesture that he was happy his friends seemed to like me.

'Of course they do.'

I smiled at the reassurance.

"Oh, see that's not fair!" Hermes pointed a long, slender finger toward us. "No internal conversations! It's rude!"

The corner of Nate's mouth curved up in a smile. "Sort of like intruding on someone's date to satisfy your own curiosity?"

"We're Elders, we're allowed," Hermes said, laughing.

"I'm quite certain that would be considered an abuse of power," Nate pointed out.

Dionysus waved a hand dismissively. "So Tessa, let me ask you this." His eyes darted to Nate, then Hermes, grinning wickedly. "Do you have any friends?"

Nate shot a glare in his direction. "Not for you! I won't have you corrupting her friends—"

"Corrupting!" Dionysus interrupted, laughing. "I'm not trying to corrupt anyone! I just think it would be fun to...triple date."

Hermes smacked the back of his head. "You're horribly unconvincing, brother." He winked at me. "He absolutely wants to corrupt your friends."

I looked at Nate. *'To be fair, I don't know that Mary would be opposed—'*

'Trust me, the last thing we need is for Mary and Dionysus to get together, in any way.'

"I see that look!" Dionysus narrowed his eyes. "What are you telling him, Tessa?"

I shook my head, holding back a laugh.

"So back to your friends..." Dionysus trailed off, a suggestive smile on his face.

I shrugged apologetically. "None that I can think of. Sorry."

"Why don't I believe you?"

"She's clearly lying," Hermes observed. "She really does think you're going to corrupt them."

"Because you absolutely will," Nate said, laughing.

"Alright, that's it!"

I yelped as Dionysus shot toward Nate, grabbing him in a head-lock and pulling him under. The two surfaced a few feet away, laughing.

"You're just mad because it's true," Nate said, somehow managing to dodge another attack. He got his arm around Dionysus' neck and pushed him under the water. The god resurfaced and spit a stream of water right into Nate's face, causing a whole new attack.

Hermes swam up beside me and tsked.

"Can you believe these two? You'd think they were raised by heathens."

I shook my head, amazed at the childish show that was being put on in front of me.

"Are they always like this?"

Hermes stretched out an arm along the wall behind me and watched as the other two continued to try to drown one another.

"Ah, the things our Nathaniel has yet to tell you," he murmured.

I pursed my lips as I eyed Nate and Dionysus, still fighting in the water.

"Do I even want to know?"

He chuckled and leaned his head back to rest on the wall.

"I'm sure we'll find out soon enough."

32

TESSA

Dionysus and Hermes stuck around for the rest of the afternoon, and I had to admit, they were a lot of fun. I'd expected all the Elders to be stiff and formal when I first came to Olympus, but nothing about them gave off an "I'm better than you" vibe.

"So why are they so laid back?" I asked Nate as I tugged my jeans up over my bathing suit.

Nate pulled his shirt over his head before answering.

"They're younger, and they've had a pretty easy go of it since they weren't around for the war. Hermes has his communication duties, but nothing overly complex is required of him. Dionysus is just... Dionysus. He's never taken anything too seriously. He's mainly an Elder in name only."

"Huh. Must be nice."

"I'm kind of glad you got to meet them."

"Oh yeah? Why's that?" I started taking the braid out of my hair and combing through the soaking wet locks.

"They're my oldest friends. I want you to know them."

"So let me ask you a question. Do you have any friends who aren't gods or centaurs?"

"Not really," he admitted as he started leading me back down toward the portal. "Chiron was my mentor long before he was my friend, and as for the other two, well, they're not much older than me. We've been friends pretty much forever."

"Not that much older than you?" I put my hands on my hips. "How much are we talking here?"

"Hermes, about four hundred years, Dionysus, I think three hundred or so?"

"Uh huh. So you haven't made any new friends in three millennia?"

"Acquaintances, sure, but I never felt like I needed more, if that makes sense."

I considered my own group of friends before responding.

"Yeah, I guess. I mean, it's always been me, Mare, and Eric. Josh and Leila were our closest human friends, although we only knew them for a few years, and Mary and I almost always had boyfriends. We knew there was probably an expiration date on those relationships, though."

We reached the portal door, and before opening it, he turned to face me, smiling as his hands came to rest on my hips.

I brought my arms up to circle his waist and narrowed my eyes.

"What is it?" he asked.

"I asked Hermes if you guys were always so crazy together. He said something about 'the things our Nathaniel has yet to tell' me."

"Did he?" He leaned down to kiss my exposed shoulder. "I might have to have a talk with him."

"Uh huh. Care to enlighten me?"

He ran a hand up my neck and into my hair, then gave a gentle tug, exposing the other side of my neck.

"Eventually," he murmured, finding a particularly sensitive spot under my ear.

"I never would've pegged you for a hair puller," I said, closing my eyes as his kisses sent heat coursing through me.

"No?" His breath tickled my skin when he spoke. "What did you peg me for?"

"Someone who clearly has devious ways of avoiding answering questions."

Laughing, he kissed my neck one more time, then pulled back so he could look at me.

"So tell me something. What's the thing you miss most about living on Earth? Aside from your guardians, of course."

I tapped my chin as I pondered his question. There were so many things in the human world that I'd taken for granted while I was there. Shopping malls, cell phones, cars, beach days, television.

"Oh!" I laughed. "I miss binge watching TV shows."

He raised his eyebrows. "Really? Of all the things you miss, you pick television?"

"If you've ever watched seven seasons of *Game of Thrones* in one month, you'd understand."

"I think that might be up there with coffee on the list of things I will never understand." He kissed my forehead and took my hand. "Let's get you home."

As soon as we stepped through the portal into Olympia, he pulled me back toward him. He intertwined the fingers of one hand with mine, then put a finger under my chin and tilted my face toward his. I smiled as he pressed his lips to mine, bringing my free arm up to wrap around his neck.

We broke apart at the sound of a loud whistle coming from just up the street.

"Yeah, Tess! You get it, girl!"

I let out an annoyed groan, then glanced over my shoulder to see Mary and Yana walking down the street toward us, each carrying paper coffee cups.

Nate chuckled as the two crossed the street and came toward us.

"I promise next time we'll go someplace where we won't keep getting interrupted," he whispered.

I smiled, feeling my heart stutter at the potential that those words held.

He laughed softly and pressed a kiss to my shoulder. "Relax,

Tessa. I just meant today would've been much more enjoyable if you hadn't been annoyed by my friends or catcalled by yours."

I relaxed into his side, then arched a brow as the girls walked up.

"Was that really necessary?"

Mary took a large gulp of her coffee. "Absolutely. You guys wanna make out in the middle of the street, you better be prepared for people to notice."

Yana pressed her lips together, the corners of her mouth turning up. "So I will take it you two had fun, then?"

Mary gestured toward me with her cup. "Of course they did. Don't you see how red her lips are?"

Nate let out a laugh. "On that note, I'll leave you ladies to do whatever it is you do. I'll see you all in the morning."

He gave me a quick peck on the forehead, then disappeared through a dark mahogany door.

"Tell us everything," Mary demanded. "Absolutely all of it."

I narrowed my eyes. "Give me your coffee and maybe I will."

Mary looked pained for a moment before handing over her steaming cup.

I took a sip, closing my eyes as the balance of sweet and bitter danced over my tongue. "Oh, my gods, this is amazing."

"I know," Mary deadpanned, crossing her arms across her chest. "Now spill. He looked all happy and not like he has a massive stick up his ass anymore, so what'd you do?"

I couldn't help but laugh at her observation. "Come on, let's go back to our room. I need to change out of this bathing suit."

Yana raised her eyebrows in shock. "Oh, so you mean you actually wore it in the water?"

I smacked her on the shoulder. "Of course I did!"

She snickered. "Well, you never know."

"Whatever. I need a shower and sweatpants. Then we'll talk."

"So hold up." Mary held up her hand. "You're telling me *Dionysus* and *Hermes* crashed your date?"

I tossed back the last of my coffee, which had grown cold, and nodded.

"Mare, it was so freaking weird. They're Nate's best friends. Can you believe that?"

"And he never mentioned this to you before today?" Yana was sitting on her bed, her face scrunched in confusion. "How does something like this not come up in conversation?"

"I don't know. I guess I should've assumed he and Hermes were close, considering how Hermes was acting the day we got here."

I pursed my lips, taking in the fascination that was clear in Mary's wide hazel eyes. "You know, Dionysus was asking if I had any friends."

Yana choked on a sip of her coffee. "Are you serious?" she asked between coughs.

"Shut up." Mary gave me a dubious look. "Seriously? Shut up."

I raised my eyebrows and smiled. "Nate didn't want me to tell you. He thinks you're going to get corrupted."

"Um, have you seen how hot Dionysus is? I may be willing to be corrupted." A grin spread across her face, but then she shook her head. "No. No way. I may be crazy but I'm not that crazy."

Yana raised her hand. "I may be."

I laughed and tossed a pillow at her. "You two are the worst."

Mary laid on her stomach and propped her chin in her hands. "Is he the best kisser ever? Now that I've seen him smiling and not all serious, he looks like he'd be a good kisser."

I nodded, unable to help the smile that took over my face. "Seriously the best." I bit my lip, smiling.

"So how long until you let him do more than just kiss you?" Mary grinned suggestively.

I blew out a breath. I leaned back against the wall and clutched a pillow to my chest. "I don't know. I mean, Caleb was the only guy I slept with before this, and we only slept together like, three times before I broke up with him. Nate's been around forever. He doesn't seem like a player or anything, but I know he's had other relationships."

"I saw the way he was looking at you," Yana said. "It does not seem like you would need to be nervous with him."

Mary nodded emphatically. "I agree. I mean yeah, he's more experienced, but is that really a bad thing? At least he won't be fumbling in the dark, completely clueless."

"Exactly," Yana said.

I shifted so I was facing her better. "Did you have a boyfriend back in Romania?"

She nodded and blew out a breath. "Dorin. We were together for about a year or so. My guardians did not care for him because he was a human, so we had to keep our relationship a secret for the most part. We broke up a few months before I left for Olympus."

Mary smiled sympathetically. "Ugh, that must've been tough."

"Eh, yes, but it is life." She adjusted herself so she was sitting cross legged on her bed and looked at Mary expectantly. "What about you? Did you have many boyfriends?"

A look of disgust crossed Mary's face. "We don't need to go there," she muttered.

"Oh, this sounds interesting." Yana smiled excitedly. "Tell me."

Mary let out a resigned sigh. "Fine. I dated some guys that were *okay*, but my first was this guy Mike Stevenson that we went to school with." She shivered in disgust. "Turned out to be a total scumbag, so I kind of just pretend he didn't happen."

Yana laughed. "What was so bad about him?"

Mary wrinkled her nose as she recalled her brief relationship with one of our human friends during junior year.

"He just turned out to be a douche. After I broke up with him, he spread all these nasty rumors about how I slept around with half the junior class." She scratched her head, then let her hand drop to her lap. "You'd think it wouldn't have bothered me, you know? We were less than a year from our transformation, so it's not like I'd be dealing with him forever. He just sucked."

"That is unfortunate, I am sorry to hear he did that to you."

"Yeah, it's water under the bridge or whatever. After that, I dated some other guys, but I never slept with anyone else."

Yana nodded. "I cannot say I blame you."

We sat in silence for a few moments. Finally, Mary rubbed her hands together and a look of excitement coated her features.

"So, weapons tomorrow! Who's ready?"

I grinned. "Me!"

I hadn't had a proper session since my last one with John, nearly two weeks ago, and I didn't realize how much I'd been itching to have a weapon in my hands.

Yana laughed. "For some reason, I am surprised that you are so eager for this aspect. You don't strike me as the type to enjoy close combat."

"I can't help it. It was my favorite part of training growing up."

"Tessa kicks ass with a staff," Mary said. "You should see her."

Yana smiled. "What do you like most, Mary?"

"The bow," she responded. "I joined the archery team freshman year of high school and fell in love."

Yana gave a knowing smile. "Ah, yes, that was always my favorite, as well. But what about for close combat?"

"Trench knife. Two weapons in one. You?"

Yana grinned. "I also like knives, although I am not too particular."

"So what do you guys think about having to train with the Titans tomorrow?" I looked toward Mary apprehensively.

"I don't know," she admitted. "I guess you can't deny their expertise, right?"

"Yeah, I'm actually kind of interested to see what they do."

"I am curious what Epimetheus will have to contribute," Yana said. "Prometheus is the soldier of the two. Epimetheus was not known for much."

"Yeah, I don't know," I responded. "He's so quiet."

A person only had to look at Prometheus' hulking form and intense expression to know he would be a formidable opponent. I'd only seen Epimetheus twice, but both times he'd hung back in his brother's shadow, silent and expressionless.

I yawned. "I think I need a nap."

"Yeah, all that making out will do that to you," Mary teased.

"Shut up. You guys probably slept all damn day."

"Whatever. It's six o'clock," Mary pointed out. "If you take a nap now, you'll be up all night."

"Nah, doubtful," I replied, crawling under the covers and nudging her away with my foot. "I'll probably sleep straight through."

"Well, you enjoy your nap." Mary stood, then pulled Yana to her feet, the latter groaning in protest. "We're gonna go get some food."

After they left, I brushed my teeth and did my normal bedtime routine, knowing I'd likely be out for the night at this point.

I laid in bed for a while, tossing and turning as I tried to shut my mind off. It had been an amazing day, and I couldn't get the feel of Nate's lips out of my head.

Smiling, I called out to him mentally.

'You there?'

'I am. Is everything okay?'

'Yup. Can't sleep. I just wanted to say thank you for today. I had a lot of fun.'

'I did, too.'

There was a pause.

'Would you like some company?'

I grinned at his teasing tone, half tempted to say yes.

'No, I'm beat. Raincheck?'

'I think that can be arranged. Goodnight, Tessa.'

'Goodnight, Nate.'

Minutes later, I was out cold.

I RAISED *one end of the staff up to meet my opponent's attack, then used the other end to slap down his attempt to change direction. The wooden*

weapons crashed against each other as I slowly beat him back toward the rock wall that rose up behind him.

Finally, I succeeded in disarming him, pinning him to the wall with one end of my weapon shoved against his sternum as his own weapon fell uselessly to the ground.

"I win." I grinned and took a step back, reaching down to grab his discarded weapon.

He laughed, then smoothed back his chin-length blond hair before taking the weapon from my outstretched hand. Throwing an arm around my shoulder, we began walking back toward the stone house that sat a few hundred yards away.

"You have improved quite a bit over the last few weeks. Mother would be proud."

"Maybe," I conceded. "She has been so unhappy recently. I do not think anything I could do would bring a smile to her face."

I frowned, noting his somber expression.

"What are you thinking? Your face looks far too serious," I asked.

He scratched his ear. "I worry for the others. And for you," he admitted. "I know he plans to come for you, to take you away."

"I can handle myself," I replied indignantly.

"You are a force to be reckoned with, there is no question, but it has become clear we have failed you over the years."

"It is not your fault—"

"It is, at least in part, and now I fear it is too late. He has vengeance on his mind. He is furious with me and will stop at nothing to hurt us. We have waited too long to prepare you for these things."

I stopped, turning to face my companion, and placed a hand on his cheek, just over the scar leftover from his most recent confrontation with a godsbane blade. It had been spelled to prevent wounds from fully healing, so his flawless face had become permanently marred, all because he'd tried to protect me.

"It will be alright," I promised.

A movement in my periphery had me looking toward the trees.

"Did you see that?" I looked back to my companion.

He glanced toward the dense forest and frowned. "No, there is nothing there. What was it?"

"I am not sure... I thought I saw someone. There was movement."

"I do not see anything. Come, we need to practice your powers. You have not been giving them enough attention."

I turned from the trees and arched a brow. "No?"

Resting my staff on my shoulder, I shot a bolt of lightning from my palm in the direction of a small tree. Instantly, it went up in flames. I followed it with a jet of water, dousing the fire and sending up a cloud of hot steam. Using a burst of wind, I blew the steam away.

"You have been getting outside help," he said, his tone disapproving.

I smirked. "Maybe I have. It does not matter; training is training, no matter who is teaching me, and my powers are sound. It is you I worry about."

He tilted his head to the side, his brow furrowed. "Why do you say that?"

I hesitated before voicing my concerns. "Because I know if something happens to me, you will leave. The others need you, and I cannot bear the thought of you abandoning them."

He gripped my shoulders and gazed at me intently. "That will not happen again, I promise you. I made a mistake before. I should not have chosen the path I did. I am here now, though, and I always will be."

I searched his eyes for any signs of uncertainty, but they were unwavering.

There was another movement in the trees, a quiet rustling sound. I looked around, searching for the source of the sound, but again, I saw nothing.

"But what if he comes for you first? I do not know that I can live in a world where you are not." Fear welled up inside of me as I imagined this man being erased from this world.

He gave me a soft smile, then hugged me fiercely, resting his chin against the top of my head. I felt tears slowly roll town my cheeks, soaking through his rough tan shirt.

"You do not need me to be with you in order to be great." He pulled back *and looked me in the eye. "You must never doubt yourself, Tessa. You will move mountains, whether I am at your side or not."*

"TESSA!"

I jerked awake at the sound of Yana's voice. She was kneeling next to me, shaking my arm. I squeezed my eyes shut, startled at the rapid change in scenery.

"Are you alright?" Yana's eyes were heavy with concern.

"Yeah." My voice came out raspy.

I leaned over to grab my bottle of water, but she was already handing it to me. I chugged down a third of the bottle before setting it back on the nightstand.

"Thanks." I tried to smile at her. "Sorry if I woke you."

"It is fine." She moved to sit on the bed next to me and put an arm around my shoulders. "I worry because this seems to be every night now."

I smiled ruefully. "I'd kind of hoped you didn't notice."

"I am woken to you thrashing about or whimpering, sometimes you seem to be crying. It is hard not to notice." She rubbed her hand up and down my back. "Have you talked to Mary? Or Nate?"

I shook my head. "I talked to Nate some." I started absently playing with the end of my ponytail.

"Have you let him look into your mind? He may be able to help."

I sighed, letting the lock drop back to my shoulder.

"No. And I know I probably should, but I'm terrified it's going to be like the first time he went in."

She gave me a sympathetic look. "I understand, but maybe it will not be so bad this time? They are memories of dreams, no?"

"Yeah. Vivid ones."

"Well then, it should not be any harder than reading your mind."

"Huh. That's actually a really good point. We talk mentally daily, so I guess it would be the same, right?"

"Yes, I would think so." She patted my shoulder and stood up. "Talk to him in the morning. You should not deal with this alone."

I smiled. "Thanks, roomie."

"Of course. Now go back to sleep. It's two in the morning."

33

NATHANIEL

Chiron was seated on the sofa when I got up the next morning, waiting for me. As he watched me walk into the living room, a wide grin spread across his face.

"So, how was it?"

"How was what?"

He arched a brow. "Are you going to tell me you weren't with Tessa all day yesterday?"

I ran a hand through my hair. "I was, but—"

He smirked and wagged a finger at me. "You're restless about a girl, Nathaniel. I haven't seen that in eons."

I sat down on the sofa and leaned back.

"I don't think it's restlessness, really. It's just...unfamiliar."

"I suppose that makes sense. Did you both enjoy yourselves?"

"You mean before or after Dionysus and Hermes decided to show up?"

Chiron fell into a fit of laughter. "Why does that not surprise me?" He wiped at the corners of his eyes. "I'm sure they terrified that poor girl."

"She did surprisingly well, considering."

"And the rest...?"

A small smile pulled at the corners of my mouth. "The rest was... good."

He arched a brow. "Just *good*?"

I stared at him in wonder, shaking my head. "You know, I expected Tessa's friends to have their heads in the gutter, but not you."

"What can I say? It's been too long since I've been able to harangue you about a woman. I like what she does for you."

I tilted my head to the side. "In what way?"

"You've been happier lately, lighter. The moment I saw her approach you after she stepped through the portal on her first day, I knew she would be something special."

I considered his words, seeing the truth in them. The happiness I'd felt during my day with Tessa was something I hadn't experienced in a long time.

"She does make me happy," I murmured.

He raised his bushy brows. "You haven't been fully forthcoming with her, have you?"

"No, I haven't."

Chiron gave me a disapproving look but knew better than to voice his thoughts.

"Alright then." He patted me on the shoulder. "Now, on to the reason I'm here. I took a trip to the library archives to try to find some information on Mimics. I found mention of one, but only in passing. If any other records exist, they're either missing or long destroyed. Nothing seems to have been recorded about him or her aside from their existence, so for all I know, they may not even have been Ischyra. Possibly a demigod or even a god. I think we may be at a dead end until we speak with Zeus."

He pursed his lips and raised his eyebrows. "Which we'll need to do soon."

"I guess we will," I said, sighing. I wasn't looking forward to bringing this to him, but it needed to be done.

"What were your plans for today?" he asked.

"We'll bring Genevieve back out once Tessa is done weapons training."

Chiron eyed me up and down. "You need to be careful, Nathaniel. There's an excellent chance you'll be called out on favoritism if you begin treating her as anything other than a recruit in public. Have Gen pull her aside and meet us out front."

"I know. To be honest, I don't know that she would stand for me to treat her any differently. She wants to succeed."

"That's good to hear." He cocked his head to the side. "Is something else bothering you?"

I tapped my finger on my elbow, debating whether I should tell him about her dreams. Despite her ability to brush the last one off, something about what she'd described hadn't been sitting right with me.

"Nathaniel?"

I blew out a breath.

"She's been having dreams... nightmares, really, and I'm concerned they may have something to do with her powers."

"What are they about?"

I launched into an explanation of what she'd been seeing, what I'd experienced with her prior to her transformation, what I'd seen while awakening her powers, and the more vivid dreams she'd been having for the last week.

When I was done, Chiron was silent, his lips pursed.

"This man that she was sparring with. You said they were using staffs?"

"Yes. That also happens to be her favorite weapon, so she tends to attribute that aspect of her dreams to real life."

He nodded slowly. "And what did he look like?"

"She said he had blond hair to about here—" I tapped the middle of my neck "—green eyes, and tall, about a head above her."

"And could she tell where they were?"

"A clearing in the woods somewhere."

"Did he have a scar, just here?" He brushed a finger across his right cheek.

"Yes, she said his face was scarred." I leaned forward, my brow creased in confusion. "What is it?"

He shook his head, looking bewildered, then laughed.

"Nathaniel, if I didn't know any better, I'd say your girl is dreaming about Atlas."

34

TESSA

"So do you think we'll get to spar with one of them?"

Mary was eyeing Prometheus and Epimetheus warily. We'd just finished our warm up—ten laps along with the fun new task of rolling small boulders around the track—and were walking into the arena. The Titans were standing in Chiron's normal spot on the sideline.

"Probably," I whispered as we headed to form lines with the rest of the recruits. "I mean they're here to train us, right?"

I took a quick look around the arena and didn't see Chiron or Nate anywhere.

"Recruits!"

All talking stopped and we stood at attention as Prometheus addressed us.

"I will keep this short," he began. "Epimetheus and I—" he gestured toward his twin, who was standing beside him, arms crossed across his chest and the picture of stoicism, "—have been asked by your trainers to assist in your hand-to-hand and weapons training. We believe you would benefit from having a variety of instructors for this task, as everyone has a different methodology. Today, we just want to see what you can do, just the basic skillset you've entered your immortal lives with."

He stepped aside and gestured toward three long tables behind him that were loaded with a variety of weapons.

"We'll start by splitting into pairs and working with your weapons of choice."

He turned to Epimetheus and whispered something. His twin shook his head but didn't speak. Prometheus stared at him for a moment, his lips pressed into a thin line, before addressing us again.

"I'll be putting you into random pairings. This may take a while as only one pair at a time will spar for now. We want to get a feel for your skill levels. When I call your names, find your partners and discuss which weapons you'll be using."

He consulted a piece of parchment in his hand, then began calling names. Once everyone was paired up, I found myself set to spar with Damien.

Lovely.

When I moved to stand next to him, he arched an eyebrow cockily.

"Hey, Damien."

"Tessa." He crossed his arms over his chest. "I hope you do not expect me to go easy on you just because you have become one of our instructor's pets."

I blinked at him, my mouth hanging open. "You're joking, right? I just walked up to you and that's what you say?"

He raised his eyebrows and crossed his arms over his chest. "Are you saying you are not in a relationship with one of our trainers?"

I laughed, trying to hide my annoyance that he'd picked up on my relationship with Nate when we'd only been on one real date.

"Even if I was, why would you think you'd have to go easy on me?"

He shook his head and gave me a patronizing smile. "You are very naïve, Tessa."

"And you clearly have no idea what you're talking about," I shot back. "I'm no one's pet."

"If you say so. What is your weapon of choice?"

"The staff," I snapped. "You?"

"Knives. I don't know how effective your staff will be against them, though."

I put my hands on my hips, ready to give him an earful, when Prometheus called the first pair to fight. Ignoring my infuriating partner, I faced the rest of the recruits. Those of us who weren't fighting had formed a large circle around the first pair to spar. Prometheus offered some general guidance before the match began but refrained from offering too many words of advice or encouragement until after the pair had finished their fight.

After about an hour, it became clear that most of the other recruits had received rigorous training prior to coming to Olympus. The speed with which some of them moved as they ducked blows and took each other down was impressive, to say the least.

Based on the way a few recruits were winded and taken down by basic moves, it was also obvious that some had not received the type of training they should have. The tense expression on Prometheus' face told me he noticed, too.

After watching ten pairs of recruits fight, Damien and I were finally called. He strode toward the weapons table and began looking over the options. He pushed the sleeves of his black training shirt up, then snagged two long-handled sparring knives. With a smirk, he walked toward the center of the circle.

I sighed, then scanned the crowd again. Still no sign of Nate or Chiron.

I looked over the weapons and saw two staffs resting at the end of the table, untouched. Both were made of smooth, dark-stained wood. I hefted one in my hands, testing the weight, noting its sturdy, balanced feel.

Giving it a twirl, I felt a sense of ease. John, Analise, and I had sparred with staffs many times, and as my skill improved, the exercise became a soothing one, the graceful flow of the weapon putting a calm, focused feeling in my mind.

Resting the wooden staff on my shoulder, I walked toward my

opponent, focused only on his cocky expression. One hand rested on his hip, his two daggers clenched in the other.

I had the sudden urge to break his nose.

As I approached, I couldn't help the smirk that came onto my face as I watched him tap the blades against his muscular thigh.

He'd have to try harder if he wanted to intimidate me.

As I stepped past Epimetheus, I saw his eyes flick to my face, then to my weapon. He uncrossed his arms and put his hands on his hips, a look of interest crossing his face.

Prometheus came to stand beside me.

"It's Tessa, right?"

I looked up at the massive Titan and nodded. His nearness set a feeling of unease in my stomach. The thought of demonstrating my skills in front of two of the old gods was taking a toll on my nerves.

His emerald eyes assessed me, then he jerked his chin toward the staff.

"That's a cumbersome weapon, not one I would've recommended for a fight like this."

I gave him a tight smile. "I'll manage."

He gave me a speculative look, then nodded. "Alright then, on you go."

I stepped slowly into the fighting circle. As I neared Damien, he straightened his back and let his hands hang loosely at his sides, a dagger in each.

"Begin."

The word was barely out of Prometheus' mouth before Damien launched himself at me. Adrenaline rushed through me, and I thrust one end of my weapon up, then the other, using the momentum to shove him back a few feet.

'You're going to have to fight dirty with this one.'

The sound of Nate's voice in my mind nearly broke my concentration, but I still managed to block the broad side of one of Damien's daggers as he brought it down toward my head.

Nate was right. Damien seemed intent on going all-out with this fight, so I had to pull out all the stops.

'Nice of you to show up. Now keep quiet.'

The fight with Damien went on for what seemed like hours, although it didn't take long before the familiar feeling of contentment swam through me, putting me at ease with my abilities. He was relentless, raining blows down as though I was an enemy and not his equal. Despite the flexibility and relative dullness of the blades, he hit me with enough force to break the skin on more than one occasion on my neck, cheek, and arms. I mentally cursed myself for rolling up my sleeves after our warmup.

I tried to maintain my composure and use the weapon the way I was taught, but he was making it difficult. My power stirred, itching to come out and fight.

I flipped the staff, holding it like a baseball bat and swung as hard as I could as Damien sent another dagger toward my chest. There was a loud CRACK as it connected with his hand, and the knife went flying, the momentum nearly sending him to the ground. I kicked his knees out and landed a hard blow on his chin as he went down, splitting the skin wide open.

He collapsed to the ground, blood dripping from his chin, and glared up at me. Flipping to his feet, he slashed toward me with his remaining dagger, but swung wide, missing my side by inches.

I smirked, then took a few steps backward, daring him to follow.

"Come on, Damien, I thought you weren't gonna take it easy on me."

He snarled with fury as he lunged toward me. I gripped my staff and swung hard toward his shoulder. He reached up with his free hand to stop the staff's momentum and used the other to push my weapon back toward me, slamming it into my chest.

I hissed and stumbled back a few feet. I barely had time to recover when he jumped at me. Ducking, I thrust the staff in the air and slammed it into his hip, sending him twisting to the ground. As he fell, he lost his grip on his remaining dagger and it fell to the sand.

I jumped up and pressed the end of the staff onto his spine, then picked up the dagger that lay beside him. He struggled to his knees, so I sent a swift kick to his torso, instantly knocking the breath out of him.

Tossing my staff aside, I planted one foot on either side of him. I grabbed his hair and yanked his head back, then pressed the point of his own weapon to his throat.

"I win."

He grunted, then slowly lifted his hands, signaling his defeat.

I tossed the dagger toward the edge of the circle, then stepped away, allowing him to stand.

Red faced and glaring, he jumped to his feet and faced me.

I arched a brow. "You want to go again or something? I'm game if you are."

His blue eyes narrowed, but I saw the corner of his mouth twitch slightly.

"No. It was a good match," he conceded.

"Great job, both of you," Prometheus said as he walked toward us. He handed Damien his other dagger which had skated off into the crowd when I had hit it out of his hand.

"Not to worry, Damien," Prometheus offered. "You can't win them all, right?"

Damien took the dagger and gave a curt nod, then stalked off to deposit his weapons back on the table.

Prometheus looked down at me, appraising. "You handle yourself well. I haven't seen anyone maneuver a staff like that in quite some time."

I grinned, still out of breath, then rested the staff on my shoulder and scraped the dried blood off of my cheek with my sleeve, the only remnant of the knife cuts that had healed almost immediately. "Thank you. My guardians were great teachers."

Prometheus glanced back toward Epimetheus, who was eyeing us warily.

"I may have to pit you against my brother one of these days," he whispered conspiratorially. "The staff has long been his favorite, and it's been quite some time since he's had a partner."

My eyes widened. "Uh—I'm sorry, what?"

He laughed and patted my shoulder. "Not to worry, it won't be until after a bit more training. You're good, but not quite that good."

I felt a slight flush come across my face, even though I had no logical reason to be embarrassed. "Sounds good."

His eyes drifted behind me and lit up. "Ah, Nathaniel, there you are!"

I turned around and saw Nate walking toward us.

"Good morning, Prometheus. How did the recruits do?"

"Good, so far. This one did wonderfully."

Nate smiled down at me. "That doesn't surprise me. Thank you for taking over today. I'm going to have to steal Tessa for a bit if you don't mind."

"Not at all. We'll catch up later." He glanced down at me. "It was good to meet you, Tessa."

I smiled, still feeling a bit weird about getting praise from a Titan. "Thank you."

Nate put a hand on my arm and began leading me toward the exit.

"Come on, Chiron needs to speak with you."

"What's up? Where've you been?" I asked him.

"I'll explain outside."

As we exited the arena, his hand found mine. He led me across the lawn in front of the arena toward where Chiron was waiting.

"Morning, Tessa." Chiron greeted me with a smile, his long, brown tail twitching. His eyes moved to Nate and he frowned.

I looked up at Nate and saw him give a quick shake of his head. I glanced between the two of them uneasily.

"What's going on?"

Nate ran a hand through his hair and blew out a breath. "I told Chiron about your dreams."

"What?" I tugged my hand away, then looked to Chiron and back at Nate. "Why would you do that without talking to me first?"

"I know, I'm sorry, I just—you need to hear what he has to say."

I folded my arms across my chest and raised my eyebrows expectantly.

"I think—" Chiron cast a worried look at Nate, then looked back at me. "Listen, I may be able to help you, Tessa, if you'll let Nate transfer the memory of your more recent dreams to me."

I looked at him incredulously. "I'm sorry, what?"

"It would be similar to the way you speak mentally, only instead of pushing words, he would push your memories."

I looked up at Nate and frowned.

He gave me a reassuring smile and put a hand on my shoulder. "Tessa, he might know who the people are in your dreams."

That drew me up short. I stood stunned for a moment, then cleared my throat.

"Well, you probably should've led with that." I blew out a breath. "I was actually going to ask if you wouldn't mind taking a look. I had another one last night."

"What was it—never mind, just let me see."

Without waiting for my okay, Nate started sifting through the memories of my dreams.

When he pulled back, he was frowning.

"Is it alright if I show Chiron?"

I looked back and forth between the two of them. "What's going on?"

"Tessa, I'm sorry, but now is not the time for questions. You know you can trust us both. Please."

I arched a brow, surprised at his impatience. "Fine. I'm surprised you didn't do it already," I muttered. "What are you going to show him?"

"Last night's dream and the one you told me about last week, where the woman was killed."

"Okay."

As Nate transferred the memory, I watched Chiron's face transform from impassive to confused, and I started to feel a glimmer of hope. It was looking like I might actually get some kind of answers today.

I folded my arms across my chest and started tapping my fingers on my arm impatiently.

When they were done, Chiron looked stunned. His mouth hung open, and his eyes were wide as he stared at me.

"How long have you been having these dreams?"

"I—uh—two or three months? I didn't actually *see* anything until Nate poked around in my head that one day. They've been pretty vivid since my transformation."

Chiron shook his head and ran his hands through his hair, causing the bushy ponytail to loosen slightly. "Tessa—the man you're sparring with. You've never seen him before?"

"No, never. Why?"

"That man," he said, his voice strained as he looked down at me from his massive height. "That's Atlas."

I blinked.

"What?" I spun to face Nate. "What is he talking about?"

"Chiron, tell her the rest."

I rubbed my hand across my forehead and closed my eyes, then turned back to Chiron.

"What else is there?"

His dark brown eyes looked hesitant. "The dream you had last week, where you saw a woman die?"

"Uh huh," I replied weakly. "What about it?"

"Nathaniel was right when he told you that you were describing the destruction of a god." He took a deep breath before continuing. "That was Clymene."

My eyes widened and I felt my heart thump loudly in my ears.

"That was..." My stomach rolled as I remembered her screams of agony as her killer pulled her life force away.

"How is that possible?" I whispered hoarsely.

Chiron shook his head. "I don't know."

"So, then the man who killed her... was Iapetus?"

Nate squeezed my shoulders. "Yes. The other—"

"Cronus. That was Cronus, wasn't it?"

Chiron pressed his lips together and nodded. "Yes, it was."

"And the witch?"

"Hecate," Nate murmured, running a hand through his hair.

"I knew she looked familiar," I said, taking a seat on a small boulder. "She was at the transition ceremony, right? Isn't she kind of reclusive?"

"More or less," Nate responded. "I was actually surprised to see her there. She rarely leaves her home."

"So she probably wouldn't be too forthcoming if we asked her exactly why she was screaming 'Chaos take her'?" I faced Chiron. "Do you think she was talking about the Void or literal chaos?"

Chiron held up his hands and shook his head. "I don't know. It was hard to tell, but that sounded like a protection spell of some sort, so I would assume the Void. I'd have to take another look to be certain."

I scrubbed my hands across my face, trying to ground myself. "Then tell me this. In these dreams, who am *I*? I'm clearly not myself, but I'm someone. Did Atlas have a lover or something? He had a bunch of daughters, right?"

A frown flickered across Chiron's face. He opened and closed his mouth a few times, then cocked his head to the side. "Atlas had many lovers over the years, and a number of daughters, none of whom he was close with. I'm not sure who you would represent in this dream."

He rubbed at his temples. "I remember...something. I don't—Nathaniel, can you help me, please?"

I stared at him, confused, then looked up at Nate curiously.

"What's wrong with him?" I asked, watching Chiron alternate between rubbing his forehead and his eyes. "Why is he doing that?"

"He can't remember," Nate murmured. "Hold on."

Nate stepped away from me and up to Chiron, then placed a hand on his friend's cheek.

Chiron looked at him, his brown eyes grateful. "Thank you," he said. "Someone...I don't know why I can't remember."

After a few moments, Nate dropped his hand and frowned. Chiron slumped back against the boulder he'd been standing in front of. His tail twitched in an agitated motion as he pressed his fingers to his eyes.

Seeing both of them so confused was freaking me out. "What is it?"

Nate shook his head, looking perplexed. "I can't tell. Something is blocking the memory. It's as though someone has gone in and erased it. There are small traces, but nothing intelligible."

Chiron's memory had been erased. This was just getting better and better.

I put my hands on my hips. "I thought that thing wasn't possible for you guys?" I looked at Chiron. "You're the son of a Titan, for gods' sake."

Chiron's jaw clenched at the mention of his parentage, and I immediately felt bad. If Cronus was my father, I wouldn't really want it thrown in my face, either.

"I'm sorry," I mumbled. "I don't get it, though."

Chiron pulled his hands away from his face and looked at me, his eyes helpless. "I wish I had answers, but I don't."

"This doesn't make any sense," Nate said, running a hand through his hair.

"Perhaps she's a descendent? He had a lot of daughters, and a descendant wouldn't be a far reach," Chiron suggested.

"That would make the most sense. Or maybe it's prophetic?" Nate asked.

Chiron cocked his head to the side. "How so?"

"We've been hoping to get Atlas to return to Olympus for quite some time now. Perhaps locating this woman, assuming she's still alive, will help with that. It seems clear they were very close."

"Yes, that's certainly a possibility," Chiron responded.

"Still right here, guys," I said.

Nate placed a hand on the small of my back and looked at me apologetically. "I'm sorry. This is just very..."

"Weird? Confusing?" I raised my eyebrows. "Yeah. I know."

He pushed a stray piece of hair off my face and brushed his thumb along my jaw. "We'll figure it out, don't worry."

His eyes drifted toward Chiron, who was staring at him, arms crossed. Nate's expression hardened.

"Not now, Chiron," Nate warned.

"Don't you think—"

"Not *now*, Chiron!"

"Nathaniel, this isn't about you," Chiron said quietly.

"What?" I looked between the two of them warily. "What's going on now?"

Nate continued to glare at Chiron, his jaw clenched. He shook his head, so quickly I almost missed it.

"If you won't take her, I will, and you know better than to challenge that," Chiron said, his voice was harsh and full of warning.

"Nate!" I snapped. "What is going on?"

He didn't respond, but looked down at me, frowning. Finally, he looked back to Chiron and nodded. "I'll take her. Go back in and keep an eye on things."

Chiron hesitated. "Shouldn't I—"

"No, it's fine." Nate looked at me, his eyes weary. "It'll be fine."

He took my hand and led me toward the portal door that stood next to the arena entrance.

"Nate, where are we going?" I pulled on his hand, trying to get him to stop.

He stopped as we reached the door, his eyes looking pained.

Finally, he gripped the sides of my face and laid a fierce kiss on my lips.

When we pulled apart, his eyes were filled with fear.

"We're going to see my parents."

35

TESSA

A surge of panic coursed through me when we stepped through the portal. Nate had avoided talking about his parents that night at the zipline field, but I knew one of them had to have been an Elder. I hadn't pushed him to tell me, and suddenly I was regretting that decision.

We came out in front of a massive and opulent one-story white building. Vibrant flowers and evergreens adorned the property, leading up a gradual incline to the building's white stucco walls. Wide arched windows that stretched the height of the walls faced outward, the inner view obscured by heavy curtains.

"Where are we?" I hissed.

"My family home." He replied, leading me toward the wide marble steps that led to the large mahogany doors that graced the front of the building.

"Nate, stop!" I'd had enough. I yanked on his hand full force as he was in mid step, causing him to lose his balance and nearly fall.

"Tell me what's going on," I demanded. "Why are we here?"

He took a deep breath, then squeezed his eyes shut.

"Tessa, I should've told you sooner and I'm sorry. I'm not—"

"Nathaniel?" A smooth voice interrupted him.

When I looked in the direction it had come from, I felt my eyes widen.

Apollo stood at the top of the stairs, arms crossed over his chest, leaning against a white column. He was dressed in a stark white suit; double breasted with gold buttons, a small silver sun gleaming on his lapel. His head was cocked to the side and his eyes narrowed, accentuating the sharp contours of his cheekbones.

I looked up at Nate, suddenly terrified. Dionysus and Hermes had been easy to get along with once I'd gotten over the initial shock of their presence, but Apollo looked nothing short of terrifying.

I was surprised to see that Nate looked furious.

"Apollo," he said tersely. He continued making his way up the last few steps, and I followed slowly behind. When we reached him, Apollo looked at us appraisingly.

"I had hoped you'd come to me first, Nathaniel."

I hoped the shock I felt wasn't as clear on my face as it was in my mind.

'Apollo is your father? You couldn't have given me a heads up?'

He pressed his lips together and flicked his eyes down toward me.

'Shut your mind down now, Tessa.'

I blinked, surprised at the malice in his words.

"I did come to you, Apollo." He shook his head and laughed. "You were useless, in case you've forgotten."

Apollo bristled at the insult, and I sucked in a breath, waiting for him to rebuke Nathaniel in some way.

Instead, he shrugged.

"I can understand why you might see it that way, but I was only trying to help."

"Help with what? I told you what was going on with her and you refused to answer any of my questions. How in all the realms was that helpful?"

Oh. They were talking about me now.

Wait.

'You talked to him about me? Before you talked to me?'

He ignored me, which was incredibly unsettling.

"There is a time and place for information to be revealed, Nathaniel, and it is not when a girl has only just completed her transformation and has so little control over her powers."

"So you know what she is, then?"

Apollo scratched his jaw, then nodded. "Yes, I know what she is."

'I am so going to kick your ass for this!'

I could feel the desperation in my thoughts, but it seemed to have no effect on him.

Apollo glanced down at me, his cold gray eyes meeting mine. A small smile flashed across his lips.

"She's upset with you, Nathaniel. Are you sure you want to do this?"

"You haven't given me much of a choice," Nate responded. "Now get out of my way."

With that, he shoved past Apollo, causing the god to stumble back several steps.

As Nate pulled me the rest of the way up the steps, I stared back at Apollo, terrified at what he would do to Nate for pushing him. Father or not, he was still an Elder and that was miles beyond inappropriate.

Surprisingly, he just straightened his jacket and followed us inside.

"A word of advice, Tessa?"

I turned my head, surprised to hear him address me.

"I'd listen to Nathaniel. If you've got any control over those mental walls of yours, now would be the time to put them up."

Before I could respond, Nate pushed open the massive wooden doors onto a long, extravagant hallway. He walked quickly, causing my sneakers to squeak on the white and beige travertine floor. We were moving so fast, I was barely able to take in the appearance of the hall, aside from the dark paneled walls inlaid with gold designs. It looked like there were quite a number of corridors that branched off, but I couldn't make out where they led.

We had walked almost the entire length of the hall and were nearly at a set of massive dark wood doors when I finally spoke.

"Nate, please talk to me," I begged. "What's going on?"

"My father will be able to help," was his only response. His words were clipped, as though he didn't want to speak.

Confused, I looked at Apollo, who had fallen in step beside me, his white shoes clicking on the marble floor.

"But I thought—"

"Oh, I'm not his father, girl." He laughed. "I'm surprised he hasn't explained his parentage yet, seeing how close you two have grown." He looked at me appraisingly. "I must say, it has been nice to see Nathaniel so interested in someone other than himself for once."

Before I could respond, Nate dropped my hand and spun on Apollo, driving him back against a statue of a woman with a bird resting in her hand, causing her to wobble precariously on her base.

"Nate!" I yelped, startled by his sudden show of violence.

"If you are going to insist on being here, it's in your best interest to keep quiet. I've had enough of your bullshit," he growled.

Apollo pushed back, sending Nate stumbling to the center of the hall. I jumped out of the way just in time to avoid being knocked over.

Apollo stormed toward him and pushed his chest, causing Nate to fall back a few more steps, then jabbed a finger in his face. "It isn't my fault you've chosen to keep things from her. You've made your choices, Nathaniel, or have you forgotten? You're the one who chose your path, not me."

"Not you?" Nate laughed, slapping Apollo's hand away from his face. "Don't act as though you're better than me, you sanctimonious bastard."

Apollo let out a wicked laugh. "No, I don't think so. You don't get to call me names, *brother*."

I sucked in a breath.

Apollo's eyes slid to mine. "Tell me Tessa, has he told you what he saw in your mind the day of your transformation? Or has he kept that from you, as well?"

Nate's eyes darted to me. His mouth opened, but no words came out. He looked back to Apollo, fury clear on his face.

Stone-faced, Apollo glared back.

Silence hung over us.

"Brother?" I frowned at Nate.

"Half-brother, technically," Apollo answered, smirking.

Suddenly, the doors burst open, nearly knocking the three of us over, and a voice, loud as thunder, roared through the hallway.

"What is going on out here?"

Zeus had just joined us, and he looked furious.

He glared expectantly at both men.

Apollo adjusted his white coat and stood up straight, while Nate schooled the angry expression off his face.

"Why do I hear the two of you out here fighting like children?" Zeus' deep voice was down to a normal level but still held a menacing rumble. Up close, he looked larger than life.

He cast a cursory glance in my direction, before looking back at both men. "In front of company, no less?"

"Zeus is your *father*?" I hissed, forgetting for a moment where I was.

The ruler in question looked down at me, his blue eyes flashing with curiosity.

Frantically, I tried to figure out how to shore up my mental walls. I felt a little click and saw Nate's jaw clench. I frowned, and he gave me a small nod.

I crossed my fingers that meant they were secure.

He folded his arms and turned back to Nate and Apollo.

"Well? Will one of you please explain what all of this is about? What are you doing here, Nathaniel?"

Apollo was his brother.

I rubbed a hand on my forehead, suddenly feeling a bit lightheaded.

Nate was an original Ischyra, and that meant one of his parents had been an Elder. So this shouldn't come as that much of a surprise. There were only so many options, really, and everyone knew Zeus got around.

I mean, it would've been nice if he'd told me his father was the ruler of Olympus, but we had only known each other for two weeks. I suppose I could see the logic in keeping that to himself, at least at first.

"Nathaniel?" A clear, lovely voice drifted through the open doors of the room Zeus had just emerged from. "Sweetheart, is that you?"

Nate rubbed a hand over his eyes, looking defeated.

"Yes," Zeus responded, as a woman stepped into the hall. "And he's brought a guest."

Hera, beautiful with her smooth tanned skin, perfect smile, and flowing lavender gown, had come to join us. Her black hair tumbled down her back in soft waves, ending just above her waist.

"I guess there were a few other things he failed to mention, hmm?" Apollo murmured as he leaned against the wall and crossed his ankles. "Like who makes up the other fifty percent of his parentage."

Nate lunged toward him, but Zeus put his massive form between them, shoving him back several feet. "That's enough! Explain yourselves!"

I pressed my fingers over my eyes, not wanting to believe what was slowly becoming clear.

"What is going on?" Hera spoke again, her voice holding an edge of impatience. "Nathaniel? Who is this girl? Why have you brought a recruit into the palace?"

I dragged my hands from my eyes, my fingers coming to rest on my lips, and looked at the goddess who stood before me.

She stared at me, her midnight blue eyes dripping with curiosity, then looked up at Nate, her expression soft, almost...

Motherly.

No. No way.

Slowly, I took a step toward Nate, and he eyed me hesitantly.

He'd lied to me. He'd pursued me and he knew that I cared for him yet neglected to tell me one of the most important things about himself. Worse, if Apollo was to be trusted, he'd kept things he knew about me to himself, too. Big things.

Steeling myself, I let my fist fly, letting it connect hard with his face.

Startled, he fell back, knocking a gold cushioned chair several feet down the hall.

"A *god*?" Ignoring the sting in my fist, I pushed him against the far wall. "You're a fucking *god*, Nate?"

"Apollo, stop her!" Hera's voice was loaded with concern.

For her *son*.

"Tessa—"

I shoved him again, and he did nothing to stop my attack.

"You didn't think that was something I should know? That the things you saw in my head weren't things I should know?"

"Tessa, wait, I wanted to—"

"No, fuck you!" I felt tears streaming down my face as I lunged toward him again. A pair of strong, white coated arms wrapped around me, preventing another assault.

"Get off of her!" Nate pushed himself off the wall and stormed toward his brother, his face contorted in outrage.

Hera went after him, pushing him back toward the wall. "Steady, Nathaniel," she murmured.

Slowly, Zeus came to stand between us.

Apollo still had my arms pinned to my sides, and my breath started to come in short gasps as I realized the enormity of the situation. I tried struggling out of his grip, but he was far too strong.

"Easy, girl," Apollo whispered. "You've just attacked a god. You may want to settle yourself."

Despite his coldness, a warm feeling began to spread through me, and I felt my body relax against him.

I repeated his words to myself, *You've just attacked a god.*

The son of Zeus and Hera, no less.

I was lucky I hadn't been struck down by lighting already.

The five of us were silent. I stared at the wall as a mixture of shame, terror, and fury coursed through me.

Zeus folded his thick arms across his chest and glared at all of us in turn.

"I'd say it's time we had a family meeting."

36

NATHANIEL

Everything was going to shit.

I'd only just found Tessa and now, I was losing her.

Tessa avoided looking at me as we walked into the main living room of my parents' palace. My venomous brother kept a firm grip on her arm, and based on her stoic expression, he was using his healing powers to keep her calm.

'Stop glaring at me, Nathaniel. She's calm and not projecting. I won't let him get into her mind.'

I clenched my jaw and gave a small nod.

At least he was good for something.

I rubbed the spot where her fist had connected with jaw. If circumstances hadn't been so dire, I would've commended her for her right hook.

"Sit," Zeus commanded. With a snap, a bit of blue lighting shot from his fingers to the kindling in the hearth, setting it ablaze.

Hera took a seat on one of the blue Victorian sofas that sat in front of the fireplace and pulled me down to sit beside her.

Tessa's eyes met mine as Apollo led her to the sofa across from us, nudging her to sit down. She was trembling. Whether it was due to fury or fear, I didn't know, but I wanted to do was go to her. Comfort her.

'Her mind is fighting you off, Apollo. You need to maintain physical contact.'

As Apollo sat down beside her, it took all my strength not to strike him again as he kept his arm and leg pressed against hers.

He was helping her. I needed to let him help her.

Zeus took a seat in a chair facing the fireplace. "Now. What is this all about?"

For a moment, my oldest brother and I both sat silent, glaring at each other. Finally, he heaved a sigh, then spoke to our father.

"The girl is a Mimic. We should've told you sooner. I've warned Nathaniel away from developing a relationship with her because I think it will distract from her training." He flicked a gaze toward me then back at Zeus. "I'm sure you will agree that her training will be of the utmost importance."

I narrowed my eyes as I heard the lie flow from his mouth.

"That's shit and you know it," I spat.

He shrugged.

Zeus turned his eyes on me.

"A Mimic? Nathaniel, you knew about this?"

I rubbed a hand across my face, suddenly hesitant. This was part of the reason I'd brought Tessa here, after all. I wanted her to know the truth, but I also needed my father to know as well. I needed him to help us figure out what was going on with her.

"Chiron and I have our *suspicions* about her abilities." I sent a scathing look at Apollo. "But we hadn't yet determined that she is, in fact, a Mimic. Clearly, my brother was already aware of her true affinity and has neglected to inform anyone, despite observing her difficulties at training for the past week."

Zeus closed his eyes and rubbed his temples, then turned to Tessa. "Is this true, girl?"

Tessa's eyes widened when Zeus addressed her.

"I—I don't really know." She pressed her lips together and swallowed nervously, finally looking at me with something other than anger. I nodded in encouragement.

"A week or so ago, I accidentally manipulated water and fire."

"Accidentally?" Hera asked, arching a brow. "How do you accidentally manipulate the elements?"

"I was there, Mother." I jerked a chin toward Apollo. "As was he. It wasn't intentional, it was instinctual. Now let her finish."

"Okay." Tessa blew out a breath. "Chiron and Nate—Nathaniel—got suspicious, so they asked me to try a few other things. They said they were going to do some more research because Mimics pretty much don't exist, so we haven't really done much since then."

"What 'things'?" Zeus crossed one leg over the other and rested a finger on his chin, his brow slightly furrowed.

"I shifted a water current and created a breeze."

His eyes widened in a rare show of surprise, then his expression turned furious as he looked between me and Apollo.

"Neither of you saw fit to inform me of this?"

"It's one of the reasons I came here." I jerked my chin toward Apollo. "I've got no clue as to why your second in command didn't tell you."

Zeus shook his head and raised his eyes to the ceiling. "Three thousand years," he groaned. "Three thousand years of childish bickering and *this* is where you finally find common ground? Keeping information from your leader—your father—that could be catastrophic in the wrong hands?"

"To be clear, we didn't find common ground," Apollo clarified. "We both simply felt it was best no one knew until the girl herself was fully aware of her abilities. There was no collaboration involved."

"Apollo, 'the girl' is sitting right next to you," Hera said calmly. "Stop treating her as though she's not."

Apollo clenched his jaw and glared into the roaring fire.

I pursed my lips to keep from smiling. My mother tolerated Apollo for Zeus' sake but never missed an opportunity to rebuke him in front of others.

"Be that as it may," my father snapped, "you both kept this from me. It's upsetting."

He rested his chin in his hand and stared silently into the fire, and I thought I actually saw a flicker of hurt in his eyes.

As the moments ticked by, I became increasingly nervous as to what was simmering in his mind in regard to Tessa. The pensive look on his face almost always indicated he was plotting.

Finally, he dropped his hand and leaned forward, resting his arms on his knees and meeting Tessa's eyes.

"It's Tessa, correct?"

She nodded.

"Tessa, do you understand why this is so significant?"

She cleared her throat. "To be honest, I don't."

He laughed, then shook his head incredulously. "You know we are on the cusp of war, correct?"

"Yes, of course."

"I know that my past may indicate otherwise, but much has changed over the years. I want you to know that I am not cruel, and I do not forcibly use others to my own end. That said, with your abilities, you have the potential to be the deadliest weapon in Olympus' arsenal."

She choked back a nervous laugh. "I'm sorry, what? All I can do is mimic other affinities! How is that any more deadly than a Mindlinker or Coercer?"

Zeus' eyebrows shot up as he looked over at me. "Nathaniel? Have you and Chiron taught her nothing?"

I sighed, then leaned forward, mirroring my father's pose. "Because you would have the ability to turn an enemy's power against them." I glanced at my brother before speaking, then back to Tessa. "Much like you did to me on your first day of training."

She tilted her head and frowned. "But I—"

"Nathaniel, what are you talking about?" Hera glared at Tessa. "She used her power on you?"

"No, it wasn't like that. She was having difficulty working with another recruit. I entered her mind to try to find a reason why she was having so much trouble, and her mind fought against me with such force it exhausted us both."

Zeus sat up straight. "She used your own powers against you on her first day of training?" He turned to glare at Tessa. "How—"

She held up her hands. "I didn't mean to, I swear."

My father stared at her, eyes wide with incredulity. "Nathaniel, is there anything else you've neglected to tell me?"

For the first time in almost three millennia, I reached out to my brother for guidance.

He stared back at me, impassive. *'Careful what you say, brother. This is far bigger than you or me.'*

'What would you suggest?'

'Avoid discussing her dreams just yet.'

"Nathaniel?" Zeus' voice was impatient.

I snapped my gaze back to his. "Her power seems very protective of her, almost sentient. Is that typical of a Mimic?"

Zeus frowned, then absently rubbed his forehead. "I can't say I've had much experience. I can't even recall the last time one existed."

"Chiron could only find record of one, and that was a passing mention. Do you know if that was in your lifetime?"

His eyes met mine, and he frowned. "I'm not sure, actually."

Hera reached over and put a hand on his knee. "Darling, are you alright?"

He looked at her, a dazed look in his eyes. I exchanged a confused glance with Tessa.

"Yes, I just—" He shook his head as though trying to clear his mind.

Apollo leaned forward, resting his elbows on his knees. He wore a perplexed expression.

"Father, do you recall any Mimics in the past?"

"I'm not sure. I thought the Fates had always reserved that power for gods, which is why it's so strange that a girl who was so recently human possesses it."

He eyed Tessa curiously.

"A god had this power?" I asked sharply.

He cocked his head to the side, that frown still marring his fore-head. "I don't remember. Hera?"

My mother opened her mouth to speak, then stopped. "No, I can't recall. Are you sure Chiron's information is accurate? Just because the power exists in theory, doesn't mean the Fates have given it to anyone."

"Yes, yes, someone had it. I'm just having trouble remembering," Zeus said, waving a hand dismissively.

They can't remember, either.' Tessa's thought was a whisper.

'You should take her home.' Apollo's voice quickly followed hers, and she gave a small jump, as though she'd heard him, too.

"I think it's time we let Tessa go back to her room." Apollo eyed her. "It doesn't appear she's got anything else to offer at present."

Zeus nodded, still frowning. "I'm sure you're correct." He pursed his lips, then looked between the three of us. "Although, I would like to see a demonstration of her abilities."

Tessa's eyes darted from Zeus to me and back again.

"She's only just discovered her powers," I pointed out. "You can't possibly expect her to do a demonstration now."

"No, no, of course not." He drummed his fingers on the arm of his chair. "I'll give her three weeks."

Apollo cleared his throat. "Father, if I may. I think we should allow her more time to perfect her powers, don't you?"

I arched a brow, surprised at his concerned tone.

Zeus glared at him. "No, I do not. We're on the verge of war. I want to know how powerful of an asset she'll be."

He turned his gaze to Tessa.

"Three weeks. I do not expect perfection in such a short time, of course, but I want to get an idea of your potential. Weapons and hand-to-hand, as well."

"Zeus—" Hera spoke up, placing a hand on his arm.

He snatched his arm away. "That is my final word on the matter!"

Hera stared at him, furious. "Fine," she snapped, standing. "Tessa, I will escort you home."

Tessa's eyes widened and I jumped to my feet.

"Mother, I can—"

"Sit down, Nathaniel." She pushed my shoulder, causing me to fall back onto the sofa, then inclined her head toward Tessa. "Look at her. She may be calmer now, but she's still full of fury. She would have torn you to pieces out there if she could."

She stepped toward Tessa, a small smile curving her lips, then reached down and pulled her off the sofa.

"No, what she needs right now is some girl talk."

"Hera, stop—" Apollo stood and reached for Tessa's arm, missing by centimeters.

"Goodnight, gentlemen." She winked, then she was gone, taking a terrified Tessa with her.

37

TESSA

Hera and I came out in front of a large, beautiful cabin in the woods.

As soon as both feet were on the ground, she released her grip on me. I took several steps back, terrified of what this goddess—an incredibly vindictive and spiteful goddess, if her reputation was anything to go by—was going to do to me.

Instead, she hitched up her dress and made her way up the wide steps, then took a seat on one of the Adirondack chairs that adorned the porch. She crooked her finger at me, then patted the seat next to her, smiling serenely.

Seeing no choice, I climbed the stairs and sat down.

"So, you're the girl who seems to have stolen my son's heart." She rested her head against the top of the chair and smiled. "You're quite pretty."

"I—thank you?"

"It's not a question, dear, it's a compliment." She sighed. "Let's move on from this stupid fear that I'm going to smite you for attacking my son, shall we? You were well within your rights. He lied to you, and quite a grievous lie, at that. I've killed men for less."

I gulped.

"I'm sorry about that," I whispered, desperately trying to squash my fear. "I just—that's not like me."

She reached over and patted my hand.

"As I said, I understand. Water under the bridge."

I smiled hesitantly. "Thank you, ma'am."

"Oh, please, drop those ridiculous human titles. You don't need to acknowledge that I'm above you when you address me; we both already know that."

I pursed my lips, not quite knowing how to react to the barely-veiled insult.

"Now, I'd like to talk to you about my son. He cares for you a great deal, from what I can see. Do you feel the same for him?"

"I do. I think. It's just—"

"You're angry with him. Trust me, I know what it's like to have your significant other lie to you," she responded bitterly.

"I don't know that I can get past this one."

She rolled her eyes. "Don't be ridiculous. Take just a moment to consider why he might have done this before jumping to that conclusion."

"Why would he, though? It's such a huge thing to keep from me. I mean, we've only known each other a couple of weeks, so it's not like he's required to tell me everything about himself. I just thought—"

Hera held up a hand to silence me.

"You thought the person who is falling in love with you might tell you who his parents are? Might tell you things he discovered about you?"

My mouth fell open at the mention of "love."

"I don't think Nate is falling in love with me. He barely knows me!"

She tapped her delicate fingers on the wide arm of the chair. "You seem to know very little of the gods and their emotions."

"I don't, I'm sorry."

"No need." Her smile seemed a bit more genuine this time. "It's important to understand that gods don't go through the same charades as humans when developing a relationship. Tell me, have you ever been in love?"

"No, I haven't," I admitted.

"Pity. Tessa, love is a reaction, pure and simple. It's not a conscious decision. There is no appropriate amount of time one should wait before expressing their love. There is no list of requirements you must check. That is a stigma your humans have placed upon it."

She wrapped her slender fingers around my hand.

"It's not logical, it just *is*. I think if you look in your mind, you'll see that the possibility of loving my son is quite present."

I turned her words over in my head. Nate and I had a lot of deep conversations over the last two weeks, and there were definitely butterflies in my stomach every time I thought about him. But love?

My power, which had been still this entire time, stirred, sending a warm feeling through my mind. I couldn't help but smile. Clearly, something within me approved, even if it had tried to mentally kick the shit out of him just last week.

I squeezed my eyes shut, unable to deal with any more weird questions at the moment.

"Yes, I think I could see that," I acknowledged, meeting her gaze. "But he broke my trust, and no matter how I feel for him, that will always be in the back of my mind."

"As it should be." She shifted so she was facing me. "But I know my son, and I know he would not have kept secrets without good reason."

"You think I should forgive him?"

"I think you should acknowledge that, despite how it made you feel, he did not keep these things from you to be malicious. You need to let him explain his reasons, then determine whether you're able to make a future with him."

Make a future with him. I was human five seconds ago and now I was talking to an Elder about "making a future" with a god.

Hera squeezed my hand and stood, straightening her dress.

"Nathaniel will be here soon. You need to make a decision as to how you wish to proceed."

"This is his house, then?"

"Yes, it is."

She held out a hand, so I let her take mine and pull me to my feet, then she gripped my shoulders and met my eyes.

"Be certain of your choice, Tessa. You're within your rights to walk away now, but if you give my son false hope, if you break his heart, I will destroy you. Remember that."

She patted my cheek and smiled. "You seem like a sweet girl, so I would prefer you stay on my good side."

Before I could stutter out a response, she was gone.

Well, now I could add death threats to today's list of crazy.

I debated for a few minutes whether I wanted to be here when Nate got back.

I knew I should hear him out. I replayed Hera's words about love and Nate's reasoning, but this was entirely new territory for me.

I still hadn't come to a decision a few minutes later when I felt a slight shift in the air around me. I looked down at the lawn and saw that Nate standing there. He hesitated when he saw me, then stuffed his hands in his pockets and slowly made his way up the stairs.

I let my hands rest in my lap and used my fingernail to scrape at a smear of blood that was on the sleeve of my uniform, a remnant of the training session from just a short while ago. It felt like days had passed since my sparring match with Damien, but it had barely been an hour.

He came to a stop in front of me.

"I guess we should talk."

"Yeah." I stopped picking at my sleeve and met his eyes. "I guess we should."

I wanted him to be the first to speak, but based on his silence and the pained way he stared off into the forest, I didn't think that was going to happen.

"Why didn't you tell me who you were, Nate?"

Instead of responding, he stood, then reached out a hand toward me. "Let's go inside, it's getting cold out here."

I deliberated for a moment, then finally took his outstretched hand.

He led me into his cabin, which was far bigger on the inside than it appeared from his porch.

"This is a nice place," I observed. "Homey."

We stepped inside to a large great room and I saw that the warm earthy tones of the forest had been seamlessly carried inside. The logs that made up the large cabin were a soft honey color, the floors paneled in wide, dark planks, covered here and there with thick, dark area rugs in deep reds. A large stone and glass fireplace was built into a column in the middle of the room, a pile of logs ready to be lit, sitting inside.

"Thank you." He gestured toward the overstuffed brown sectional that faced the fireplace. "Come on, let's sit down."

We each took seats, him in the corner, me on the end, facing each other.

Nate scrubbed his hands over his face before dropping them into his lap. I was surprised to see his eyes looked red.

"Tessa, I'm so sorry. I shouldn't have kept so much from you." His voice held a twinge of sadness, mirrored in his downturned eyes.

"Nate—" I took a deep breath. "No, screw it. You knew I cared for you. In all those hours we've spent together these last few weeks, you didn't think it was worth mentioning that, not only are you a god, you're the son of the two Elders who rule Olympus? Why would you keep that from me?"

He slumped against the back of the sofa, a look of defeat on his face. "The day I met you, I didn't tell you because I didn't see a need. When we talked about the original Ischyra...I don't know, I just didn't have it in me to get into it that night. After that..."

He pressed his fingers to his eyes and took a deep breath.

"Tessa, if I had come to you, pursued you, and you knew I was a god, how would you have reacted? Would you have been so quick to spend time with me one on one? Or would you have assumed I was simply playing games?"

"Wait, you're going to try to put this on me?" I couldn't help but laugh. "Unbelievable."

"No, that's not what I'm doing. Just... okay, look at how you reacted when you met Hermes on your first day and when he and Dionysus arrived yesterday." He raised his eyebrows. "They intimidated you."

"Well yeah, but—"

"But they're Elders? You're telling me you wouldn't have had the same reaction if they were just Zeus' sons, minus the title?"

"Okay, fine, I guess I see your point, but I got over that quick enough."

"I wanted us to know each other without that stigma hanging over my head. I acknowledge that may not have been the best course of action."

I pressed my lips together, trying to hold back the tears of hurt that threatened my eyes. I let out a deep, shuddering breath.

"Gods, Nate, it's like you just threw a wrench in everything," I whispered.

"Believe me, Tessa, no one knows that more than me. There were so many times I thought it was time to tell you and lost my nerve. The longer I waited, the more I dreaded having to tell you who I really am."

"Is that really all there is? Or does it have something to do with Apollo, too?"

"He tried to tell me to leave you be, but that had nothing to do with my choice not to tell you."

I raised my eyebrows. "You guys looked ready to kill each other back there, Nate."

He took a deep breath and rubbed at his eyes before responding. "That's...complicated."

"Screw complicated. If you want any chance of forgiveness from me, you need to stop bullshitting around everything and tell me what's going on. If you don't care about forgiveness, then I'm happy to be on my way."

"No, no, that's not what I meant." He reached out a hand to stop me from standing. "Please, don't leave."

"Then talk to me."

He nodded, then stood and walked over to a long cabinet that ran behind the couch, emerging with two tumblers and a bottle of red wine. Based on the purplish blossoms floating inside, I guessed it to be ambrosia. He sat back down, poured glasses for each of us, and slid one down the glass coffee table toward me.

I eyed it warily, then picked it up, needing something to do with my hands.

Nate took a large swallow of his wine, then set the glass on the table with a *clink* before turning to me.

"Do you remember when I told you about Karis?"

I frowned. "Yes, I remember."

"I told you how she died, correct?"

"Godsbane arrow, right?"

"Yes. There was a bit more to it than that, though." He picked up his glass and tossed back the rest of his wine, then refilled it before continuing.

"Back then, Apollo was in charge of the Ischyra, and I would often advise him. One of his main duties was determining where Ischyra were assigned, and he usually based decisions on a soldier's individual skills. If a soldier was particularly good at dispatching giants, for example, he or she would be sent to lead a team in an area where giants were causing problems, typically in the larger mountain ranges."

"That makes sense. Is it not the same today?"

"It is, but Apollo didn't always follow that rule."

He tapped a finger on his tumbler.

"He took issue with my relationship with Karis, much like he seems to have taken issue with my relationship with you. He felt she was beneath me, saw her as a distraction, and considered her the reason I'd begun drifting away from my life as a god. So, he took it upon himself to remove that distraction."

"But I thought Zeus considered you and Karis a good match?"

"He did. My brother disagreed."

I felt the blood drain from my face. "So he had her killed?"

"Not directly. Karis was an amazing fighter, but she never did well against Sirens. Ischyra are supposed to have enough of a resistance to a Siren song to be able to get out of hearing range, but Karis lacked that ability. Her resistance was minimal. The song wouldn't kill her, but it would weaken her. Knowing that, Apollo sent her to join a team he'd dispatched to Venice to deal with a Siren problem in the canals."

He paused and took a deep breath.

"I confronted him on her behalf, tried to get him to change his mind, see reason. He wouldn't listen, said she needed to 'adapt' if she was going to be a worthwhile Ischyra and that I needed to step back and let her do her job."

He took another slow sip of his wine.

"Needless to say, she did not return from that mission alive. According to one of the soldiers on her team, a Siren had disabled her, and a human, of all things, shot her through with a poisoned arrow.

"I blamed my brother for her death. Zeus sided with me, but only because he thought Apollo's attempt to teach Karis a lesson was ill-conceived. He thought Apollo had needlessly sacrificed the life of a valuable soldier. He didn't say it outright, but he believed part of Apollo's motivation had been spite.

"My brother didn't like that I was making choices that were different from what he saw as 'right.' For whatever reason, he never felt he had a choice when it came to how he served Olympus. I took that choice, and he resented me for it."

"What happened after Zeus stepped in?" I asked.

The corner of his mouth turned up in a wry smile. "Apollo got demoted. Ares and Athena were brought to lead the Ischyra. It was a good decision in the end. They're better suited for the job than my brother. Of course, he blamed me for his demotion. We've barely spoken since, and when we do, well..."

"It's like what I saw today?"

"Much worse when we were younger." He smirked. "Those fights usually ended in physical violence. Once Zeus and Hera finally kicked us out of the palace, we avoided each other whenever possible. When we do speak, it tends to be a struggle in civility."

I pursed my lips, going over everything he'd just told me and trying to phrase what I wanted to say.

"Can I ask a question?"

He smiled. "Of course."

"I understand why you had a falling out. But...it's been almost three thousand years, Nate. Why hold onto that anger for so long?"

He ran his hand through his hair, and I fought back the urge to smooth it back down.

"I wish I had an answer for you. I moved on from Karis long ago, but he and I have always clashed. Sometimes it just seems easier to hate him than work out our issues."

"What about the rest of your family? It seems like you keep your distance from the top half of the mountain, but don't you have, like, a million siblings? Do you ever spend time with them?"

He smiled. "There are quite a few. Ares and Hephaestus are the only two *full* siblings who really interact with those of us on Olympus. Eileithyia travels all over the realms, tending to childbirths, Angelos spends all her time in the Underworld, and Hebe decided she wanted to live among humans as a college professor. Enyo gets involved with Ischyra on Earth sometimes, but her methods tend to be a bit more destructive than Ares' and Athena's, so she spends her time in the war-torn parts of the world. And Eris just skips around the realms causing trouble."

He grinned. "You'd like her. She reminds me of Mary, in a way, only a bit more insane."

"Are you calling my best friend insane?"

"She's a little bit crazy, Tessa. If you'd heard the threats she was tossing at me when we first met, you'd agree."

"Speaking of threats...your mother is terrifying."

His eyes widened. "Tell me she didn't threaten you."

"Maybe a little."

He groaned. "I'm sorry about that. She can be very overprotective."

"That's one word for it," I said as I set my glass down on the table. "Now. Explain what Apollo was talking about when he said you saw something at my transformation."

He scratched his forehead. "It was strange. When I funneled the magic into your mind to awaken your power, all of these images and emotions flashed through. They were fighting against both of us, so I forced them into your subconscious."

He sighed, then met my eyes.

"Everything you've been dreaming about was there, and more, only I didn't know it at the time. Atlas, Iapetus, Clymene, and others, but they were moving so fast it was hard to make out much."

I leaned forward and rested my elbows on my knees, then tapped my index fingers on my lips, trying to decide whether to be furious, scared, or aggravated.

"You should've told me." I struggled to keep my voice even.

"I didn't want to—"

"Worry me?" I dropped my hands and stared at him, dumbfounded. "What the fuck, Nate! This is not about you! You see weird visions in my head that just happen to coincide with these messed up nightmares, and you don't think I should know? Gods, Nate, I'm not a child!"

"I know, I just...if you had seen yourself that day outside your school, I couldn't—I couldn't see you like that again. I couldn't put you through that again."

"That was completely different. Both of us were caught off guard." I sighed and pressed my fingers to my eyes. "You need to trust me to handle these things on my own, Nate."

"I know," he murmured. "I'm so sorry."

We sat in awkward silence for a moment. I picked up my glass and took a gulp before speaking again.

"So, your father wants a demonstration? What does that mean?"

"He just wants to see what you can do. He knows you won't have perfected much within such a short span of time, so it's not as bad as you think." He took a sip of wine, his eyes darting away from me.

I narrowed my eyes. "What aren't you telling me?"

He winced. "There's going to be a bit of a change in your training, starting tomorrow."

"What kind of change?"

"Zeus wants Chiron and me back with the recruits, and I don't think he trusts me to train you properly. So...Ares and Athena will be taking over."

I nearly dropped the glass I'd been holding.

"What?! How the—" I took a deep breath to try to steady myself. "Why are two Elders taking on my training?"

"Zeus thinks a Mimic should have more specialized training, and I think he's right."

"Of course you do," I muttered.

"It'll be fine. You'll do wonderfully."

"Not so sure about that." I tried to ignore all of the conflicting thoughts running through my mind. I wanted to bury my face into a pillow and forget the last hour had happened, but I also had so many questions I wanted to ask. This whole new aspect of Nate had been revealed, and as angry as I was, my curiosity was killing me.

Nate's eyes searched my own, and he reached out a hand to hold mine. "Tessa—"

"Don't." I pulled my hand out of his and tried to ignore the look of hurt that washed over his face. "This day has just been too much. I can't deal with hashing out relationship issues just yet." I took a deep breath before meeting his eyes. "Just give me some time to process everything, okay? I just had about a dozen bombs drop on me at once."

"I understand," he murmured. He looked like he wanted to say more, but he pressed his lips together and stayed silent.

"Look, I'm hurt and I'm not sure my trust in you will be quick to return, but I don't have the mental capacity to harbor anger right now. You had your reasons for keeping things from me, and whether I agree with them or not doesn't matter. I don't believe you did any of that maliciously. I just need some time, that's all."

I gave myself a mental pat on the back for being so mature. A huge part of me wanted to punch him again.

"Tessa, I promise I won't put you in the same position I put you in today ever again. I didn't think—"

"You don't have to explain it to me. I think I get it."

"Alright." He smiled sheepishly. "I'm guessing you want to go home?"

"It's probably better if I do. I don't suppose you want to send me back the easy way, do you? Since you're a god and all?"

He let out a shaky laugh.

"Of course."

He held out a hand, and a second later, he'd teleported us to the entrance to my dorm.

I huffed out a breath at the clear evidence of his godliness.

I paused before going inside, then turned to look up at him. Slowly, I wrapped my arms around his waist, pressing my head to his chest. His arms circled around me, squeezing me tight as tears leaked from my eyes.

"I'm sorry, Tessa. I truly am." He kissed the top of my head, then stepped back.

"I know," I whispered, wiping my eyes. "I'll see you soon."

He gave me a pained smile, then disappeared.

I stared up at the dormitory, not quite ready to go in.

This freaking day had turned into a dumpster fire of epic proportion.

My sort-of boyfriend was a god, and his crazy mother had threatened my life. I was being forced to train with two Elders, away from my peers and mentors, so that I could give Zeus a demonstration of my powers in three weeks. Not to mention witches were erasing memories, I was dreaming about a missing Titan, and there were apparently a ton of weird visions in my head that Nate had hidden from me.

Feeling defeated, I sat down in the middle of the street and rested my head on my knees.

Screw this day and the horse it rode in on.

38

TESSA

I walked around Olympia for the next few hours, not quite ready to be enclosed in my dorm. As I walked through the quiet streets, my mind continued to reel at all the new information I'd acquired.

The issues with Nate aside, I was more curious about why in all the realms I was dreaming about Atlas. Other than his part in the war, he was kind of a non-entity in my history lessons. He existed, but I'd never had cause to think about him outside of the few lessons he'd been mentioned in. Of all the things I'd learned today, that made the least sense.

As the sun slipped closer to the horizon, I began to make my way back to the dorms, working out what I was going to say to Yana and Mary when I returned.

Of course, they were waiting to pounce the moment I walked into my room. They were both still in their training uniforms, and when I looked at the clock, I realized they must've just returned.

"Hey, guys," I said as I walked in. I dropped down onto my bed and toed off my shoes. "What's up?"

"Seriously? 'What's up?'" Mary rolled her eyes. "You've been missing all day. Where'd you go?"

"Yes, you missed watching me put Eric on his ass," Yana boasted. "It was glorious."

"Gods, I would've loved to have seen that." I let out a heavy sigh. "So...yeah. I think we should talk."

Mary arched a brow in question. "About..?"

"You guys are not going to believe the day I've had."

I proceeded to tell them about everything that had gone down over the last couple of hours. About Nate's lies, his confrontation with Apollo, the revelation that Zeus and Hera were his parents, Hera threatening my life, and finally, about me. I told them all about Nate and Chiron's suspicions about my powers and about what we'd uncovered about my dreams. Somehow, I managed to get through it all with minimal tears.

They listened quietly, but a range of emotions went across their faces as I spoke.

Mary looked mainly hurt. "Tess, why couldn't you tell me? Did they tell you that you couldn't or something?"

I shook my head and sniffed, wiping the dampness from my eyes. "No, I just...I don't know. I just felt weird about it, plus there wasn't anything definitive really until today. I guess I didn't want to make a thing of it until I knew there was something more concrete."

"I guess." She picked at a fuzz on the pillow in her lap. "It just seems like, since Nate came around—"

I held up a hand to cut her off. "No. Don't start that. You know me well enough to know I wouldn't bail on you for a guy. The only reason he knew any of this was because he was there when we figured it out."

"Ugh, I know!" She tossed the pillow to the side. "It just sucks. It's like he suddenly knows all this stuff about you that I don't."

The three of us sat in silence for a few moments before Yana spoke.

"I think what is most important here," she said slowly, "is that Tessa should not handle these things alone. Mary, I know you are hurting, but I think we need to focus. If Tessa is a Mimic, well..." She eyed me sympathetically. "Then Zeus is right, and you will be a valuable weapon."

"Gods, Yana, she's not a weapon," Mary snapped, still not meeting my eyes. "She's a person."

"It's okay, Mare, I get what she's saying, and I don't disagree," I said.

"I knew there was something off about that guy," she grumbled. "Didn't I tell you?"

"Even you couldn't have guessed he was a god."

"Yeah, well...I knew he wasn't any good for you."

"I don't think it's that he's bad for me, necessarily," I began. "I mean—"

Mary groaned. "Let me guess. You 'kind of get it.' Yeah. So do I. But it's still shitty."

"Fair enough."

"So now what?" Mary finally looked me in the eye. "Now what happens? You're seriously going to be training with Ares and Athena?"

"I guess. That's what he said."

Yana let out a low whistle. "I still cannot believe that. I suppose I understand the logic, but I cannot imagine how you must be feeling."

"Scared shitless, basically." I let out a shaky breath. "They're fucking war gods, you guys."

"Not that I care what he thinks," Mary said, rolling her eyes, "but did Nate seem to think you'd be ok with them?"

"Yeah, definitely," I assured her. "He said I'd be totally fine."

Mary let out a small grunt. "Well, I guess that's something."

"Mary, I really don't believe Nate was being malicious when he kept all this stuff from me. He just—"

"Tessa, stop." Mary sighed. "Whatever his intentions, Nate kept things from you that were about you, not just about him. If he didn't want to tell you he was a freaking god, fine, that's his prerogative. He shouldn't have kept those visions from you."

"I agree one hundred percent, trust me."

She arched a brow. "But you're still going to give him another chance?"

I sighed, then pulled my pillow into my lap and squeezed it against my chest, resting my chin on top.

"I don't know," I muttered. "I really don't."

"Mary, I do not think it is necessarily fair to consider Nate a bad guy just yet," Yana said, eying my best friend hesitantly.

"Yeah? Why's that?"

Yana glanced at me before continuing. "Because... I think, if I were in his position, I would have done the same. If what he says is true, he was trying to prevent Tessa from reliving that first experience. It sounds as though that was somewhat traumatic for him, as well. I can understand wanting to spare a person that type of pain. He may have been misguided, I will acknowledge that, but I do not think it makes him a bad person."

Mary looked at her incredulously. "You would seriously file away weird visions into your boyfriend's head, not tell him about it, and decide to figure it out later?" She threw up her hands in defeat. "When did I become the reasonable one here?"

I bit back a smile.

"You care about your friend," Yana said gently. "I do not think you are wrong to feel the way you do, but I can also see why Nate would do what he did."

Mary sighed, then gave me an exasperated look. "Listen, Tess, I'll back you no matter what you decide, you know that. But please, *please* take some time before you decide whether you want to give him another chance. Aside from the fact that he needs to regain your trust, his mother just threatened to kill you if you hurt him. So please, be really fucking sure before you make a choice, because I'd kind of like you to not be dead."

I grinned, then leaned over and gave her a hug. "I'd kind of like that, too."

~

MY APPREHENSION and excitement must've won out in my sleep, because I woke before my alarm on my first morning of training with Ares and Athena.

Quietly, I tiptoed into the bathroom to avoid disturbing Yana. I pulled on my black training pants and sports bra, then started my normal morning routine.

After a minute or so, I heard the blare of the alarm clock. Yana grunted as she pulled herself out of bed and began opening drawers.

There was a knock at the door, and I grinned, feeling bad for whoever was about to get a dose Yana's early morning snark.

"Tessa!" she called out.

I leaned over the sink and spit out my mouthful of toothpaste. "Yeah?"

"You—ah—company!"

I frowned, grabbing my shirt off the hook on the door and slipping my arms through. I had it halfway to my head when I saw who our guests were.

"Good morning, Tessa," Ares said, arching one dark eyebrow. His short, dark hair looked damp, and a small smirk played on his lips. He wore a loose-fitting gray Henley and black pants that looked similar to the ones I had on.

Athena stood next to him wearing a green, knee-length tunic woven through with gold thread over dark-gray leggings. Her long brown hair was in a braid that fell down her back. She cocked her head to the side and smiled.

"Our brother told you we would be training you today, correct?"

Their brother. Nate. Right.

Hastily, I turned my back to them and finished pulling my shirt on before responding.

"He did. I'm sorry, I thought that meant I would be meeting you at the arena."

Yana had backed away from the door and was staring at me wide-eyed.

"Yes, well, we wanted to get going a bit earlier than the rest," Athena explained, giving me a quick smile. "Are you ready to go?"

I ran a hand over my hair, which I'd yet to brush.

"Can I just—I need to put my hair up if that's alright?"

"Go on, finish up," Ares said brusquely, waving a hand toward the bathroom. He slowly began pacing the room, stopping to examine the various framed photos Yana and I had set up on the bookshelf between our bed.

I darted back into the bathroom and began yanking my brush through my hair. Yana followed me in and took the brush, then rapidly twisted my hair into a tight braid.

"There," she whispered, patting my shoulders. "Good luck."

I smiled gratefully. "Thank you."

"Tessa? We really must get going," Athena called.

"Yes, sorry!" I hurried back into my room and grabbed my shoes from under the bed. "Ready!"

Ares placed one hand on my back and the other on Athena's and teleported us out of my room.

Surprisingly, we came out on the zipline field instead of the arena. It looked different in the light of day—bigger, more open.

I looked around, confused. "We aren't going to the arena?"

"No, we'd prefer you be somewhere your friends are not," Ares responded, releasing my arm.

"Yes, there are fewer distractions out here," Athena added.

"I see."

I couldn't help the disappointment that washed over me. The only solace I'd had when Nate told me I'd be training with the two Elders was that I thought I'd still be close to my friends. I assumed we'd train outside the arena like I had been with Nate and Chiron, but I didn't think I'd be completely isolated like this.

Athena tilted her head, frowning. "Is that not acceptable to you?"

My eyes widened. "Oh, no, I'm sorry. I didn't mean—"

She smiled, seemingly amused at my flustered state. "It's fine, Tessa. We aren't here to scare you, are we?" She nudged Ares with her elbow.

The dark-haired god flicked a glance in her direction before looking me up and down, his blue eyes narrowed. "Is Father certain this girl is a Mimic?"

Athena shrugged. "That's what Apollo and Nathaniel have both said, and it's rare that those two agree on anything."

His chiseled jaw twitched, then he let out a sigh. "Alright, then. Let's get started."

Athena sat cross-legged on the grass, then gestured with her hand for me to do the same. Ares took a seat beside her, stretching his legs out in front of him.

"Nathaniel gave us a bit of information," Athena said, "but why don't you tell us what you know of your power so far?"

"To be honest, these last couple of weeks have been a bit of a blur," I began as I got comfortable in the soft grass. "But Nate noticed—"

"Nate?" Ares snorted, interrupting me. "He must love that."

"Shush. I think it's quite adorable," Athena said, giving me a conspiratorial wink. I immediately felt a bit more comfortable with her.

"You only say that because he's your favorite brother," Ares grumbled.

Athena smirked but didn't dispute Ares' assertion. "You were saying, Tessa?"

I cleared my throat. "Right. Nate noticed something was off when I used my power to hurl a ball of water at my friend on the first day of training, then later that night I put out a candle. I thought I was using my telekinesis, but apparently that's not how it works."

Ares nodded. "Anything else?"

"Well, I was also having some problems working with my partner, Damien. He was trying to perform a mind link, and I was having trouble controlling my power enough to let him in. When Nate tried to look through my mind to figure out what was going on, I had to fight to allow him access."

"You engaged in mental combat with my brother?" Ares' words sounded accusing, but his furrowed brow told me he was more curious than angry.

"Not intentionally. I *was* trying to let him in. I wanted to know why I was...failing so miserably, but it was as though my power was fighting against me just as much as him."

"Chiron thought that may have been you using Nathaniel's own powers of Coercion, correct?" Athena asked.

"Yes, that was his thinking. Nate was the first one to use his powers on me, back when I was still human."

I snapped my mouth shut, unsure whether they knew about the vision Nate and I had seen.

Athena eyed me speculatively but didn't question me on it. "So what else? Wind, correct?"

"Yes."

"Alright, then. Has anyone else used their powers on you or in your presence?"

"All of the Mentalist recruits and my mentors used their powers in front of me the night of our transition. Oh, and my roommate is an Electrokinetic. She zapped one of my friends the other day. None of them actually used their powers on me, though."

"Neither did the fire user, from what I understand?"

"No, he was just showing off," I responded.

She smiled, then stood and brushed off her tunic. She reached out a delicate hand and pulled me to my feet.

"We'll start with electrokinesis, then."

"Not with fire?" I couldn't help the disappointment that crept into my voice.

Ares raised his brows. "That upsets you?"

I nodded. "Actually, I had really hoped I'd get a fire affinity."

He shook his head and frowned. "I'll never understand why you recruits always think fire is the most interesting affinity. Water and wind are far more destructive."

"You don't need to understand," Athena said. "You just need to train her."

She put her hands on her hips and drummed her fingers contemplatively as she stared at me.

"I'd say let's just start with some sparks." She wiggled her slender fingers. "Nice and small. See if you can muster some up."

"Do you recall how you used the other powers?" Ares asked.

"I do, but it might take a minute."

"Take your time," he said.

I closed my eyes, thinking back to the morning of my bathing suit date with Nate when Yana had shocked Mary. She had still been sparking when I came out of the bathroom, so I focused on that. As soon as I set my attention on the memory, her power was clear as day. A pale green glow surrounded the electricity that was slowly receding back into her skin. Sure enough, just as I'd seen with Andrei's wind power, a pale green speck, no bigger than my fingertip, floated toward me and found its home in my chest.

"Tessa?"

I opened my eyes and met Athena's questioning gaze.

"Hmm?"

"Look at your hands."

She looked down, and when I followed her gaze, I saw green electricity sparking all around my hands. It didn't seem to have a purpose; it was just there, curving around my fingers and palms like gloves.

"Can you direct it?" Ares asked.

"I—I don't know. Let me see."

I focused my thoughts on what I wanted the electricity to do. After a few seconds, it slowly shrunk back until it was only visible on the tips of my fingers.

"Perfect," Athena stated. "Now let's try something else. On the day of your transformation, Charlise let you all try out your powers, yes? And your telekinesis worked well?"

"Yes, very well."

She tapped her finger on her chin. "I would say, for today, let's try teleportation. It's more complex than telekinesis, but it's the only other one that doesn't require interaction with another person. We'll work on some of the more intricate mental affinities when we bring in some of the mentors."

"Okay, I'll try."

I closed my eyes and tried to think back to when Lara, the Teleporter, had demonstrated her powers on the first night. The spark was there—purple, this time—but I couldn't quite figure out how to access it and make it work.

"I'm sorry," I said after a few minutes with no success. "The power is definitely there, but I can't really figure out how to get to it."

"Hmm." Athena tapped her fingers over her lips. "Did you have trouble when you used Coercion?"

"I'm not really sure," I hedged, not wanting to get into how sentient my power felt. "Sort of, I guess."

Ares arched a brow. "Sort of? How do you mean?"

I exhaled a large breath. "That wasn't really...*me*. It was my power. It just reacted when Nate entered my mind that day at training. Kind of like a self-defense mechanism or something."

"Was it just as he entered your mind or once he began sorting through your thoughts?"

"Almost immediately. It was fighting against us both. It didn't want to let him in, and it didn't want to let me let him in."

"That could just be the Coercion resisting Coercion," Ares guessed. "It's inherently just as defensive as it is offensive, so if your mind felt as though it was under attack, it's not unreasonable to think your power would react defensively."

"That would make the most sense," Athena agreed.

She clapped her hands together.

"Alright, then. We'll file that away for future examination. Let's try a different one. There's a Psychometric in your group, right?"

"Yes, a girl named Sylvi."

"Let's go for that, then. It might be a bit simpler since there's no real physical aspect." Athena handed me a zipline hook that had been on a nearby bench. "See if you can tell me who the last person was to use this."

I took the hook from her and turned it over in my hands. Remembering Sylvi's power was nearly effortless; I immediately tapped into the memory and saw the bright yellow spark drift toward me. Within seconds, I had my answer.

"Chris, the Tempest. He's a mentor this generation."

"Can you tell us how he used it?" she asked.

I cocked my head to the side and frowned. "I'm sorry?"

Ares gestured toward the zipline towers with his hand. "Which tower did he use when he began?"

"Oh. Okay." I closed my eyes and wrapped my fingers around the hook again. After a moment, I saw it.

I opened my eyes and pointed at the tower at the far end of the field.

"That one, down there. And he came out just over there," I added, pointing toward the tower directly across from us.

Athena grinned, then took the hook back from me.

"So far you've manipulated at least three elements and have utilized three mentalist affinities. That's quite impressive."

She patted her brother on the back and grinned up at him. "It looks like our brothers were right, Ares. We've got a Mimic on our hands."

39

NATE

'*She's doing fine, Nathaniel. You can stop using me as your spy now.*'

Athena's indignance rang clear in her tone.

'*I'm not spying, I'm just worried about her.*'

'*Call it what you want, it's all the same. I'm going to ignore you now.*'

I felt the slight push from her mind that told me she had, in fact, blocked me out.

"Goddammit," I muttered as I made my way toward the track behind the arena. The mentors had brought the recruits out for their morning laps, and it was taking all I had not to leave and go find Tessa and my siblings.

Chiron fell into step beside me.

"Talking to yourself?"

"Yes," I bit out, sliding a glare at him.

"Ah." He nodded his head knowingly. "I take it things didn't go well last night?"

"You could say that."

"Want to talk about it?"

"Go ask Apollo. I'm sure he'd love to give you a recap."

"Nathaniel..."

I stopped and stared at him expectantly. "What? Would you like to tell me that I royally fucked things up here? That I should've told Tessa everything from day one? Save it. I already know." I pushed past him and started walking toward the exit.

"Alright," he said, hurrying to catch up. "Then what do you plan to do about it?"

"There's nothing I can do. She made it very clear that she needs time and space. I'm going to give her that. I dropped a bomb on her, Chiron. Several, in fact. I can't force her to be okay with who I am and what I kept from her."

"The fact that you acknowledge that is a testament to your character. She knows you, Nathaniel. She won't abandon you."

"Why not? I'm sure that's exactly what she thinks I did. I threw her to the goddamn wolves, bringing her there. I don't know what I was thinking."

"Alright, you need to stop." He gripped my arm and stopped me in my tracks. "Look at me."

I pulled my arm from his grasp and glared at him.

He gripped me by the shoulders and gave me a quick shake. "You're letting all this get to your head. You need to take a step back and see that driving yourself mad and lashing out at those around you is not the way to keep her in your life."

He took a step back and folded his arms across his chest. "Now, tell me. What else has got you so worked up? This is more than just anger with yourself."

I put my hands on my waist and stared down the length of the arena.

"It was Apollo," I said after a moment. "If you could've seen his face. He was almost...gleeful. He wanted her to find out everything so badly, and I don't understand why."

I watched Chiron's face as he pondered my words.

"I think," he said after a moment, "that we may find there is more to Apollo's actions than your feud. He is often misguided in the way he handles things, but he isn't cruel. You know that as well as I."

I rubbed a hand on the back on my neck and sighed. "I know."

Chiron pressed his lips together and arched a brow, a sign he was trying to bite his tongue.

I raised my eyebrows.

"Just spit it out."

He blew out a breath. "It's been three thousand years, Nathaniel. You moved on from Karis long ago. Don't you think—"

"Don't start," I groaned. "Please, not now."

"He's your brother," he said evenly. "You've been able to avoid working closely with him for a long time, but if ever there was a time to reconcile, now would be it."

I stared at him impassively.

When he realized I wasn't going to respond, he ran a hand through his wild hair and sighed. "Fine. I'm assuming Athena's already blocked you out?"

"What do you think?"

He laughed, then shook his head. "Would you like me to check in with her and Ares later to see how Tessa's doing?"

"I would appreciate that greatly."

He gave me a tight smile and patted me on the back. "Come, let's get to training. Keep your focus on the recruits for now and let the rest sort itself out."

I snorted. "If only it were that easy."

I remained at the arena until all the recruits and mentors had trickled out. By the time I got home, it was nearly dusk.

I had just put my hand on the doorknob when I realized I wasn't alone.

I let out a heavy sigh, then turned and faced my oldest brother, who'd taken up residence in one of the porch chairs, feet propped up on the railing.

"What are you doing here, Apollo?"

"I came to apologize," he replied, keeping his gaze focused on the forest. "I didn't handle things well last night."

I folded my arms across my chest and stared down at him, willing him to look at me.

"Shouldn't you be apologizing to Tessa?"

He arched a brow but still wouldn't meet my eyes. "Shouldn't you?"

"I already have," I said through gritted teeth. "You made things far worse than they needed to be."

He shifted in his seat to face me. "I acknowledge that, Nathaniel, which is why I'm here. I did not intend for things to turn so...ugly."

"You were taunting her, Apollo. It was completely intentional."

"Intending to aggravate the two of you and intending for you to hit me are two different things."

"Why bother with either? You couldn't get through to me, so now you're going to make sure she knows just how bad I am for her?"

He rolled his eyes. "Will you sit down for gods' sake? You're too damn tall for me to keep looking up."

"You could always stand."

"Petulance. Lovely."

"More like disdain, but let's not split hairs. Now answer the question," I demanded.

With a sigh, Apollo stood and straightened his jacket, then leaned back against the railing. "For what it's worth, I don't think you're bad for her. Quite the opposite, actually. That said, there are things at play here that are bigger than you or I or that damn girl, things I'm not at liberty to disclose at this time. You need to trust that I am working in her *and* your best interest."

He held up a hand to stop me from interrupting. "I understand you may not like that response, but it's the best I can give you right now."

My eyebrows shot up. "That's it? You want me to trust you, yet you won't give me any reason why? What part of that makes sense to you?"

His jaw twitched as he stared at me, a look of annoyance crossed his face. "Fine then, I guess we're done here," he said, standing. He was quiet for a moment, then he huffed out a breath. "I understand you may think I do things intentionally to hurt you, but I assure you, that isn't the case."

"You've got a funny way of showing it," I muttered. "Goodnight, Apollo."

"Goodnight, Nathaniel."

Once he was gone, I dropped down into a chair and closed my eyes, letting the quiet sounds of the forest calm me.

I didn't know how long I sat there before I heard the thud of hooves coming up the steps.

I gave Chiron a tight smile as he rested his shoulder against one of the porch posts.

"Did I miss something?" I asked. "I seem to be popular tonight."

"Apollo muttered something about you sitting here wallowing in self-pity. I thought I'd come see for myself."

"I'm not wallowing. He doesn't know what he's talking about, and I was fine until I got home and saw him sitting on my porch."

Chiron's tail twitched and a look of interest filled his features. "Interesting. What did he want?"

"To apologize for letting things get out of hand with Tessa last night." I drummed my fingers on the wide arms of the chair. "And to tell me I need to trust that he's working in our best interest, despite the fact that he won't give me a single damn reason why I should."

"I see. That's a bit odd."

"That's one word for it."

"Nathaniel!" Hermes' voice boomed out over the front lawn. "We come bearing gifts!"

I looked at Chiron, eyebrows raised.

"Sorry, I needed backup," he explained. "You're absolutely wallowing."

"Oh, come on," I groaned.

A moment later, Hermes and Dionysus ran up the porch steps.

"Beer and pizza?" I raised my eyebrows. "What is this?"

Hermes was carrying three six-packs of beer, and Dionysus had two pizza boxes balanced on either hand.

Dionysus set the pizza down on the floor and handed me a beer. "Isn't this what the humans do when they go through a break up? Eat bad food and get drunk?"

"Seeing as I'm not human, I really can't answer that," I said, setting the beer down on the floor next to my chair.

"I told him that was what human women do, but he didn't want to hear it," Hermes explained, dropping down in the chair next to me and opening his own bottle.

"And I told *him* that human women would drink wine and eat ice cream. This is far manlier," Dionysus explained, twisting the cap off his beer. "Even if it won't technically get you drunk."

Chiron opened one of the pizza boxes and pulled out a slice. He took a bite, then grinned down at me. "Besides, Nico's pizza is delicious, human or not. Even I know that."

"Look, I appreciate this," I offered, "but I'm really not in the mood for company right now."

"Which is exactly why we're here," Hermes said. "When Apollo, of all people, is telling us you're miserable and in need of company, we figured we should listen."

"Apollo is—"

"A patronizing ass who is completely devoid of emotion?" Dionysus rolled his eyes and took a bite of pizza. "Clearly, only the first part is true, otherwise we wouldn't be here."

I arched a brow and smiled. "Or he knew I wanted to be alone and sent you all to annoy me."

"Enough about Apollo," Hermes said, opening my discarded beer and shoving it into my hands, setting the cap on the arm of my chair. "What do you plan to do about Tessa?"

"There's nothing to do. She needs time to deal with what I've done. Maybe she'll get past it, maybe she won't."

I took a sip of beer to wash down the bad taste that sentence left in my mouth. As much as I didn't want it to be true, I knew there was a real possibility she would never forgive me.

"You know her better than I do, but even I can see that she cares too much for you to write you off completely," Chiron said.

"Have you told her that you love her?"

I looked down at Dionysus, who'd just spoken around a mouthful of pizza, and frowned.

"No," I said after a moment. "It's too soon."

He shrugged. "Maybe for a human. We're gods. It's different for us."

"She doesn't understand that."

Hermes pulled himself up onto the railing and raised his eyebrows. "So explain it to her."

I laughed. "Hera already did. I don't think—"

"Once again, you give her too little credit," Chiron said. "We don't apply arbitrary timelines to these things, and I can see by the way she looks at you that she doesn't, either."

"That may have been the case yesterday morning. Now, I'm not so sure."

Dionysus groaned. "Gods, do I need to get Apollo back here to lighten the mood?"

I flicked my bottle cap at him, hitting him square in the forehead.

"I was being serious, Nathaniel. His snark might be preferable to your self-pity." He rolled his eyes and took another bite of pizza. "We all know damn well that Tessa is going to find her way back to you. I'm sure even he would agree with that."

"Apollo seems to be doing all he can to prevent that, actually."

He leaned over and flicked my forehead. "Think, Nathaniel! Unless he's suddenly found himself in love with this girl, I'm sure he's got a damn good reason for being such a prick."

"Since when does he need a reason to be a prick?" I shot back. "That's been his M.O. his entire life."

"That's not true and you know it," Hermes said. "You and he are two sides of the same coin, you just don't want to admit it."

"I don't have to admit it. I know it isn't true."

"No? You mean you don't make stupid decisions based on misguided attempts to protect those you love?"

I stared at him incredulously. "You're joking, right? You can't compare—"

"Enough," Chiron interrupted, shooting Hermes a glare. "We're here to cheer him up, remember?"

"Oh, is that why you're here? I thought we were just recounting all of the shitty things that currently exist in my life."

Dionysus laughed. "Now you really do sound like Apollo."

Hermes laughed, then ruffled my hair, a move he knew I hated. "Like I said, Nathaniel. Two sides of the same coin."

40

TESSA

I trained with Ares and Athena for eight hours every day for the next three weeks.

The first few days were touch and go as we tried to figure out which powers I could manipulate and which ones I needed to learn, but once we got past that, we spent each day focusing on something new.

It was incredible but still felt a bit haphazard. I was relieved when they brought Genevieve in to help give me pointers on the Elemental powers. Charlise and Fletch traded off working with me on Mentalist powers until I felt I had a pretty good grip on them.

With the guidance of a few of the other mentors, I created small wind storms, set fire to piles of leaves, then doused flames with blasts of water. I froze patches of dew-soaked grass and even managed to bend the light a bit to make myself hazy, although I couldn't go full invisible. I used psychometry to learn new weapons skills, I used Coercion to shatter illusions, mentally tracked mentors through the forest, and finally, after several hours of practice on the tenth day of training, I was able to teleport. It was only a few feet, but it was progress.

At the end of the second week of training, they decided to change things up.

"Today we're going to talk about how we can weaponize your powers," Athena explained when we were five days from my demonstration. Genevieve was standing beside her and Ares, awaiting instruction.

Excitement and fear ran through me as I thought of the possibilities.

"It's what they've started doing with the other recruits," Genevieve explained. "Ye need to, as well."

"Yeah, Mary and Yana told me. What should I do?"

"Genevieve is going to show you a few tricks she's cooked up over the years," Athena replied.

"Sounds great. What's first?"

"I think I'll have ye start with fire," Gen said, tapping her finger to her chin.

"What are your thoughts?" Ares asked her.

A slow grin spread across Genevieve's face. "Whips."

My eyes widened. "Whips? You want me to make fire whips? Like the kind I'd use on a horse?"

"It's an incredibly efficient way to weaponize fire. Watch." Without further warning, a long rope of fire sprung from Genevieve's palm. She wrapped her hand around it and flicked her wrist, sending a ripple through the length of it, scorching the grass ten feet away.

She closed her hand to reel the fire back in.

"See? You can do that with electricity, as well, and even water, if you get the right amount of ice worked in."

Ares crossed his arms over his chest. "Do you think you can do that, Tessa?"

I eyed the blackened patch of grass warily. "Maybe?"

"There's been no indication that you wouldn't be able to, so there's no need to be apprehensive," he said.

I put my hands on my hips and nodded, looking the war god directly in the eye. It seemed like the only person doubting my abilities was me.

"Yes, I think I can. Gen, can you show that to me again?"

THAT EVENING, after several more hours of practicing with
Genevieve's whips, I opted to walk home. I was exhausted, but
weaponizing my powers had left me on edge, and I needed to burn
off some energy.

When I entered the courtyard, I was surprised to see Eric sitting
on one of the benches.

"Hey, Tess," he said.

"Hey. You waiting for someone?" I asked, sitting down next
to him.

He smiled and turned toward me. "I was actually hoping to catch
you. How's training going? I haven't seen you much these last few
weeks."

I leaned back against the edge of the fountain and stared up at the
darkening sky. I'd given Mary the okay to let Eric in on what was
going on with me. I knew he wouldn't blab to the other recruits, and I
also didn't want him to drive her nuts with questions.

"It's going well. I'm having a lot of fun, even though Ares and
Athena are kind of terrifying. Genevieve is cool, though. How about
you?"

"It's going, I guess. I'm really getting the hang of these fire balls
Genevieve's been showing us." He grinned. "They're like little fire
bullets."

"Oh, that's awesome. Can you show me?"

"Yeah, here."

He created a small ball of fire in the air in front of him. Slowly, it
split off into small chunks, each taking the form of a bullet.

"Now you can fire them off wherever you want." He turned
around and fired them into the fountain, each one sending up a hiss
of steam when it hit the water.

"Cool," I told him. "I'll definitely keep those in mind."

He smiled. "So, what did Gen show you?"

"Fire whips."

His eyes widened. "Whips? Can I see?"

"Sure. It's not as fancy as hers, but you'll get the idea."

I opened my hand and called up fire, forming it into a smaller version of Genevieve's rope. I gave it a light flick so he could see the way it moved.

"Cool, huh?" I closed my hand.

"Wow, that's..." He shook his head, looking amazed. "That's awesome."

"Yeah, I thought so, too. She's crazy talented."

"She is," he agreed.

"So what's up? You said you were waiting for me?"

"Yeah." He cleared his throat, suddenly looking uncomfortable. "So that thing with you and the Coercer...that's done, right?"

I sighed and stared down at my shoes. I'd barely spoken to anyone about my situation with Nate after I'd explained everything to Yana and Mary more than two weeks ago. It still hurt to think about, much less talk about.

"I don't really know, to be honest. Things are a bit weird right now." I frowned. "Why?"

A hopeful smile bloomed on his face. "Well, I was thinking that maybe...Igor is thinking about asking Yana out and I wanted to see if you maybe wanted to do something with them."

Shit.

I shouldn't have been surprised. The crush he had on me was never a total secret, even if he tried to conceal it. It was frustrating because he still represented a much simpler time in my life. Every now and then, I wished I could go back to that time where my biggest worries were trying to convince my guardians to let me skip training for a day. I was pretty certain being with someone like Eric would be as easy as breathing.

And yet...

I gave him a sympathetic look.

"Eric, I just don't—I'm sorry, I just don't feel that way about you. I wish that weren't the case."

He slumped, looking crestfallen. "Yeah, I guess I kind of figured it was a long shot." His tone was laced with bitterness. "You're super important now, anyway. You need a super important boyfriend."

"I don't 'need' a boyfriend, Eric. I need my friends, and I think you know me well enough to know I wouldn't turn my back on you guys just because I have this freakish power."

"I know," he mumbled. "Still sucks, though."

Against my better judgement, I wrapped my arms around him in a sideways hug and rested my chin on his shoulder. "You'll always be one of my best friends, you know that, right?"

"Friendzone. Woo hoo."

"Stop that. You're going to find yourself someone amazing one of these days, and when you do, I'm going to be happy for you. I need you to do the same for me."

I pulled back and turned his chin to face me.

"Please, Eric. If you can't just be my friend, then tell me now."

"No, I can. It just might take some time, ya know?"

I smiled. "I know."

"Tessa! There you are."

I turned and saw Mary walking into the courtyard.

"I was just coming out to see if you'd gotten back yet. Hey, Eric." She eyed the two of us suspiciously. "What's going on?"

Eric and I stood, and I reached up to give him a hug.

"We good?" I asked him.

"Yeah," he whispered. He gave me a quick squeeze, then avoided my gaze as he said goodnight to Mary and walked off.

Mary linked her arm through mine and we started walking back to our rooms.

"What was that all about?"

"Nothing important. So how was your day?"

"Good! I learned how to make knives out of ice. My mentor said a bow and arrow isn't always practical but thought knife throwing might be something worth looking into." She gave me a self-satisfied smile. "And I kicked ass, of course."

"Of course you did," I said, returning her smile with one of my own.

Mary's initial concerns that she wouldn't do well had been squashed by the end of her first week. Her mentors turned out to be fantastic, and she'd managed every task they threw at her with ease.

I pushed open the door to our hall. "Anette asleep?"

"Yeah. I was waiting for you with Yana and got worried when you were late."

"I needed to burn off some energy, so I walked home."

"Ah, gotcha."

I opened the door to my room and found Yana sprawled out on her bed, her pillow over her face.

"Hey," I greeted her.

She pulled the pillow away from her face. "Hey. How was training?"

"Long and exhausting," I said, sitting down on the edge of my bed and pulling off my shoes. "You?"

"The same," she replied, then grinned at Mary. "Mary and I learned a cool trick, though."

Mary's eyes lit up. "Ahh, I forgot to tell you! Tess, it's so cool."

I raised my eyebrows. "Can you show me, or do I need to guess?"

"We can't really show you," she explained. "But basically, you know how if you stand in water that's touching an electric current, you'll get electrocuted?"

"Yeah..."

"Well, the mentors had me form a big puddle of water on the ground, then Yana shot a jet of electricity at it. It was crazy. Anyone who'd been standing in the water would've been toast."

"Huh. That is pretty cool. Definitely useful."

"Yes, I think my favorite part has become working with the others," Yana said.

"Must be nice," I muttered, sliding my sneakers under the bed.

"Aw, Tess, she didn't mean it that way," Mary said, giving me a sympathetic look.

"I know." I sighed. "It just sucks sometimes, you know? You guys are all getting to explore this stuff together and I'm just kind of on my own."

Yana frowned. "Is there a reason they have not let you back to work with us?"

"Not that I know of."

"Well, maybe tomorrow you could ask them," Mary suggested.

I rubbed a hand across my eyes.

"I don't know. I'm beat. I just need to go to shower and sleep."

Mary gave my leg a squeeze before getting up to leave. "Talk to them tomorrow. You never know."

"Yeah, I'll see what they say." I tried to smile, but I didn't know if it was as convincing as I'd hoped. "I won't know until I ask, right?"

She smiled. "Exactly. See ya in the morning."

"Night."

I RECOGNIZED the dream walk as soon as I opened my eyes. I almost expected Hestia's garden again and to see the beautiful redhead waiting to speak to me.

Instead, I saw the clearing where I'd been sparring with Atlas, the stone house about one hundred yards away on the edge of a cliff.

In front of me stood a tall and imposing dark-haired man.

"Hello, Tessa."

He was massive—easily a foot taller than me; his chest a broad expanse of muscle straining under a black shirt. His gray pants looked dirty, like what you'd expect to see on a mechanic, only the dirt looked...off somehow. He had wavy black hair tucked behind his ears, revealing a chiseled jaw, sharply defined cheekbones, and piercing black eyes. About two days' worth of scruff covered his chin. A long, silver knife hung loosely in one hand, its blade glistening an iridescent shade of blue.

"Who are you?" I glanced at our surroundings. "Where have you taken me?"

"I haven't taken you anywhere. You're still tucked safely in your bed. We're just having a conversation."

I eyed the knife warily, the shimmering blue color sending chills through my body. A familiar sensation tugged at my memory.

"Who are you?"

He laughed as though I'd just made a joke. "Oh, you'll figure that out quite soon, I'm sure. I just thought I'd pay you a visit and see for myself that you exist."

"What are you talking about? Of course I exist."

His eyes widened and his lips parted in a disbelieving expression. "That blasted witch did quite the number on you all, didn't she?"

"Witch? Hecate?" I narrowed my eyes. "What do you know?"

"Plenty, sweet Tessa, plenty. Personally, I enjoy watching you drown in your own ignorance, though, so you won't get anything from me." He cocked his head, eyeing me curiously. "You know, the resemblance to Atlas truly is astounding. You've been dreaming about him quite often, haven't you?"

I felt my heart start to sprint.

"What—" I stopped myself as I thought back to the rustling bushes and feelings of being watched. My blood ran cold as I realized this man had been stalking my dreams long before tonight.

"That was you, wasn't it? In my other dreams, in the forest?"

One corner of his mouth curled up in a leer.

He didn't answer, instead just tapped the knife softly against his dirty pants. "You know, I've always wondered something about these dream walks." He looked around at the trees that encircled us.

"What's that?" I asked, my voice barely above a whisper.

His eyes met mine, and a cruel smirk formed on his lips. "If someone were to say, *die* while we were here, what would happen to your body in the waking world?"

He began to stalk closer, causing me to stumble backward into a tree. Before I could raise my hands in defense, he'd shoved me against the wide trunk, crushing me against the rough bark. He pressed a large hand to my throat. Something flashed, an image of a darkened forest, but it vanished before I could latch on.

"For example," he growled, raising the knife to my throat. "If I were to cut into your skin with this godsbane blade and let the poison run through your veins, would you ever wake up to see the people you love? Or would the poison eat through your body before they even realized you were gone?"

"Please," I begged, my voice hoarse. Desperately, my hands scratched against his as I tried to fight him off, but my nails brushed uselessly against his skin. I tried to access my power, but all it did was thrash against me, unable to escape.

He pressed harder against my neck, bringing the knife dangerously close to my throat, and grinned.

"Tell me, has anyone told you how painful pure godsbane is when it touches your skin?"

He grabbed my hair and yanked my head to the side. Slowly, he pressed the flat edge of the knife against my neck, sending a searing pain across my skin.

I cried out, struggling uselessly against his grip as I felt the sting of poison on my skin.

"It's pure torture," he whispered.

"Tessa!"

Distantly, I heard someone calling my name, but when I tried to respond, he just put more pressure on my throat. Black spots clouded my vision. Desperately, I tried again to access my power, but it felt like it had been locked in a cage. If I could just tap into Coercion...

"Ah, you think you can Coerce me into letting you go? I guess your mentors haven't taught you how to fight against someone who can disable your powers, have they?"

His laugh was cruel as he pulled the knife from my neck and brushed it against my cheek.

"You were always shit with mental abilities, anyway."

I thrashed against him as tears leaked from my eyes. The pain of the blade over my bare skin was nauseating, and the fear that I'd never wake up began to consume me.

He began dragging the poisonous blade along my body, leaving trails of blistering pain everywhere it touched.

"What are they going to do with you when they realize you aren't as perfect as they think?"

I heard the voice call my name again, and a weird vibration went through my body.

"Stop—please—" I begged.

Finally, he dropped the knife and released me.

I crumpled to the ground, my chest heaving against the fiery pain that coated my skin. Too weak to do much else, I lifted my face and glared at him.

"Why—" I brought myself up to a kneeling position and leaned back against the tree he'd just pinned me against. "Why won't you tell me who you are?"

He leaned down so that his face was level with mine, and pure malice flashed through his eyes. "I'll see you soon, Tessa."

With that, he clamped a rough hand to my face and sent me back to the waking world.

41

NATHANIEL

'*N*ate, you son of a bitch you need to get here now! Tessa needs you!'

Mary's voice jolted me out of a deep sleep.

'Mary?'

'*Yes, it's Mary, now get over here! I've been calling you for ten minutes!*'

I stumbled out of bed, grabbed the clothes closest to me, and teleported to the dormitories.

Before I could knock, the door swung open and Mary grabbed me, pushing me toward Tessa's bed.

"Fucking help her!"

"What—Tessa!"

She sat on her mattress, knees drawn to her chest. Her beautiful face was red, tears dripping down her cheeks and running in rivulets down her neck and chest. Her long ponytail had come out of its tie, and pieces of hair were plastered to her skin.

Her face, neck, chest, and arms were all covered with vicious red burns.

I dropped down beside her and gently placed a hand on her back, careful to only touch the fabric of her tank top.

"Tessa?" I brought my hand up to her head and stroked her hair. "Can you hear me?"

She raised her eyes to me, and a shudder rocked through her body. Anger welled up inside of me as I stared at the burns that marred her skin.

"Nate, I think—"

My gaze snapped to Mary, who was hovering next to Yana and Anette, their expressions tense.

"You think what? Who did this to her?"

"We think you need to enter her mind," Yana said. "We cannot get her to speak. It took all we had just to wake her. I tried—I had to go get Mary..." She swallowed and rubbed her hands up and down her arms.

"She was thrashing, screaming, and these marks kept appearing on her skin," Anette whispered, her eyes wide.

"This happened while she was sleeping?" I asked.

Mary nodded, sniffling, her face streaked with tears.

Without further deliberation, I dove into her mind, and for once, her power didn't fight me.

I watched as she was taunted, then attacked, then tortured by a monster I knew all too well.

Cutting the connection, I lifted her into my arms and held her tight against me. Her hands gripped my shirt as she shuddered and pressed her face to my chest.

"What are you doing?" Mary moved to stand in front of me, blocking my path.

"I'm taking her to my brother."

"What—Nate, what did you see?"

"It was Menoetius. He's gotten into her head."

"Nate!"

Ignoring her, I teleported us directly to my brother's front lawn.

I kicked open the front doors so forcefully they crashed against the walls.

"Apollo!"

I stormed down the hall toward the living room. I'd just raised my foot to kick them open when Apollo stepped out, looking furious.

"Nathaniel, what do you think—" Apollo's expression transformed from angry to confused. "What's happened?"

He stepped out of the way and let me set Tessa down on his sofa.

As soon as I released her, she began to shiver.

"Nate?" Her voice was a harsh whisper, and her eyes were wide as she met mine.

"I'm here." I sat down next to her, still careful not to touch too much of her bare skin as I wrapped my arms around her.

She leaned into me, resting her head on my shoulder, and I pressed my lips to her hair.

Frowning, Apollo pulled a blanket off the back of the couch and handed it to me, then sat down on the coffee table, so close his knees almost touched mine as he looked her over.

"Nathaniel, what's happened?"

"Menoetius attacked her in a dream walk," I said flatly, wrapping the blanket around Tessa.

He gave me a look of alarm, then leaned forward to examine her injuries. He touched one of the fading red lines on her cheek.

"Is this from—"

"Godsbane," I bit out. "He pinned her against a fucking tree and tortured her with it."

His eyes widened in surprise. "Show me what you saw," he demanded. "Her thoughts are too jumbled. I can't get a good read on her memory."

"Aren't you going to ask my permission first?"

I looked down at Tessa and smiled in relief when I saw that her tears had dried and her shaking had ceased.

"Not this time, love. Sorry."

She nodded, and she buried her face into my chest.

"Okay."

When Apollo saw the events of Menoetius' dream walk, and Mary and Yana's description of Tessa's state, he paled.

"This is...not good."

I stared at him, incredulous. "Not good? No shit! How does he know who she is?"

He opened his mouth to speak, then snapped his jaw shut. Reaching toward the end table, he picked up a tumbler of wine and took a large swallow. I was surprised to see his hand trembling slightly.

"Nathaniel, I can't tell you that."

Rage coursed through me. Tessa must've known what I was feeling because she twined her fingers through mine and squeezed, the soft gesture instantly settling me.

Taking a deep breath, she faced Apollo. "Why can't you tell us?"

He scratched the back of his neck, then moved to sit in a chair on the opposite side of the sofa and met her gaze wearily.

He ran a hand over his face and exhaled sharply before speaking. "Do you know what an interdiction is?"

"No, I don't."

Suddenly, I understood.

"Who placed it?" I demanded.

"What's an interdiction?" Tessa said, her voice stronger now.

"It's similar to what humans call a gag order," Apollo explained, setting his glass down. "Only for the gods, a gag order isn't in writing, it's performed by a witch. I would quite literally be rendered speechless if I tried to disclose certain information to you."

He turned his gaze to me.

"It's why I haven't been able to tell you anything about her, Nathaniel. I know you may not believe that, but it's the truth."

I ran a hand through my hair and exhaled a heavy breath. "Why didn't you tell me this sooner?"

"I'd hoped I could simply convince you to stay away from her. I wanted to avoid certain... questions being raised. I suppose I should have learned long ago that wouldn't work."

I drummed my fingers against the arm of the sofa. "I'll ask again; who placed it?"

"It was Hecate, wasn't it?"

Apollo turned his eyes to Tessa and arched a brow. "I can't answer that."

Defeated, I fell against the back of the sofa and stared at my brother.

"So what do you suggest? We can't just leave her to be attacked again."

"I don't think he'll be back," Tessa said. "It seemed like he just wanted to scare me."

"I wouldn't count on that," I replied.

"Neither would I," Apollo agreed. He pressed his lips into a thin line as he assessed us both. His eyes drifted to where Tessa's hand was clutched in mine and he sighed.

"Take her home with you," he said, looking at me. "There's nothing I can do for her here, and with your powers, you should be able to force her to wake if it happens again. She should stay with you until—" His jaw snapped shut once again. He pinched the bridge of his nose and huffed out a breath. "She should stay with you... for the time being. You'll be able to keep her safe."

I looked at Tessa, who'd let her head come to rest on my shoulder.

"Is that alright with you?" I asked her.

"Now is not the time for politeness," Apollo snapped. "Just take her with you."

Tessa's head jerked up and she stared at him, wide eyed. "Shouldn't I get a say in this?"

"No."

"Tessa, I think—" I sat forward and turned her face toward me. "I think he's right. It would be safer if you stayed with me."

She rubbed her hands over face, then dropped them to her lap and met my eyes. "Fine. Let's go."

"I'll go speak with Ares and Athena," Apollo offered. "We'll adjust her training for tomorrow."

"Thank you." I appreciated the gesture, even if it wasn't meant for me.

With no further acknowledgement, he vanished, leaving Tessa and me alone in his living room.

"We need to go back to my room," Tessa said. "I need clothes, and I can't leave the girls hanging after this."

"Of course." I reached for her hand. "Whatever you need."

42

TESSA

By the time we made it back to Nate's house, it was nearly four in the morning. Mary had convinced Anette to go back to bed before I returned, but she and Yana had waited up for me. They'd been reluctant to let me out of their sight but agreed that Nate's place was safest for me at the moment. The fact that I'd calmed down and the burns had faded helped reassure them.

Nate rubbed the back of his neck as he looked around the living room.

"So, ah...My room is right through there." He pointed toward a short hall behind the fireplace. "I can take the couch."

I looked in the direction he was pointing, then arched a brow.

"Isn't the whole point for you to be able to wake me up if he comes back?"

"Yes, but I just thought—"

"Nate, I think we're both adult enough to share a bed," I said wearily.

Nate nodded, then took my bag and led me into his bedroom.

His room held the same comfortable feel as the rest of the house. The floors were made up of the same dark wood planks as the living room, but the walls had been covered with smooth, white plaster, a sharp contrast to the honey colored logs in the main part of the house. A large oriental carpet took up most of the floorspace, and a fireplace was built into the wall on the right side of the room, flanked by two large picture windows that faced the mountain. Facing the fireplace was a king-sized bed topped with sage green sheets on an ash wood frame. Matching nightstands sat on either side, and a door beside it opened into a closet. Across the room from the entrance was another door I assumed led to a bathroom.

I eyed the rumpled comforter and pillow that had fallen to the floor. Between that, his wrinkled clothes, and messy hair, it didn't take much to deduce he'd left in a hurry once he'd gotten Mary's call.

Reaching up, I pulled the hair tie from my hair and began combing through it with my fingers. I forced back a shudder as my mind flashed back to the pain I'd felt when Menoetius had yanked my head to the side.

I wasn't sure I could speak without crying, so after using the bathroom and splashing cold water on my face, I crawled silently into his bed and pulled the covers up around me. His clean, woodsy scent surrounded me, putting me at ease.

After a few moments, he turned out the light, bathing the room in moonlight. I heard the rustle of clothing as he put his pajamas back on, then he slid into bed next to me.

"Come here," he whispered, pulling me into him.

Accepting his offer of comfort, I clung to him, pressing my face to his chest as silent tears began to make their way down my cheeks.

"I'm so sorry you had to endure that," he whispered, resting his chin on my head.

I sniffed and pulled back to look at him.

"You don't have anything to be sorry for, Nate. There's no way you could've prevented this."

He brought one hand up to my face and used his thumb to wipe away my tears. "Maybe not. It doesn't change how I feel."

"And how is that?"

"Like I failed you. Like I should've known something like this might happen."

"That's ridiculous. There's no possible way—"

"Zeus said it himself; you're incredibly powerful. There's clearly a connection to Atlas, which means a connection to Menoetius. A dream walk is the only way to reach someone mentally for a face-to-face conversation. He's leading a damn rebellion against us. If he somehow got word of the existence of a Mimic..."

"That's a huge stretch and you know it," I said. "Besides, even if you had thought of it, what could you have done?"

"What I'm doing now." His eyes searched mine as he spoke. "Making sure I'm by your side if anything happens."

"What—ohh." Understanding dawned in my mind. "You think—"

"Tessa, if I hadn't ruined things with you, I might've been with you when this happened."

He pulled back to look at me, keeping his arm around my waist. "Am I wrong?"

I bit my lip, unsure how to respond.

Was he right? Was it so crazy to think I would've been sleeping in his bed if he hadn't put such a rift in the relationship we were building?

I closed my eyes against the onslaught of conflicting emotions that swirled through me. The memories of Menoetius' dream walk still burned within me, but they were being overwhelmed by my need to be happy. To feel loved.

I opened my eyes and looked into his. A soft smile turned up the corners of his mouth.

I felt my cheeks redden. "I was shouting again, wasn't I?"

"A little."

I scooched up on my pillow so I could look him in the eye.

"You didn't ruin things, Nate, you just put a kink in them. I needed time to wrap my head around everything, that's all."

"And have you? Wrapped your head around things?"

"I think so. I think tonight kind of put it all in perspective, you know?"

"How so?"

"I'm pretty positive I would've died tonight if Menoetius wanted me to," I said, shuddering slightly. "But I didn't, and now I'm here. This might sound nuts, but I've been thinking a lot about some of the things Hera said to me that day. One of the things she talked about was how stupid humans were for waiting for an opportune time to voice feelings. I thought it was crazy at first, but I think she's right. I've spent so much time these last couple of weeks thinking about whether I should forgive you, and I'm realizing now, I already have. I just felt like I should make you wait, suffer a little."

I smiled up at him. "After tonight, I'm realizing how stupid that was."

He smiled back and brushed his thumb along my jaw. "Does that mean I get another chance?"

I smiled apprehensively. "Yes. I mean, if you want one."

He pulled me in tighter and kissed my forehead.

"There's nothing I'd love more," he murmured.

My lips curved up into a smile. "So should we, like, kiss or some-thing?" I asked, trying to keep my tone teasing.

He laughed quietly, then tilted his head down and laid his lips on mine. He ran his fingers through my hair and down my arm before linking them with mine.

Suddenly, a question that had been bugging me for a while popped into my head. I pulled back and frowned.

"Hey, speaking of your mother, can I ask a weird question?"

He gave me a dubious look. "I suppose."

"How did your parents come up with your name? It's so…"

He laughed. "Human? Yes, I know. I was wondering when you'd ask about it, actually." He sighed and rolled his eyes. "That was all Hera. According to Ares, she and Zeus had been fighting quite a lot while she was pregnant with me. I'm not sure what about, exactly, but most likely my father's lack of fidelity. Apparently she threatened to give me the most human name she could think of if he didn't shape up. He didn't, and he was absent for my birth, so he ultimately had no say."

My mouth dropped open.

"Hold on." I shook my head in disbelief. "You're telling me that your mother named you Nathaniel purely to spite your father?"

He gave me a wry smile. "Does that really surprise you?"

"Yes! Why didn't he just change it?"

"A god's name can't be changed once it's given. The Fates don't allow it. So, I got stuck with Nathaniel while all of my siblings got the best names."

"Eh." I shrugged. "At least your name is easy to shorten. You can't really do that with many of the others."

He chuckled, then kissed my forehead. "I guess there's always a silver lining. You should sleep. I'm not sure what time Ares and Athena will be expecting you, but I know you'll be required to train tomorrow. Or today, technically."

I looked out the picture window next to his bed and saw that the sky was turning a pale purple.

I groaned. "Can't you write me a note or something?"

He laughed. "You'll be fine. I'm going with you this time. *Every* time, if I have anything to say about it."

"Good. I've hated not seeing you these last few weeks," I admitted.

"I wish you knew how badly I wanted to come find you," he said. "Giving you space took more self-control than I thought I had."

"Well, I don't need space anymore."

He kissed my forehead and pulled the covers up around my shoulders. "I'm happy you're here, Tessa."

I wrapped my arm around his waist and snuggled closer. "I'm happy, too."

43

TESSA

"Well, it looks like you two had a productive evening."

A smooth voice startled me out of a dead sleep a few hours later. Nate and I had fallen asleep wrapped up in each other, our arms and legs a tangled mess.

Nate let out a groan as he rolled off of me and pulled a pillow over his head.

I peeked over the edge of the blanket to see Apollo smirking down at us.

"Good morning Tessa. Would you be so kind as to wake your lover?"

My eyes widened and I shot an elbow into Nate's side, causing him to grunt.

"I'm awake," he mumbled, pulling the pillow from his face and rubbing his eyes. "And just because you're an Elder and my brother doesn't mean you shouldn't knock. It's rude."

"I'd just assumed you'd let her get some sleep, that's all. Now come on, it's time to get up."

Nate lifted his head and glared at his brother who'd just taken a seat at the foot of the bed.

"She did sleep, Apollo. Now go away."

"I'd like to avoid any morning—" he eyed us both "—shenani-gans, if possible, so I think I'll stay until I'm certain that won't be happening."

Just then, the door opened, and Athena stepped into the room. "Oh, good, they're awake." She smiled sweetly at me. "Tessa, dear, it's time to get moving."

"Oh, for the love of—is this entirely necessary?" Nate sat up, glaring at both of them.

"What's the problem? Is this relationship a secret?" Athena glanced between us, her brow furrowed. "No one told me."

"This is mortifying," I muttered, covering my face with my hands and thanking the gods that we hadn't done more than kiss the previous night.

"Gods, I hate you both," Nate groaned.

"Come, Athena," Apollo said, his lips twitching as though he was trying not to smile. "I think we've embarrassed the poor girl enough for one morning."

"Of course," Athena said. "Oh, here, Tessa. I brought you some coffee. Nathaniel had mentioned you liked it, and Apollo explained what happened last night so I thought it might help this morning." She walked over and set the to-go cup on the nightstand next to me. Her lips wobbled, as though she was trying not to smile. "Although it, um, seems as though you're feeling better."

"Out!" Nate threw a pillow at his sister. "Now!"

"Thank you for the coffee," I said. She flashed me a quick smile, then grabbed Apollo's arm and dragged him into the living room.

As soon as the door clicked shut, I sat bolt upright.

I looked at Nate, my mind reeling from the Elders' sudden presence.

"What just happened? Is that normal? For your siblings to just show up in your room?"

Nate got up and started digging through his drawers, emerging a few seconds later with a dark red t-shirt. He started to change, and it took all my willpower not to openly appreciate what I saw.

He grinned, and I realized he'd likely heard my thoughts.

"So...is that normal?" I asked, steering my thoughts back to my original questions.

"For Athena, yes. Hermes and Dionysus also have no boundaries, as I'm sure you've gathered. Apollo hasn't been here in ages, though."

"They totally think we slept together, don't they?"

"That would be my guess." He sat down next to me and took my hand. "I'm sorry about that."

"It's okay, I guess," I said with a shrug. "I probably would've thought the same."

I picked up the coffee cup and took a sip, letting out a small groan as the flavor hit my tongue.

"Really?"

I opened my eyes and saw Nate staring at me in disbelief. "Hey, don't knock it 'til you've tried it."

I held out the steaming cup. "Here."

He gave me a crooked smile as he pulled on clean socks. "No."

"Come on. You'll love it."

"I can promise I won't."

"One sip."

He stared down at me and I could see that he was considering it. Finally, he reached down and took the cup. He took a small sip, then wrinkled his nose and handed the cup back to me.

"Like I said, burnt bean water."

"Will you two please come on!" Apollo's irritated voice drifted through the door.

"We should go before he comes back in," Nate said, depositing my black suitcase on the bed before walking into the bathroom to brush his teeth.

I sighed. "Definitely wouldn't want that."

"So considering recent events, we've decided that we're going to take a break from practicing your powers today," Athena said when we arrived at the zipline field. "Ares and Apollo thought it might be best for you to work with weapons since we haven't done that much yet."

"Oh. Okay." I tried to hide my disappointment. I wanted to get back into the work I'd done with Genevieve and her whips.

Ares, who'd been waiting for us when we arrived, arched a brow. "Disappointed?"

"Maybe a little. I like what we were doing yesterday with those whips, and I was hoping to get in some more practice with Mentalist powers."

"I understand, but unfortunately, Menoetius did have a point when he threatened you last night," Ares explained. "We haven't trained you to defend yourself against an attacker who can disable powers. To our knowledge, he's the only one capable of such a feat, but you still need to be prepared for all manner of attack. You need to understand the gravity of this situation, Tessa. He very well could have killed you."

I pressed my lips together and nodded, not wanting him to see how much that possibility terrified me.

He cast a glance at Apollo who folded his arms across his chest.

A stony look overtook Apollo's face as he addressed me. "Are you able to shore up your mental walls thoroughly? We'll be having some guests today who should probably not be apprised of last night's attack, and I'd rather not let that cat out of the bag just yet."

"Yes, I think so." I'd been working on it quite a bit over the last couple of weeks, but my control was still spotty at times.

I frowned and looked up at Nate.

"She has a tendency to shout at times, though," he said. "What's going on?"

Before Ares could answer, the air shifted around us.

"Lock up tight, Tessa," Ares warned, just as Prometheus and Epimetheus emerged out of thin air.

Nate choked back a laugh. "You're going to have her fight with a Titan? Are you insane?"

"You have too little faith in her skills, Nathaniel," Prometheus said, smiling as he handed me a staff. "Haven't you seen her with one of these?"

"Of course I have. It doesn't change the fact that you've got several thousand years of experience on her."

"It's fine, Nate, really," I murmured.

"Don't worry, Nathaniel," Prometheus said, handing Epimetheus the other staff. "My brother won't hurt her, and I told Tessa I was going to set them up to spar one of these days."

I looked at Epimetheus and saw that he was eyeing me warily.

"Is that so?" Nate looked down at me and raised a brow.

"Yes, he did tell me that," I replied, ignoring Nate's look of annoyance. "It was about two seconds before I met your parents, though, so back off. It's just sparring, Nate. Even if I do get hurt, I'll heal in two seconds, anyway."

Nate sighed, then gave me a quick kiss on the top of my head. "Alright. Good luck, then." He moved aside and took a place next to Ares, arms folded across his chest.

Prometheus gave his brother a light shove in my direction.

Epimetheus stopped a few feet away, then gave me a tight smile. "If it's any consolation, I told him that this was a bad idea," he said quietly.

I stared at him, stunned to hear actual words come out of his mouth. His voice had the same baritone as Prometheus, but it was quieter, not as assertive. Calming, even.

Before I could respond, he took advantage of my shock and shot one end of his staff at me.

"Shit!" I jumped back, narrowly avoiding a stinging hit to my collarbone.

As he moved to take another swing, I whipped my staff up and let it crack against his, then gave a heavy shove and sent him stumbling back a step. He twirled his own weapon gracefully as he slowly made his way forward, and the next time he lunged, I was ready for him. I shot the staff forward, hitting him full-force in the sternum.

He'd barely had a chance to hiss out a breath when I swung low, cracking the staff against his knee. He let out a growl and charged, barely giving me time to react before taking me to the ground, sending my weapon skittering off to the side.

Before he could let go, I grabbed his hair and yanked his head back, using his own momentum to flip him to his back. I scrambled backward and jumped to my feet, dancing back a few steps to grab my staff. I'd barely gotten a grip on it when he lunged toward me again.

As we fought, I began to see signs of life on his face. A determined look or the flash of a dimple as a smile spread across his face. He looked like he was having fun, and I could easily say the same for myself.

Yet no matter how long we fought, neither of us gained the higher ground.

His movements seemed unique but felt predictable. Too often, I found myself blocking a move that he'd barely begun. He moved with the speed you'd expect of a Titan, but he didn't land any blows.

"Are you going..." I brought the end of my staff up to block a swing toward my shoulder. "—easy on me?"

"Not at all," he said. He flipped his weapon so that he was holding it like a baseball bat and swung toward my torso. I dodged out of the way and was about to launch a counter attack when Ares cut us off.

"Okay, let's stop there," he said.

Epimetheus and I both stepped back, and let our weapons fall to the ground. Grabbing a small towel off a nearby bench, I wiped the sweat from my hands and arms, then took a few large swallows of water.

Ares came to stand beside me.

"Epimetheus, why aren't you challenging her?"

Epimetheus raised his eyebrows, which were glistening with sweat. "I am. As my brother said, she's a very good fighter."

I glanced over at Nate, but he just shrugged.

"Okay then," Ares said. "Tessa, you can spar with me next."

I gaped at him, then laughed. "Are you—seriously?"

He cocked his head to the side and gave me a confused look. "You're more concerned with fighting me than a Titan?"

"I, uh—" I looked to Epimetheus, who had an impassive expression, not wanting to offend him. "No offense, but he is a war god."

"None taken."

"You need to fight someone who will challenge you," Ares said. "After me, you'll fight Athena."

"Great," I muttered.

"You totally went easy on me," I said breathlessly, glowering at Epimetheus. "There's no other explanation."

I'd just finished my fifth sparring session, this time with Athena, who'd wielded a pair of her silver arrows that were most certainly *not* for sparring, and now I was sitting, bruised, bloody and aching, on the ground. Nate sat down beside me and handed me my bottle of water. Thankful, I gulped down half of it in one shot.

Epimetheus sat down on one of the long wooden benches along the side of the field. "I promise, I did not. I'm just out of practice."

"You two have very similar fighting styles, that's all," Prometheus said.

I used my sleeve to brush dried blood off my neck from where Athena had pricked me with one of her arrows.

"It's alright, Tessa." Athena sat down on the other side of me and set her arrows down in the grass.

She bumped me with her shoulder.

"You did wonderfully, considering you haven't fought against any gods before."

"I guess," I said, wincing as I laid back on the cool grass. "Can we go back to practicing powers tomorrow? They're a lot less painful."

"I'd like her to get one more day with weapons and some hand-to-hand," Apollo said from his spot next to Prometheus. "She's demonstrated adequate skill with her powers, but this can't be how she fights in front of Zeus, and it certainly can't be how she faces Menoetius."

I sat up and glared at him.

"Hey! I think I did pretty well, considering you just pitted me against two war gods and a Titan!"

He raised his eyebrows, an amused look on his pale face. "Oh? Tell me, how does your back feel after that final blow my sister just dealt? What would your reaction have been if that happened while in combat? Do you think Menoetius would have reached out a hand and helped you up like Athena did? He would've gutted you in a heartbeat," he said, his tone dripping with disdain.

"Enough, Apollo," Nate said sternly. "She's been fighting for hours."

"This is not the time to defend her, Nathaniel," Apollo snapped. "She needs to focus, not be coddled. There are no fatigue breaks in war."

"No one is coddling her," Nate snapped. "You're expecting too much."

"Expecting too much?" Apollo laughed. "I don't think it's unreasonable to think—"

"Enough!" Ares barked. "If you two cannot be civil, then leave. Bicker all you want, but do it elsewhere."

"Imagine putting up with this for three millennia," Athena whispered, leaning close. "Stick around long enough and you'll want to throw them both to the crows."

I bit back a smile as Nate and Apollo sent identical glares at their sister. I bit my lip, trying not to laugh at how similar their facial expressions were.

"Fortunately for us, it's not up to either of you," Athena said. "Tessa is done for the day. Nathaniel, take her home and let her get some rest. The next few days are going to be difficult."

"Worse than today?" I asked.

Ares reached out a hand and pulled me to my feet. "You've only got three more days, Tessa. I think you'll survive."

44

TESSA

Three days later, on the morning of my demonstration, I woke up exhausted. We'd spent the last few days working with various weapons. Some, like the bow and arrow, I knew from my training with John and Analise and my brief stint on the archery team with Mary in freshman year. Others, like the throwing stars, were new to me. Athena brought out several used weapons so I could practice using psychometry, which gave me a bit of a leg up. I was able to learn how the weapons were supposed to be used, see the skill required for them, but full mastery would take some time.

I'd gone to bed the night before my demonstration anxious as to how this day would play out, and it had kept me awake most of the night.

"Would you like me to get you some coffee?" Nate asked as I pulled my black uniform top on.

"Yes, please. That would be amazing."

"Of course." He leaned over and kissed me. "I'll be right back."

While he was gone, I stood in front of the bathroom mirror and attempted to French braid my long hair. Repeatedly, I tried to mimic the way Yana had shown me how to twist the strands, but the pieces kept slipping through my fingers.

"Ugh!" I let the long strands drop after my third attempt. "Stupid hair."

"You still have not figured that out?"

I looked in the mirror and nearly cried in relief when I saw Yana and Mary standing behind me. I spun and leapt at them, forcing them into a three-person hug.

I pulled away and grinned. "What are you guys doing here? Please tell me you're here to do my hair."

Yana laughed. "Of course. Turn around."

"Nate came and got us," Mary said, leaning against the door frame. "He thought you could use some moral support since you're about to go show off for Zeus and all." She arched a brow. "Anything you'd like to tell us?"

"Like what?"

Mary pulled a hand towel off the rack and tossed it in my direction.

"Tessa Avery, you know exactly what!" She pointed a finger at me. "You've been sleeping here for the last three nights, and then Nate came to get us after he went and got you coffee. Coffee! Guys don't get coffee this early unless they're getting something in return."

"That's a horrible gender stereotype," Nate called from the bedroom. "And incredibly untrue."

"Shut it, I'm still pissed at you, even if she's not!"

"Nothing happened," I said, blushing.

She sighed. "But you're together now?"

"Yes."

She huffed and folded her arms across her chest. "Alright, well, if you're happy, I'm happy. But he's still not off my shit list, just so you know."

I grinned. "So are you guys coming with me?"

"Yes," Nate said, coming to stand beside Mary. He handed me my coffee. "I've already cleared it with Zeus. It's Saturday, so they don't have training."

"Not that it would matter, even if we didn't," Mary said, elbowing him.

He rolled his eyes, then brushed a hand over my neatly braided hair. "Finish your coffee, we have to leave in fifteen minutes."

⁓

"Huh," Mary said when we reached the arena floor. "I thought there'd be more of them."

Only a handful of spectators were in attendance. Zeus and Hera, Ares, Athena, Hestia, Apollo, plus Prometheus and Epimetheus, stood waiting on the sideline of the arena floor. Chiron, Charlise, Genevieve, Mary's mentor, Alex, and another Illusionist named Olivette stood waiting to challenge me.

When Hestia saw me, she gave me a small smile.

"Don't let them intimidate you," Nate said, slipping his arm around my shoulders. "You'll be—"

I held up a hand to cut him off. "Nate, if you say 'you'll be fine,' I will punch you in the face. I don't care how pretty you are."

Mary snorted.

"Fine," he murmured, pressing his lips to my hair. I felt them curve into a smile. "You're going to do terribly."

"I don't think that is helpful, either," Yana said dryly.

"No, it's really not," I agreed.

I took a deep breath as we approached Zeus who was standing with Hera, Ares, Apollo, Chiron, and Athena at the base of the stairs leading up into the stands. Butterflies took up residence in my stomach as a thousand doubts and questions started running through my mind. I tried to push them aside and give myself a quick pep talk, but it was a struggle.

"Never doubt yourself, Tessa."

I came up short and latched onto Nate's arm.

He looked down at me curiously. "Tessa?"

I flicked a glance toward the gods standing nearby, then gave my mental walls a poke.

'Can they hear us?' I asked him.

'No. What is it?'

'My dream, Nate. The one I had a few weeks ago. Atlas called me by name.'

I pushed the memory of that specific moment into his mind and watched as his eyes widened. I mentally kicked myself for not letting him see the whole dream when I'd had it.

'How is that possible?' I asked.

He shook his head, his forehead furrowed in confusion.

'I don't know, Tessa, but I think it's time we bring this to Prometheus and Epimetheus.'

"Ah, Tessa! There you are."

I jumped at the sound of Zeus' voice as he approached. His eyes crinkled as he smiled down at me.

"How are you feeling this morning? Is Nathaniel giving you one last pep talk?"

I forced a smile on my face. "I—yes, he is. I'm not sure how much it's helping, though."

Zeus let out a laugh and patted my shoulder. "No need to be nervous. I've heard from your trainers that you're doing well. You even bested Epimetheus in a fight, correct?"

I let out a nervous laugh. "I think he might've been going a little easy on me."

"Nonsense! Prometheus says you're a promising fighter. I'm eager to see what you can do. Now, let's begin, shall we?" He arched a brow at Nate. "Nathaniel, it's time to let go now."

Nate leaned down so he was eye level with me, then put one hand on either side of my face and kissed me.

"Good luck," he whispered. *'I'm going to show Apollo your dream and see what he can make of it.'*

I gave him a weak smile and nodded.

As if I needed anything else to worry about.

"You're gonna do great, Tess," Mary said wrapping her arms around my waist.

Yana squeezed my shoulder. "Yes, I think we might have to find some wine tonight so we can celebrate." She eyed Nate. "I suppose he can come."

"Thanks," he said, laughing.

Mary and Yana followed Nate up the stairs to take seats in the first row. I was about to head over to Athena, Ares, and Chiron for instruction when Hera stopped me.

"Tessa, a moment please?"

"Oh, um, sure." I smiled and let her lead me to a spot about ten feet away. "How are you?"

"I'm well." She cast a quick glance in Nate's direction before facing me. "I take it you've made a decision about my Nathaniel?"

"Yes, I have."

She clasped her fingers in front of her. "You're certain of your choice?"

"Completely," I responded, forcing as much conviction into my voice as possible.

A smile spread across her lovely face. "I'm happy to hear that." She reached out and took my hands, her delicate fingers wrapping tightly around mine. "As I said, you seem like a very nice girl. You've brought something out of Nathaniel that I haven't seen in some time."

"I appreciate you saying that. He really does mean the world to me."

"Good. I'm glad you were able to get past his mistakes."

"I am, too."

She gave my hands a quick squeeze before letting go. "Good luck, Tessa. I'm sorry my insufferable husband is making you go through this farce."

"It's okay. It's better to know what I can do now, right?"

She laughed, then patted me on the cheek. "Whatever you say, dear. Now, off you go. You'll be starting in just a few moments."

With one last smile, she went and joined her family.

I blew out a heavy breath, then made my way to my trainers.

I grinned at Chiron. "I didn't expect to see you here today," I said.

He laughed. "I've missed seeing your progress. Ares and Athena have kept me up to speed, but I wanted to see how you were doing myself."

"Well, I'm glad you're here. One more friendly face definitely helps."

"You'll always have my support Tessa," he said, squeezing my shoulder.

I gave him a tight-lipped smile, then turned to Ares and Athena. "So, how is this going to play out?"

"It's nothing too complex," Athena. "You'll do a bit of weaponry work, but Zeus isn't terribly concerned about that, considering your Psychometric ability. Aside from that, you'll be pitted against mentors to show what you can do with your powers. You'll want to be sure to use as wide a range as possible."

"Okay." I nodded. "So what's first?"

"Weapons," Ares said, tossing me a staff. "We'll stick with this since it's what you're most proficient in. After that, it will be up to you to determine which powers to use to defend yourself."

"Got it." I turned the weapon over in my hands, checking it over for splinter or cracks. "Who am I fighting first?"

"That would be me," Prometheus said, coming to a stop next to me.

I gaped at him, then looked back to Ares and Athena. "You said mentors!"

Athena laughed. "A wide range of opponents is the best way to demonstrate your skills."

"This sounds like a terrible idea."

"It's really quite a good one," Prometheus said. "It was Epimetheus' idea, actually."

I arched a brow at his quiet brother, who just shrugged. I put my hands on my hips and faced Prometheus. "You're about a thousand times better than I am."

"You fought my brother, Ares, and Athena yesterday. There's no need to be fearful of me."

"Your brother didn't fight me, he let me win... even if he won't admit it. Ares and Athena kicked my ass. How could I possibly demonstrate my abilities against someone who's probably going to lay me out in five seconds?"

"Because you're not going to let me lay you out in five seconds." He took the second staff from Ares and walked to the middle of the field.

Athena came over and put her arm around me. "I've seen you fight, Tessa, and so has he," she whispered. "We wouldn't pit you against him if we didn't think you could handle it."

"You guys put way too much faith in me," I replied, trying desperately to squash my aching case of nerves.

"Never," she said. She gave me a small push. "Now go. And remember, use your powers. You'll want to show your skill with a weapon, certainly, but don't ever feel restricted by it. Your powers are weapons, too."

"Got it. Power is my weapon." I rolled my neck and let out a few cracks, then walked onto the field to where Prometheus was waiting for me, grinning.

"Don't look so nervous, Tessa. The staff isn't my normal weapon, so you've got a leg up there. Just look at this as no more than a sparring session. A scrimmage."

"No, I know, it's just that you're really big and scary."

"And my twin wasn't?"

"No."

He barked out a laugh, then looked over my shoulder. I looked back and saw that all the bystanders had taken seats and were waiting for us to begin. Nathaniel had taken a seat just behind Apollo. Both wore tense expressions, so I assumed Nate had told him about my dream.

"Ignore them," Prometheus whispered. "Just treat this as another practice session and focus on me."

"Easy for you to say," I muttered. I lifted my weapon and got into a fighting stance.

"Let's begin!" Zeus bellowed from his place in the front row.

"Alright, Tessa. Let's show them what you've got."

Without warning, Prometheus swung one end of his staff up

toward my face. I barely got my own up in time to avoid a bruised jaw. I scowled, then responded with an upward thrust to the sternum, aiming for the soft area just between his ribs.

He grinned as he dodged the hit, and we began moving at a rapid pace. He landed several blows, but I pushed back just as hard. He was far more skilled than his twin. I felt bruises bloom and heal all over my body. I could tell quickly that there was no way I'd be winning this fight without using my powers.

Finally, when he had me pinned by the neck to the wall, he sighed. "Now would be a good time to start using those powers."

I tossed my weapon aside, then pressed my hand to his chest and let out a bolt of green electricity. I heard Yana let out a whoop as she saw her own power shoot from my hands.

Prometheus fell back, wincing as he clutched his chest. "There's a girl." He dropped his hands and advanced on me, his singed shirt still smoking.

I pulled moisture from the air and let it fall onto the sandy floor, then froze it under his feet. As he jumped aside to avoid slipping, I began moving toward the center of the arena.

Hands latched onto me from behind. Reaching up, I flipped my attacker over my back, then used the power of Earth to open the ground beneath her. The crevasse I formed caused Genevieve to stumble, then quickly right herself.

I glared at her, then a swirling tornado surrounded her, holding her in place. I threw a whip of fire around her ankles, pulling her to her knees. The second she hit the ground, she went invisible. Surprised, my grip on the whip loosened and I lost focus on the small cyclone.

Suddenly, she was on top of me, pinning me to the ground and knocking the wind out of me. I gave a hard shove, knocking her backward, then used my telekinesis to send her sliding twenty feet down the arena floor.

Prometheus was back up, and he'd been joined by Charlise. Genevieve jumped up, and the three stalked toward me. Alex joined them, freezing the ground beneath my feet, causing me to focus hard on not falling. I fired off a handful of fire bullets, breaking his focus long enough for me to melt the frozen ground. Genevieve cracked a whip of fire toward me, and I met it with a water whip of my own, then hit her with a blast of Coercion, halting her in her tracks.

Just as I finished dispatching her, images of those I loved flickered around me.

Everywhere I looked I was confronted by the faces of John and Analise, Mary, Yana, Eric, Leila, Josh, and Nate. I spun, unsure who I needed to take out in order to break the illusion. Charlise was right in front of me, but Olivette had just walked onto the field, too.

I was jolted from the side as another body crashed into me, knocking me to the ground.

"Don't let the illusions distract you," Epimetheus whispered as he wrapped me in a headlock. "Ignore them."

I went invisible, and his arms loosened just a hair, allowing me to slip through. I threw a gust of wind that sent him sailing to the other side of the arena, then did the same for Olivette, causing the illusions to flicker out. As Genevieve started back up with her fire whip, I responded by dousing her with icy water. When Charlise tried to take over my body with a mind link, I used Coercion to force her back out.

I felt a sharp sting on my ear. I spun around and saw Athena coming toward me with her bow and arrow, a second arrow already nocked.

Shit. They weren't messing around.

She aimed and fired three more silver arrows, nicking my arm and leg, tearing holes in my uniform. Taking a gamble, I used telekinesis to pull the bow out of her hands, then I tossed it into the upper level of the arena. She glared at me, but I thought I saw a hint of admiration.

I didn't know how long I'd been fighting when Charlise finally caught me in a trap of illusions. One moment, I was preparing to fight off yet another attack by Prometheus, and the next, I was surrounded by a dozen mirror images of my former mentor.

I rushed forward, but a gale force wind pushed me back. I turned in the opposite direction and was met with the same resistance.

Clearly, she was getting help from Genevieve's wind power. I tried to use Coercion to get into Gen's head, but this time, it was locked down tight.

Still feeling the pressure of Genevieve's wind on all sides, I racked my mind for things that could break Charlise's illusion.

"Having trouble, Tessa?"

Charlise's sweet southern drawl sounded almost menacing. Her words echoed off one another, like too many radios playing the same station at once.

"There aren't many things that can shatter an illusion, you know."

I spun in a circle, examining each version of the blond-haired mentor before me. "Care to enlighten me?"

"Look around, Tessa. Who holds the most powerful weapon in this arena, aside from you?"

Frantically, I scanned the scant number of onlookers. Ares and Athena used physical weapons, Nate's Coercion clearly wasn't an option, Hera had nothing to offer, and Mary, Yana, and the mentors all had powers I had easy access to but were useless on illusions.

Then suddenly, I knew.

I looked between two of Charlise's illusions and saw Zeus sitting in the front row, arms folded across his chest.

I felt a smile pull at the corners of my mouth.

"'Atta girl," Charlise whispered, sounding pleased.

Then with all my strength, I forced out a thunderbolt of blue lightning that sent a shockwave through the entire arena, destroying the images of Charlise that surrounded me.

A look of shock came across Zeus' face as he and the rest of the onlookers were thrown back in their seats.

Before I could rejoice at my success, I felt a ripping sensation. Everything inside of me shattered, as though the lightning was splintering my soul into a thousand pieces.

Daggers of pain tore through my mind, causing me to stumble. I bent at the waist and gripped the sides of my head, trying to will it all away, but the emotion, the feeling of it all began to overwhelm me. Something crawled from my subconscious, a memory of someone that had long been forgotten, and beat against me, digging into my brain like railroad spikes. It was strong, familiar, and really freaking determined.

I tried to open my eyes, but each time I dragged them open, all I saw was blinding blue light. Visions began to flood my consciousness, no more than rapid flashes of light and color, but they were pulling me under.

Strong arms caught me as I fell to my knees.

Something hot sparked all around me, sending vicious pain across my skin. The arms that had caught me fell away.

"Zeus!"

I tried to focus on the voices that were yelling nearby, but the pain was too much.

I reached out for something to lean on but found nothing.

Instead, I fell, crashing to the sandy floor, and slowly began to fade into darkness.

45

NATHANIEL

The shockwave from Tessa's burst of power rippled through the arena, sending all of us slamming against the backs of our seats. Everyone in the stands sat, stunned, as we watched my father's lightning dance across her body. Charlise, who'd been standing next to Tessa and had attempted to catch her as she fell, lay unconscious on the ground beside her. The moment she'd touched Tessa, she'd been shocked with the full force of my father's lightning. It would take days for her to heal from that.

There was a beat of silence before anyone reacted.

Slowly, Zeus stood. He swayed, then put a hand out to steady himself on the rail in front of him. Hera sat beside him, her head clutched in her hands. A soft whimper sounded from below me, and I looked down to see Athena leaning against the arena wall rubbing her temples, her bow and arrow lying on the ground beside her.

"Athena, what is it?"

"Something hurts," she murmured, squeezing her eyes shut. "My head—" Her eyes sprung open and met mine. "We need to go to her." Her voice quavered, and I thought I saw a hint of fear in the set of her mouth.

"This is not how this was supposed to happen," Apollo

murmured, sounding resigned. I noticed he was one of the few who didn't appear to be in pain. "Come on, Nathaniel."

Before I could voice my anger, he stood and hurried down the steps toward Tessa. I followed, and I was quickly joined by Athena, her hand tucked tightly in mine as she pulled me after him.

We'd nearly reached Tessa when Zeus leapt over the rail and stormed forward.

"How in all the realms was this girl able to use my power?" Zeus roared, taking several unsteady steps toward Tessa's still form.

"She's a Mimic, Father. What did you expect?" Athena rubbed her forehead as Zeus came to stand beside us. "Gods, that hurt."

"Get her up," Zeus snapped. "We'll get to the bottom of this."

Tessa groaned, and slowly struggled to her hands and knees as the lightning continued to roll over her.

Before I could move toward her, Apollo gripped me by the shoulders and pulled me back.

"She's still channeling his power, Nathaniel. You can't touch her."

I spun around, turning my back on Tessa as I glared at him in disbelief. I pushed him back toward the arena wall. "Can you tell us all what's wrong with her now, Apollo? Or does your interdiction prevent that, too?" I shoved him again, and he did nothing to stop me.

Zeus stepped in front of me before I could go after him again.

"What is he talking about?"

Apollo opened his mouth to respond but was cut off by a quiet voice.

"Tessa?"

I tore my gaze from them as Epimetheus approached.

His voice was almost childlike as he moved slowly toward Tessa. When he reached her, he sucked in a breath, one hand covering his mouth.

Then he fell to his knees beside her. Tears began to run down his cheeks as he slowly moved one shaking hand toward her.

Prometheus reached out a hand to stop him.

"Epimetheus, you can't—" His hand stopped in midair, and his eyes grew wide as he stared down at the pair.

Hesitantly, Epimetheus rubbed one hand up and down Tessa's arm, using the other to cup her cheek. He winced, but the electricity that had been sparking all around her slowly began to still.

"There you go," he whispered, stroking her arm and pulling her to her knees. "Take it back in."

Her green eyes fluttered open, and she smiled.

"Epimetheus," she breathed, leaning forward to rest her forehead on his shoulder. He wrapped an arm around her and pressed his cheek to her head.

When he looked to his twin, his eyes were full of tears and wide with disbelief. "You see her, don't you, Prometheus? It's really her?" His voice was full of hope.

"How is this possible?" Prometheus' voice came out as a harsh whisper. He turned his eyes on Zeus. "My memories—" His voice turned cold. "How?"

I frowned, unable to tear my eyes from Epimetheus' emotional display.

"I think we should take this back to the palace," Apollo said, his tone urgent.

Prometheus grabbed his arm and glared at him. "I am not going anywhere until you answer me." He jabbed a finger toward Tessa. "How is this possible? This girl has been in front of us for weeks!"

Apollo jerked his arm from the Titan's grasp. "There's a very complex answer to that, Prometheus. The short answer is a spell. Several, actually. The long answer will take a bit more time to explain."

Epimetheus stood, scooping Tessa up into his arms. I walked toward them and gently laid a hand to Tessa's forehead. Her eyes flickered open for a moment, but they stared at me blankly before sliding closed again.

"Hold on." My father stepped forward, elbowing me out of the way as he moved toward Epimetheus. He looked down at Tessa with a curious expression before lifting his wide eyes to meet Epimetheus' gaze.

"Is that—"

"Yes," Epimetheus whispered, his voice thick with emotion.

"Good gods..." Athena whispered as she stared down at Tessa with tear-filled eyes, the fingers of one hand resting on her lips.

Zeus turned to Apollo, eyes wide.

"What is it?" I asked, placing a hand on Athena's arm.

She took a shuddering breath before slumping against me, tears freely flowing down her cheeks. I barely had time to catch her before she slid to the ground.

I heard shouting and saw Mary and Yana trying to force their way past Chiron and Ares.

"As I said," Apollo said. "I think we should take this elsewhere."

Zeus nodded. "Yes, I think you're right," he murmured, his focus back on Tessa, a stunned expression plastered on his face. "Back to the palace, now."

Without waiting for acknowledgement, he vanished, and the twins, Apollo, Athena, and I followed behind.

THE MOMENT we stepped onto my parents' front lawn, Zeus charged up the stairs, threw open the front doors, and stormed inside. Halfway to the living room, he gestured to one of the hallways that led off toward the guest wing where Prometheus and Epimetheus had been living.

"Go, lay her down in one of the guest suites and make sure she's comfortable. Nathaniel, where is your blasted—Athena!"

"Yes, Father, I'm here," she said from just behind me, her voice wobbling and face ashen. It was unnerving; I couldn't remember the last time I'd seen her in such a state.

"Get in there and get the girl taken care of. Do not let any of the servants in, whatever you do. The rest of you, in the living room, now!"

His tone left no room for questions.

I made to follow Epimetheus and Athena down the hall, but my father grabbed me by the back of my shirt and dragged me down the hall with them.

"No, you and your scheming brother are coming with me."

"What are you—I haven't done anything!" I protested, struggling against his grip.

"Father, really, he—"

My father used his other hand to smack the back of Apollo's head, sending his blond hair falling across his forehead.

"Quiet. You're not going to start defending each other now after spitting on one another for nearly three thousand goddamn years."

He threw open the doors to the living room and pushed us both inside. Prometheus followed us in, stone faced.

Zeus shoved us both inside, then advanced on Apollo.

Before my father could speak, Prometheus pushed him aside. He grabbed my brother by the collar of his white shirt, lifting him several inches off the ground until he was eye level.

"Start talking now, Apollo. Tell me why I shouldn't murder you for hiding her away."

Apollo pressed his lips together and pushed against Prometheus. "I haven't hidden—"

I slammed my fist into the wall. "Will someone please tell me what the fuck is going on?"

Tessa was hurt. I needed to go to her, and I couldn't deal with these games.

Prometheus straightened, dropping Apollo back to his feet, not sparing him a glance as he stumbled back several feet. He glared at me. "You truly don't know?"

"Know *what*?"

"Nathaniel, I wanted to tell—"

"No!" I roared at Apollo. "You don't get to speak!"

"Your lover," Prometheus spoke, his breathing heavy as he eyed me curiously. "She's no Ischyra. She's my sister, and your brother has been hiding her from me."

"YOU MEAN to tell me a spell was cast on Tessa to make her unrecognizable? To take away all of our memories of her?"

My father paced slowly in front of his fireplace, listening as Apollo detailed his story.

"Yes. Hecate cast it at Clymene's bidding," my brother explained wearily. He ran a hand over his face, then rested his elbow on the arm of the sofa.

"Yes, Hecate will be dealt with later," Zeus growled.

Ignoring him, Apollo continued his story.

"Clymene wanted her daughter protected from the Titans. She knew Cronus wanted to take her, harness her power, and use it as a weapon in the war. She had Hecate cast a protection spell to fake Tessa's death, sending her soul into Chaos where they couldn't reach her."

His gaze drifted to Prometheus, who stood leaning against the wall.

"Eighteen years ago, Hecate temporarily erased all memory of Tessa from existence and she was reborn in human form."

"She's been here for over a month!" Zeus roared, slamming his fist on the mantle. Small cracks spiderwebbed across the front of the stone surface. "First, you don't tell me—or her, for that matter— about her true identity, now you're telling me our most powerful witch altered all of our memories?"

"Hecate placed an interdiction on Hestia and myself," Apollo said. "I was powerless to tell you any of it."

"Are you telling me she gave neither of you a choice? She placed it without your consent?"

Apollo slumped back in his seat. "No," he admitted. "I had a choice."

I frowned at him. "Why would you agree to something like that?"

His gaze slid to me, and for once, the look we shared wasn't filled with anger or malice. "You may not believe this, Nathaniel, but I had her best interest at heart."

"Why now?" Prometheus' voice was rough. "Why was she brought back to us now?"

"Because the Fates decreed it," Apollo replied. "Hecate will have to explain that aspect in further detail."

"Her nightmares," I said. "Hestia told me that the first vision was a memory. Are you telling me all of her nightmares have been memories of her past life?"

"What nightmares?" Zeus looked between Apollo and me, confused. "What are you talking about?"

I arched a brow at my brother.

"Yes, her dreams were her memories coming to the surface," Apollo responded, ignoring our father's question. "When she shattered Charlise's illusion during her demonstration, the spell that protected her mind and cloaked her identity dissolved, as well."

Zeus banged his fist on the mantle again, sending white dust to the carpet below. "What nightmares?" he roared.

"She's been having them for months," I explained. "Recently, we discovered Atlas was a prominent figure in them."

"She's been dreaming of our brother?" Prometheus pushed himself off the wall and stepped toward me. "When did you discover this?"

"Just a few weeks ago."

"Weeks?" My father stared at me, aghast. "For weeks she's been dreaming about the Titan we've been trying to access for years, and again, you neglected to tell me?" He glared down at Apollo. "And you—"

Apollo's hand drifted from his face. "Yes, Father, I knew, as well."

"What I don't understand," I said to Prometheus, "is why she was dreaming of him. She dreamt of your mother's death as well as her own, but outside of that one instance, he was the focus. I'd just assumed she was a lover, until Menoetius mentioned the physical resemblance."

"Nathaniel!" Apollo snapped.

Prometheus' eyes widened. "She's seen Menoetius? When?"

"He came to her in a dream walk a few nights ago."

Prometheus paled. "Show me," he demanded.

"Me, as well," Zeus said through clenched teeth.

I hesitated, then shared the memory of her dream with them both.

As they watched the events of the dream walk unfold, Zeus cursed, and Prometheus began to look nauseous. He closed his eyes against the vision of her torture, and fresh tears began to fall from his eyes.

"He'll go to any length to torment her," he whispered. He raised his eyes to mine. "He despised her from the moment she was born."

Before I could respond, my father spoke.

"How could you not bring this to me?"

"I'm sorry—" I began.

"It's just as much my doing as it is his," Apollo interrupted. "He brought her to me just after the dream walk occurred."

"I should banish you both to Tartarus for all you've kept from me," Zeus spat, turning to rest his hands on the mantle. "First her powers and now this. It's inexcusable."

I exchanged a glance with Apollo before turning back to Prometheus.

"It seems clear she's close to Epimetheus, but he never appeared in her dreams. Was her relationship with Atlas different?" I asked him.

Prometheus rubbed a hand over his eyes, wiping away the last of the tears, then sighed. "Very much so. They're twins, Nathaniel. Inseparable since birth. Her and Clymene's deaths tore what remained of our family apart and nearly killed him. She was, quite literally, his other half."

46

TESSA

"Tessa, honey, it's time to wake up."

A gentle, honey-sweet voice spoke beside me.

I dragged my eyelids open, then slammed them back shut at the onslaught of color and light that surrounded me.

A warm hand rubbed circles on my back.

"No, sweetheart, none of that. Too many people are waiting for you."

Slowly, I opened my eyes and stared into the porcelain face of Hestia. Her flame-red hair flowed over her shoulders in waves. A tall, slender woman with long, curly black hair, light brown skin, and full, bow-shaped lips stood next to her. Three glittering moons were pinned in her hair.

"There you are," Hestia said, smiling as she stroked my cheek.

"Come, let's sit up, dear," the black-haired woman said. Gently, she helped lift me to a sitting position.

We were sitting on the edge of one of the hot springs. The aqua water steamed in front of me as purple flowers rioted around us.

"Why are we here?"

Hestia tucked my hair behind my ear. "You've got fond memories here, don't you?"

I let my bare feet dangle into the hot water, then closed my eyes.

That's right. I'd been here with Nate.

"Yes," I whispered. "This is where—"

"Where you first realized you could love our Nathaniel." She gave me a knowing smile. "He's a good boy, you know. Quite perfect for you. A true kindred spirit."

I smiled at the memory. I'd thought that, as well.

It seemed so long ago.

"It's different now," I said. I turned to meet Hestia's eyes. "I'm different. All of these memories..."

I squeezed my eyes shut as the blurred memories of my life before swirled through my mind. "What's happening to me?"

"You're waking up," Hestia said, smiling.

"It's been quite some time coming," the other goddess said.

I gazed up at her, then recognition dawned. "You're Hecate," I said. "You were at the transformation ceremony."

"I was. I wanted to see for myself that you'd returned to us."

"You were in my dream, too." I frowned. "I don't understand..."

She gave me a sad smile. "It's a sad story, and I'm sorry I have to be the one to tell it." She twined her long fingers through my own and gazed at me with a look of sorrow. Her eyes were a stormy gray, nearly the same color as her soft sweater, and full of emotion.

"Just before the war started, Cronus discovered a way to steal power from other immortals. Gods, witches, anything with power. He wanted to be invincible, and utilizing the affinities possessed by other immortals was his means to an end."

She squeezed her eyes shut and took a deep breath.

"When your mother discovered Cronus' plan to capture you and use your power to his own gain, she made a deal with me."

"You need to know that your mother loved you very much," Hestia cut in, placing a hand on my back. "Everything she did was for her children."

I frowned, then looked to Hecate. "What kind of deal did she make with you?"

Her eyes searched mine for a moment before she responded. "Her life in exchange for your protection."

"What? No." My eyes darted between them. "Iapetus killed my mother, I watched it happen. You were there."

"Let her finish," Hestia said gently.

"Your mother went to that clearing willingly, Tessa, knowing her life would end. She knew what Cronus expected of Iapetus. The only way I could do what she asked—send your consciousness, your soul, into Chaos for safekeeping—was to use the energy of a powerful immortal being."

"Why not Iapetus? Or anyone else?" My voice wobbled as I struggled to maintain some semblance of composure.

"They wished you harm, dear. Their energy would have done little to protect your soul. Hers was full of love, a desire to protect. Cronus wanted your power, so we needed to hide you away. Had you stayed in this realm, he would have found you. So, when your father killed your mother, I directed her energy toward you instead of allowing it to flow freely back into Chaos."

I stared down at the warm blue pool as I took in her meaning.

"Then my mother...she wasn't murdered?" I whispered.

"No, honey," Hestia said. "She sacrificed herself."

I sucked in a sharp breath as tears filled my eyes. Clymene's screams of anguish echoed through my mind. I felt myself slowly slump into Hestia's arms as sobs began to tear at my body.

She'd done that—endured that horrific pain—for me.

Hestia wrapped an arm around me and rested her head against mine. "I'm so sorry," she whispered. "I wish I could've told you all of this sooner."

I sniffed, then pulled back to look at her. "Why couldn't you?"

"That was my doing," Hecate said. "The Fates came to me eighteen years ago and told me you'd been reborn, your memories of your life as a Titan stored safely in your deep consciousness. I needed someone I could trust with the information to keep watch over you. I erased all memory of you, then placed an interdiction on Hestia and Apollo and instructed them to keep you focused on your training.

Once you were strong enough, I intended to explain it all to you myself."

Annoyance flashed through her eyes when she looked at Hestia.

"Things became a bit more rushed once Hestia found a loophole and flagged that memory in your subconscious. Your Coercer saw it immediately when he looked into your mind."

"So the other dreams...the ones I had before, where I couldn't see anything?"

"Those dreams were your memories peeking through, that's true, but they were, for the most part, locked down tightly. Once that first one was let loose from your subconscious, it left a crack for others to seep through. When Nathaniel opened your mind during your transformation ceremony, more slipped free. That's why you began having such vivid dreams after your powers were awakened."

I stared at the steam as it rose lazily from the water, trying to take in all she was telling me.

"Those memories are from an earlier time, Tessa, but they don't change who you are," Hecate said.

I huffed out a small breath.

Easy for you to say, I thought.

I turned to Hestia. "You said something to me, back when I was still human. Something about gaining a piece of myself that had been dormant? Being the same Tessa I was, but complete. Is this what you meant?"

"It is," she said, smiling sadly.

"But I feel so broken," I protested as tears once again threatened to fall. "I have vague memories of being a Titaness, and I remember the way it felt to be sent into Chaos, but I don't remember actually being there. It's as though I went from Titaness to human, and there's this huge blank spot in the middle."

"It's as Hestia said," Hecate responded. "That piece of you was dormant until you were reborn. A soul is not a being with awareness of its surroundings. It needs a lifeforce, a living being, in order to truly exist and create memories."

"Why now?"

"I'd hoped to bring you back after the war, once Cronus was destroyed, but Zeus decided to sentence him to Tartarus, instead. After a time, the Fates became concerned that your soul would begin to deteriorate if it didn't have a lifeforce to attach to, so when they said it was time to bring you back, I acquiesced to their demands. When you were an infant, I cast a cloaking spell that hid your memories and memories of your prior existence from those who knew you."

"Wouldn't it have been better to return me to my brothers? You know they would've protected me," I asked Hecate.

"Your brothers were...difficult when it came to you, Tessa. You'll remember that in time. Prometheus and Epimetheus would've gone back to being overprotective. They'd have kept you locked in a bubble of safety, only permitting you freedom when you took it by force." She gave me a fond look. "Which you did, often and loudly, as you'll soon recall. Maybe it sounds silly, but I wanted more for you than that. I thought it much more prudent to send you into a life where you'd be given freedoms to become your own person."

She smiled and ran her hand over my hair. "I knew your mother, Tessa, and I'm certain that's what she would have wanted for you."

"Wait, if you put this spell on everyone that might recognize me, how did Menoetius know who I was?"

"Ah. Yes, Menoetius is tricky," Hecate said. "He has the ability to disable powers, even my own if he puts his mind to it. Creating an illusion or casting a spell on someone with that power can be incredibly difficult. You had no memory of him, but due to his abilities, his memories of you were much harder to erase."

"I see."

I was quiet for a moment as I tried to shake off the memory of his blade against my skin.

"And Atlas? What about my twin?"

"Atlas is..." Hecate stared absently into the water, gently trailing her bare feet back and forth. "He blamed himself a great deal for your death. Zeus was unaware that Atlas had left Cronus' side, so when he found him, he imprisoned him. At that point, Atlas' grief turned him into little more than a shell of the man you knew, so he did nothing to clear his name."

"But Zeus released him! Why hasn't he returned?"

"He did release him," Hestia said gently. "Once he knew the truth, not two years later. Atlas has been punishing himself for centuries for your death."

I narrowed my eyes. "Then why wouldn't he have returned once his memories of me disappeared? Once he had no reason to grieve anymore?"

"Unfortunately, that's something neither of us has an answer for," she replied. "Hopefully in time, you'll discover his reasons."

A sudden warmth surrounded me, and I felt a slight pressure on my waist.

"Tessa, it's time for you to return to the waking world," Hecate said. "Everyone is waiting for you. Zeus can explain the rest of your brother's story now that my spell has been lifted.'

I nodded, blinking back tears.

Here in this quiet world, I was safe with Hestia and Hecate. They knew my story, they knew who I was, and they didn't seem to care.

Out there in the waking world were the people who loved me. Or at least, the Ischyra version of me.

Would they still love me as a Titaness?

I felt tears dripping down my cheeks. I looked down at my wrist and ran a thumb over the shimmery purple Ischyra mark. It seemed like eons had passed since my transformation.

"What if they don't want me?" I sniffed and wiped at my eyes. "I want my brothers back, but I also want everyone from the last eighteen years back, too. Mary, Nate, all of them. I don't think I can live in a world where that isn't possible."

"Oh, honey," Hestia whispered, her eyes brimming with tears as she pulled me in for a hug. "They all love you more than you know. You'll see."

We sat like that for a few more moments before she finally placed a hand on my cheek.

"Are you ready?" Hestia asked.

I nodded, wiping away my tears one more time. "I am."

She laid a kiss to my forehead. "Then off you go."

47

TESSA

When I woke, my eyes still burned with tears. I groaned and buried my face in the soft pillow under my head, blocking out the sunlight that was streaming through the massive, richly draped windows.

After a few moments, I slowly opened my eyes and took in my surroundings. Epimetheus was asleep in a chair next to the bed, arms crossed over his chest and feet propped on an ottoman.

Mary was curled on a tan chaise that had been pulled up next to him, her hands tucked under her chin and knees pulled to her chest. Her wavy brown hair was a mess, and a small frown rested on her face.

Something tightened on my waist, and I realized that there was a strong arm wrapped around me.

"Tessa?"

A whispered voice spoke next to me and a soft hand touched my shoulder. I rolled onto my back and was greeted with the sight of Nate's midnight blue eyes, full of concern, looking down at me.

"Hi," I whispered, my voice coming out raspy.

A smile broke across his face and he brushed a hand along my cheek. "Hi."

I looked around the bedroom, not recognizing the cherry-stained wood or Grecian style furniture.

"Where are we?"

He put a finger to his lips and switched over to mental speak.

'One of the guest wings at my parents' house.' His brow furrowed as his eyes continued to search my face. *'We brought you back here after...'*

I loosened my grip on his hand.

'So you know...everything?'

'Yes, Apollo explained most of it, then Hecate and Hestia gave us the rest. My father is furious, and the twins are beside themselves. Hestia convinced them all to let you rest.'

A smile pulled at the corners of my mouth.

'Then why are there three people in here with me?'

'Epimetheus has refused to leave. After I spoke with Hestia, I thought it might be good if Mary was here when you woke up, so I snuck her in yesterday.'

'And you?' The fear of rejection that I'd had during my dream walk with Hestia and Hecate returned. *'Why are you here?'*

He suddenly looked uncomfortable.

'Do you...not want me to be? She seemed to think—'

My eyes widened at his insinuation, and I gripped the fabric of his shirt.

'No! Gods, no, that's not what I meant.' I put a hand on his cheek. *'I want you here more than you could possibly know.'*

He closed his eyes and pressed his forehead to mine.

'Is it ok if I take a few more minutes with you before we wake the others?'

'Yes, please.'

He tightened his arm around my waist and pulled me close, letting me bury my face into his chest. I inhaled his clean, familiar scent and tried to get a handle on my spinning thoughts.

"Oh, thank the gods, you're awake," a relieved voice said.

I shifted and saw that Mary had woken up. Groggily, she climbed into the bed next to me and wrapped her arm around my waist, nudging Nate's out of the way.

For a moment, she just lay there quietly, her head pressed against my shoulder.

"You scared me, Tessa," she finally whispered.

I rolled over and looked into her pretty hazel eyes. "I'm sorry," I whispered.

"Just promise me that you're still my BFF and we're all good," she said as tears filled her eyes. "If he gets to stick around, I do, too."

"Always," I whispered, pressing my forehead to hers. "I'm so goddamn confused right now, but you will always be my number one."

She lifted her head and arched a brow at Nate.

"You hear that? I'm her number one."

"Yes, I heard," he said dryly. "We should go see the others. The last two days have been...difficult."

I nodded, then squeezed my eyes shut as I tried to sort through the mash up of memories that kept swirling around in my mind.

"Are you okay?" Mary whispered.

"I'm still having some trouble working all of this out in my mind. I have all of these memories and they're just...floating around. My old memories keep fighting with new ones. It's like my mind can't figure out what's real."

I looked over at Epimetheus' sleeping form.

"They're my brothers, but my memories of loving them are clashing with memories of being terrified of them. My mind keeps wanting to disregard one or the other. They're just so muddled."

"I think you should take your time trying to work out how you're going to adapt to all of this," Nate said. "They'll need to adapt, as well. You're not the same sister they lost."

I stared up at the crystal chandelier that hung down from the recessed ceiling.

Sister.

"What if they won't accept that?" I asked.

"If you'd seen them these last two days, you'd know that would never be the case," he replied.

"He's right," Mary added. "Epimetheus hasn't moved since they brought you here."

"I hope you're right," I murmured.

Nate kissed my forehead and slid off the bed. I tried to push myself up, but my arms felt weak. Nate saw my struggle and came around to help me.

"Thanks," I whispered, smiling up at him as he slid me into a sitting position. I noticed someone had changed me out of my training outfit and into the skinny jeans I'd bought at Goddesses, a plain, pink tank top, and a white hoodie.

"Did you dress me?" I asked Mary.

"Yeah, Nate asked me to bring you clothes, and you love those jeans, so..."

"Thanks," I said, leaning in for a hug, trying to ignore how restricted I felt in the tight clothing. Somewhere in the back of my mind, I itched for the soft, flowing fabric of jewel colored dresses.

"Here." Nate handed me a glass of water from the nightstand.

I accepted it gratefully and took a large sip.

"Tessa?" Epimetheus' quiet voice spoke from the corner.

Slowly, he sat forward in the chair, and for a moment, we assessed each other.

"We'll let you two have some privacy," Nate said, pulling Mary off the bed.

Mary opened her mouth to protest but he shook his head.

"Come on, we'll go update Yana and Eric," Nate said.

"Fine," she grumbled. "But you better bring me back." She leaned down and gave me a hug, then gripped me by the shoulders and met my eyes. "We'll talk soon, okay?"

I nodded, then squeezed her hands. "Sounds good."

After Nate had teleported them away, I met Epimetheus' gaze and waited for him to speak.

"Do you remember...anything?"

"I do," I said, absently picking at a loose thread on the blue quilt over my legs. "It's a little confusing, though." I dropped my hands and sighed. "Very confusing, actually."

He rested his arms on his knees and tapped his fingers together. Finally, he raised his eyes to mine.

"What happens now, Tessa? You're my sister, my best friend, yet it's as though you don't even know me."

"I do know you, Epimetheus." I threw back the blanket and moved to sit on the ottoman by his feet. "I'm just having troubling reconciling my old life with my new one. Two days ago, you were helping me train. I was terrified to fight you. That memory doesn't fit with my original memories of you. It's going to take time to work through all of that."

"I understand. It's just—"

He leaned forward and rested his head in his hands.

"What is it?" I put my hand on his head and ran my hand through his messy, dark blond curls. I had vague memories of doing the same thing to soothe him when we were younger.

He lifted his head to look at me, and I saw tears falling down his cheeks.

"After you and Mother died," he began. "We all...well, we all sort of spiraled a bit when you were taken from us. Watching your bodies burn on your funeral pyre...we all became lost in our own way."

I had to blink back more tears as I realized exactly what they'd had to live through once they'd thought me dead. They'd had to burn our bodies, watch as our ashes returned to nature, and learn how to live without us. Two pieces of their hearts had been ripped away in a way they'd believed to be irrevocable.

I closed my eyes, willing myself not to cry again, then met Epimetheus' gaze.

He ran a hand through his hair and sighed. "Prometheus blamed himself, of course, and closed himself off to everyone. He felt he should've seen it coming, so he wrote off Olympus entirely and went to go live in the human world. Atlas lost the will to live, and I...I became so lonely, Tessa. Nothing made sense to me anymore."

He lowered his head and stared at the floor for a moment before continuing.

"Without you and our brothers, I was so, so lonely," he whispered, his voice thick with tears. "Lonely enough that I accepted Pandora from Zeus without even considering what the consequences might be. I thought if I could start a family of my own, it might get better. I had no idea..." He wiped his eyes with the back of his hand. "And then she was taken from me, too. I know it wasn't real, but I'd tasted love, or the illusion of love. Then it was ripped away, and I was forced to watch as humans suffered for my mistakes."

"Gods, Epimetheus," I murmured, pulling him into my arms. He pressed his face to my shoulder and gripped my arms as sobs began to rack his body. In that moment, fury at Zeus and all who helped him trick my brother sparked in my mind. I knew they'd atoned, I knew that Zeus had released my brothers from their prisons, and I knew he felt horrifically guilty about all he'd done. Yet here, holding Epimetheus as he cried, I hated him.

I held him until his crying jag ended. After a few moments, he pulled back and let out a laugh.

"I thought this would be a happy reunion."

I gave him a watery smile. "It'll just take some time to...get back to normal, I guess. Or as close to normal as possible." I rubbed a hand across my forehead. "I don't even know what normal is right now."

"I'll give you all the time you need," he promised. "Prometheus, too, I'll make sure."

"Thank you." I frowned, considering my thoughts just a few moments earlier. "Epimetheus, can I ask you something?"

"Of course."

"Are you really okay with all of this? Working with Zeus, I mean, after what he did to you?"

His eyes searched my face for a few seconds before responding. "I am. If you'd asked me that two thousand years ago, my answer might have been different, but yes, I can say that I'm okay allying myself with him once again."

"You've got no concerns at all?"

He cocked his head to the side and smiled. "You're asking a lot of questions for someone who just woke up after a three thousand year-long nap."

I swatted his shoulder and laughed.

"Very funny. Seriously, though. None?"

"If I didn't have concerns, I'd be a fool. I think we've all learned from our mistakes, but I won't ever forget what he did, or what I did."

I nodded slowly, digesting his words. "Okay. If you can do it, I can, too."

He smiled and ruffled my hair. "You know, I realized something today," he said, letting his hand drop back to his lap. "When we were sparring, you told me I was going easy on you after you won. I think I've figured out why."

The corner of my mouth pulled up in a grin as a dim memory tugged at my mind. "Because you could never win against me?"

He laughed, and I let him wrap his massive hands around mine.

"Once you started your weapons training, Atlas would always call our matches because we took too long." He smiled softly. "You do remember."

I squeezed his hand. "I'm starting to."

I sighed and looked at the heavy wood door that separated us from whoever still waited outside.

"I guess I should go face everyone?"

"You can teleport now," he said with a grin. "I'll give you a head start if you want to take off for a bit."

I considered it for a moment, then shook my head. "No, I can't hide from this." I stood, then rolled my neck a few times to ease the stiffness two days in a bed had left.

"No, I don't suppose you can," Epimetheus said as he rose from the chair and took my hand.

Just as he was about to open the door, Prometheus walked in. He stopped when he saw us, and his eyes ran over my face. His mouth opened, but no sound came out. Finally, he closed the distance between us and pulled me to his chest in a bone-crushing hug.

"Ease back, Prometheus," Epimetheus murmured. "She's still a bit fragile."

Prometheus released me, only pulling back far enough to keep his hands on my shoulders. "Are you alright?"

"I am." I smiled. "A little woozy and pretty confused still, but I think I'm okay."

"Tessa—" A pained expression came across his face. "I don't know how I didn't know...gods, you were right in front of me. I should've—"

"You think you should've known about this?"

"Well, I am the—"

"Don't pull that 'god of forethought' nonsense right now." I put my hands on his cheeks and looked him in the eye. "That makes you intuitive, not all knowing. Please, stop."

He closed his eyes and nodded. "We should go. Zeus wants to see you, and I'm quite sure Hera wants to ensure that you don't intend to seduce her husband now that you're a Titaness again."

My eyes widened. "You—did she say that? Ew! That's Nate's father!"

Prometheus laughed and brushed a hand over my hair. "I think your time as an Ischyra has had a detrimental effect on your vocabulary," he said. "And Hera hasn't outright said as much, but you know how she can be."

"Yes, I do," I muttered. I ran my fingers through my hair and immediately hit several snags. "Hang on, I need to do something with my hair." Someone had left a hair tie on my wrist, so I began to pull it into a ponytail.

"Here, let me," Epimetheus said, taking the tie from me.

I smiled as another long-forgotten memory flashed in my mind.

"Clymene... Mother taught you how to braid my hair," I said fondly. "I remember that."

He laughed as he began combing through the strands, twisting them into a loose braid. "Yes, well, you hated to have your hair down and she got tired of doing it. You couldn't do it on your own, so I offered."

"I couldn't manage it in this life, either. Yana, my roommate, tried to teach me."

"Don't think so highly of him just yet," Prometheus said, laughing. "He only wanted to be on your good side so you'd put in a word with Athena."

"Yes, well, do you blame me?" Epimetheus said, giving my shoulders a quick squeeze as he finished up my hair.

I paused, trying to remember.

I looked up at Prometheus. "Athena and I—we were friends. Right?"

"Damn good ones."

I nodded, trying to recapture the memories of our friendship. "Does she know?"

"She does. She's waiting with the others."

"Alright," I said with a sigh. "Let's go, then."

We made our way out to the living room and found Zeus sitting in an arm chair facing the fire, gazing into the flames. Apollo stood next to the fireplace, sipping a glass of amber liquid and staring at the floor. Hera and Hestia were sitting on one of the Victorian style sofas and Athena was sitting across from them. Her feet were bare and tucked underneath her legs, and her brow was furrowed.

They looked like they were sitting vigil.

The moment we stepped into the room, Zeus' head shot up, and Athena jumped from her seat and faced me. She wobbled a bit, as though she might take a step in my direction but thought better of it. Apollo eyed me curiously, then sat down on the sofa next to Hestia, who was smiling softly. Hera arched a brow and looked at me appraisingly.

Zeus cleared his throat and stood. He ran his fingers through his wavy blond hair and put a hand on his hip, looking decidedly awkward. "How are you—please, sit down," he said, gesturing toward the long blue sofa that Athena sat on.

I offered them all a wavering smile, suddenly wishing I'd brought the glass of water with me.

"I'm...alright, I guess," I said once I'd taken a seat next to Athena. Prometheus and Epimetheus hovered behind the sofa. "I'm still trying to wrap my head around everything."

"Here," Athena whispered. She handed me a bottle of honeysuckle water.

"Thank you," I said, smiling gratefully.

She gave me a hesitant smile in return.

"Do you remember anything?" Zeus leaned forward and rested his elbows on his knees. "About your life before?"

"It's coming back," I admitted. "It's still pretty murky. The more recent memories are very clear. They're making it hard to remember the old ones, so there are still a lot of blank spots."

"Yes, that's likely going to take some time." Hestia gave me a sympathetic smile. "Not all of us can understand how it feels to remember two lives."

"That must be confusing," Athena said. She looked at her lap and started tapping her fingers against one another. "Do you—what do you remember?"

I smiled. "I know that we were friends. Good friends, and I think that's part of the reason we got along so well when you were training me."

She let out a heavy breath, then gave me a relieved smile. "That's good to hear."

"Like I said, it's beginning to come back in small pieces." I waved my hand in the air next to my head. "Right now, everything is just... trying to figure out where it fits, if that makes sense."

Zeus eyed me warily. "I suppose it does," he said with a sigh. He leaned back in his chair and rubbed his hands across his face.

I could sense disappointment coming off of him.

"I know that you're hoping I'll be able to help with your war, and I plan to do all I can, but I can't promise that it won't take time to figure out how to be who I was before."

"I understand that," Zeus replied. "It doesn't make it any less disappointing."

Epimetheus squeezed my shoulder reassuringly. "We all understand that, Tessa. No one is expecting you to bounce right back."

I looked up at him, then let my gaze meet those of everyone else in the room.

"I appreciate that," I said slowly. "I just don't know how 'back' I'll ever be."

"You're a Titaness," Apollo said brusquely. "You'll return to your former self soon enough."

Hestia laid a hand on his arm. "I wouldn't be so sure of that," she warned. "She's been through quite an ordeal. A separate life. That changes a person."

Apollo pressed his lips into a hard line and eyed me speculatively. "I suppose we'll see," he said.

Before anyone could respond, the door opened and Nate walked in.

Relief flooded me at the sight of his tall frame and warm smile.

He crossed the room and sat down next to me, stretching one arm out on the back of the sofa behind me. Smiling up at him, I relaxed into his side.

"I left Mary at the dorms to fill in Yana and Eric," he said, absently running his thumb along the back of my neck.

"Thank you," I murmured. "I'll go see them when we're done here."

He brought his arm down and laced his fingers between mine. "There's no rush, Tessa. They understand you need time."

Apollo arched a brow. "It seems some things haven't taken long to return," he muttered.

"Quiet," Hestia said, admonishing him.

Hera cleared her throat, cutting off any response. "So, you plan to continue your relationship with my son, then?"

Apollo snorted and Athena let out a huff.

Nate made a sound of annoyance. "Really, mother?"

"Hera, that's hardly relevant here," Zeus chided.

She shrugged. "I only have my son's best interests at heart. That's all."

"Your son is three thousand years old," Nate said. "And I'm quite certain there are more pressing issues here than my love life."

"Can I please speak?" I looked between them both, then turned my focus to Hera.

"There are very few things that stick out clearly in my mind from either of my lives. Nate is one of them. I can tell you unequivocally that my feelings for him are as strong as they were two days ago."

She eyed me speculatively. "Alright then. I just hope you recall our conversation. If not, I'm happy to refresh your memory."

I bit back a smile. "Yes, I remember."

"Can we get back to the bigger picture here?" Prometheus said. "My sister needs to be protected. Somehow, Menoetius knows she's back. I've no doubts he's more motivated than ever to find a way to release Cronus and my father from Tartarus. They'll come for her the moment they're free."

"I'm aware," Zeus said dryly. "I've already been in contact with Hades. He'll be arriving tomorrow to discuss how we might proceed."

I felt a weird tugging sensation in my mind at the mention of the god of the Underworld. I couldn't quite place the feeling, although it felt something akin to irritation. I made a mental note to ask Athena about it later.

"Are you both forgetting that she's no longer the weak recruit we were training just a few days ago?" Athena asked, looking annoyed. "She's a Titaness, not a child. She has her full strength now, right?"

"I think so," I said, looking at Hestia. "Right?"

Hestia nodded. "Yes, when your memory returned, so did all of your deific abilities."

"She's still a Titaness with an unclear memory of being such," Zeus snapped. "Therefore, she needs protection."

Athena groaned. "Here we go again. You all nearly smothered the life out of her in the name of 'protection' back then. Don't you understand how detrimental that was?"

Prometheus glared at her indignantly, but Zeus held up a hand before either of the twins could respond. "Enough. For the time being, until we're certain Tessa is back up to her full strength, I agree that she needs an added layer of security." He looked between my brothers and Nate. "Nathaniel—"

"No," Nate said firmly. "She'll stay with me. Titaness or not, as of right now, I've still got the best chance of waking her up if Menoetius tries another dream walk." He looked at me, then added, "If that's alright with you."

I raised my eyebrows and smiled. "It doesn't sound like I have much of a choice." I frowned at Hestia. "Hang on. Menoetius threatened to kill me in that dream walk. If he knew who I was, wouldn't he have known that wasn't possible?"

Hestia cast a glance at Zeus. He met her gaze briefly, then went back to staring into the fire.

"If I had to hazard a guess," Hestia said, "I'd say he was likely just taking pleasure in tormenting you. Your brother enjoys mental torture nearly as much as physical."

"Oh." I frowned as something flickered in the back of my mind, another memory trying to break through. It felt almost...dirty. Black.

Before I could force it forward, Zeus let out a rumble of annoyance.

"As to our current situation," he said. "Tessa, what do you plan to do now?"

I looked back at my brothers, then around the room at everyone else.

"Well," I said slowly, meeting Zeus' eyes. "There is something I need to do before I do anything else."

"What might that be?"

"I need you to tell me everything you know about Atlas. I think—no I *need* to go find my brother. Wherever he is right now, I need to bring him home."

If you enjoyed *Chaos* and want to see a bit more into the world of Olympus, signup for my newsletter here to get some exciting bonus scenes!

Continue reading for a preview of Paradox, book 2 of Tessa's story…

TESSA

1

When I was about ten, a blizzard came through my little hometown of Renville, Pennsylvania. After going through all the DVDs we'd stockpiled over the years, John and Analise had insisted we watch the *Lord of the Rings* trilogy. I grumbled and complained because I was ten and annoying, but I finally gave in when Analise promised to make blueberry pancakes for dinner.

I had rolled my eyes when John complained about the discrepancies between the books and the movies while Analise gushed over how handsome Aragorn was. And of course, Legolas, the beautiful blond elf, quickly became my first movie crush.

I mean, who doesn't love a guy who can sling arrows like that?

Even at ten, the gravity of Frodo's journey resonated with me. I was in awe of his bravery as he made his way to Mordor, where he would likely meet certain death. Yet despite being surrounded by trained warriors and faced with impossible circumstances, he had succeeded. He'd destroyed the ring, saved the world, and lived to tell his tale.

And in the end, he went home, hoping to return to his old life.

Yet who could endure what Frodo did and just pick up right where he left off?

No one, that's who.

Now, sitting in Zeus' living room, taking in the faces of my family and friends and recalling vague memories of both my old life and new, I was beginning to feel a bit like Frodo when he'd sat as his desk, penning the words to his book as he tried to figure out how to move forward after so much had changed.

The strands of my life as a Titaness were scattered about like bits of thread on a sewing room floor, trying desperately to force themselves into the tapestry of my life as an Ischyra, a human gifted with immortality and the powers of the gods of Olympus. I had been irrevocably changed, and not a single person in my life—god, Ischyra, or otherwise—could help put things back in their place. I couldn't simply go back to being Tessa, Titaness of Olympus, twin sister to Atlas and daughter of Iapetus and Clymene any more than I could go back to being Tessa Lynn Avery of Renville, Pennsylvania.

Somehow, I had to be both.

But first, I had to rescue my brother, and it was starting to look like that might not be an easy feat.

Propping my elbows on my knees, I pressed my fingers to my eyes. After a moment, I let my hands drop to my lap and stared at Zeus, aghast at the information he'd just shared with me.

"You're telling me my brother has been wasting away in a cave in *Morocco* for nearly three thousand years?" I asked.

Our leader cleared his throat and shifted in his seat, then looked around the room at the others who were present. I followed his gaze and noticed everyone seemed equally as uncomfortable as he did.

Turning accusing eyes on my brothers, twins Prometheus and Epimetheus, I frowned. "You two could've teleported in and taken him ages ago! Why wouldn't you have gone to him?"

"When we told you he was inaccessible, it wasn't because we couldn't find him," Prometheus explained. "He refuses to see reason. He's been punishing himself for your death, and for our mother's."

"But it wasn't his fault," I protested. "Iapetus and Cronus are the ones responsible."

Epimetheus walked around the sofa and knelt in front of me, pulling my hands into his. Green eyes—the same as mine and our brothers'—bore into mine. "We all know that, Tessa. That's never been a question. Please believe that."

"I just don't understand why he's punishing himself so harshly," I whispered.

"He's your twin," Apollo said. He tapped a long, pale finger on the crystal wine glass in his hand. "Your other half, born of the same energy. Did you truly think the loss of your energy wouldn't affect him profoundly? As a twin myself, I can say it would certainly affect me."

"You and Artemis are hardly the poster children for strong sibling relationships, so I find that hard to believe," Prometheus said.

"Be that as it may, the point remains the same. Were my twin to die, her soul destroyed, my psyche would be affected. That's just the way it is."

"But I wasn't really dead," I argued. "My soul wasn't destroyed, it was just hidden away. I'd expect grief, not insanity."

"Chaos is another dimension, Tessa," Hestia explained, her blue eyes soft. She tucked a lock of fiery red hair behind her ear and matched my position. "That connection would have been damaged, at the very *least*, the moment Hecate sent your soul there."

"Fine, but once I was reborn a human, shouldn't that have fixed things?" My heart ached at the thought of my brother—strong, unshakeable Atlas—deteriorating in a cave all these years due to my absence.

"It's possible," Nate said, running a thumb along the back of my neck. "The likelihood is, he was too far gone by then to know what was real from what wasn't."

"Have any of you attempted to speak to him?" I asked.

"We have," Prometheus confirmed. "He won't see us. The first time we went, not long after Zeus lifted his sentence, he said we were too painful a reminder of the sister he'd let die. We've gone back many times over the centuries to no avail. The most recent attempt, about two years ago, ended with Epimetheus nearly losing an arm."

My eyes widened as I turned back toward Epimetheus. "He attacked you?"

"He's become unstable over the years," Athena explained, her tone gentle. "At first, he was simply reclusive. Content to live in solitude. Now, though...well, he hasn't actually spoken to anyone in centuries, that we know of."

I shook my head. "That still doesn't explain why you all didn't just go into that cave and take him."

Apollo sighed and sent a look toward Zeus.

I looked back and forth between the two of them, brow furrowed. "What?"

"We—" Zeus cut himself off when Hestia cleared her throat. "I felt it...unwise to bring him back here in such a state. His instability on the mountain would have likely caused more trouble than—"

My eyebrows shot up.

"Than he's worth?" I snorted. "Unbelievable."

Hera let out an annoyed huff, her dark, exotic eyes flashing. "Oh, for the love of us all. He's one of the strongest warriors to ever come off this mountain. It doesn't matter why he's there or how much of a lunatic he's become; his place is *here*. Tessa, go to Morocco and bring your damned brother home." She sniffed and adjusted her deep-green skirts. "I don't see why you're all making this so complicated."

"She wanted details, Hera," Athena said. "With what she's been through, she's entitled to that, at least."

Hera waved a hand dismissively, and the gold bracelets on her slender wrist made a musical tinkling sound. "Deal with the details later. Just go and get this thing done already. He'll be much easier to handle now that his twin has returned."

Apollo set his glass on the coffee table and looked at me. "I have to say that I agree with Hera on this. You're almost certainly the only person that will get him out of that mountain without further harm to himself or anyone else. Sitting here talking about it won't make it any more, or less, true."

I let out a heavy breath and stared down at Epimetheus. He was my older brother by a good hundred years, and even though my memories had barely begun to filter in, I knew, without question, he would tell me what I needed to hear.

His eyes searched mine, then he smiled softly. "You're his twin. If anything can bring him home to us, it's you."

I struggled with his confidence in me. At best, I felt like I was half of who I used to be. Confusion as to who I was still swirled in my mind, and I had no idea how long it would take for the rest of my memories to sort themselves out. I loved my brothers and wanted us all to be together again, but Atlas had been in isolation for almost three thousand years.

What if he was damaged beyond repair?

The ache I'd felt moments earlier started working its way through my chest as I realized just how possible it was that I would never get my twin back. I'd barely had time to remember the man I'd shared a childhood with, and now I was being faced with the task of saving him myself or risk losing him for good.

I closed my eyes against the pain. Quietly, the words he'd whispered to me flowed through the chaos in my mind.

Never doubt your greatness, Tessa. You will move mountains.

I'd heard those words since the moment I stepped through the portal into Olympia, and if ever there was a time I needed Atlas' faith in me, it was now. Yet here, thousands of miles from where he'd holed himself up in a mountain, that faith felt nearly nonexistent.

'Don't think like that.'

A smile flickered across my face as Nate picked up on my thoughts. As a Coercer, his ability to communicate telepathically was far stronger than the other gods, so my mental walls, the walls that kept everyone else out, barely had to falter for him to get a sense of where my mind had gone.

"Okay." I rubbed my hands on my legs nervously. "It looks like we're going to Morocco. When do we leave?"

No one spoke for a moment, and I saw Epimetheus slide a glance toward his twin.

"What?" My eyes darted between them. "You just said—"

Epimetheus gave me a sympathetic smile. "Tessa, we want to go as soon as possible, but don't you think you should take a bit of time to acclimate? You've only just gotten your memories back."

"She barely *has* her memories back, you mean," Apollo muttered.

"So?" I frowned at the twins, ignoring Apollo's usual snark. "Our brother needs our help. I don't need my memories to know that."

Nate slid a hand down my arm and twined his fingers through mine. "He's right. Give yourself a few days, at least, before making plans like this. See if more of your memories come back first."

"I have to agree with Nathaniel," Zeus said, sounding reluctant as he drummed his fingers on the arm of his chair. There was a shrewd look in his eye that made me shift uncomfortably in my seat.

"We've been trying to get Atlas to come out of that hole for years," Hera argued. "Why wait any longer?"

"Because there's a better chance of success if she's got her damn wits about her," Zeus snapped.

"Tessa, dear, a few days won't make a difference," Hestia said. "You've barely woken up. Why not see if your mind clears a bit more? Train up a little, just to make sure you'll be able to defend yourself, should something go wrong."

I looked at Athena, the beautiful brunette sitting beside me, and one of my oldest friends. I arched a brow in question.

She smirked. "You wouldn't have to ask me twice, you know that."

"At least I've got one ally," I grumbled.

"Two impetuous goddesses going hunting for an unstable Titan is the last thing we need," Prometheus said.

"Oh, but what about your friend, that Mary girl? We could bring her," Athena suggested, her eyes twinkling. "If she and I are to be friends, this would be a wonderful bonding experience."

"That's a great idea." I grinned. "She'd be so upset if she missed out on this. Eric, too, probably."

"Lovely, it's settled then."

"That's just what we need," Nate muttered.

"Enough!" Zeus snapped.

I pressed my lips together, trying to contain my laughter, and Athena's gray eyes sparkled as she looked at her father.

"Tessa, I understand that you are still becoming accustomed to your true self, but I would encourage you to try to leave some of your human proclivities behind. You cannot include recruits in a mission like this," Zeus said.

I arched a brow. "I can't change who I was the last eighteen years, Zeus. I won't just write them out of my life."

"Then take them out to dinner. Get roaring drunk, for all I care. It doesn't change the fact that recruits have no business coming on this trip."

"But why not?" Hera challenged him. "This—what's her name?"

"Mary," Epimetheus said.

"Yes, thank you," Hera said before continuing. "This Mary girl will be going off to battle soon enough. Surely a trip to some dusty mountain won't kill her."

Zeus let out a sound of frustration. "For once, can you not challenge me?"

"Can we get back to the matter at hand?" Apollo interrupted.

"I thought this was the matter at hand?" Athena frowned up at him. "Weren't we discussing who will be joining us on the mission to retrieve Atlas?"

"No," Apollo said slowly. "We were discussing when Tessa would be *able* to make that trip. She and I seem to be the only ones who think she's capable now, despite her... limitations."

"I think she's capable!" Athena countered.

"No, you just want to be contrary. There's a difference."

"Alright, let me put an end to this," I said, holding up a hand to quiet the bickering siblings. "Although I'd like to leave immediately, I acknowledge that some of you have made valid points. I need to take time to get my bearings. I'll give you three days; four, at most, but then I'm going to get Atlas, whether I have your support or not. In the meantime, I'll brush up on whatever it is you all think I need to brush up on."

"That sounds fair," Nate said, squeezing my hand. "No need to rush."

I looked at Zeus. "You said Hades will be here tomorrow to talk about the security of Tartarus?"

Once again, the strange rippling feeling went through my mind as the last time Hades had been brought up. This time it was accompanied by the brief flash of memory, too quick to latch on to.

"Yes, he should be here midday," Zeus replied. "He's currently speaking with his guards and inspecting the security of the walls and wards that surround the realm. We need to be certain your father and Cronus have no means of escape."

Tensing, I tried to control the panic that set in as I thought of them escaping. "Has he said anything about whether my father and Cronus are still secure?"

"As of yesterday, they were still locked in. We'll get more details from him tomorrow, though."

Something in Zeus' tone sent unease through me. "Okay," I said, brushing off the odd sensation. "Until then, I have a few things I need to address."

"And you should probably get some rest, as well," Hestia said.

"She just slept for two days," Prometheus pointed out.

"My mind is also trying to bombard me with almost a thousand years' worth of memories," I told him. "My body isn't tired, my brain is."

"Alright," he said with a sigh, then rubbed his hand across his face. "I was just hoping—"

"She needs to rest if she's to find herself, Prometheus," Hestia interrupted. "Let's not push too hard today."

I smiled at her appreciatively as Epimetheus stood and held out a hand. I let him pull me to my feet, then he wrapped his muscular arms around me in a crushing hug.

"I can't tell you how happy I am that you're here, Tessa," he whispered, his voice raspy with emotion. "Take all the time you need. I'm not going anywhere."

I hugged him back, then pulled away and pressed a hand to his cheek. "Neither am I."

He grinned, then handed me off to Prometheus, who took me from his twin and placed a hand on each shoulder and looked me in the eyes. "Don't feel pressured to do things faster than you're able. As much as I want our family back together, I need you to be ready for that to happen."

"Thank you." I wrapped my arms around his waist and let him envelop me in a hug. "I promise, we'll all be together soon."

"I know," he whispered. "Now, go do what you need to do. We'll speak in the morning."

Ten minutes later, Nate and I stood outside of the dorms, listening to the voices of recruits in the courtyard.

Turning to face him, I shook my head. "I can't go in there. Who knows what they've been saying about me?"

Nate eyed the entryway warily, then raked a hand through his sandy-brown hair.

"I'm not crazy about you being thrown into the midst of that group, myself," he admitted.

Just then, Eric Anderson, one of my oldest friends, came rushing through the gate. His shaggy blond hair, blue eyes, and lean, muscular build gave him a classic surfer look, but the wide, relieved smile he wore as he jogged toward me was almost boyish.

"Tessa! I thought that was you." He gave Nate a tight-lipped smile in greeting. "You don't want to go in there. Come on, I'll take you guys around the back."

"Why?" I looked past him toward the courtyard, where voices still chattered loudly.

He put his hand on the small of my back and started leading me toward the side of the building. "So far, only Mary, Yana, and I know what actually happened to you," he explained quietly as he took us down the narrow alleyway between the dorms and the apartments next door. "Everyone in there is waiting for you to make an appearance."

"Who's in there? What are they saying?" Nate demanded as we came out on the lawn that spread out from the back of the building.

Eric rolled his eyes and let out a sound of annoyance. "About a dozen recruits with nothing better to do than wait around in the courtyard gossiping any time we're not at training. So far, I've heard you've tried to kill Charlise and Zeus, stolen Zeus' power, you're pregnant with Zeus' baby, you're trying to overthrow Olympus, are in cahoots with the rebels, and probably a few other things that I haven't heard yet."

My eyes widened. "What the—are you serious?"

Nate chuckled. "That's far less creative than I would've expected."

"Yeah. The three of us have been taking shifts when we're not at training, waiting to catch you before you came in."

"How come?" I asked.

He cocked his head in the direction we'd just come from. "Because those dicks in there are annoying."

A sense of relief washed over me at his words. The last time Eric and I had spoken, he'd asked me out and I'd turned him down. At the time, I wasn't sure if our friendship would be able to recover. Despite Mary's earlier reassurance that my friends were still my friends, a small part of me had worried the rift between me and Eric—the result of my rejection of him—would increase, once he realized I wasn't the girl he'd grown up with.

Overcome with emotion, I threw my arms around his waist and hugged him. "You don't know how happy it makes me to hear you say that," I whispered.

He tightened the embrace and rested his chin on my head. "I know, Mary told us," he murmured. Pulling back, he smiled down at me. "You don't have to worry about us bailing on you, Tess. That'll never happen."

Quietly, Nate knocked on the window. A few seconds later, Yana's face was pressed to the glass. When she saw us, she flung open the window.

"Tessa! Thank the gods! Come, get in here quickly."

Nate grabbed me by the waist and boosted me up. I pulled myself through, falling to the floor between Yana's bed and my own, grunting as my elbow smacked into the hardwood.

"Isn't your kind supposed to be a bit more graceful than that?"

I looked up and saw Mary leaning over me. Her light brown hair was wet and hanging over her shoulder, dripping onto the floor. She'd changed into ripped, black jeans and a white sweater with patches of pink lace sewn on in random places.

I scowled at her. "Yes, well, apparently, I haven't figured that part out yet, so leave me alone. You're dripping on me."

She reached down and helped me stand, then went about wrapping her hair up into a bun as Eric and Nate hoisted themselves through the tiny window.

Yana stood at the foot of her bed, still in her uniform, with her hands on her hips and her wide blue eyes narrowed in my direction. Her black hair was still up in the tight braid she always wore for training.

"This window gets far more use as a doorway than I anticipated," she observed, pursing her lips. She met my eyes and gave me a hesitant smile.

There was an awkward silence as my friends and I looked at each other. Finally, I sat down on my bed and pulled Nate down next to me. The others perched on Yana's bed, facing us.

"So...how are you feeling?" Yana asked after a moment.

"I'm alright. Still a little weird in the head."

"I still cannot believe it," she said, shaking her head slowly. "How does this kind of thing happen?"

"Scheming between Titans and witches, apparently," I replied before diving into the full story. Nate and Mary supplied a few details they'd learned while I was still asleep.

"You remember it all, then?" Yana asked when we finished our tale, her eyes wide. "Your life before?"

"Hardly anything yet. The more recent stuff is the clearest, but I'm hoping it'll all come back quickly."

Eric cleared his throat. "So...how old are you, anyway?"

Mary smacked his chest with the back of her hand. "Rude!"

He winced and pulled back. "What? You were both wondering, too."

"I certainly was," Yana said in her deadpan voice.

"About four thousand years," I replied, laughing. "A little less."

"That's her chronological age," Nate added. "Technically, she's only been alive for about seven hundred years.

"Geez. Here I thought Nate was the cradle robber," Mary muttered, then shifted curious eyes to Nate. "How old are you, anyway?"

"I'm just over three thousand," he said, his lips wobbling with humor.

Mary narrowed her eyes. "How much over?"

He winced. "About thirty-two hundred. I honestly couldn't tell you the exact number."

"So, this is life now," Yana said, her expression amused. "Friends who are so old they do not know how old they are."

"Where will you be staying now?" Mary asked. "I'm assuming you aren't going to be coming back here."

I thought I detected a note of sadness in her voice.

"I can't. It's just not safe," I said. "Titaness or not, Menoetius might still be able to dream walk into my head, and Nate has the best chance of waking me if that happens."

"Gods, you would think being a Titaness would give you some immunities to that bastard," Eric grumbled.

"He's a Titan, too, and I'm still not one hundred percent yet. Not even close." I looked back and forth between them. "You guys are really okay with all of this? I honestly expected you to run for the hills."

"It is weird, I will grant you that," Yana admitted. "I certainly had some conflicting feelings at first. Mary has told us that you are still you, though."

I nodded. "She's right, more or less. There's just a little bit more of 'me' to deal with now."

"That's part of why we had Mary stay with you when you were asleep," Nate explained gently. "Hestia and Apollo were able to give her the entire story."

Mary grinned. "Apollo was super grumbly about it, too. He's kind of a dick, isn't he?" She raised her eyebrows at Nate.

A smile twitched at the corners of his mouth. "As he is my brother and an Elder, I'm going to refrain from answering that."

She nodded knowingly. "Uh huh." She turned her smiling eyes back to me. "Besides, how many recruits can say one of their best friends is a Titaness? Oh, and can I have your bed? It's way more comfortable than mine."

"Nice to see your priorities are in order," I said dryly.

"I wouldn't be me if they weren't."

TESSA

2

When Nate and I left the dorms a short while later, I felt like a weight had been lifted from my chest. At some point between saying goodbye to Mary at the palace and arriving at the dorms, I'd convinced myself that my friends would want nothing to do with me. Hearing confirmation that they were still the same loving and loyal people they'd been a few days earlier brought me a huge sense of relief.

"I think I need to start training," I said to Nate once we'd arrived back at his cabin.

He toed off his shoes and fell back onto his overstuffed leather sectional. I dropped the suitcase of belongings that I'd packed from my room, then sat down next to him and rested my head against his chest.

He began twirling the end of my braid around his fingers. "So soon?"

I shrugged. "No time like the present, right?"

I looked down at my wrist and brushed a thumb over the three wavy purple lines on the inside of my wrist; the mark of an Ischyra. I'd had it since birth—my human birth, that is—and now they represented a part of me that I desperately wanted to cling to.

"I don't think going back to training with the Ischyra is the best way to go about that," he said cautiously.

"No, of course not. And stop reading my mind," I said, looking up at him teasingly.

"I'm not," he said, pulling me back against him. "I'm just pretty sure I know where your thoughts are right now."

"I just feel useless." Absently, I drew circles on his chest, focusing on the way my finger moved so I could force myself not to focus on what I was actually feeling. "Everyone else has their power and knows how to use it, and here I am with this awesome gift that I've barely scratched the surface of."

"Who did you train with before you were an Ischyra?"

"My brothers, I guess." I sat up and scrubbed my hands over my face in annoyance. "I don't remember."

He gave me a sympathetic smile. "You will, just give yourself time. Until then, I'll help however I can, and I'm sure your friends will do the same."

I snorted. "A Titaness being trained by Ischyra. Who'd have thought that's where my life would be?"

"You can learn from anyone, love. Rank doesn't matter here."

"I know. It's just...a few days ago, the thought of training with two Titans was both thrilling and terrifying. Now I'm the Titan, and the last thing I want is to be terrifying."

He cupped my cheek in his hand and gave me a soft kiss. "Your friends will never see you as terrifying, Tessa. Deep down, you know that."

I tapped my thumbs together on my knees as I considered the idea. "I don't know, we'll see. They have their own training to do; they don't need to be wasting time with me."

"That's entirely your call, but I can assure you, they won't consider it a waste of time." He stood, then took my hand and pulled me to my feet. "Come on, let's go get some rest."

The last thing I felt like doing just then was going back to sleep, but I knew he was probably right. Like I'd told the twins, my brain was tired. I felt better now that I'd spoken to my friends, but my mind still felt a bit like mush.

When we got into his bedroom, I dug through my suitcase and pulled out my pajamas and bag of toiletries, then went into the bathroom, closing the door behind me.

Away from the distraction of conversation with friends and family, my mind began to resume its own little civil war, causing a dull ache to bloom in my head. Flashes of color and light danced through my thoughts, old and new memories asking for recollection.

I let out a heavy sigh, then turned on the shower, letting the water heat up as I stared at my reflection in the mirror above the sink.

Thanks to Hecate's spell, my appearance was the same now as it had been in my previous life. My blonde hair, green eyes, and golden tan skin looked just as they had when I was a Titaness. I was unsure why she'd crafted it that way, but I was beyond thankful that she did. I didn't know what I would've done if my face didn't match my twin's.

An array of emotions flitted through my mind and across my features.

Curiosity. Hope. Wonder.

Happiness at having been given the opportunity to meet John and Analise, Mary, Eric, Nate, and all the other people I'd lived through the last eighteen years with.

Anger that my Titan family had been torn apart because of my mother's decision to put my protection over her own life.

I understood why Clymene had done it; I might have even done the same for my own child, had I been in her shoes. But it didn't change the fact that our family had been destroyed as a result.

My brothers had been beaten down psychologically, and I'd missed out on thousands of years of life, only to return just in time to fight a war against the same monster who'd wanted to suck me dry of my power so long ago.

Gritting my teeth, I thought of everyone who'd been party to the recent events of my life. Cronus, Menoetius, and Iapetus for wanting to use me; my mother for choosing to end her life and letting the world think I was dead; Hecate for going along with her plan; Apollo and Hestia for agreeing to guard the truth.

The list went on, and the more I added to it, the angrier I got.

Calm yourself, Tessa.

I flinched, startled by the whispered words in my mind. The voice was familiar and...irritated.

Yet another memory of another time, no doubt.

Regardless of who'd spoken to me and when, I heeded their advice. Anger wouldn't get me anywhere.

I closed my eyes and took a deep breath, willing my swirling emotions to settle, grabbing onto the positive emotions and squashing down the bad.

After a few seconds, I straightened my back, then stared at the girl in the mirror once more, unsure which version of me was staring back. Fear was written all over her face. I dared that fear to challenge my determination, to tell me not to be angry, not to scream or cry or break things and people and gods, until I got all of my fury, grief, and sadness out.

My life had been taken from me, and I had every damn right to be pissed about it.

Taking a deep breath, I forced myself to focus on the good things. I'd been reunited with my brothers. My friends from both lives still stood by me, and there was a man waiting for me in the next room who cared for me deeply. Maybe even loved me.

Despite the changing nature of my life, their support didn't seem to be wavering.

I clung to that, hoping to all the gods that it wouldn't change.

WHEN I EMERGED from the bathroom a short while later, showered and in my pajamas, Nate was lying on the bed, one arm thrown over his face.

He lifted his arm and smiled when he heard me walk in, then

held out a hand, beckoning me over. I slid in next to him and let him wrap a strong arm around me.

"Hi," he murmured, kissing my temple. "How are you feeling?"

I sighed, breathing in his clean, woodsy scent, and closed my eyes. "I don't know. All over the place."

"How so?"

I shifted so I was looking up at him before speaking. "I'm just so... angry, with all of them. I wouldn't trade the last eighteen years for the world, but gods, I'm so fucking angry."

His eyes searched mine as he brushed my wet hair off my forehead. "Would you like to leave for a while, digest all of this somewhere that isn't here?"

I smiled ruefully. "Only if you come with me."

He put one finger under my chin, tilting my mouth toward his, and brushed his lips gently across mine. When he pulled back, his midnight eyes bore into mine. "Just say the word and we're gone," he whispered.

"Okay." I swallowed back the lump in my throat. "For now... Can you just kiss me again?"

Shifting so we were laying face-to-face, he cupped my face in his hand and drew my lips to his. His kiss was gentle at first, testing, then deepened when my fingers curled in the soft material of his shirt.

Parting my lips for his, I slid my fingers into his hair and arched my back, pulling his body against mine.

Tears pricked the corners of my eyes as I realized just how happy I was to have him here, and how content he was being here. I needed to feel him close to me, to feel happiness so I could beat back everything that was threatening to unravel inside me. Everything in me ached as I tried to reconcile the unfamiliar feelings of the past with the comfortable, familiar ones of the present. Pushing it all back, I let myself get lost in Nate's arms.

After a few moments, he pulled back and met my eyes, taking in my tears. Gently, he brushed one away, then another, before kissing my forehead. "Get some rest. We can talk more tomorrow."

I nodded, then let him pull me closer to him, tucking my head in under his chin.

"Hey, Nate?"

"Hmm?"

"Thank you."

~

MY DREAMS STARTED OUT HAZY, as though memories were trying to work their way to the surface while I slept.

I was in the process of trying to coax a memory through, when the dream shifted focus and I found myself standing in the clearing Menoetius had brought me to in our last dream walk. Cheery sunlight filtered through the trees, belying the feeling of doom that permeated this place. Whatever memories had yet to resurface, I knew none of them reflected this small bit of forest in a positive light.

A cloudy sensation of immobility rippled through me as screams of pain echoed in my mind, but just like last time, the thought slipped away before I could grab hold.

Dread washed through me when I realized why I was back here.

"Hello there, Tessa." Menoetius' voice was smooth, and an evil smirk twisted his lips as he took in my expression. He held the same silver knife that he'd tortured me with, less than a week ago, in his hand. It made a soft thudding sound as he tapped it lightly against his dark pants. "Something bothering you?"

"Not a thing," I said, trying to keep my voice from shaking.

"That's good to hear." He took a slow step forward. "Tell me, have you figured it all out yet?"

"Can't you just read my mind and find out?"

His jaw clenched and he eyed me shrewdly. "Mind reading is not an affinity. It's an innate part of an immortal's being. I can't disable your ability to prevent my reading your thoughts any more than I can disable your ability to walk." Realization flashed in his eyes, and he laughed cruelly. "You haven't gotten your memories back yet, have you?"

I narrowed my eyes. "I don't know what you're talking about. And how are you able to do a dream walk if you can't read my mind?"

He laughed, then pointed the knife in my direction. "You've always been terrible at keeping your walls up while asleep, so it's easy to get past the barriers meant to keep me out. I can disable your power in here—" he pointed at the ground with his dagger "—because your mind is weak out there."

I shrugged, trying not to let him see how much his words terrified me.

"So? Have your memories returned yet?" He twirled the dagger around in his hand and smirked. "I'm quite anxious to know how you're handling some of my favorites."

"Of course they have." I didn't bother keeping up the 'I'm just an Ischyra' farce. He knew the truth.

"Ah, wonderful. Then I'm sure you remember my fondness for this place, yes?" He looked around, staring disdainfully at the sky. "It's much lovelier at night, don't you agree?"

My heart slammed against my ribs as Menoetius snapped his fingers and the clearing was suddenly bathed in moonlight. A battle warred in my mind, one half trying to reclaim the memory, while the other half rebelled, scrambling to force it back. Something awful had happened here, something I wasn't entirely sure I wanted to remember.

He took another step toward me, and I felt a sudden sting on my wrists. I glanced down but saw nothing there.

"Your ignorance truly does amuse me."

Nate. Where was Nate?

'Nate!'

Slowly, my oldest brother began to stalk closer. I cast a quick glance over my shoulder and saw the massive tree looming barely a foot behind me.

I tried to shift to the side, hoping to avoid having my back against anything solid, but he was too quick. He leapt forward and grabbed my shoulders, slamming me against the trunk. I hissed as the rough bark tore through the fabric of my shirt. Pain, razor-sharp, wrapped around my wrists and ankles.

"Tell me, Tessa," he whispered, his breath hot as his lips pressed to my ear. "Do you remember your final days? I have to say, of all of the memories I have of you, those are some of my favorite."

I swallowed hard, not wanting to give him any more confirmation that I had absolutely no idea what he was talking about.

"You need to let me go," I said, my voice barely above a whisper.

He leaned back and ran his eyes over my face. I tried to look away from his hate-filled stare, but he gripped my chin in his massive hand and jerked my face toward his. "Tell me...has Zeus told you what he thinks he has in store for me?"

He pressed the tip of his blade to my neck. I sucked in a breath and tried to pull away, then forced myself to remember that the godsbane-infused blade couldn't kill me.

Pain, I could deal with. Maybe not easily, but deep down, something in my mind told me I could do it if I had to.

I gritted my teeth as he turned the flat side of the blade against my throat, pressing it into the flesh. "I don't know what you're talking about. He doesn't tell me anything."

He dragged the blade lightly across my skin. I tensed in anticipation of the pain I knew the poisonous blade would deliver.

"And that son of his? What has he told you? Or have you been too busy being a whore for him to learn anything useful?"

"I don't know anything," I said through gritted teeth, struggling uselessly against his power.

"Don't lie to me, little girl. I know all about you. Zeus thinks he'll use you as a weapon against me, doesn't he? He thinks you can stop me from bringing my father home?"

He pressed the cool blade harder against my neck, just barely breaking the skin.

I struggled against his grip as the godsbane trickled into my blood.

"Even if Zeus did think that," I hissed out, "I wouldn't be much use against you, would I?"

A cruel laugh rumbled through his chest. "You don't know him well at all, do you?"

He turned the blade, letting the sharp tip slice through the thin flesh that covered my collarbone. I was unable to hold back a cry of pain as I felt the knife brushing against bone as more poison entered my body.

A maniacal gleam sparked in his eyes as he dragged the knife across my shoulder and slowly started to dig it into my upper arm. The more I screamed, the brighter his eyes became, full of enjoyment at my agony.

"I bet if I pushed this in just a little further, every single memory of yours would return," he said, a grin slowly spreading across his face. He put more pressure on the blade, and I felt blood slowly begin to trickle down my arm. "Would you like me to do that for you? Wouldn't you rather just get it over with?"

Black dots danced across my vision as the blade continued to pierce my flesh, tearing through my shirt as if it were paper. I pressed my lips together as waves of nausea began to roar through me, and my body rapidly began losing strength. I wanted to scream, cry, try to fight back, but the godsbane was making me weak. Soon, I'd be unconscious. That thought terrified me more than anything.

"I'd step away from her," a menacing voice said.

Menoetius froze, and his smile grew wider. "Hello, little brothers," he said, pressing the blade farther into my shoulder, the pain sending a torrent of tears down my cheeks. It was nearly halfway through my shoulder now. "How nice of you to join us."

I struggled uselessly as my vision began to go red and my breaths started to come in heaving gasps. Again, I wanted to cry out, beg my brothers to help me, but I couldn't muster the strength for more than a whimper.

Without warning, Menoetius yanked the blade out. I screamed at the sudden absence of pressure, and he shoved me to the ground. My chest heaved as I tried to see through the fire that was tearing through my body. Slowly, my vision began to clear, and the pain began to dull to a burning ache.

"She's going to wake up now, and you're going to leave her be," Epimetheus growled.

"My, my." Menoetius wiped the tip of the blade on his pants, smearing my blood across the fabric, then slid the weapon back into its leather sheath. "Is baby brother finally growing a backbone?"

I cast a glance toward Epimetheus and just barely saw his eyes flick toward Menoetius' midsection. The knife.

I lowered my eyes and saw that his sheath was less than a foot away from me, the handle of the knife tilted slightly back. Willing myself not to vomit, I pulled my body into a crouch.

"I was hoping you might finally tell us why you insist on tormenting her," Prometheus replied, his tone almost conversational.

Before Menoetius could respond, I jerked forward and grabbed the knife, using what strength I had to shove it into his side, jamming it to the hilt.

He roared in pain as the godsbane flowed into his body.

I felt a rough shaking sensation and a hard pressure in my mind. The scenery around me began to waver, and Prometheus and Epimetheus disappeared from view.

Just as Menoetius pulled the knife from his side and spun toward me, I woke up.

ACKNOWLEDGMENTS

To my husband, whose sage advice to "write the damn book" has finally been put to good use.

To Shay (but not Katrina) because, well, you know. (Just kidding. Love you both.)

To my crazy cousins, who could make "supporting your family" a competitive sport.

To my betas, ARC readers, and my beta-turned-alpha, Eric, who might be the only person to actually like Mary's character. None of you told me what you thought I wanted to hear, and my work is better for it.

To the BBs. Despite having never met any you, you've been some of my biggest cheerleaders throughout this process. You may not know it, but every bit of encouragement you offered gave me confidence to do this.

To Brittany at TBR Editing & Design for my gorgeous cover—thank you for putting up with my pickiness.

To Jenifer, my amazing editor for putting her shining touch to my words.

To all of the authors who've inspired me over the years—I may never meet you, but I thank you, nonetheless.

Finally, to all of the readers who've chosen to take a chance on me. Writing has become my heart and soul, and I'm thankful for all of you who've taken the time to read my work.

ABOUT THE AUTHOR

Lucy grew up "down the shore" in New Jersey, where her love of the mythological was born when her middle school English teacher introduced her to the Odyssey. After high school, she received Bachelor's degrees in Psychology and English Literature before continuing on to her Master's degree in Library and Information Science. In her spare time, Lucy loves to read, cook, and go hiking with her husband and two daughters. Chaos is her debut novel.

Stay up to date! Hop over to www.lucyroyauthor.com to sign up for Lucy's newsletter, follow her on social media, and read up on news and other bookish things!

- tiktok.com/@lucyroywrites
- instagram.com/lucyroywrites
- facebook.com/authorlucyroy
- x.com/LucyRoyAuthor
- pinterest.com/authorlucyroy
- bookbub.com/profile/lucy-roy

www.ingramcontent.com/pod-product-compliance
Lightning Source LLC
Chambersburg PA
CBHW020229110726
47898CB00004B/1210